"HAIR-RAISING...
WELL-WRITTEN...
EXCELLENT."
—*Tampa Tribune*

"IMAGINATIVE AND
THRILLING...NONSTOP
SUSPENSE."
—*Sunday Oklahoman*

"A FUN, ACTION-FILLED
ADVENTURE."
—*Roanoke Times* (VA)

"TENSE DIALOGUE
AND SURPRISING
INGENUITY...MELTZER'S
MOST ORIGINAL NOVEL."
—*Style Weekly*

PRAISE FOR *THE MILLIONAIRES* AND BRAD MELTZER

"A giddy thriller . . . banking, cyber-theft, and Disney World in a fast-paced tale of financial adventure."

—*Publishers Weekly*

"Meltzer's *First Counsel* was a winner and THE MILLIONAIRES is guaranteed to score with readers."

—*Southern Pines Pilot* (NC)

"Meltzer has mastered the art of baiting and hooking readers quickly into a fast-moving plot."

—*USA Today*

"Good fun. . . . Meltzer, often called the Grisham of financial thrillers, has a knack for keeping a story moving while still throwing in plenty of insider information."

—*Booklist*

"A wild financial thriller . . . a Mad Hatter ride leading to the audience singing Brad Meltzer's praise for an enlightening, exciting, and entertaining story."

—*Midwest Book Review*

"One critic has predicted that Meltzer would be 'the next John Grisham'; there's no need for that, for Meltzer does quite well being Brad Meltzer."

—*Richmond Times*

more . . .

THE MILLIONAIRES

ALSO BY BRAD MELTZER

Dead Even

The Tenth Justice

The First Counsel

THE
MILLIONAIRES

BRAD MELTZER

WARNER
VISION
BOOKS

An AOL Time Warner Company

WARNER BOOKS EDITION

Copyright © 2002 by Forty-four Steps, Inc.
All rights reserved. No part of this book may be reproduced in any form or by any electronic or mechanical means, including information storage and retrieval systems, without permission in writing from the publisher, except by a reviewer who may quote brief passages in a review.

Cove design by Tony Greco and Associates

Warner Vision is a registered trademarks of Warner Books, Inc.

Warner Books, Inc.
1271 Avenue of the Americas
New York, NY 10020

Visit our Web site at
www.twbookmark.com.

An AOL Time Warner Company

Printed in the United States of America

Originally published in hardcover by Warner Books
First International Paperback Printing: August 2002
First U.S. Paperback Printing: November 2002

10 9 8 7 6 5 4 3 2 1

For Cori,
who every single day
amazes me

For Dotty Rubin and Evelyn Meltzer,
Nanny and Grandma,
for teaching me my past,
and in the process,
showing me my future

And in memory of
Ben Rubin and Sol Meltzer,
Poppy and Grandpa,
whose legacies still touch our entire family

ACKNOWLEDGMENTS

I'd like to thank the following people, whose constant support is the only reason this book exists: First of all, Cori. There are so many words in this world, but none is good enough to express what she means to me. I'm not just in love with Cori—I'm astounded by her. By who she is, by what she does, and by who she helps me to be. She's my tether to reality, and without a doubt, the best reason for me to leave my Land of Make-Believe is to see her at the end of every day. C—thank you for editing, for brainstorming, for putting up with me, and most of all, for believing in every one of our dreams; Jill Kneerim, friend, agent, and every writer's dream, who embraced and nurtured this book from the absolute start. She has always understood me as a writer, and her Zen way of approaching my manuscripts is more than just a pleasure—it's pure magic; Elaine Rogers, for always taking such good care of us; Ike Williams, Hope Denekamp, Andrea Dudley, and all the other incredible people who watch out for us at the Hill & Barlow Agency.

I also want to thank my parents for the life they gave me in Brooklyn and all the love they've given me since. They're the ones who first taught me the importance of always being myself, and they're the reason I'm here today; my sister, Bari, the Charlie to my Oliver and the Oliver to my Charlie. The love these characters have for each other is only possi-

ble because of the wonderfully insane childhood I shared
with my sister; Bobby, Dale, and Adam Flam and Ami and
Matt Kuttler help with everything that needs helping and
always make me feel like family; Judd Winick, partner in
crime, fellow schemer of the scheme, and the friend who
brought me the eureka moment that led to this entire book.
Judd, I'm giving you the full salute (like Hawkeye in the last
M*A*S*H). Thanks, Max; Noah Kuttler, one of the first people I turn to, for his astonishing patience, brilliant intuition,
and his neverending ability to challenge me as a writer. I'm
humbled by what he brings to the novels and, more important, to our friendship; Ethan and Sally Kline, who have
proven that even an ocean between us won't stop them from
helping me with everything from editing to plot twisting;
Paul Brennan, Matt Oshinsky, Paulo Pacheco, Joel Rose, and
Chris Weiss kept this book honest. Their input is critical to
everything I write and I hope they know how important they
are to me. Brothers, indeed. Chuck and Lenore Cohen, our
family in D.C., who gave new meaning to the term "opened
their home" as they turned their house over to the creative
process. I couldn't have finished this book without them.

   When I started this novel, it was the first time I had to step
into a world that I knew absolutely nothing about. For that
reason, I owe enormous thank-yous to the following people
for showing me around: Without a doubt, Jo Ayn "Joey"
Glanzer was the most brilliant investigative teacher anyone
could ask for. She took me through the details, dragged me
down the back alleys, and brought one of my favorite characters to life. More important, she's a true friend; Len
Zawistowski and Rob Ward are amazing investigators and
incredibly nice guys whom I turned to without hesitation.
Thanks for all the plotting and planning; Eljay Bowron, John
Tomlinson, Greg Regan, Marc Connolly, and Jim Mackin

were my guides to the incredible organization known as the Secret Service, and I can't thank them enough for their trust. They're the actual good guys, and I respect them (and the Service) more than they know; Bill Spellings, my director of high-tech gadgetry, who puts James Bond to shame; Robin Manix and Bob West, for taking the time to make sure I had every banking detail I needed; Ashima Dayal, Tom DePont, Mike Higgins, Alex Khutorsky, David Leit, Mary Riley, Denis Russ, Jim Sloan, Don Stebbins, and Ken van Wyk answered question after question, no matter how silly or inane; Bill Warren and Deborah Warner at Disney, for all their fantastic help in taking me backstage at the Magic Kingdom. The place is just amazing, and their support is much appreciated; Chuck Vance and Larry Sheafe (who are just the best), Bill Carroll, Andy Podolak, and all the incredible minds over at Vance International, for teaching me how to track people down; Richard Bert, Sheri James, and the other wonderfully kind people at FinCEN, who taught me so much about financial crime and law enforcement; Glen Dershowitz, Joe Epstein, Rob Friedsam, Steven Heineman, Roman Krawciw, Amanda Parness, P. J. Solit, Greg Stuppler, and Jon Weiner, for taking me through the financial world; John Byrne, Tom Lasich, Laura Mouck, Charles Nelson, and Bob Powis, for their insight into the intricacies of money laundering; Chris Campos, Louis Digeronimo, Nancie Freitas, Mary Alice Hurst, Terry Lenzner, Ted O'Donnell, Rob Russell, Robert Smith, and Joseph T. Wells, who shared their privacy and investigative techniques; Steve Bernd, David Boyd, Greg Hammond, Peter Migala, and Sean Rogers, who were the rest of my high-tech surveillance team; Cindy Bonnette, Jeannine Butcavage, Vincent Conlon, Mike Martinson, and Bill Spiro, for their expertise on the banking industry; Noel Hillman and Dan Gitner, for the legal advice;

Cary Lubetsky, Eric Meier, and Roger White, who reintroduced me to my hometown; Sue Cocking, Greg Cohen, Jon Constine, Tom Deardorff, Edna Farley, Michele and Tom Heidenberger, Karen Kutger, Ray McAllister, Ken Robson, Sharon Silva-Lamberson, Joao Morgado, Debra Roberts, Sheryl Sandberg, Tom Shaw, and my dad, for walking me through the rest of the details; Rob Weisbach, for being the first to say yes; every one of my male friends (you know who you are—if you just grinned, I'm talking about you), for being the brothers who live in this book; and, as always, to my family and friends, whose names inhabit these pages.

Finally, I'd like to thank my family at Warner Books: Larry Kirshbaum, Maureen Egen, Tina Andreadis, Emi Battaglia, Karen Torres, Martha Otis, Chris Barba, the hardest working sales force in show business, and the rest of the amazingly nice people who always make me feel at home there. Sincere thanks and a huge hug also go to Jamie Raab, for her dead-on editing, her tremendous enthusiasm, and for always cheering in our corner. Jamie, I can't thank you enough for bringing us into the family. Finally, I want to say a massive thank-you to my editor, Rob McMahon, who does all the heavy lifting. Simply put, Rob is a prince among men. His editorial input is as honest as his demeanor, and his suggestions always push me to reach for what's better. Thank you, Rob, for your friendship, and most important, your faith.

Twenty-three percent of people
say they would steal if they couldn't get caught.

. . . but to live outside the law, you must be honest.

—Bob Dylan

THE
MILLIONAIRES

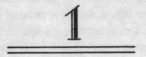

1

I know where I'm going. And I know who I want to be. That's why I took this job in the first place . . . and why, four years later, I still put up with the clients. And their demands. And their wads of money. Most of the time, they just want to keep a low profile, which is actually the bank's specialty. Other times, they want a little . . . personal touch. My phone rings and I tee up the charm. "This is Oliver," I answer. "How can I help you?"

"Where the hell's your boss!?" a Southern chainsaw of a voice explodes in my ear.

"E-Excuse me?"

"Don't piss on this, Caruso! I want my *money!*"

It's not until he says the word "money," that I recognize the accent. Tanner Drew, the largest developer of luxury skyscrapers in New York City and chief patriarch of the Drew Family Office. In the world of high-net-worth individuals, a family office is as high as you get. Rockefeller. Rothschild. Gates and Soros. Once hired, the family office supervises all the advisors, lawyers, and bankers who manage the family's money. Paid professionals to maximize

every last penny. You don't speak to the family anymore—
you speak to the office. So if the head of the clan is calling
me directly . . . I'm about to get some teeth pulled.

"Has the transfer not posted yet, Mr. Drew?"

"You're damn right it hasn't posted yet, smartass! Now
what the hell you gonna do to make that right? Your boss
promised me it'd be here by two o'clock! *Two o'clock!*" he
screams.

"I'm sorry, sir, but Mr. Lapidus is—"

"I don't give a raccoon's ass where he is—the guy at
Forbes gave me a deadline of today; I gave *your boss* that
deadline, and now I'm giving *you* that deadline! What the
hell else we need to discuss!?"

My mouth goes dry. Every year, the Forbes 400 lists the
wealthiest 400 individuals in the United States. Last year,
Tanner Drew was number 403. He wasn't pleased. So this
year, he's determined to bump himself up a notch. Or three.
Too bad for me, the only thing standing in his way is a forty-
million-dollar transfer to his personal account that we apparently still haven't released.

"Hold on one second, sir, I . . ."

"Don't you dare put me on h—"

I push the hold button and pray for rain. A quick extension
later, I'm waiting to hear the voice of Judy Sklar, Lapidus's
secretary. All I get is voicemail. With the boss at a partners
retreat for the rest of the day, she's got no reason to stick
around. I hang up and start again. This time, I go straight to
DEFCON One. Henry Lapidus's cell phone. On the first
ring, no one answers. Same on the second. By the third, all
I can do is stare at the blinking red light on my phone.
Tanner Drew is still waiting.

I click back to him and grab my own cell phone.

"I'm just waiting for a callback from Mr. Lapidus," I explain.

"Son, if you ever put me on hold again . . ."

Whatever he's saying, I'm not listening. Instead, my fingers snake across my cell, rapidly dialing Lapidus's pager. The moment I hear the beep, I enter my extension and add the number "1822." The ultimate emergency: 911 doubled.

". . . nother one of your sorry-ass excuses—all I want to hear is that the transfer's complete!"

"I understand, sir."

"No, son. You don't."

C'mon, I beg, staring at my cell. *Ring!*

"What time does your last transfer go out?" he barks.

"Actually, we officially close at three . . ." The clock on my wall says a quarter past three.

". . . but sometimes we can extend it until four." When he doesn't respond, I add, "Now what's the account number and bank it's supposed to go to?"

He quickly relays the details, which I scribble on a nearby Post-it. Eventually, he adds, "Oliver Caruso, right? That's your name?" His voice is soft and smooth.

"Y-Yes, sir."

"Okay, Mr. Caruso. That's all I need to know." With that, he hangs up. I look at my silent cell phone. Still nothing.

Within three minutes, I've paged and dialed every other partner I have access to. No one answers. This is a hundred-and-twenty-five-million-dollar account. I pull off my coat and claw at my tie. With a quick scan of our network's Rolodex, I find the number for the University Club—home of the partners retreat. By the time I start dialing, I swear I can hear my own heartbeat.

"You've reached the University Club," a female voice answers.

"Hi, I'm looking for Henry Lapi—"

"If you'd like to speak to the club operator or to a guest room, please press zero," the recorded voice continues.

I pound zero and another mechanized voice says, "All operators are busy—please continue to hold." Grabbing my cell, I dial frantically, looking for anyone with authority. Baraff . . . Bernstein . . . Mary in Accounting—Gone, Gone, and Gone.

I hate Fridays close to Christmas. Where the hell is everyone?

In my ear, the mechanized female voice repeats, "All operators are busy—please continue to hold."

I'm tempted to hit the panic button and call Shep, who's in charge of the bank's security, but . . . no . . . too much of a stickler . . . without the right signatures, he'll never let me get away with it. So if I can't find someone with transfer authority, I need to at least find someone in the back office who can—

I got it.

My brother.

With my receiver in one ear and my cell in the other, I shut my eyes and listen as his phone rings. Once . . . twice . . .

"I'm Charlie," he answers.

"You're still here!?"

"Nope—I left an hour ago," he deadpans. "Figment of your imagination."

I ignore the joke. "Do you still know where Mary in Accounting keeps her username and password?"

"I think so . . . why?"

"Don't go anywhere! I'll be right down."

My fingers dance like lightning across my phone's keypad, forwarding my line to my cell phone—just in case the University Club picks up.

Dashing out of my office, I make a sharp right and head straight for the private elevator at the end of the dark mahogany-paneled hallway. I don't care if it's just for clients. I enter Lapidus's six-digit code at the keypad above the call buttons, and the doors slide open. Shep in Security wouldn't like that one either.

The instant I step inside, I spin around and pound the *Door Close* button. Last week, I read in some business book that *Door Close* buttons in elevators are almost always disconnected—they're just there to make hurried people feel like they're in control. Wiping a forehead full of sweat back through my dark brown hair, I push the button anyway. Then I push it again. Three floors to go.

"Well, well, well," Charlie announces, looking up from a stack of papers with his forever-boyish grin. Lowering his chin, he peers over his vintage horn-rimmed glasses. He's been wearing the glasses for years—way before they were fashionable. The same holds true for his white shirt and rumpled slacks. Both are hand-me-downs from my closet, but somehow, the way they hang on his lean frame, they look perfect. Downtown stylish; never preppy. "Look who's slumming!" he cheers. "Hey, where's your *'I'm no longer a member of the proletariat'* button?"

I ignore the jab. It's something I've had to get used to over the past few months. Six months, to be exact—which is how long it's been since I got him the job at the bank. He needed the money, and mom and I needed help with the bills. If it were just gas, electric, and rent, we'd be fine. But our tab at the hospital—for Charlie, that's always been personal. It's the only reason he took the job in the first place. And while I know he just sees it as a way to pitch in while he writes his music, it can't be easy for him to see me up in a private office with a walnut desk and a leather chair, while he's down here with the cubicles and beige Formica.

"Whatsa matter?" he asks as I rub my eyes. "The fluorescent light making you sick? If you want, I'll go upstairs and get your lamp—or maybe I should bring down your mini-Persian rug—I know how the industrial carpet hurts your—"

"Can you please shut up for a second!"

"What happened?" he asks, suddenly concerned. "Is it mom?"

That's always his first question when he sees me upset—especially after the debt collectors gave her a scare last month. "No, it's not mom . . ."

"Then don't do that! You almost gave me a vomit attack!"

"I'm sorry . . . I just . . . I'm running out of time. One of our clients . . . Lapidus was supposed to put through a transfer, and I just got my ass handed to me because it still hasn't arrived."

Kicking his clunky black shoes up on his desk, Charlie tips his chair back on its hind legs and grabs a yellow can of Play-Doh from the corner of his desk. Lifting it to his nose, he cracks open the top, steals a sniff of childhood, and lets out a laugh. It's a typical high-pitched, little-brother laugh.

"How can you think this is funny?" I demand.

"That's what you're worried about? Some guy didn't get his walking-around money? Tell him to wait until Monday."

"Why don't you tell him—his name's Tanner Drew."

Charlie's chair drops to the floor. "Are you serious?" he asks. "How much?"

I don't answer.

"C'mon, Ollie, I won't make a big deal."

I still don't say a word.

"Listen, if you didn't want to tell me, why'd you come down?"

There's no debating that one. My answer's a whisper. "Forty million dollars."

"Forty mil!?" he screams. *"Are you on the pipe!?"*

"You said you wouldn't make a big deal!"

"Ollie, this isn't like shorting some goober a roll of quarters. When you're talking eight figures . . . even to Tanner that's not spare change—and the guy already owns half of downt—"

"Charlie!" I shout.

He stops right there—he already knows I'm wound too tight.

"I could really use your help," I add, watching his reaction.

For anyone else, it'd be a moment to treasure—an admission of weakness that could forever retip the scales between walnut desks and beige Formica. To be honest, I probably have it coming.

My brother looks me straight in the eye. "Tell me what you need me to do," he says.

Sitting in Charlie's chair, I enter Lapidus's username and password. I may not be squatting at the top of the totem pole, but I'm still an associate. The youngest associate—and the only one assigned directly to Lapidus. In a place with only twelve partners, that alone gets me further than most. Like me, Lapidus didn't grow up with a money clip in his pocket. But the right job, with the right boss, led him to the right business school, which launched him up through the private elevators. Now he's ready to return the favor. As he taught me on my first day, the simple plans work best. I help him; he helps me. Like Charlie, we all have our ways of getting out of debt.

As I scooch forward in the chair, I wait for the computer to kick in. Behind me, Charlie's sidesaddle on the armrest, leaning on my back and the edge of my shoulder for balance. When I angle my head just right, I see our warped images in the curve of the computer screen. If I squint real quick, we look like kids. But just like that, Tanner Drew's corporate account lights up the screen—and everything else is gone.

Charlie's eyes go straight to the balance: $126,023,164.27. "*A la peanut butter sandwiches!* My balance is so low I don't order sodas with my meals anymore, and this guy thinks he's got a right to complain?"

It's hard to argue—even to a bank like us, that's a lot of change. Of course, saying Greene & Greene is just a bank is like saying Einstein's "good at math."

Greene & Greene is what's known as a "private bank." That's our main service: privacy—which is why we don't take just anyone's money. In fact, when it comes to clients, they don't choose us; we choose them. And like most banks, we require a minimum deposit. The difference is, our minimum is two million dollars. And that's just to *open* your account. If you have five million, we say, "That's good—a nice start." At fifteen million, "We'd like to talk." And at seventy-five million and above, we gas up the private jet and come see you right away, Mr. Drew, sir, yes, sir.

"I knew it," I say, pointing at the screen. "Lapidus didn't even cue it in the system. He must've completely forgotten the whole thing." Using another one of Lapidus's passwords, I quickly type in the first part of the request.

"Are you sure it's okay to use his password like that?"

"Don't worry—it'll be fine."

"Maybe we should call Security and Shep can—"

"I don't want to call Shep!" I insist, knowing the outcome.

Shaking his head, Charlie looks back at the screen. Under

Current Activity, he spots three check disbursements—all of them to "Kelli Turnley."

"I bet that's his mistress," he says.

"Why?" I ask. "Because she has a name like *Kelli?*"

"You better believe it, Watson. Jenni, Candi, Brandi—it's like a family pass to the Playboy Mansion—show the 'i' and you get right in."

"First of all, you're wrong. Second of all, without exaggeration, that's the stupidest thing I've ever heard. And third . . ."

"What was dad's first girlfriend's name? Lemme think . . . was it . . . *Randi?*" With a quick shove, I push my chair back, knock Charlie off the sidesaddle, and storm out of his cubicle.

"Don't you want to hear her turn-ons and turn-offs?" he calls out behind me.

Heading up the hallway, I'm lost in my cell phone, still listening to recorded greetings of the University Club. Enraged, I hang up and start again. This time, I actually get a voice.

"University Club—how may I assist you?"

"I'm trying to reach Henry Lapidus—he's in a meeting in one of your conference rooms."

"Please hold, sir, and I'll . . ."

"Don't transfer me! I need to find him *now*."

"I'm just the operator, sir—the best I can do is transfer you down there."

There's a click and another noise. "You've reached the University Club's Conference Center. All operators are busy—please continue to hold."

Clutching the phone even tighter, I race up the hallway and stop at an unmarked metal door. *The Cage*, as it's known throughout the bank, is one of the few private offices on the floor and also home to our entire money transfer system. Cash, checks, wires—it all starts here.

Naturally, there's a punch-code lock above the doorknob. Lapidus's code gets me in. Managing Director goes everywhere.

Ten steps behind me, Charlie enters the six-person office. The rectangular room runs along the back wall of the fourth floor, but inside, it's the same as the cubes: fluorescent lights, modular desks, gray carpet. The only differences are the industrial-sized adding machines that decorate everyone's desks. Accounting's version of Play-Doh.

"Why do you always have to blow up like that?" Charlie asks as he catches up.

"Can we please not talk about it here?"

"Just tell me why you—"

"Because I work here!" I shout, spinning around. "And you work here—and our personal lives should stay at home! Is that okay?" In his hands, he's holding a pen and his small notepad. The student of life. "And don't start writing this down," I warn. "I don't need this in one of your songs."

Charlie stares at the floor, wondering if it's worth an argument. "Whatever you want," he says, lowering the pad. He never fights about his art.

"Thank you," I offer, heading deeper into the office. But just as I approach Mary's desk, I hear scribbling behind me. "What're you doing?"

"I'm sorry," he laughs, jotting a few final words in his notepad. "Okay, I'm done."

"What'd you write?" I demand.

"Nothing, just a—"

"What'd you write!?"

He holds up the notepad. "*I don't need this in one of your songs*," he relays. "How good of an album title is that?"

Without responding, I once again look back at Mary's desk. "Can you please just show me where she keeps her password?"

Strolling over to the neatest, most organized desk in the room, he mockingly brushes off Mary's seat, slides into her chair, and reaches for the three plastic picture frames that stand next to her computer. There's a twelve-year-old boy holding a football, a nine-year-old boy in a baseball uniform, and a six-year-old girl posing with a soccer ball. Charlie goes straight for the one with the football and turns it upside down. Under the base of the frame is her username and password: marydamski—3BUG5E. Charlie shakes his head, smiling. "Firstborn kid—always loved the most."

"How did you . . . ?"

"She may be the queen of numbers, but she hates computers. One day I came in, she asked me for a good hiding spot, and I told her to try the photos."

Typical Charlie. Everyone's pal.

I turn on Mary's computer and glance at the clock on the wall: 3:37 P.M. Barely twenty-five minutes to go. Using her password, I go straight to *Funds Disbursement*. There's Tanner's transfer queued up on Mary's screen—waiting for final approval. I type in the code for Tanner's bank, as well as the account number he gave me.

"Requested Amount?" It almost hurts to enter: *$40,000,000.00*.

"That's a lot of sweet potatoes," Charlie says.

I look up at the clock on the wall: 3:45 P.M. Fifteen minutes to spare.

Behind me, Charlie's once again jotting something in his notepad. That's his mantra: G*rab the world; eat a dandelion.* I move the cursor to *Send*. Almost done.

"Can I ask you a question?" Charlie calls out. Before I can

answer, he adds, "How cool would it be if this whole thing was a scam?"

"What?"

"The whole thing . . . the phone call, the yelling . . ." He laughs as he plays it out in his head. "With all the chaos blowing, how do you know that was the real Tanner Drew?"

My body stiffens. *"Excuse me?"*

"I mean, the guy has a family office—how do you even know what his voice sounds like?"

I let go of the mouse and try to ignore the chill that licks the hairs on the back of my neck. I turn around to face my brother. He's stopped writing.

2

What're you saying? You think it's fake?"

"I have no idea—but just think how easy that was: Some guy calls up, threatens that he wants his forty million bucks, then gives you an account number and says 'Make it happen.'"

I stare back at the eleven-digit account number that's glowing on the screen in front of me. "No," I insist. "It can't be."

"Can't be? It's just like that novel they release every year—the villain sets up the overachiever hero right at the beginning . . ."

"This isn't a stupid book!" I shout. "It's my life!"

"It's both our lives," he adds. "And all I'm saying is the moment you hit that button, the money could be headed straight to some bank in the Bahamas."

My eyes stay locked on the glow of the account number. The more I look at it, the brighter it burns.

"And you know who gets hit if that money disappears . . ."

He's careful the way he says that. As we both know, Greene & Greene isn't like a normal bank. Citibank, Bank of America—they're big faceless corporations. Not here. Here, we're still a closely held partnership. For our clients, it keeps us exempt from some of the government's reporting requirements, which helps us maintain our low profile, which keeps our names out of the papers, which allows us to pick only the clients we want. Like I said: You don't open an account at Greene. We open one with you.

In return, the partners get to manage a significant amount of wealth under an incredibly small roof. More important— as I stare at Tanner's forty-million-dollar transfer—each partner is personally liable for *all* of the bank's holdings. At last count, we had thirteen billion dollars under management. That's *billion*. With a B. Divided by twelve partners.

Forget Tanner—all I can think of now is Lapidus. My boss. And the one person who'll shove the walking papers down my throat if I lose one of the bank's biggest clients. "I'm telling you, there's no way it's all a setup," I insist. "I overheard Lapidus talking about the transfer last week. I mean, it's not like Tanner's calling up out of nowhere."

"Unless, of course, Lapidus is in on it . . ."

"Will you stop already? You're starting to sound like . . . like . . ."

"Like someone who knows what he's talking about?"

"No, like a paranoid lunatic divorced from reality."

"I'll have you know, I'm offended by the word *lunatic*. And the word *from*."

"Maybe we should just call him to be safe."

"Not a bad idea," Charlie agrees.

The clock on the wall says I have four minutes. What's the worst a phone call can do?

I quickly scan the Client Directory for Tanner's home number. All it has is his family office. Sometimes, privacy sucks. With no other choice, I dial the number and look at the clock. Three and a half minutes.

"Drew Family Office," a woman answers.

"This is Oliver Caruso at Greene & Greene—I need to talk to Mr. Drew. It's an emergency."

"What kind of emergency?" she snips. I can practically hear the sneer.

"A forty-million-dollar one."

There's a pause. "Please hold."

"Are they getting him?" Charlie asks.

Ignoring the question, I click back to the wire transfer menu and put the cursor on *Send*. Charlie's back on sidesaddle, grabbing the shoulder of my shirt in an anxious fist.

"Momma needs a new pair of stilettos . . ." he whispers.

Thirty seconds later, I hear the secretary back on the line. "I'm sorry, Mr. Caruso—he's not answering his work line."

"Does he have a cell phone?"

"Sir, I'm not sure you understand . . ."

"Actually, I understand just fine. Now what's your name, so I can tell Mr. Drew who I was talking to?"

Again, a pause. "Please hold."

We're down to a minute and ten seconds. I know the bank is synchronized with the Fed, but you can only cut these things so close.

"What're you gonna do?" Charlie asks.

"We'll make it," I tell him.

Fifty seconds.

My eyes are glued to the digital button marked *Send*. At the top of the screen, I've already scrolled past the line that reads "$40,000,000.00," but right now, that's all I see. I put the phone on *Speaker* to free my hands. On my shoulder, I feel the grip of Charlie's fist tighten.

Thirty seconds.

"Where the hell is this woman?"

My hand's shaking so hard against the mouse, it's moving the cursor onscreen. We don't have a chance.

"This is it," Charlie says. "Time to make a decision."

He's right about that one. The problem is . . . I . . . I just can't. Searching for help, I look over my shoulder, back to my brother. He doesn't say a word, but I hear it all. He knows where we're from. He knows I've spent four years killing myself here. For all of us, this job is our way out of the emergency room. With twenty seconds to go, he nods his head ever so slightly.

That's all I need—just a nudge to eat the dandelions. I turn back to the monitor. *Push the button*, I tell myself. But just as I go to do it, my whole body freezes. My stomach craters and the world starts to blur.

"C'mon!" Charlie shouts.

The words echo, but they're lost. We're in final seconds.

"Oliver, push the damn button!"

He says something else, but all I feel is the sharp yank on the back of my shirt. Pulling me out of the way, Charlie leans forward. I watch his hand come thundering down, pounding the mouse with a tight fist. On screen, the *Send* icon blinks into a negative of itself, then back again. A rectangular box appears three seconds later:

Status: Pending.

"Does that mean we—?"

Status: Approved.

Charlie now realizes what we're looking at. So do I.

Status: Paid.

That's it. All sent. The forty-million-dollar e-mail.

We both look at the speakerphone, waiting for a response. All we get is a cruel silence. My mouth hangs open. Charlie finally lets go of my shirt. Our chests rise and fall at the same pace . . . but for entirely different reasons. Fight and flight. I turn to my brother . . . my younger brother . . . but he won't say a word. And then, there's a crackle from the phone. A voice.

"Caruso," Tanner Drew growls in a Southern accent that's now as unmistakable as a fork in the eye, "if this isn't a confirmation call, you better start praying to heaven above."

"I-It is, sir," I say, fighting back a grin. "Just a confirmation."

"Fine. Goodbye." With a slam, it's over.

I turn around, but it's too late. My brother's already gone.

Racing out of The Cage, I scan for Charlie—but as always, he's too fast. At his cubicle, I grab on to the top edges of his wall, boost myself up, and peek inside. With his feet up on his desk, he's scribbling in a spiral green notebook, pen cap in mouth and lost in thought.

"So was Tanner happy?" he asks without turning around.

"Yeah, he was thrilled. All he could do was thank me— over and over and over. Finally, I was like, 'No, you don't have to include me in the *Forbes* profile—just having you make the top 400 is all the thanks I need.'"

"That's great," Charlie says, finally facing me. "I'm glad it worked out."

I hate it when he does that. "Go ahead," I beg. "Just say it."

He drops his feet to the floor and tosses his notebook on his desk. It lands right next to the Play-Doh, which is only a few inches from his collection of green army men, which is right below the black-and-white bumper sticker on his computer monitor which reads, "I sell out to The Man every day!"

"Listen, I'm sorry for freezing like that," I tell him.

"Don't worry about it, bro—happens to everyone."

God, to have that temperament. "So you're not disappointed with me?"

"Disappointed? That was your puppy, not mine."

"I know . . . it's just . . . you're always teasing me about getting soft . . ."

"Oh, you're definitely soft—all this high living and elbow-rubbing—you're a full-fledged baby's bottom."

"Charlie . . . !"

"But not a soft baby's bottom—one of those completely hard ones—like a sumo baby or something."

I can't help but smile at the joke. It's not nearly as good as the one three months ago, when he tried to talk in a pirate voice for an entire day (which he did), but it'll do. "How about coming over tonight and letting me say thank you with some dinner?"

Charlie pauses, studying me. "Only if we don't take a private car."

"Will you stop? You know the bank would pay for it after everything we did tonight."

He shakes his head disapprovingly. "You've changed, man—I don't even know you anymore . . ."

"Fine, fine, forget the car. How about a cab?"

"How 'bout the subway?"

"I'll pay for the cab."

"A cab it is."

Ten minutes later, after a quick stop in my office, we're up on the seventh floor, waiting for the elevator. "Think they'll give you a medal?"

"For what?" I ask. "For doing my job?"

"*Doing your job?* Aw, now you sound like one of those neighborhood heroes who pulled a dozen kittens out of a burning building. Face facts, Superman—you just saved this place from a forty-million-dollar nightmare—and not the good kind either."

"Yeah, well, just do me a favor and tone down the advertising for a bit. Even if it was for a good reason, we were still stealing other people's passwords to do it."

"So?"

"So you know how they are with security around here—"

Before I can finish, the elevator pings and the doors slide open. At this hour, I expect it to be empty, but instead, a thick man with a football-player-sized chest is leaning against the back wall. Shep Graves—the bank's VP of Security. Dressed in a shirt and tie that could've only been bought at the local Big & Tall, Shep knows how to hold his shoulders back so his late-thirties frame looks as young and strong as possible. For his job—protecting our thirteen billion—he has to. Even with the most state-of-the-art technology at his fingertips, there's still no deterrent like fear—which is why, as we step into the elevator, I decide to end our discussion of Tanner Drew. Indeed, when it comes to Shep, except for some minor chitchat, no one in the bank really talks to him.

"*Shep!*" Charlie shouts as soon as he sees him. "How's my favorite manhandler of misappropriation?" Shep puts his hand out and Charlie taps his fingers like they're piano keys.

"You see what they got going at Madison?" Shep asks with a clumsy boxer's grin. There's a trace of a Brooklyn accent, but wherever he's been, they trained it out of him. "They got a girl who wants to play boys varsity b-ball."

"Good—that's the way it should be. When do we see her play?" Charlie asks.

"There's a scrimmage in two weeks . . ."

Charlie grins. "You drive; I'll pay."

"Scrimmages are free."

"Fine, I'll pay for you too," Charlie says. Noticing my silence, he motions me into the elevator. "Shep, you ever meet my brother, Oliver?"

We both nod our cordial nods. "Nice to see you," we say simultaneously.

"Shep went to Madison," Charlie says, proudly referring to our old rival high school in Brooklyn.

"So you also went to Sheepshead Bay?" Shep asks. It's a simple question, but the tone of his voice—it feels like an interrogation.

I nod and turn around to hit the *Door Close* button. Then I hit it again. Finally, the doors slide shut.

"So what're you guys doing here with everyone else gone?" he asks. "Anything interesting?"

"No," I blurt. "Same as usual."

Charlie shoots me an annoyed look. "Didja know Shep used to be in the Secret Service?" he asks.

"That's great," I say, my eyes focused on the five-course menu that's posted above the call buttons. The bank has its own private chef just for client visits. It's the easiest way to impress. Today they served lamb chops and rosemary risotto appetizers. I'm guessing a twenty- to twenty-five-million-dollar client. Lamb chops only come out if you're over fifteen.

The elevator slows at the fifth floor and Shep elbows himself off the back wall. "This is me," he announces, heading for the doors. "Enjoy the weekend."

"You too," Charlie calls out. Neither of us says another word until the doors shut. "What's wrong with you?" Charlie lays into me. "When'd you become such a sourpuss?"

"Sourpuss? That's all you got, Grandma?"

"I'm serious—he's a nice guy—you didn't have to blow him off like that."

"What do you want me to say, Charlie? All the guy ever does is lurk around and act suspicious. Then suddenly, you walk in and he's Mr. Sunshine."

"See, there's where you're wrong. He's always Mr. Sunshine—in fact, he's a rainbow of fruit flavors—but you're so busy angling with Lapidus and Tanner Drew and all the other bigshots, you forget that the little people know how to talk too."

"I asked you to stop with that . . ."

"When was the last time you spoke to a cab driver, Ollie? And I'm not talking about saying '53rd and Lex'—I'm talking a full-fledged conversation: 'How ya been? What time'd you start? You ever see anyone shaking their yummies in the backseat?'"

"So that's what you think? That I'm an intellectual snob?"

"You're not smart enough to be an intellectual snob—but you are a cultural one." The elevator doors open, and Charlie races into the lobby, which is filled with a grid of gorgeous antique rolltop desks that add just the right old-money feel. When clients come in and the hive is buzzing with bankers, it's the first thing they see—that is, unless we're trying to close someone big, in which case we bring them through the private entrance around back and lead them straight past Chef Charles and his just-for-us, oh-you-should-check-out-our-million-dollar kitchen. Charlie blows past it. I'm right behind him. "Don't worry, though," he calls out. "I still love you . . . even if Shep doesn't."

Reaching the side exit, we punch in our codes at the keypad just inside the thick metal door. It clicks open and leads us into a short anteroom with a revolving door on the far end. In the industry, we call it a man-trap. The revolving door doesn't open until the door behind us is closed. If there's a problem, they both shut and you're nabbed.

Without a care, Charlie closes the metal door behind himself and there's a slight hiss. Titanium bolts clamp shut. When it's done, there's a loud thunk straight ahead. Magnetic locks on the revolving door slide open. On both ends of the room, two cameras are so well hidden, we don't even know where they are.

"C'mon," Charlie says, charging forward. We spin through the revolving doors and get dumped out on the black-snow-lined streets of Park Avenue. Behind us, the bank's subdued brick facade fades inconspicuously into the low-rise landscape—which is really why you go to a private bank in the first place. Like an American version of a Swiss bank, we're there to keep your secrets. That's why the only sign out front is a designed-to-be-missed brass plaque that reads, *"Greene & Greene, est. 1870."* And while most people have never heard of private banks, they're closer than anyone thinks. It's the small, understated building people pass by every day—the unmarked one, not far from the ATM, where people always wonder, "What's in there anyway?" That's us. Right in front of everyone's face. We're just good at keeping quiet.

So is that worth the extra fees? Here's what we ask the clients: Have you gotten any credit card offers in the mail recently? If the answer's yes, it means someone sold you out. Most likely, it was your bank, who culled through your personal info and painted a bull's-eye on your back. From your balance, to your home address, to your Social Security number, it's all there for the world to see. And buy. Needless to say, rich people don't like that.

Hurdling over some recently shoveled snow, Charlie goes straight for the street. A hand in the air gets us a cab; a gas pedal sends us downtown; and a look from my brother has me asking the cab driver, "How's your day going?"

"Pretty okay," the cabbie says. "How 'bout yourself?"

"Great," I say, my eyes locked out the window on the dark sky. An hour ago, I touched forty million dollars. Right now, I'm in the back of a beat-up cab. As we hit the Brooklyn Bridge, I glance over my shoulder. The whole city—with its burning lights and soaring skyline—the whole scene is framed by the back window of the cab. The further we go, the smaller the picture gets. By the time we get home, it's completely disappeared.

Eventually, the cab pulls up to a 1920s brownstone just outside of Brooklyn Heights. Technically, it's part of the rougher Red Hook district, but the address is still Brooklyn. True, the front stairs have a brick or two that're loose or missing, the metal bars on my basement apartment's windows are cracked and rotting, and the front walk is still glazed with a layer of unshoveled ice, but the cheap rent lets me live on my own in a neighborhood I'm proud to call home. That alone calms me down—that is, until I see who's waiting for me on my front steps.

Oh, God. Not now.

Our eyes lock and I know I'm in trouble.

Reading my expression, Charlie follows my gaze. "Oh, jeez," he whispers under his breath. "Nice knowing you."

3

Here! Pay!" I shout, tossing Charlie my wallet and kicking open the door to the cab. He fishes out a twenty, tells the cabbie to keep the change, and bounces his butt out of there. No way he's missing this.

Skidding across the ice, I'm already in apology mode: "Beth, I'm so sorry—I totally forgot!"

"Forgot what?" she asks, her voice as calm and pleasant as can be.

"Our dinner . . . inviting you out here . . ."

"Don't worry—it's already done." As she talks, I notice that she's blown her long brown hair completely straight.

"No bounce," Charlie whispers, acting innocent behind me.

"I have my own key, remember?" Beth asks. She steps around me, but I'm still confused.

"Where're you going?"

"Soda. You were all out."

"Beth, why don't you let me . . ."

"Go relax—I'll be right back." She turns away from me, and it's the first time she sees Charlie.

"What's shakin', bacon?" He opens his arms for a huge hug. She doesn't take him up on it.

"Hi, Charlie."

She tries to step around him, but he cuts in front of her. "So how's the world of corporate accounting?" he asks.

"It's good."

"And your clients?"

"They're good."

"And your family—how're they?"

"Good," she smiles, putting up her best defense. Not an annoyed smile; not a jaded smile; not even an angry get-outta-my-face-you-overhyper-little-gnat kinda smile. Just a nice, calming Beth smile.

"And whattya think of vanilla as an ice cream flavor?" Charlie asks, raising a devilish eyebrow.

"*Charlie*," I warn.

"What?" Turning to Beth, he adds, "So you sure you don't mind if I crash all over your dinner?"

She looks to me, then back at Charlie. "Maybe it'd be better if I left you two alone."

"Don't be silly," I jump in.

"It's okay," she adds with a wave that tells me not to worry about it. She's never one to complain. "You two should have some time together. Oliver, I'll call you later."

Before either of us can stop her, she walks up the block. Charlie's eyes are on her L.L. Bean duck boots. "My God— my whole sorority had those," he whispers. I pinch the skin on his back and give it a twist. It doesn't shut him up. As Beth walks, her beige camel-hair coat fans out behind her. "Like Darth Vader—only boring," Charlie adds.

He knows she can't hear him, which only makes it worse.

"I'd give my left nut to see her slip on her ass," he says as she disappears up the block. "No such luck. Bye-bye, baby."

I shoot Charlie a look. "Why do you always have to make fun of her like that?"

"I'm sorry—she just makes it so easy."

I spin around and storm for the door.

"What?" he asks.

I yell without facing him. Just like dad. "You can be a real jerk-off, y'know that?"

He thinks about it for a second. "I guess I can."

Once again, I refuse to face him. He knows he's pushed too far. "C'mon, Ollie—I'm only teasing," he says, chasing me down the wobbly-brick stairway. "I only say it because I'm secretly in love with her."

I stuff my key in the door and pretend he's not there. That lasts about two seconds. "Why do you hate her so much?"

"I don't hate *her*, I just . . . I hate everything she stands for. Everything she represents. The boots, the quiet smile, the inability to express anything approaching an opinion . . . that's not what I— It's not what you should want for yourself."

"Really?"

"I'm serious," he says as I work on the third deadbolt. "It's the same thing as this teeny basement apartment. I mean, no offense, but it's like taking the blue pill and waking up in a young urban twentysomething sitcom nightmare."

"You just don't like Brooklyn Heights."

"You don't live in Brooklyn Heights," he insists. "You live in Red Hook. Understand? Red. Hook."

As I shove open the door, Charlie follows me into the apartment.

"Well, bust out the Magic Markers and color me impressed," he says, wandering inside. "Look who's decorated."

"I don't know what you're talking about."

"Don't play modest with me, Versace. When you first moved in, you had a used, stained mattress from Goodwill, a dresser you stole from our old bedroom, and the table and chairs mom and I bought from Kmart as a housewarming gift. Today, what's that I see on the bed? A knockoff Calvin Klein comforter? Plus the Martha Stewart faux-antique crackle-paint on the dresser, and the table that's now sporting the imitation Ralph Lauren tablecloth, perfectly set for two. Don't think I missed that sweetheart touch. And while I appreciate what you're trying to do, it's like the existence of show towels, bro—the whole thing's a symptom of a deeper problem."

He repeats the last few words to himself. *"Symptom of a deeper problem."* Stopping in the kitchen, he pulls out his notepad and jots them down. *"For some, life is an audition,"* he adds. His head bobs in place as he puts together a quick melody. When he gets like this, it takes a few minutes, so I leave him be. On his notepad, his hand suddenly stops, then starts scribbling. The pen scratches furiously against the page. As he flips to the next sheet, I spot a tiny, perfect sketch of a man bowing in front of a curtain. He's done writing—now he's drawing.

It's the first thing that came naturally to him, and when he wants to, Charlie can be an incredible artist. So incredible, in fact, that the New York School of Visual Arts was willing to overlook his spotty high school record and give him a full college scholarship. Two years into it, they tried to steer him into commercial work, like advertising and illustration. "It's a nice living," they told him. But the instant Charlie saw career and art converge, he dropped out and finished his last two years at Brooklyn College studying music. I yelled at him for two days straight. He told me there's more to life than designing the new logo for a bottle of detergent.

Across the room, I hear him wandering through the rest of the apartment and sniffing the air. "Mmmmm . . . smells like Oliver," he announces. "Air freshener and loafer whiff."

"Get out of my bathroom," I call out from my bed, where I've already opened my briefcase to flip through some paperwork.

"Don't you ever stop?" Charlie asks. "It's the weekend— relax already."

"I need to finish this," I shoot back.

"Listen, I'm sorry about the vanilla joke . . ."

"*I need to finish this*," I insist.

He knows that tone. Letting the silence sink in, he curls up on the foot of the bed.

Two minutes later, the lack of noise does the trick. "Sometimes I hate rich people," I finally moan.

"No, you don't," he teases. "You love 'em. You've always loved 'em. The more money, the merrier."

"I'm serious," I say. "It's like, once they get some cash— bam!—there goes their grasp of reality. I mean, look at this guy . . ." I pull the top sheet from the paper pile and wing it his way. "This moron misplaces three million dollars for five years. *Five years* he's forgotten about it! But when we tell him we're about to take it away from him—that's when he wakes up and wants it back."

He reads the letter signed by someone named Marty Duckworth—"*Thank you for your correspondence . . . please be aware that I've opened a new account at the following New York bank . . . please forward the balance of my funds there.*"—but to Charlie, it still looks like just another normal wire request. "I don't understand."

I wave the short paper stack in front of him. "It's an abandoned account." Knowing he's lost, I add, "Under New York law, when a customer doesn't use an account for five years, the money gets turned over to the state."

"That doesn't make sense—who would ever abandon their own cash?"

"Mostly dead people," I say. "It happens in every bank in the country—when someone dies, or gets sick, sometimes they forget to tell their family about their account. The cash just sits there for years—and if there's no activity on the account, it eventually gets labeled *inactive*."

"So after year five, we just ship that money to the government?"

"That's part of what I'm working on. When it hits year four and a half, we're required to send out a warning letter saying '*Your account's going to be turned over to the state.*' At that point, anyone who's still alive usually responds, which is better for us, since it keeps the money in the bank."

"So that's your responsibility? Dealing with dead people? Man, and I thought my customer service skills were bad."

"Don't laugh—some of these folks are still alive. They just forget where they put their cash."

"Y'mean like Mr. Three-Million-Dollar Duckworth over here."

"That's our boy," I say. "The only bad part is, he wants to transfer it somewhere else."

Looking down, Charlie rereads the grainy type on the faxed letter. He runs his fingers across the blurry signature. Then, his eyes shoot to the top of the page. Something catches his eye. I follow his fingers. The phone number on the top of the fax. He makes that face like he smells sewage.

"When'd you get this letter again?" Charlie asks.

"Sometime today, why?"

"And when does the money get turned over to the state?"

"Monday—which is why I assume he sent it by fax."

"Yeah," Charlie nods, though I can tell he's barely listening. His whole face flushes red. Here we go.

"What's wrong?" I ask.

"Lookie here," he says, pointing to the return fax number at the top of the letter. "Does this number look familiar to you?"

I grab the sheet and study it close. "Never seen it before in my life. Why? You know it?"

"You could say that . . ."

"Charlie, get to the point—tell me what's—"

"It's the Kinko's around the corner from the bank."

I force a nervous laugh. "What're you talking about?"

"I'm telling you—the bank doesn't let us use the fax for personal business—so when Franklin or Royce need to send me sheet music, it goes straight to Kinko's—and straight to that number."

I look down at the letter. "Why would a millionaire, who can buy ten thousand fax machines of his own, and can walk right into the bank, send us a fax from a copy shop that's right around the corner?"

Charlie shoots me a way-too-excited grin. "Maybe we're not dealing with a millionaire."

"What're you saying? You think Duckworth didn't send this letter?"

"You tell me—have you spoken to him lately?"

"We're not required to—" I cut myself off, suddenly seeing what he's driving at. "All we do is send a letter to his last known address, and one to his family," I begin. "But if we want to be safe, there's one place open late . . ." I sit up in bed, flick on the speakerphone, and start dialing.

"Who're you calling?"

The first thing we hear is a recorded voice. "Welcome to Social Se—"

Without even listening, I hit one, then zero, then two on the phone. I've been here before. The speaker fills with Muzak.

"The Beatles. 'Let It Be,'" Charlie points out.

"Shhh," I hiss.

"Thank you for calling Social Security," a female voice eventually picks up. "How can I help you?"

"Hi, this is Oliver Caruso calling from Greene & Greene Bank in New York," I say in that overly sweet voice I know turns Charlie's stomach. It's the tone I save for customer service reps—and no matter how much Charlie despises it, deep down, he knows it works. "I'm wondering if you can help us out," I continue. "We have a loan application that we're working on, and we just wanted to verify the applicant's Social Security number."

"Do you have a routing number?" the woman asks.

I give her the bank's nine-digit ID. Once they get that, we get all the private info. That's the law. God bless America.

Waiting for clearance and unable to sit still, I pick at the seams of my sage green comforter. It doesn't take long to come undone.

"And the number you'd like to check?" the woman asks.

Reading from the printout of abandoned accounts, I give her Duckworth's Social Security number. "It's under the name Marty or Martin."

A second passes. Then another. "Did you say this was for a loan application?" the woman asks, confused.

"Yeah," I say anxiously. "Why?"

"Because according to our files here, I have a June twelfth date of death."

"I don't understand."

"I'm just telling you what it says, sir. If you're looking for Martin Duckworth, he died six months ago."

4

I hang up the phone, and Charlie and I stare down at the fax. "I don't believe this."

"Me either," Charlie sings. "How *X-Files* is this moment?"

"It's not a joke," I insist. "Whoever sent this—they almost walked away with three million dollars."

"What're you talking about?"

"It's a perfect crime when you think about it. Pose as a dead person, ask for his money, and once the account's reactivated, you close up shop and disappear. It's not like Marty Duckworth's going to complain."

"But what about the government?" Charlie asks. "Won't they notice their money's missing?"

"They have no idea," I say, waving the master list of abandoned accounts. "We send them a printout, minus anything that's been reactivated. They're just happy to get some free cash."

Charlie bounces restlessly on the bed, and I can see his wheels spinning. When you eat the dandelions, everything's a thrill ride. "Who do you think did it?" he blurts.

"Got me—but it has to be someone in the bank."

Now his eyes go wide. "You think?"

"Who else would know when we sent out the final notice letters? Not to mention the fact that they're faxing from a Kinko's around the corner . . ."

Charlie nods his head in steady rhythm. "So what do we do now?"

"Are you kidding? We wait until Monday, and then we turn this bastard in."

No more nodding. "Are you sure?"

"What do you mean, *Am I sure?* What else are we gonna do? Take it ourselves?"

"I'm not saying that, but . . ." Once again, Charlie's face flushes red. "How cool would it be to have three million dollars? I mean, that'd be like . . . it'd be like—"

"It'd be like having money," I interrupt.

"And not just any money—we're talkin' three million monies." Charlie jumps to his feet and his voice picks up speed. "You give me cash like that and I'd . . . I'd get me a white suit and hold up a glass of red wine and say things like, 'I'm having an old friend for dinner . . .'"

"Not me," I say, shaking my head. "I'd pay off the hospital, take care of the bills, then take every last penny and invest it."

"Oh, c'mon, Scrooge—what's wrong with you? You have to have some insane wastefulness . . . do the full Elvis . . . now what would you buy?"

"And I have to buy something?" I think about it for a moment. "I'd get wall-to-wall carpeting . . ."

"*Wall-to-wall carpeting?* That's the best you can . . . ?"

"For my blimp!" I shout. "A blimp that we'd keep chained in the yard."

Charlie laughs out loud at that one. The game is on. His eyes squint at the challenge. "I'd buy a circus."

"I'd buy Cirque du Soleil."

"I'd buy Cirque du Soleil and rename it Cirque du Sole. It'd be a three-ring all-fish extravaganza."

I fight a smile, refusing to give up. "In my bathrooms, I'd get fur-covered toilet seats—the really good kind—like you're crapping right on top of an expensive rodent."

"Those're sweet," Charlie agrees. "But not as sweet as my *gold-plated pasta!*"

"Diamond-crusted mondel-bread."

"Sapphire-studded blueberry muffins."

"Lobsters stuffed with spare-ribs . . . or spare-ribs stuffed with lobsters! Maybe even both!" I shout.

Charlie nods. "I'd buy me the Internet—and all the porn sites."

"Nice. Very tasteful."

"I try."

"I know you do—that's why I'd buy you Orlando."

"We talking *Tony Orlando*, or we talking *Florida?*" Charlie asks.

I look him straight in the eye. "Both."

"Both?" Charlie laughs, finally impressed.

"There's the pause! Count it right there!" I shout. It's been a long time since he's been the first to give up. Still, I'll take it. It's not every day you get to beat a master at his own game.

"See, now that's what I'm talking about," he eventually says. "Why would we spend another day busting our humps at the bank when we can get ourselves blimps and Internets and lobsters?"

"You're so right, Charles," I say in my best British accent.

"And the best part is, no one would know the money was gone."

Charlie stops. "They wouldn't, would they?"

I come out of character. "What're you talking about?"

"Is it really that crazy, Ollie?" he asks, his voice now serious. "I mean, who's really gonna miss that cash? The owner's dead . . . it's about to be stolen by someone else . . . and if the government gets it . . . oh, they'll really put the funds to good use."

Just like that, I sit up straight. "Charlie, I hate to burst your seventeenth fantasy for the day, but what you're talking about is *illegal*. Say it out loud . . . *illll-eeeeeegal.*"

He shoots me a look that I haven't seen since our last fight about mom. Son of a bitch. He's not joking.

"You said it yourself, Oliver—it's the perfect crime—"

"That doesn't mean it's right!"

"Don't talk to me about right—rich people . . . big companies . . . they steal from the government all day long and no one says a word—but instead of *stealing*, we just call 'em *loopholes* and *corporate welfare.*"

Typical dreamer. "C'mon, Charlie, you know the world's not perfect . . ."

"I'm not asking for perfect—but you know how many breaks the tax code has for the rich? Or for a big corporation that can afford a good lobbyist? When people like Tanner Drew file their 1040EZ, they barely pay a dollar in income tax. But mom—who's barely making twenty-eight grand a year—half of what she owns goes straight to Uncle Sam."

"That's not true; I had the planners at the bank—"

"Don't tell me they're saving her a few bucks, Oliver. It's not gonna make a difference. Between the mortgage, and the credit cards, and everything else dad stuck us with when he left—you have any idea how long that'll take to pay off?

And that's not even including what we owe the hospital. What's that at now? Eighty thousand? Eighty-two thousand?"

"Eighty-one thousand four hundred and fifty dollars," I clarify. "But just because you feel guilty about the hospital, doesn't mean we have to—"

"It's not about guilt—it's about eighty thousand dollars, Ollie! Do you even realize how much that is? And it's still growing every time we head back to the doctor!"

"I have a plan—"

"Oh, that's right, your great, fifty-step plan! How's it go again? Lapidus and the bank bring you to business school, which'll bring you up the ladder, which'll make all our debt disappear? Does that about cover it? 'Cause I hate to break it to you, Ollie, but you've been there four years and mom's still breathing hospital fumes. We're barely making a dent—this is our chance to set her free. Think about how many years that'll add to her life! She doesn't have to be second-class anymore . . ."

"She's not second-class."

"She is, Ollie. And so are we," Charlie insists. "Now I'm sorry if that ruins your priceless self-image, but it's time to find a way to get her out. Everyone deserves a fresh start—especially mom."

As the words leave Charlie's lips, I feel them tear at my belly. He knows exactly what he's doing. Taking care of mom has always been top priority. For both of us. Of course, that doesn't mean I have to follow him over the cliff. "I don't need to be a thief."

"Who said anything about thieves?" Charlie challenges. "Thieves steal from *people*. This money doesn't belong to anyone. Duckworth's dead—you tried to contact his family—he's got no one. All we'd be taking is some cash that would never be missed. And even if something goes wrong, we can just blame it on whoever faxed us that letter. I mean, it's not like he's in any position to tell on us."

"Oh, okay, Lenin, so when we're done redistributing the wealth, we'll just take this show on the road and go on the run for the rest of our lives. That's clearly the best way to help mom—just abandon her and—"

"We don't have to abandon anyone," he insists. "We'll do exactly what this guy's doing—transfer the money out, and then we don't touch it until we know it's safe. After seven years, the FBI closes the investigation."

"Says who?"

"I read this article in the *Village Voice*—"

"The *Village Voice*?"

"No screwing around—all it takes is seven years—then we're just another unsolved file. Case closed."

"And then what do we do? Retire on the beach, open a bar, and write sappy little songs for the rest of our lives?"

"It's a lot better than wasting another four years kissing corporate ass and going nowhere."

I hop off the bed and he knows he's overstepped the boundaries. "You *know* business school is the best way out, and you *know* I can't go there directly after college," I insist, shoving a finger in his face. "You have to work a couple years first."

"Fine. A couple years—that's two. You're finishing four."

Taking a breath, I try not to lose it. "Charlie, I'm applying to the top schools in the country. Harvard, Penn, Chicago, Columbia. That's where I want to go—anything else is second best and doesn't help anyone, including mom."

"And who decided that, you or Lapidus?"

"What's that supposed to mean?"

"How many opportunities did you give up because Lapidus put his grand plan about B-school in your head? How many companies have you refused offers from? You know it as well as I do—you should've left the bank years ago. Instead, it's been back-to-back B-school rejection letters. And you think this year's gonna be any different? Broaden your horizons a little. I mean, it's just like dating Beth—sure, you make a nice picture, but that's all it is—a nice picture, Oliver—a Sears portrait of how you think things should be. You're one of the most brilliant, dynamic people I know. Stop being so scared of living."

"Then stop judging me!" I explode.

"I'm not judging you . . ."

"No, you're just asking me to steal three million dollars—that'll solve all my problems!"

"I'm not saying it's the answer to every prayer, but it's the only way we're ever gonna dig out of this."

"See, that's where you're wrong!" I shout. "You may be thrilled nursing paper cuts in the file room, but I've got my eyes on something bigger. Trust me on this one, Charlie—once I'm done with business school, mom's never gonna see another bill again. You can tease and joke all you want—sure, the path is safe, and it may be simple—but all that matters right now is that it works. And when the payoff hits, that three million dollars is gonna look like bus fare from Brooklyn."

"And that's what it's all about, isn't it? Well, let me tell you something, buddy-boy—you may think you're all private jet going straight to the summit, but from my side of the river, all you're doing is standing in line like the rest of the lower-level drones you used to hate. A drone like dad."

I want to smack him across the face, but I've been there

before. I don't need another fistfight. "You don't know what you're talking about," I growl.

"Really? So you think that even though you're one of the bank's top associates, and even though you've single-handedly brought in over twelve million dollars' worth of new accounts for Lapidus just by scouring the NYU alumni magazine, and even though almost every partner in the firm went to one of the four business schools you're applying to, it's still possible that you've been rejected two years in a row?"

"That's enough!"

"Uh-oh, sore spot! You've already thought it yourself, haven't you?"

"Shut up, Charlie!"

"I'm not saying Lapidus planned it from the start, but do you have any idea what a pain it is for him to hire someone new and train him to think exactly like he does? You gotta find the right kid . . . preferably a poor one with no connections . . ."

"I said, shut up!"

". . . promise him a job that'll keep him there for a few years so he can pay off his debt . . ."

"Charlie, I swear to God . . . !"

". . . then keep stringing him along until the poor fool actually realizes he and his whole family are going nowhere . . ."

"*Shut up!*" I yell, rushing forward. I'm in full rage. My hands go straight for the collar of his shirt.

Always the better athlete, Charlie ducks under my grasp and races back toward the eat-in kitchen. On the table, he spots a B-school catalogue from Columbia and a file folder with the word "Applications" on it.

"Are these . . . ?"

"Don't touch them!"

That's all it takes. He goes straight for the file. But just as he flips it open, a letter-sized blue-and-white envelope falls to the floor. There's a signature across the back, right where it's sealed. Henry Lapidus.

The signature on the envelope is required by all four schools—to make sure I don't open it. Indeed, the typed pages inside are the most important part of any business school application—the boss's recommendation.

"Okay, who wants to play detective?" Charlie sings, waving the envelope over his head so it scrapes the basement's low ceiling.

"Give it back!" I demand.

"Oh, c'mon, Oliver, it's been four years already—if Lapidus is locking you in the dungeon, at least this way, you get the truth."

"I already know the truth!" I yell, lunging forward and reaching out for the envelope. Once again, he ducks and spins under the attack.

Back by the bed, Charlie's no longer dangling it in front of me. For once, he's serious. "You know something's screwy, Oliver—I can see it in your eyes. This guy took four years of your life. Four years in shackles on the promise of a later payoff. If he's bashing you in the letter—forget about the fact that all the B-schools keep it on file—he's ruined the whole plan. Your way out—how to pay mom's debts— everything you were counting on. And even if you think you can start over, do you know how hard it is to move to a new job without a recommendation? Not exactly the ideal situation for covering the hospital bills and mom's mortgage payments, now is it? So why don't we just tear this bad boy open and—"

"*Let go of it!*" I explode. I plow straight at him, ready for the sidestep. But instead of ducking under, he hops backwards onto my bed and bounces like a seven-year-old. "Laaaaadies aaaaaaaaaaand geeeeentlemen, the heavyweight champion of the wooooooorld!" He sings the last part, then imitates a crowd cheering wildly. When we were little, this is where I'd dive at his feet. Sometimes I'd catch him, sometimes I'd miss—but eventually, the four-year age difference would catch up with him.

"Get off my bed!" I shout. "You'll pop one of the springs!"

Right there, Charlie stops. He's still on the bed, but he's done jumping. "I love you when I say this, Oliver—but that last statement—that's exactly the problem."

He steps to the edge of the mattress, and in one smooth move, drops himself on his butt, bounces off the bed, and springboards to his feet. No matter how risky, no matter how wild—always a perfect landing.

"Oliver, I don't care about the money," he says as he slaps the envelope against my chest. "But if you don't start making some changes soon, you're gonna be that guy who—when he hits his forty-third birthday—hates his life."

I stare him straight in the eye, unmoved by the comment. "At least I won't be living with my mother in Brooklyn."

His shoulders fall and he steps backwards. I don't care.

"Get out," I add.

At first, he just stands there.

"You heard me, Charlie—get out."

Shaking his head, he finally heads toward the door. First slow, then fast. As he turns, I swear there's a grin on his face. The door slams behind him and I look through the peephole. Doop, doop, doop—Charlie bounds up the stairs. "Open it and find out!" he shouts from outside. And just like that, he's gone.

*　*　*　*

Ten minutes after Charlie leaves, I'm sitting at my kitchen table, staring down at the envelope. Behind me, the refrigerator's humming. The radiator's clanging. And the water in the teapot is just starting to boil. I tell myself it's because I'm in the mood for some instant coffee, but my subconscious doesn't buy it for a second.

It's not like I'm talking about stealing the money. It's just about my boss. It's important to know what he thinks.

Outside, a car whizzes by, thumping through the crater-sized pothole that's in front of the brownstone. Through the tops of my windows, I see the car's black wheels. That's the only view I get from the basement. The sight of things moving on.

The water starts boiling—hitting its high note and screaming wildly through my mostly bare kitchen. Within a minute, the high-pitched shriek feels like it's been going for a year. Or two. Or four.

Across the table, I spot the most recent bill from Coney Island Hospital: $81,450. That's what happens when you miss an insurance payment to juggle your other bills. It's another two decades of mom's life. Two decades of worrying. Two decades of being trapped. Unless I can get her out.

My eyes go straight to the blue-and-white envelope. Whatever's inside . . . whatever he wrote . . . I need to know. For all of us.

I grab the envelope and shoot out of my seat so fast, I knock the chair to the floor. Before I know it, I'm standing in front of the tea kettle, watching the geyser of steam pound through the air. With a quick flick of my thumb, I open the tea kettle's spout. The whistling stops and the column of steam gets thicker.

In my hands, the envelope's shaking. Lapidus's signature, perfect as it is, becomes a mess of movement. I hold my breath and struggle to keep it steady. All I have to do is put it in the steam. But just as I go to do it, I freeze. My heart drops and everything starts to blur. It's just like what happened with the wire transfer . . . but this time . . . No. Not this time.

Tightening my grip on the envelope, I tell myself this has nothing to do with Charlie. Nothing at all. Then, in one quick moment, I hold on to the bottom of the envelope, lower the sealed side into the steam, and pray to God this works just like it does in the movies.

Almost immediately, the envelope wrinkles from the condensation. Working the corners first, I angle the edge toward the tea kettle. The steam warms my hands, but when I bring it too close, it burns the tips of my fingers. As carefully as I can, I slide my thumb into the edge of the envelope and pry open the smallest of spaces. Letting it fill with steam, I work my thumb in deeper and try to inch the flap open. It looks like it's about to rip . . . but just as I'm about to give up . . . the glue gives way. From there, I peel it like I'm pulling the back from a Band-Aid.

Tossing aside the envelope, I yank open the two-page letter. My eyes start skimming, looking for buzzwords, but it's like opening a college acceptance letter—I can barely read. *Slow down, Oliver. Start at the top.*

Dear Dean Milligan. *Personalized. Good.* I'm writing on behalf of Oliver Caruso, who is applying as a fall candidate for your MBA program . . . *blah, blah, blah* . . . Oliver's supervisor for the past four years . . . *blah and more blah* . . . sorry to say . . . *Sorry to say?* . . . that I cannot in good conscience recommend Oliver as a candidate to your school . . . much as it pains me . . . lack of professionalism . . . maturity issues . . , for his own sake, would benefit from another year of professional work experience . . .

I can barely stand. My hands clamp tightly around the letter, chewing the sides to pieces. My eyes flood with tears. And somewhere . . . beyond the potholes . . . across the bridge . . . I swear I hear someone laughing. And someone else saying, "I told you so."

Spinning around, I race to the closet and pull out my coat. If Charlie's taking the bus, I can still catch him. Gripping the letter as I fight my coat on, I yank open the door and—

"So?" Charlie asks, sitting there on my front steps. "What's new in Whoville?"

I screech to a halt and don't say a word. My head's down. The letter's crumpled in my fist.

Charlie studies me in an instant. "I'm sorry, Ollie."

I nod, seething. "Were you serious about before?" I ask him.

"Y'mean with the—"

"Yeah," I interrupt, thinking about mom's face when all the bills are paid. "With that."

He cocks his head to the side, narrowing his eyes. "Whatchu' talkin' 'bout, Willis?"

"No more playing around, Charlie. If you're still up for it—" I cut myself off mid-sentence. In my head, I'm working through the permutations. There's still a lot to do . . . but right now . . . all I have for him are two words: "I'm in."

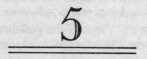

5

So whatta we do now?" Charlie asks as he shuts the door to my office early Monday morning.

"Just what we talked about," I say, pulling weekend work from my briefcase and dumping it on my desk. I'm moving at my typical frantic pace, rushing from desk to filing cabinet back to desk, but today . . .

"You've got some bounce in your step," Charlie decides, suddenly excited. "And not just the hamster-on-a-treadmill thing you've usually got going."

"You don't know what you're talking about."

"Oh, yeah I do." He watches me carefully, consuming every move. "Arms swaying . . . shoulders rising . . . even under the suit— Yeah, brother. Let freedom ring."

I grab the fax from Friday night and slide it in front of my computer. At noon today, the abandoned accounts have to be sent to the state or returned to their owners. That gives us three hours to steal three million dollars. Just as I'm about to start, I crack my knuckles.

"Don't hesitate," Charlie warns.

He's worried I'll talk myself out of it. I crack my knuckles one last time and start copying from the Duckworth fax.

"Now what're you doing?" Charlie asks.

"Same thing our mystery person did—writing a fake letter that claims the money—but this one puts the cash in an account for us."

Charlie nods and grins. "Y'know last night was a full moon," he points out. "I bet that's why they took it in the first place."

"Can you please not get all creepy on me?"

"Don't mock the moon," Charlie warns. "You can bathe in all the left-brain logic you want, but when I was working that telemarketing job taking consumer complaints, we got seventy percent more calls on nights when the moon was full. No joking—that's when all the crazies come out to dance." He falls silent, but he can barely sit still. "So any new ideas on who the original thief was?"

"Actually, that was going to be my next . . ." Picking up the phone, I read the number from the Duckworth fax and start dialing. Before Charlie can even ask the question, I put the phone on speaker so he can hear.

"Directory Assistance," a mechanized female voice says. "For what city?"

"Manhattan," I say.

"What listing?"

I read from the fax. "Midland National Bank." Where the thief wanted to transfer the money.

"Why're you . . ."

"Shhhh," I say as I dial the new number.

Charlie shakes his head, clearly amused. He's used to being the little brother.

"Midland National," a female voice answers. "How can I help you?"

"Hi," I say, back in my customer service voice. "My name is Marty Duckworth, and I just wanted to confirm the details for an upcoming wire transfer."

"I'll do my best—what's your account number, sir?"

I once again read it straight from the letter, and even throw in Duckworth's Social Security number as a bonus. "First name Martin," I add.

We hear a quiet clicking as she types it in. "Now what can I help you with today, Mr. Duckworth?"

Charlie leans forward on my desk. "Ask her name," he whispers.

"I'm sorry, what's your name again?" I add. It's the same trick Tanner Drew used on me—ask their names and they're suddenly accountable.

"Sandy," she answers quickly.

"Okay, Sandy, I just wanted to confirm . . ."

". . . the wire instructions for the incoming transfer," she offers a bit too enthusiastically. "I have it right here, sir. The transfer will be coming from the Greene & Greene Bank in New York City, and then, upon receipt, we have your instructions to send it to TPM Limited at the Bank of London, into account number B2178692792."

The faster writer, Charlie scribbles down the number as quickly as he can. Next to *TPM Ltd.*, I take his pen and write, *Fake company. Smart.* "Wonderful. Thanks, Sandy . . ."

"Is there anything else I can help you with, Mr. Duckworth?"

I look Charlie's way, and he moves closer to the speakerphone. Dropping his voice down to his best impersonation of me, he adds, "Actually, as long as I have you on the line . . . I haven't gotten my last few statements—can you please check and see if you have my right address?"

Oh, the boy's good.

"Let me take a look," Sandy says.

When I was nine years old and sick with a hundred and three fever, Charlie made me a peanut butter and mayo sandwich that he said would make me feel better. It made me barf everywhere. Today, Charlie's voice is as sweet as ever. There's a thin smirk across his face. All these years, I thought he was trying to be helpful. Now I wonder if he's just plain ruthless.

"Okay, I think I see the problem," Sandy interrupts. "Which address do you want us to send it to?"

Confused, Charlie hesitates.

"You have more than one?" I jump in.

"Well, there's the one in New York: 405 . . ."

". . . Amsterdam Avenue, Apartment 2B," I agree, reading from the address on the letter.

"And then I have another in Miami . . ."

Charlie flings me a Post-it, and I dive for a pen. We're only going to get this once.

"1004 Tenth Street, Miami Beach, Florida, 33139," she announces.

Instinctively, Charlie writes down city, state, and zip. I write down the street address. It's the way we used to remember phone numbers: I get the first half; he gets the last. "Story of my life," he used to say.

"If you want, I can change it to the New York one," Sandy explains.

"No, no, leave it as is. As long as I know where to look for—"

There's a loud knock on my office door. I jerk myself around just in time to see it open. "Anyone home?" a deep voice asks.

Charlie grabs the letter. I grab the receiver, killing the

speakerphone. "Okay, thanks again for the help." With a crash, I'm off.

"H-Hey, Shep," Charlie sings, putting on his happy face for the head of Security.

"Everything okay?" Shep asks, stepping toward us.

"Yeah," Charlie says.

"Absolutely," I add.

"What could possibly be wrong?"

The last one's Charlie's and he kicks himself as soon as it leaves his lips.

"So what can I help you with today, Shep?" I ask.

"Actually, I was hoping to help *you*," Shep blurts. There go the kid gloves.

"Excuse me?" I ask.

"I just wanted to talk to you about that transfer you made to Tanner Drew . . ."

Charlie's shoulders sag with instant dread. He's no good with confrontation.

"That was a perfectly legal transfer," I challenge.

"*Listen,*" Shep interrupts. "Spare me the tone." Sensing that he has our attention, he adds, "I already spoke to Lapidus—he's thrilled you had the balls to take charge. Tanner Drew's happy; all is well. But from my side of the desk . . . well, I don't like seeing forty million dollars go zip . . . especially when you're using someone else's password."

How'd he know we—

"You think they hired me for my looks?" Shep asks, laughing. "With thirteen billion at risk, we've got the best security money can buy."

"Well, if you need any backup, I've got a pretty good bike lock," Charlie adds, trying to keep things light.

Shep turns directly toward him. "Oh, man, would you

love it, Charlie—I got this one option—you ever heard of Investigator software?"

Charlie shakes his head. He's out of jokes.

"It lets you do keystroke monitoring," Shep adds, all his attention now on me. "Which means when you're sitting at your computer, I can see every word you're typing. E-mail, letters, passwords . . . as soon as you hit the key, it pops up on my screen."

"You sure that's legal?" I ask.

"You kiddin'? It's like standard issue these days— Exxon, Delta Airlines, even bitchy spouses who want to see what their husbands are doing in chat rooms—they all use it. I mean, why do you think the bank puts all our computers on one network—so you can send in-house e-mail? Big Brother ain't comin'—he's been here for years."

I glance over at Charlie, who's staring way too intently at the computer screen. Oh, jeez. The fake letter . . .

"It's really amazin'," Shep continues. "You can program it like an alarm—so if someone's using Mary's password, and the security system says she's no longer in the building . . . it'll pop up on your screen and tell you what's going on."

"Listen, I'm sorry I hadda do that . . ."

"So there's the Brooklyn accent," Shep grins. "What, it only comes out when you're nervous? Is that when you forget to hide it?"

"No, it's just . . . under the circumstances, I didn't know what to . . ."

"Donworryaboudit," Shep says, rubbing in the old neighborhood. "Like I said, Lapidus didn't give a squat. When it comes to the tech stuff, he doesn't care that I can see when someone types in Mary's name, or his name . . ." Shep glances over my shoulder and his voice slows down. ". . . or even that I can see when someone's using a company computer to write a fraudulent letter."

Charlie shoots up in his seat, and suddenly I'm not the only one wearing the constipated mask.

"I'll tell ya, they never had that when I was in the Service," Shep continues, taking a few steps toward us and rolling up his shirtsleeves. He scratches his forearms—first right, then left—and I see for the first time how massive they are. "These days . . . with the computers . . . you can have 'em notify you of anything . . ." he adds, the old neighborhood now long gone. ". . . forty-million-dollar transfers to Tanner Drew . . . or three-million-dollar transfers to Marty Duckworth . . ."

Son of a bitch.

I'm paralyzed. I can't move.

"It's over, son. We know what you're up to."

Charlie jumps out of his seat and pumps a little laughter into his voice. "Whoa, whoa, whoa, Shep—easy on the nightstick—you don't think we—"

Shep plows past him, a finger pointed straight at my face. "Do I look blind to you, Oliver!?" Looking down, I don't answer. "I asked you a question, son: Do you really think I'm that much of a moron? I knew from the second you sent that first fax, it was just a matter of time until you blew it."

"The first fax?" Charlie blurts. "The Kinko's one? You think that was *us?*" He puts a hand on Shep's shoulder, hoping to buy a second or two. "I swear to you, buddy—we never sent that—in fact . . . in fact, when we got in this morning . . . we were . . . we were trying to catch the thief ourselves . . . isn't that right, Oliver? We were doing the same thing as you!"

Ghost white, I just sit there. Charlie knows I'm lost. He glares my way. *Dammit, Ollie . . . get with it. Please.*

Turning back to Shep, Charlie laughs like it's a riot. "I swear to you, Shep. We were trying to track the thief oursel—"

"Knock, knock—anyone home?" a scratchy voice shouts as the door to my office swings open. Shep spins around and finds the source of the voice—the paunchy, but still impeccably dressed middle-aged man who's now approaching my desk—Francis A. Quincy, head financial partner of the firm. Behind him is the boss himself. Henry Lapidus.

I throw on a phony grin, but down low, my toes dig toward the carpet.

"Look who it is—the forty-million-dollar man!" Lapidus sings my way. "Believe it or not, I hear Tanner Drew's holding a spot for you in his will." As he says the words, he wipes his hand across his mostly bald head—it's part of his constant state of kinetic motion. Despite his towering six-foot-three frame, Lapidus is like a hummingbird in human form . . . flap, flap, flap, all day long. I used to think it was an energy that couldn't be contained. Charlie used to say it was hemorrhoids. They always show up around assholes.

"And guess who we brought for you?" Lapidus asks. Stepping aside, he reveals a nebbishy turtle-faced kid slicked up in a way-too-expensive Italian suit. He's our age and looks familiar, but I . . .

"Kenny?" Charlie blurts.

Kenny Owens. My freshman year roommate at NYU. Obnoxious Long Island rich kid. Haven't seen him in years—but the suit alone tells me nothing's changed. Still a putz.

"Been a long time, huh?" Kenny asks. He's waiting for an answer, but Charlie and I are both eyeing Shep.

"I thought you'd like some time to catch up," Lapidus says, sounding like he's setting us up on a date.

"Old friends and all that . . ." Quincy adds.

Cocking his head, Charlie knows something's up. As a rule, Quincy hates everyone. Like most CFOs, all he cares about is the money. But today . . . today, we're all family. And if Lapidus and Quincy are personally taking Kenny around . . . he must be interviewing for a job.

Before anyone can get a word in, Lapidus follows our gaze to Shep. "And what're you doing here?" Lapidus asks, sounding pleasantly surprised. "More lecturing about Tanner Drew?"

"Yeah," Shep says dryly. "All about Tanner Drew."

"Well, why don't you save it for later," Lapidus adds. "Let these boys have some time alone."

"Actually, this is more important," Shep challenges.

"Maybe you didn't understand," Quincy jumps in. "We want these boys to have some time alone." Right there, the fight's over. CFO outranks Security.

"Thanks again for doing this," Lapidus says to me. Leaning in close, he whispers, "And take it from me, Oliver—helping us get Kenny—it's a perfect way to round out your B-school applications."

Charlie and I sit there silently as Shep grudgingly follows Lapidus and Quincy to the door. Just as they leave, Shep turns around and pegs Charlie with a javelin glare that pins him through the heart. The door slams shut, but there's no doubt about it. All we've done is prolong the pain.

"So do I look good, or do I look good?" Kenny asks as soon as they're gone.

Charlie's still in shock.

"What're you doing here?" I blurt.

"Nice to see you too," Kenny says, taking a seat in front of the desk. "You always so warm to your guests?"

"Yeah . . . no. . . . Sorry—just one of those days," I stammer. I'm trying to keep it calm—even if it's obvious I'm failing.

Kenny says something else, but all I can think about is Shep. I look at Charlie, and he looks at me. There's nothing worse than fear in your brother's eyes.

"So tell us what's going on," I say to Kenny. "What position are you interviewing for?"

"Interviewing?" Kenny laughs. "I'm not here for a job— I'm here as a client."

I rocket up in my seat.

That's all Kenny needs to see. Big putz grin. "I'm telling you, real estate is always hot," he adds, the canary still fresh in his teeth. "Seventeen million—and that's just from the buyout. Where else you gonna get free cash like that? I mean, without getting arrested, of course."

The instant the door slams behind Kenny, I sink down in my seat. Charlie's up and moving, unable to stop. "Maybe we should call Shep," he says as he starts pacing. "He's still my friend . . . he'll listen to reason . . ."

"Just give me a minute . . ."

"We don't have a minute—you know he's gonna be here any second . . . and if all we do is sit around . . . I mean, what're we still doing here anyway? It's like pulling the pin and waiting with the grenade in our pants." He wheels around, all set for me to argue, but to his surprise, I give him nothing but silence. "What?" he asks. "What'd I do now?"

"Repeat what you just said."

"About the grenade in our pants?"

"No—before that."

He thinks for a second. "What're we still doing here?"

"That's the one," I say, my voice now cruising down the runway. "How do you answer that?"

"I don't understand."

"What *are* we still doing here?" I ask as I stand from my seat. "Shep just had us nailed for swiping three million bucks—but does he tell Lapidus? Does he tell Quincy? Does he call in his buddies from the Secret Service? No, no, and no. He walks away and saves the conversation for later."

"So?" Charlie says with a shrug.

"So what's the first rule of Law Enforcement 101?"

"Be a power-mad donkey's ass every time you pull someone over?"

"I'm serious, Charlie—it's page one in the rulebook: Don't let the bad guys get away. If Shep smells something wrong, he's supposed to go straight to the boss."

"See, now you're reaching. Maybe he's just giving us a chance to explain."

"Or maybe he's—" I stop mid-step. Up goes the suspicious eyebrow. "How well do you know this guy, Charlie?"

"Oh, c'mon . . ." he says with a roll of his eyes. "Now you think *Shep's* the thief?"

"It makes perfect sense when you think about it. How else would he know about the original Duckworth fax?"

"He told you, Sherlock—he saw it come in . . ."

"Charlie, do you have any idea how many hundreds of faxes come in here every day? Unless Shep spends his days hunting through every fax in the building, there's no way he'd find it. So either someone tipped him off before it got here . . . or somehow, some way . . ."

". . . he knew it was coming," he says, completing my thought. His mouth gapes open. His body stiffens, like his blood's running cold. "You really think he . . ."

"You don't know him at all, do you?" I ask.

"W-We hang out at work."

"We should get out of here," I blurt. I take off and rush to the door.

"Right now?"

"The longer we sit here, the more likely we'll be tagged as scapegoa—" Tearing the door open, I look up. There's a figure in the doorway.

With his chest in my face, Shep steps forward, forcing me to step back. Once he's in the room, he whips the door shut. He studies Charlie, then stares at me. His thick neck keeps his head brutally arched, but it's not an attack—he's taking our measure. Weighing. Calculating. It's like one of those silences at the end of a first date—where decisions get made.

"I'll split it with you," Shep says.

6

"Excuse me?" I ask as Charlie moves in next to me.

"No joke," Shep says. "Three ways—a million each."

"You gotta be kidding," Charlie blurts.

"So it *was* you who sent the first letter," I say.

Shep stays silent.

So does Charlie. His teeth flick against his bottom lip.
Half of it's disbelief and the other half's . . .

Charlie's whole face lights up.

. . . pure adrenalized excitement.

"This could easily be the single best day of my life,"
Charlie beams. The boy couldn't hold a grudge if it was
glued to his chest. I'm different.

Turning to Shep, I add, "You were just in here blaming us,
and now you expect us to hold hands and be partners?"

"Listen, Oliver, you can chew my head off all you want,
but just realize if you blow the whistle on me, I'm gonna
blow it right back on you."

I cock my head sideways. "Are you threatening me?"

"That depends what you want the outcome to be," Shep
shoots back.

Standing in front of my desk, I watch Shep carefully. Deep down, I may not be a thief, but I'm also no sucker.

"We're all here for the same thing," Shep quickly adds. "So you can either be a mule and get nothing, or you can share the profits and walk away with a little something in your pocket."

"I vote for the profits," Charlie interrupts.

"Screw this," I say, storming to the door. "Even I'm not that stupid."

Shep reaches out and grabs me by the biceps. Not hard—just enough to stop me. "It's not stupid, Oliver." As Shep says the words, the swagger's gone. So's the Secret Service. "If I wanted to blame it on you . . . or turn you in . . . I'd be talking to Lapidus right now. Instead, I'm here."

Even as I pull away, Shep has my undivided attention.

He looks up at the NYU diploma on my wall and studies it carefully. "You think you're the only ones who have that dream? When I first signed up with the Service, I thought I was going straight to the White House. Maybe start with the Vice President . . . work my way up to the First Lady—it's a nice life when you think about it. What I didn't realize was that before you get on Protective, you usually spend five years or so on Investigations: counterfeiting, financial crimes, all the scut work we never get credit for.

"So there I am, a few years out of Brooklyn College, in our Miami office in Florida. Anyway, on the drive from Miami to Melbourne, there was this wide-open stretch of unlit highway. Drug-runners would land their planes there, dump duffel bags full of money and drugs, and then have their partners pick it up and drive it down to Miami.

"Night after night, I'd fantasize about finding these guys—and every time, the dream was the same: In the sky, I'd see the red lights of a fleeing plane. Instinctively, I'd cut my own lights, slow the car, and stumble upon an army green duffel bag full of ten million dollars in cash." Turning back to us, Shep adds, "If it ever happened, I'd throw the bag in my trunk, leave my badge behind, and just keep on driving.

"Of course, the only problem was, I never found the plane. And after missing four consecutive promotions and barely surviving on government pay, I realized that I don't want to work until the day they put me in the ground. I saw what it did to my dad . . . forty years for a handshake and a fake gold plaque. There's got to be more to life than that. And with Duckworth . . . a dead man with three million dollars . . . it may not be as much as the clients here have, but I'll tell you . . . for guys like us . . . it's as good as we're gonna get."

Charlie nods his head ever so slightly. The way Shep talks about his dad . . . there're some things you can't make up. "So how do we know you won't play Take the Money and Run?" I ask.

"What if I let you pick where the transfers go? You can start over from scratch . . . put it in whatever fake company you want. I mean . . . with your mom here . . . you're not going on the run for two million dollars—that's the only guarantee I need," Shep says, ignoring Charlie and watching my reaction. He knows who he has to work on.

"And you really think it'll work?" I ask.

"Oliver, I've been watching this one for almost a year," Shep says, his voice picking up speed. "In life, there're only two perfect—and I mean *perfect*—crimes where you can't be caught: One is where you're killed, which isn't too great an option. And the other is when no one knows that a crime took place." Swinging his sausage-shaped forearm through the air, he motions to the paperwork on my desk. "That's what's here on a silver platter. That's the beauty of it, Oliver," he says as he lowers his voice. "No one'll ever know. Whether the three million goes to Duckworth or to the government, it was always leaving the bank. And since it's supposed to be gone, we don't have to go on the run or give up our lives. All we do is say thank you to the forgetful dead millionaire." Pausing to drive it home, he adds, "People wait their whole lives and never get an opportunity this good. It's even better than the plane and the duffel bag—the bank spent the last six months trying to contact his family—no one's there. No one knows. No one but us."

It's a good point. Actually, it's a great point . . . and the best insurance that Shep'll stay quiet. If he toots his horn to anyone, he risks his own share too.

"So whattya say, Oliver?" he adds.

The Art Deco clock on my wall was last year's holiday gift from Lapidus. I stare up at it, studying the minute hand. Two and a half hours to go. After that, the opportunity's gone. The money'll be transferred to the state. And all I'll be left with is a clock, a handshake, and eighty thousand dollars' worth of hospital bills.

"It's okay to want something more," Charlie says. "Think of what we can do for mom . . . all the debt."

Back in my seat, I take a deep breath and spread my palms flat on my desk. "You know we're gonna regret this," I say.

They both break into smiles. Two kids.

"We have a deal?" Shep asks, extending a hand.

I shake Shep's hand and watch my brother. "So what do we do now?" I ask.

"Know any good fake companies?" Shep replies.

That's my department. When Arthur Mannheim divorced his wife, Lapidus and I opened a holding company and an

Antigua bank account in a total of an hour and a half. It's
Lapidus's favorite dirty trick—and one I know all too well.
I reach for the phone.

"No, no, no, no, no," Shep scolds, pulling my hand
away. "You can't call these people yourself anymore.
Everything you touch, everything you do—all of it's a link,
just like a fingerprint. That's why you need a go-
between—and not just some schlub off the street—you
want a professional who can protect your interests so no
one ever sees you. Someone who you can send a thousand
dollars and say, 'Make this phone call for me and don't ask
any questions . . .'"

"Like a mob lawyer," Charlie blurts.

"Exactly," Shep grins. "Just like a mob lawyer." Before
I can even ask, Shep stands up and leaves my office. Thirty
seconds later, he returns with a phonebook under each arm.
One for New York; one for Jersey. He tosses them on my
desk and they hit with a thud.

"Time to find the stutterers," Shep says.

Charlie and I look at each other. We're lost.

"You've seen 'em in every phonebook," Shep explains.
"The first alphabetical entries in every category. AAAAAA
Flower Shop. AAAAAA Laundromat. And the most pathetic and desperate of all the stutterers—the ones most likely to
do anything for a buck: AAAAAA Attorneys At Law."

I nod. Charlie grins wide. Par for the course. Without a
word, we dive for the phonebooks. I get New York; Charlie
gets Jersey; Shep reads over our shoulders. Flipping as fast as
I can, I go straight for the Lawyer section. The first one I spot
is "A Able Accident Attorneys."

"Too specialized," Shep says. "We want a general practi-
tioner—not an ambulance chaser."

My finger scrolls up the page. "A AAAA Attorneys." On

the next line are the words, "All Your Needs—Lowest Prices."

"Not bad," Shep says.

"I got it!" Charlie shouts. Shep and I both shush him down to a whisper. "Sorry . . . sorry," he says, barely audible. He spins his book around and shoves it in front of my face, knocking my own phonebook straight into my lap. His pointer finger jabs right to the spot. All it says is "A." Under it, the text has one word: *Lawyer.*

"I still vote for mine," I say. "You gotta like the low price guarantee."

"Are you on crack?" Charlie asks. "All. Mine's. Using. Is. An. A."

"Mine's got five As—all in a row."

Charlie looks me straight in the eye. "Mine's from Jersey."

"We have a winner," Shep announces.

This time, Charlie's the one who leaps for the phone. Shep pounds him in the knuckles. "Not from here," Shep says. Heading for the door, he adds, "That's why God invented payphones."

"Are you crazy?" I ask. "All three of us hovering over a payphone? Yeah, that's inconspicuous."

"I suppose you have a better idea?"

"I work with rich people every day," I say, stepping in front of Shep and taking a quick glance at the clock. "You think I don't know the best places to hide money from the government?"

7

"Hi," Charlie coos with a beauty pageant smile as he glides up to the black granite reception desk. We're on the fourth floor of the Wayne & Portnoy building, a sterile cavernous structure that, even though it has all the architectural charm of an empty shoebox, still has two redeeming qualities: First, it's across the street from the bank, and second, it's home to the largest stuffed-shirt law firm in the city.

Behind the desk, an overdressed, overexcited receptionist is yammering into her headset, which is exactly what Charlie's counting on. Sneaking in may be my idea, but we both know who's better face-to-face. We all play to our strengths. "Hi," he says for the second time, knowing it'll charm. "I'm waiting for Bert Collier to come down . . . and I was wondering if I could use a phone for a quick private call." I smile to myself. Norbert Collier was just one of a hundred names listed on the firm directory in the lobby. By calling him Bert, Charlie has them sounding like old friends.

"Back past the elevators," the receptionist says without even hesitating.

Still hiding out of sight around the corner, Shep and I wait for Charlie to pass, then fall in line behind him. I point him to the wood-paneled door and usher them into a small conference room. The words *Client Services* are on a brass nameplate just outside the door. It's not a huge room. Small mahogany table, a few upholstered chairs, bagels and cream cheese on the sideboard, a fax machine against the wall, and four separate telephones. Everything we need to do some damage.

"Nice choice," Shep says, dumping his pea coat on the back of a chair. "Even if they trace it . . ."

". . . all they'll find are some Wayne & Portnoy clients," I add, throwing my coat on top.

"You're all geniuses," Charlie adds. "Now can we get going on our stutterer? Tick-tock, tick-tock."

Shep slides into a seat, pulls the number from his pocket, and grabs the phone in a meaty paw. As he dials, Charlie hits the *Hands-Free* button on the starfish speakerphone system that's at the center of the table. Everybody loves conference calls.

It rings three times before someone picks up. "Law offices," a male voice answers.

Shep keeps it cool and calm. "Hello, I'm looking for a lawyer and was wondering what type of law Mr. . . . uh . . . Mr. . . ."

"Bendini."

"Right . . . Bendini . . ." Shep repeats, writing it down. "I was wondering what type of law Mr. Bendini specializes in."

"What type of law are you looking for?"

Shep nods to the two of us. The only thing fishier is Starkist. Here's our man. "Actually, we're looking for someone who specializes in keeping things . . . well, we're hoping to keep things low-profile . . ."

There's a short pause on the other line. "Talk to me," Bendini says.

Bam, Shep's out of his seat. He paces slightly, though his big frame makes it look more like lumbering. I can't tell if he's thrilled or scared. I'm betting thrilled. All those years behind the desk, he's feeling his inner James Bond. "I'm gonna put on my associate," he tells Bendini. Shep nods to me as I strain to get as close as I can to the speakerphone.

"You lean in any more, you're gonna start humping it," Charlie teases.

"Mr. Bendini . . . ?" I ask.

No one answers.

Shep shakes his head. Charlie laughs and pretends it's a cough.

Catching on, I start over. Without using names. "Here's the story: I want you to listen carefully, and I want you to call the following number . . ." *I want, I want, I want*, I say, driving home my point. Charlie sticks his chest out at my newfound tone. He's happy to see me strong . . . more demanding. At least I learned something from Lapidus after all these years.

"The place is called Purchase Out International, and you want to ask for Arnie," I explain. "Don't let them give you anyone else. Arnie's the only one we deal with. When you get him on the line, tell him you need a same-day four-layer cake, endzone in Antigua. He'll know what it is."

"Believe me, kid, I know how to stack corporations," Bendini interrupts in a brickyard Jersey accent.

"Don't back down," Charlie whispers. I'm not. My eyes are sharp, my face is flushed. I'm finally feeling my pulse.

"What name you want to put it in?" Bendini adds.

"Martin Duckworth," all three of us say simultaneously.

I swear, I hear Bendini roll his eyes. "Fine—Martin Duckworth," he repeats. "And for initial ownership?"

He needs another fake name. This one doesn't matter— everything's ultimately owned by Duckworth. "Ribbie Henson," I say, using the name of Charlie's imaginary friend from when he was six.

"Fine—Ribbie Henson. Now how do you wanna pay Arnie's bill?"

Damn. I hadn't even thought of that.

Charlie and Shep both go to jump in, but I wave them back. "Tell him we'll pay when we request the original paperwork—right now all we need is a fax," I decide. Before Bendini can argue, I add, "It's what he does with the big fish—they don't pay until the money hits. Tell him we're whales."

Charlie looks at me like he's never seen me before. "Now we're talking," he whispers to Shep.

"And when do you need it by?" Bendini asks.

"How's a half-hour sound?" I reply.

Again, there's a short pause. "I'll do what I can," Bendini says, unfazed. Clearing his throat for emphasis, he adds, "Now how'm *I* gonna get paid?"

I look at Charlie. He looks to Shep. Bendini doesn't sound like the kinda guy you just say "bill me" to.

"Tell me your rates," Shep says.

"Tell me what it's worth," Bendini shoots back.

Smacking the *Hands-Free* button, I shut off the speakerphone. "Don't dicker!" I hiss. "We're running out of—"

"I'll give you a thousand cash if you can do it in a half-hour," Shep says as he turns the phone back on.

"A *grand?*" Bendini asks. "Boys, I don't piss for a grand—even when I have to. The minimum is five."

Shep shoots a panicked look to me, and I go back to

Charlie. My brother shakes his head. His cookie jar's always empty. As my eyes drop down to my watch, I press my lips together. Takes money to make money. Looking back at Shep, I can't help but nod. Charlie knows what it means. There go some B-school funds—and hospital bills.

"Don't worry," Charlie whispers with a hand on my shoulder. "It's another staple we're gonna put in Lapidus's head."

"Okay, you got it," Shep tells Bendini. "We'll wire it as soon as we hang up." Reading from the white sticker on the fax machine, Shep relays our phone and fax numbers, thanks the price-gouger, and hangs up the phone.

The room is corpse silent.

"Well I think that went great," Charlie announces, swinging his arm through the air aw-shucks style.

"We'll be fine," Shep interrupts.

I nod my head quickly. Then slower. "So you think it'll work?" I ask anxiously.

"There we go—three full seconds," Charlie says. "The old Oliver's back."

"As long as your buddy Arnie comes through . . ." Shep says.

"Trust me, Arnie'll have it done in ten minutes. Fifteen at the most," I add, watching Charlie's reaction. He thinks I'm rationalizing. "Arnie's this hippie leftover who lives in the Marshall Islands, makes pro-level margaritas, and sticks it to the government by plucking shelf corps off the wall all day long."

"Shelf corps?" Charlie asks.

"Corps . . . corporations. Arnie registers them all across the world—gives them names, addresses, even boards of directors. You've seen the classified ads—they're in every in-flight airline magazine in existence: Hate the IRS? Paying

Too Much in Taxes? Private Offshore Companies! Guaranteed Privacy!"

"And you think he's gonna be able to set up an entire company in the next half-hour?" Charlie asks.

"Trust me, he's set these up months ago. ABC Corp. DEF Corp. GHI Corp. All the paperwork's already done . . . each corporation is just a notebook on a shelf. When we call, he scribbles our fake name into the few blanks that are left and gives it a quick notary stamp. To be honest, I'm surprised it's taking this l—"

The phone rings and Charlie leaps forward, answering it through the speakerphone. "H-Hello."

"Congratulations," Bendini says in full Jersey accent. "Ribbie Henson is now the proud owner and sole shareholder of Sunshine Distributors Partnership, Limited, in the Virgin Islands, which is owned by CEP Worldwide in Nauru, which is owned by Maritime Holding Services in Vanuatu, which is owned by Martin Duckworth in Antigua."

Four layers—endzone in Antigua. When law enforcement digs, it'll take 'em months to sort through all the paperwork.

"Sounds like you boys are in business. Just make sure you wire my cash."

The moment the line goes dead, the fax machine hums to life. I swear, it almost gives me a heart attack.

Over the next five minutes, the fax machine vomits up the rest of the paperwork—from bylaws to articles of incorporation—everything we need to open up a brand-new corporate account. I check the clock on the wall: two hours to go. Mary asked for the paperwork by noon. Damn. All three of us know this can't be like Tanner Drew. No stolen passwords. It's gotta be done by the book.

"Can we make it?" Charlie asks.

"If you want, we can hand the original letter to Mary right

now," Shep offers. "My Duckworth accounts are already set up, since they belonged to the real Duckworth—"

"Not a chance," I interrupt. "Like you said—we pick the places where the money goes."

Shep's tempted to argue, but quickly realizes he can't win. If the first transfer goes to him, he's got his duffel bag of cash, and we risk getting nothing. Even Charlie's not willing to take that risk.

"Fine," Shep says. "But if you're not going to use the already existing Duckworth account, I'd go offshore as soon as possible. That'll get it out of the United States and away from the reporting requirements. You know the law—anything that looks suspicious gets reported to the IRS, which means they'll track it anywhere."

Nodding, Charlie pulls a thin stack of red paper from my briefcase. The Red Sheet—the partners' master list of favorite foreign banks, including the ones that're open twenty-four hours. It's on red paper so no one can photocopy it.

"I vote for Switzerland," Charlie adds. "One of those bad-ass numbered accounts with an unguessable password."

"I hate to break it to you, shortie, but Swiss bank accounts aren't what they used to be," Shep says. "Contrary to what Hollywood wants you to think, anonymous Swiss accounts have been abolished since 1977."

"What about the Cayman Islands?"

"Too Grisham," Shep shoots back. "Besides, even those are opening up. People got so many ideas after reading *The Firm*, the U.S. had to step in. Since then, they've been working with law enforcement for years."

"So what's the best—"

"Don't focus so much on one place," Shep says. "A quick transfer from New York to the Caymans is suspicious no matter who it's from, and if the bank clerk raises an eyebrow—

it's hello IRS. It's the first principle for laundering money: You want to send it to the foreign banks because they're the ones who're least likely to cooperate with law enforcement. But if you transfer it there too fast, the reputable banks over here will tag it as suspicious, and quickly put the IRS on your tail. So whattya do? Focus on short jumps—logical jumps— that way you won't get a double take." Pulling a bagel from the breakfast spread, Shep slaps it on the table. "Here we are in the U.S.—now what's the number one location where we bank abroad?"

"England," I say.

"England it is," Shep replies, slapping another bagel down a few inches from the first. "The epicenter of international banking—Mary does almost thirty transfers there a day. She won't think twice. Now once you're in London, what's close by?" He slaps another bagel down. "France is the easiest— nothing suspicious about that, right? And once your money's there—their regulations are softer, which means the world opens up a little." Another bagel hits. "Personally, I like Latvia—nearby . . . slightly smarmy . . . the government hasn't decided if it likes us yet. And for international investi- gations, they only help us about half the time, which means it's a perfect place to waste an investigator's day." Rapid-fire, two more bagels hit. "From there you slam the Marshall Islands, and from there, you bounce it close to home in Antigua. By the time it gets there, what started out as dirty cash is now so untraceable, it's clean."

"And that's it?" Charlie asks, looking from Shep to me.

"Do you even realize how long it takes to investigate in a foreign territory?" Shep points to the first bagel, then the second, then the third. "Bing, bing, bing, bing, bing. That's why they call it the Rule of Five. Five well-chosen countries and you're gone. In the Service, it'd take us six months to a year to investigate with no guarantees."

"Ohhh, baby, pass me the cream cheese," Charlie sings.

Even I grin. I try to bury it down, but Charlie spots it in my eyes. That alone makes him happy.

Leaning on the desk, I skim through the Red Sheet and pick out a bank for each territory. Five banks in an hour. It's going to be close.

"Listen, I should go check in with Lapidus," Shep says, pulling his coat from the chair. "How 'bout we meet back in my office at eleven-thirty?"

I nod, Charlie says *thanks,* and Shep hightails it out of the office.

The moment the door shuts, I once again dive for the speakerphone, rehump the table, and punch in the phone number for the Antigua bank.

"I have a calling card in case it doesn't go through," Charlie offers.

I shake my head. There's a reason I picked the law firm. "Hi, I'd like to speak to Rupa Missakian," I read from the sheet.

Within five minutes, I've relayed the tax ID number and all the other vital stats for Sunshine Distributors's first bank account. To really sell it, I throw in Duckworth's birthday and a personally selected password. They never once give us a hard time. Thank you, Red Sheet.

As I shut off the speakerphone, Charlie points to his Wonder Woman watch with the magic lasso second-hand. Twenty minutes, start to finish. Forty minutes left and four more accounts to open. Not good enough.

"C'mon, coach, I got my skates on," Charlie says. "Get me in the game."

Without a word, I rip two pages from the Red Sheet and

slide them across the table. One says *France,* the other *Marshall Islands.* Charlie darts to the phone on his far right; I race to the one on mine. Opposite corners. Our fingers flick across the keypads.

"Do you speak English?" I ask a stranger from Latvia. "Yes . . . I'm looking for Feodor Svantanich or whoever's handling his accounts."

"Hi, I'm trying to reach Lucinda Llanos," Charlie says. "Or whoever has her accounts."

There's a short pause.

"Hi," we both say simultaneously. "I'd like to open a corporate account."

"Okay, and can you read me the number one more time?" Charlie asks a French man who he keeps calling Inspector Clouseau. He scribbles down the number and calls it out to me. "Tell your English bloke it's HB7272250."

"Here we go—HB7272250," I say to the rep from London. "Once it comes in, we want it transferred there as soon as possible."

"Thanks again for the help, Clouseau," Charlie adds. "I'm gonna tell all my rich friends about you."

"Wonderful," I say. "I'll look for it tomorrow—and then hopefully we can start talking about some of our other overseas business."

Translation: Do me this solid and I'll throw you so much business, it'll make this three million look like gum money. It's the third time we've played this game—relaying the account number of one bank to the bank that precedes it.

"Yeah . . . yeah . . . that'd be great," Charlie says, switching to his I-really-gotta-run voice. "Have a croissant on me."

Charlie hops out of his seat as I lower the receiver.

"Aaaaaaannnnnnnd . . . we're done," he says as soon as the phone hits the cradle.

My eyes go straight to the clock. Eleven thirty-five. "Damn," I whisper under my breath. In a blur, I rake the loose pages of the Red Sheet back into one pile and stuff them in my briefcase. "C'mon, let's go," Charlie demands, flying toward the door. As I run, I shove the chairs back under the table. Charlie sweeps the bagels back on their tray. Neat and perfect. Just like we found it.

"I got the coats," I say, grabbing them from the chair.

He doesn't care. He just keeps running. And before the receptionist notices the blur in front of her desk, we're gone.

"Where the hell were you guys—braiding each other's hair?" Shep asks as we plow into his office. Ten minutes and counting. I throw the coats on the leather sofa; Shep leaps out of his seat and jams a sheet of paper in front of my face.

"What's this?" I ask.

"Transfer request—all you need to do is fill in where it's going."

Ripping the mess of paperwork from my briefcase, I flip to the Red Sheet marked *England*. Charlie bends over so I can use his back as a desk. I scribble as fast as I can and copy the account info. Almost done.

"So where's it finally going?" Shep asks.

Charlie stands up, and I stop writing. "What're you talking about?"

"The last transfer. Where're we putting it?"

I look to Charlie, but he returns a blank stare. "I thought you said . . ."

". . . that you could pick where the money goes," Shep interrupts. "I did—and you can bounce it wherever you want—but you better believe I want to know the final stop."

"That wasn't part of the deal," I growl.

"Guys, can we just save this one for later?" Charlie pleads.

Shep leans in, plenty annoyed. "The deal was to give the two of you control . . . not to freeze me out altogether."

"So suddenly you're worried we're going to keep the cake?" I ask.

"Fellas, please," Charlie begs. "We're almost out of time . . ."

"Don't fuck with me, Oliver—all I'm asking for is a taste of some insurance."

"No, all you're asking for is *our* insurance. This is what's supposed to keep us safe."

"I just hope you both realize you're about to blow this whole thing," Charlie says. Neither of us cares. That's how it always is with money—everything gets personal.

"Just tell me where the damn bank is!" Shep explodes.

"Why? So you can live your duffel bag fantasy and leave us chewing dirt?"

"Dammit, you two, no one's leaving anyone!" Charlie shouts. Shoving himself between us, he reaches out and grabs my stack of Red Sheets.

"What're you doing?" I yell, pulling them back.

"Let . . . *go!*" Charlie insists with one last yank. The top two pages tear in half and I fly backwards. I'm fast enough to regain my footing, but not fast enough to stop him. Spinning toward Shep, he flips to the bottom of the pile, pulls out the Red Sheet marked *Antigua*, and folds it back so you can only see one bank on the list.

"*Charlie . . . don't!*"

Too late. He covers the account number with his finger and rams it in Shep's face. "You got it?"

Shep studies it with a quick look. "Thank you . . . that's all I ask."

"What the hell is wrong with you?" I shout.

"I don't want to hear it," Charlie shoots back. "If we sit here arguing, no one's getting anything—so finish the damn paperwork and get going. We've got only a few minutes!"

Spinning toward the clock, I check for myself.

"Eyes on the prize, Oliver. Eyes on the prize," Shep says.

"Go, go, go!" Charlie shouts as I jot in the last line. He just gave away our entire insurance policy—but it's still not worth losing everything. Not when we're this close. Charlie stuffs the Red Sheets back in my briefcase; I've got a stack of forty abandoned accounts under my arm. Stumbling out the door, I don't once look back. Just forward.

"That's the way, bro," Charlie calls out.

Here we go. Time to nab some cash.

8

Charlie slams the door behind me and I rush down the fifth-floor hallway, still juggling a mound of paper. On my right, the doors to the public elevator slide shut, which is why I double my pace and head straight for the private one in the back.

The indicator panel above the doors is lit up at eight . . . then seven . . . then six . . . I can still catch it. I rush forward and punch in the six-digit code as fast as I can. Just as I hit the last digit, the abandoned accounts pile gives way. I pull the full stack against my chest, but the pages are already sliding down my stomach. They crash to the floor and spread out amoeba-style. Dropping to my knees, I madly shuffle them back into place. That's when the elevator sounds. The doors slide open and I'm staring at two sets of nice shoes. And not just anyone's nice shoes . . .

"Can I help you with that, Oliver?" Lapidus asks as I look up to see his wide grin.

"Still using the boss's code, huh?" Quincy adds, jamming his arm in front of the door to hold it open.

I force a strained smile—and feel the blood seep from my face.

"Do you need some . . ."

"No. I got it," I insist. "You two go ahead."

"Don't worry," Quincy teases. "We're thrilled to wait."

Seeing that they're not leaving, I straighten the pile, scramble to my feet, and join them inside the elevator.

"What floor would you like, sir?" Quincy adds.

"Sorry," I stutter. Once again forcing a grin, I reach forward and press four. My finger shakes as it taps the button.

"Don't let him get to you, Oliver," Lapidus offers. "He's just mad he doesn't have his own protégé." Like always, it's the perfect reaction to the situation. Like always, it's exactly what I want to hear. And like always . . . just as he pulls me close for the fatherly hug, he's carving his initials straight into my back. Drop dead, Lapidus. The whipping boy is moving on.

There's a ping and the elevator doors glide open. "See you tomorrow," I say, feeling like I'm about to vomit.

Quincy nods; Lapidus pats me on the shoulder.

"By the way," Lapidus calls out, "did you have a nice conversation with Kenny?"

"Oh, yeah," I say, leaving them behind. "It was just perfect."

Fighting the vertigo that's pounding my head, I speed-walk down the hallway. Eyes front. Stay on course. By the time I approach The Cage, my whole body's numb. Hands, feet, chest—I can't feel a thing. In fact, as I reach down to open the door, my hands are so sweaty, and the doorknob's so cold, I'm worried I'm going to spot-weld right to it. My stomach caves out from under me, begging me to stop—but it's too late—the door's already open.

"About time," Mary says as I enter The Cage. "You had me worried, Oliver."

"Are you kidding?" I ask, smiling anxious hellos to the other four officemates who look up as I cross the industrial carpet. "I still have a good three—" The door slams behind me and I jump at the crash. I almost forgot . . . in The Cage, the door shuts automatically.

"You okay there?" Mary asks, immediately shifting to mother hen.

"Y-Yeah . . . of course," I say, struggling to pull it together. "I was just saying . . . we still have at least three minutes . . ."

"And worse comes to worst, you can always do it yourself, right?" As she asks the question, she wipes a smudge from the glass of her oldest son's picture frame. The one with her password . . .

"Listen, about Tanner Drew . . ." I beg. "I shouldn't have . . . I'm sorry . . ."

"I'm sure you are." She lowers her head, refusing to face me. No question, she's ready to blow. But out of nowhere, her high-pitched laugh cuts through the room. Then Polly, who sits next to her, joins in. Then Francine. All of them laughing. "C'mon, Oliver, we're only teasing," Mary finally adds, a big smile on her face.

"Y-You're not mad?"

"Honey, you did the best you could with what you had . . . but if I ever find out you use my password again . . ."

I wince slightly, waiting for the rest of the threat.

Once again, Mary smiles wide. "It's a joke, Oliver . . . it won't kill you to laugh." She pulls the stack of abandoned accounts from my hand and lightly slaps me across the chest with it. "You take things too seriously, y'know that?"

I try to answer, but nothing comes out. All I see are the forms as they wave through the air.

Turning to her computer, Mary clips the whole stack to the vertical clipboard attached to her monitor. She knows the deadline. No time to waste. Luckily, the transfers are already keyed in—all she has to do is enter the destinations. "I don't see why the state gets this," she adds as she opens the *Abandoned Accounts* file. "Personally I'd rather see it go to charity . . ."

She says something else, but it's drowned out by the blood rushing through my ears. On the screen, a twenty-thousand-dollar account gets zapped to New York's Unclaimed Funds Division. Then a three-hundred-dollar one. Then a twelve-thousand. One by one, she works her way through the pile earmarked for the state. One by one, she hits that *Send* button.

"So I think you're going to be able to steal it," Mary eventually says.

A hot jolt stabs me in the legs, like someone shoving a knife in my thigh. I can barely stand. "E-Excuse me?"

"I said, we're going to be able to go on our ski trip," Mary adds. "Justin's knee isn't as bad as we thought." Turning around, Mary catches me wiping a wave of sweat from my forehead. "Are you sure you're okay, Oliver?"

"Of course," I reply. "Just one of those days."

"More like one of those years, the way you're always running around. I'm telling you, Oliver, if you don't start taking it easy, the people here'll kill you."

There's no arguing with fact.

Flipping to the next sheet in the pile, Mary finally gets to a four-hundred-thousand-dollar transfer to someone named Alexander Reed. I expect her to make some comment about the amount, but at this point, she's dead to it. She sees it every day.

And so do I. Hundred-thousand-dollar checks . . . finding

decorators for their Tuscan villas . . . the dessert chef at L'Aubergine who knows exactly the right crispiness they like for their chocolate soufflés. It's a nice life. But it's not mine.

It takes Mary a total of ten seconds to type in the account number and hit *Send*. Ten seconds. Ten seconds to change my life. It's what my dad was always chasing, but never found. Finally . . . a way out.

Mary licks her fingertips for a touch of traction, leafs to the next sheet in the pile, and lowers her fingers to the keyboard. There it is: *Duckworth and Sunshine Distributors*.

"So what'd you do this weekend?" I ask, my voice racing.

"Oh, same as every weekend for the last month—tried to show up all my relatives by buying them better holiday presents than the ones they bought me."

Onscreen, the name of our London bank clicks into place. *C.M.W. Walsh Bank.*

"That sounds great," I say vacantly.

Digit by digit, the account number follows.

"That sounds great?" Mary laughs. "Oliver, you've really got to get out more."

The cursor glides to the *Send* button and I start saying my goodbyes. I could still stop it, but . . .

The *Send* icon blinks to a negative and then back again. The words are so small, but I know them like the Big E on the eye chart:

Status: Pending.

Status: Approved.

Status: Paid.

"Listen, I should be getting back to my office . . ."

"Don't worry about it," Mary says without even turning around. "I can handle it from here."

9

Staring at his computer screen and running his tongue across a cold sore inside his lip, he had to admit, he didn't think Oliver would go through with it. Charlie, maybe. But not Oliver. Sure, he sometimes showed moments of greatness . . . the Tanner Drew incident being the most recent . . . but deep down, Oliver Caruso was still as scared as the day he started at Greene & Greene.

Still, the proof was always in the pudding—and right now, the pudding looked like it was about to be sent to London, England. Using the same technology he knew Shep had, he called up Martin Duckworth's account and scanned the column marked *Current Activity*. The last entry—*Balance of Account to C.M.W. Walsh Bank*—was still marked *Pending*. It wasn't going to be long now.

He pulled a pen from his jacket pocket and jotted down the bank's name, followed by the account number. Sure, he could call the London bank . . . try to catch the money . . . but by the time he got through, it'd almost certainly be gone Besides, why interfere now?

His phone started ringing and he picked up immediately. "Hello?" he answered, standardly confident.

"Well . . . ?" a gruff voice asked.

"*Well,* what?"

"Don't jerk me around," the man warned. "Did they take it?"

"Any second now . . ." he said, his eyes still focused on the screen. At the very bottom of the account, there was a quick blink—and *Pending* . . . became *Paid.*

"There it goes," he added with a grin. Shep . . . Charlie . . . Oliver . . . if they only knew what was coming.

"So that's it?" the man asked.

"That's it," he replied. "The snowball's officially rolling."

10

There's someone watching me. I didn't notice him when I said goodbye to Lapidus and left the bank—it was after six and the December sky was already dark. And I didn't see him trail me down the grimy subway stairs or follow me through the turnstile—there're way too many commuters crisscrossing through the urban anthills to notice any one person. But as I reach the subway platform, I swear I hear someone whisper my name.

I spin around to check, but all that's there is the typical Park Avenue post-work crowd: men, women, short, tall, young, old, a few black, mostly white. All of them in overcoats or heavy jackets. The majority stare down at reading material—a few lose themselves in their headphones—and one, just as I turn around, abruptly lifts a *Wall Street Journal* to cover his face.

I crane my neck, trying to get a look at his shoes or pants—anything for a context clue—but at the height of rush hour, the density of the crowd's too thick. In no mood to take chances, I head further up the platform, away from the *Journal* man. At the last second, I once again look over my shoulder. A few more commuters fill out the crowd, but for the most part, no one moves—no one except the man, who once again—like a villain in a bad Cold War movie— lifts the *Journal* to cover his face.

Don't get nuts, I tell myself—but before my brain can buy it, a quiet rumble fills the air. Here comes the train, which barrels into the station and blows my hair into an instant comb-over. Brushing it back into place with my fingers, I make my way toward the subway car and take one last peek down the platform. Every twenty feet, there's a small crowd shoving itself toward an open door. I don't know if he's on board or gave up, but the man with the *Journal* is gone.

I fight my way onto the already overstuffed subway car, where I'm smashed between a Hispanic woman in a puffy gray ski jacket, and a balding man in a flasher overcoat. As the train makes its way downtown, the crowd slowly begins to thin and a few seats actually open. Indeed, when I transfer at Bleecker and pick up the D train at the Broadway-Lafayette stop, all the downtown fashion plates wearing black shoes, black jeans, and black leather jackets make their way off. It's not the last stop before we head to Brooklyn, but it is the last *cool* stop.

Enjoying the extra space on the car, I lean up against a nearby metal pole. It's the first time since I left the office that I actually catch my breath—that is, until I see who's waiting for me at the far end of the car—the man hiding behind the *Wall Street Journal.*

Without the crowds and the distance, it's easy to give him the quick once-over. That's all I need. I plow toward him without even thinking. He lifts the paper a little higher, but it's too late. With a sharp swipe, I rip it from his hands and reveal who's been stalking me for the past fifteen minutes. "What the hell are you doing here, Charlie?"

My brother ekes out a playful grin, but it doesn't help.

"Answer me!" I demand.

Charlie looks up, almost impressed. "Wow—the full *Starsky & Hutch*. What if I was a spy . . . or a man with a hook?"

"I saw your shoes, dimwit—now what do you think you're doing?"

Pointing with his chin, Charlie motions to the crowd in the car, all of whom are now staring. Before I can react, he slips out from under me, heads to the other end of the subway car, and invites me to follow. As we pass, a few people look up, but only for a second. Typical New York.

"Now you want to tell me what this is about, or should I just add it to your ever-growing list of stupid moves?" I scold as we continue to move through the train.

"Ever-growing?" he asks, weaving his way through the crowd. "I don't know what you're—?"

"With Shep," I snarl, feeling the vein throb in my forehead. "How could you give him our final location?"

Turning my way, but refusing to slow down, Charlie waves a hand through the air as if it's an absurd question. "C'mon, Oliver—you're still in a huff over that?"

"Dammit, Charlie, enough with the jokes," I say, chasing after him. "Do you have any idea what you've done? I mean, do you ever actually stop and think about the consequences, or do you just jump off the cliff, content with being the town idiot?"

At the far end of the car, he stops dead in his tracks and turns around, glaring straight at me. "Do I look that stupid to you?"

"Well, considering what you—"

"I didn't give him anything," Charlie growls in a low whisper. "He has no idea where it is."

I pause as the train skids into Grand Street—the last subway stop in Manhattan. The moment the doors open, dozens of hunched-over Chinese men and women flood the car carrying pink plastic shopping bags that reek of fresh fish. Chinatown for groceries—then on the subway, back to Brooklyn. "What're you talking about?" I ask.

"When I showed him the Red Sheet . . . I pointed to the wrong bank. On purpose, Ollie." Stepping in close, he adds, "I gave him some random place in Antigua where we have nothing. Not even a shiny dime. Of course—and this is really the best part—you were so busy yelling, he believed every word." It takes me a second to process. "Don't have a brain blow, Oliver. I'm not letting anyone take our cash."

With a sharp tug, he tries to slide open the service door between the two subway cars. It's locked. Annoyed, he cuts around me, heading back exactly the way we came. Before I can say a word, the train chugs forward . . . and my brother's lost in the crowd.

"Charlie!" I shout, racing after him. "You're a genius!"

"I still don't understand when you planned it," I say as we walk up the broken concrete sidewalks of Avenue U in Sheepshead Bay, Brooklyn.

"I didn't," Charlie admits. "I thought of it as I was folding over the Red Sheet."

"Are you kidding me?" I ask, laughing. "Oh, man—he never knew what hit him!"

I wait for him to laugh back, but it never happens. Nothing but silence.

"What?" I ask. "Now I can't be happy the money's safe? I'm just relieved you—"

"Oliver, have you been listening to yourself? You spend the whole day crying a river and saying we have to play it cool, but then the moment I tell you I screwed over Shep, you're acting like the guy who got the last pair of Zeppelin tickets."

Heading up the block, I stare around at the mom-and-pop storefronts that dot the Avenue U landscape—pizza parlors, cigar stores, discount shoes, a barely breathing barber shop. Except for the pizza place, they're all closed for the night. When we were little, that meant the owners shut the lights and locked the doors. Today, it means lowering a roll-down steel-reinforced shield that looks like a metal garage door. No doubt about it, trust isn't what it used to be.

"C'mon, Charlie—I know you love taking in the lost puppy, but you barely know this guy—"

"It doesn't matter!" Charlie interrupts. "We're still screwing him over and twisting the butter knife in his back!" Nearing the corner of the block, he stretches his arm out and lets his fingertips skate along the metal shield that hides the used bookstore. "Damn!" Charlie shouts, punching the metal as hard as he can. "He trusted us t—" He grits his teeth and cuts himself off. "It's exactly what I hate about money . . ."

He makes a sharp right on Bedford Avenue, and the garage door storefronts give way to an uninspired 1950s-era six-story apartment building.

"I see handsome men!" a female voice shouts from a window on the fourth floor. I don't even have to look up to know who it is.

"Thanks, mom," I mutter under my breath. Keep the routine, I tell myself as I follow Charlie toward the lobby.

Monday night is Family Night. Even when you don't want it to be.

By the time the elevator reaches the fourth floor and we head to mom's apartment, Charlie's yet to say a single word to me. That's how he always gets when he's upset—shutdown and turned off. The same way dad solved his problems. Naturally, if he were dealing with anyone else, they'd be able to read it on his face, but with mom . . .

"Who wants a nice baked ziti!?" she shouts, opening the door even before we hit the doorbell. As always, her smile's wide and her arms are outstretched, searching for a hug.

"Ziti!?" Charlie sings, jumping forward and hugging her back. "We talking original or extra-crispy?" As corny as the joke is, mom laughs hysterically . . . and pulls Charlie even closer.

"So when do we eat?" he asks, sidestepping her and pulling the sauce-covered wooden spoon from her hand.

"Charlie, don't . . ."

It's too late. He shoves the spoon in his mouth, taking an early taste of the sauce.

"Are you happy?" she laughs, turning around to watch him. "Now you've got your germs all over it."

Holding the spoon like a lollipop, he presses it flat against his dangling tongue. "Aaaaaaaaaaaa," he moans, his tongue still out of his mouth. "Ah ott o ehrrs."

"You do too have germs," she continues to laugh, facing him directly.

"Hi, ma," I say, still waiting at the door.

She turns back immediately, the wide smile never leaving her face. "Ooooh, my *big* boy," she says, taking me in. "You know I love seeing you in a suit. So professional . . ."

"What about *my* suit?" Charlie calls out, pointing to his blue button-down and creased khakis.

"Handsome boys like you don't have to wear suits," she says in her best Mary Poppins tone.

"So that means I'm not handsome?" I ask.

"Or does that mean I look bad in a suit?" Charlie adds.

Even she knows when the joke's gone too far. "Okay, Frick and Frack—everybody inside."

Following my mom through the living room and past the framed painting Charlie did of the Brooklyn Bridge, I breathe deep and take a full whiff of my youth. Rubber erasers . . . crayons . . . homemade tomato sauce. Charlie has Play-Doh—I have Monday night dinners. Sure, some of the knickknacks shift, but the big things—grandma's dining room set, the glass coffee table I cut my head on when I was six—the big things are always the same. Including my mom.

Weighing in at over a hundred and eighty pounds, my mom's never been a petite woman . . . or an insecure one. When her hair went gray, she never dyed it. When it started thinning, she cut it short. After my dad left, the physical nonsense didn't matter anymore—all she cared about were me and Charlie. So even with the hospital bills, and the credit cards, and the bankruptcy dad left us with . . . even after losing her job at the secondhand store, and all the seamstress jobs she's had to do since . . . she's always had more than enough love to go around. The least we can do is pay her back.

Heading straight for the kitchen, I reach for the Charlie Brown cookie jar and tug on its ceramic head.

"Ow," Charlie says, using his favorite joke since fourth grade.

The head pops off, and I pull a small stack of papers from inside.

"Oliver, please don't do this . . ." mom says.

"Okay," I say, ignoring her and carrying the stack to the dining room table.

"I'm serious—it's not right. You don't have to pay my bills."

"Why? You helped me pay for college."

"You still had a job . . ."

". . . thanks to the guy you were dating. Four years of easy money—that's the only reason I could afford tuition."

"I don't care, Oliver. It's bad enough you paid for the apartment."

"I didn't pay for the apartment—all I did was ask the bank to work out better financing."

"And you helped with the down payment . . ."

"Mom, that was just to get you on your feet. You'd been renting this place for twenty-five years. You know how much money you threw away?"

"That's because your—" She cuts herself off. She doesn't like blaming my father.

"Ma, you don't have to worry. This is a pleasure."

"But you're my son . . ."

"And you're my mom."

It's hard to argue with that one. Besides, if she didn't need the help, the bills wouldn't be where I could find them, and we'd be eating chicken or steak instead of ziti. Her lips slightly quiver and she bites nervously at the Band-Aids that cover her fingertips. The life of a seamstress—too many pins and too many hems. We've always lived paycheck to paycheck, but the lines on her face are starting to show her age. Without a word, she opens the window in the kitchen and leans outside into the cold air.

At first, I assume she must've spotted Mrs. Finkelstein — mom's best friend and our old babysitter—whose window is

directly across the alley between our buildings. But when I
hear the familiar squeaky churn of the clothesline we share
with The Fink, I realize mom's bringing in the rest of
today's work. That's where I learned it—how to lose yourself in your job. When she's done, she turns back to the sink
and washes off Charlie's spoon.

The second it's clean, Charlie grabs it from her and presses it against his tongue. "Aaaaaaaaaaa," he hums. My mom
fights as hard as she can, but she still laughs. End of argument.

One by one, I flip through the monthly bills, totaling them
up and figuring out which ones to pay. Sometimes I just do
the credit cards and the hospital . . . other times, when the
heating gets high, I do utilities. Charlie always does insurance. As I said, for him, it's personal.

"So how was work?" mom asks Charlie.

He ignores the question, and she decides to let it go. She
had the same hands-off approach two years ago when
Charlie became Buddhist for a month. And then again a
year and a half ago when he switched to Hinduism. I
swear, sometimes she knows us better than we know ourselves.

Scanning through the credit card bill, my bank instincts
kick in. Check the charges; protect the client; make sure
nothing's out of place. Groceries . . . sewing materials . . .
music store . . . Vic Winick Dance Studio?

"What's this Vic Winick place?" I ask, leaning my chair
back toward the kitchen.

"Dance lessons," my mother says.

"*Dance lessons?* Who do you take dance lessons with?"

"Wif me!" Charlie shouts in his best French accent. He
takes the wooden spoon, grips it like a flower between his

teeth, grabs my mother, and pulls her close. "And a-one . . . and a-two . . . right-foot-first-now . . ." Breaking into a quick lindy, they bob and weave around the narrow kitchen. My mother is positively flying, her head held higher than . . . well, even higher than when I graduated college.

Twisting his neck, Charlie wings the spoon in the sink. "Not bad, huh?" he says.

"So how do we look?" she asks as they bang into the oven and nearly knock the pot of sauce to the floor.

"G-Great . . . just great," I say, my eyes falling back to the bills. I don't know why I'm surprised. I may've always had her head and her pocketbook, but Charlie . . . Charlie's always had her heart.

"Lookin' good, sweet momma—lookin' good!" Charlie yells, his hand waving in the air. "You're gonna be sleepin' easy tonight!"

I've made this walk 1,048 times. Out from the subway sauna, up the never-clean stairs, slalom-skiing through the freshly showered crowd, and straight up Park Avenue until I hit the bank. 1,048 times. That's four years, not including weekends—some of which I also worked. But today . . . I'm done counting the days I've put in. From now on, it's a countdown until we leave.

By my estimate, Charlie should be the first out—maybe a month or two from now. After that, when everything's long settled, it's a coin toss between me and Shep. For all we know, he may want to stay. Personally, I don't have that problem.

Continuing up Park Avenue toward 36th Street, I can practically taste the conversation. "I just wanted to let you know I think it's time I moved on," I'll tell Lapidus. No need to burn bridges or bring up the B-school letters—just a mention of "other opportunities elsewhere" and a thank-you for being the best mentor anyone could ever ask for. The fake bullshit will be oozing through my teeth. Just like he does to me. Still, the whole thing brings a smile to my face . . . that is, until I see the two navy blue sedans parked in front of the bank. Actually, forget parked. Stopped. Like they raced in for an emergency. I've seen enough black limos and privately driven town-cars to know they're not clients. And I don't need sirens to tell me the rest. Unmarked cop cars stand out everywhere.

My chest constricts and I take a few steps back. No, keep walking. Don't panic. As I edge toward the car, my eyes skate from the city-soot eyebrows at the top of the windshield, down to the blue-and-white "U.S. Government" placard sitting on the dashboard. These aren't cops. They're feds.

I'm tempted to turn and run, but . . . not yet. Don't get mental—keep it calm and get answers. There's no way anyone knows about the money.

Praying I'm right, I shove my way through the revolving door and search frantically for the early-arriving co-workers who sit at the wide-open web of desks that fill the first floor. To my relief, everyone's in place, first cup of coffee already in hand.

"Excuse me, sir, can I speak with you for a second?" a deep voice asks.

On my left, in front of the mahogany reception desk, a tall man with stiff shoulders and light blond hair approaches with a clipboard. "I just need your name," he explains.

"W-What for?"

"I'm sorry—I'm from Para-Protect—we're just trying to

figure out if we need to increase security in the welcoming area."

It's a clean answer with a clean explanation, but last I checked, we weren't having security issues.

"And your name?" he reiterates, keeping the tone friendly.

"Oliver Caruso," I offer.

He looks up—not startled—but just fast enough that I notice. He grins. I grin. Everybody's happy. Too bad I'm ready to pass out.

On the clipboard, he puts a small check next to my name. There's no check next to Charlie's. Not here yet. As the blond man leans against his clipboard, his jacket slides open and I get a quick peek at his leather shoulder-strap. This guy's carrying a gun. Behind me, I take one last glance at the unmarked cars. Security company, my ass. We're in trouble.

"Thank you, Mr. Caruso—you have a nice day now."

"You too," I say, forcing a smile. The only good sign is that he lets me pass. They don't know who they're looking for. But they are looking. They just don't want anyone to know.

That's it, I decide. Time to get some help. Blowing through the lobby and past the bullpen of rolltop desks, I head for the public elevator, but quickly change course and keep walking toward the back. I use Lapidus's code every day. Don't call attention to it by stopping now.

By the time I reach the private elevator, I'm a sweaty mess—my chest, my back—I feel like I'm soaking through my suit and wool coat. From there, it only gets worse. Stepping into the elevator's wood-paneled embrace, I go to loosen my tie. That's when I remember the surveillance camera in the corner. My fingers bounce off my tie and scratch an imaginary itch on my neck. The doors slam shut. My throat goes dry. I just ignore it.

My first instinct is to go see Shep, but it's no time to be stupid. Instead, I pound the button for the seventh floor. If I want to get to the bottom of this, I need to start at the top.

"He's been waiting for you," Lapidus's secretary warns as I fly past her desk.

"How many stars?" I call out, knowing how she rates Lapidus's moods. Four stars is good; one is a disaster.

"Total eclipse," she blurts.

I stop in my tracks. The last time Lapidus was that upset, it came with divorce papers. "Any idea what happened?" I ask, struggling to keep it together.

"I'm not sure, but have you ever seen a live volcano . . . ?"

Taking a quick gulp of air, I reach for the bronze doorknob.

". . . *I don't care what they want!*" Lapidus screams into his phone. "*Tell them it's a computer problem . . . blame it on a virus—until they hear otherwise, it's staying shut down—and if Mary has a problem with that, tell her she can take it up with the agent in charge!*" He slams the receiver just as I shut the door. Following the sound, he jerks his head toward me—but I'm too busy staring at the person sitting in the antique chair on the opposite side of his desk. Shep. He shakes his head ever so slightly. We're dead.

"Where the hell've you been!?" Lapidus yells.

My eyes are still on Shep.

"*Oliver, I'm talking to you!*"

I jump, turning back to my boss. "I-I'm sorry. What?"

Before I can answer, there's a knock on the door behind me. "Come in!" Lapidus barks.

Quincy opens it halfway and sticks his head in. He's got the same look as Lapidus. Gritted teeth. Manic head movements. The way he surveys the room—me . . . Shep . . . the couch . . . even the antiques—everything gets a look. Sure, he's a born analyzer, but this is different. The pale look on his face. It's not anger. It's fear.

"I have the reports," he says anxiously.

"So? Let's hear 'em," Lapidus says.

Standing on the threshold and still refusing to enter the room, Quincy tightens his glance. Partners only.

With a swift push away from the desk, Lapidus climbs out of his leather wingback and heads for the door. The moment he's gone, I go straight for Shep.

"What the hell is going on?" I ask, fighting to keep it to a whisper. "Did they—"

"Was this you?" Shep shoots back.

"Was *what* me?"

He looks away, completely overwhelmed. "I don't even know how they did it . . ."

"Did what?"

"They set us up, Oliver. Whoever took it, they were watching the entire time . . ."

I grab him by the shoulder. "Dammit, Shep, tell me w—"

The door swings wide and Lapidus storms back in the room. "Shep—your friend Agent Gallo's waiting in the conference room—do you want to—?"

"Yeah," Shep interrupts, leaping from his seat.

I shoot him a sideways glance. *You called in the Service? Don't ask,* he motions, shaking his head.

"Oliver, I need you to do me a favor," Lapidus adds, his voice on fire. He flips through a stack of papers, looking for . . .

"There," I say, pointing to his reading glasses.

He snatches them and stuffs them in his jacket pocket. No time for thank-yous. "I want someone downstairs as people start coming in," he says. "No offense to the Service, but they don't know our staff."

"I don't underst—"

"Stay by the door and watch reactions," he barks, his patience long gone. "I know we've got an agent taking attendance . . . but whoever did this . . . they're too smart to call in sick. That's why I want you to keep an eye on people when they walk in. If they've got a guilty conscience, the agent alone'll freak them out . . . you can't hide panic. Even if it's just a pause or an open mouth. You know the people, Oliver. Find out who did it for me." He puts an arm on my shoulder and rushes me toward the door. Lapidus and Shep march off to the conference room. Searching for options, I head downstairs. I just need a second to think.

By the time the elevator doors open in the lobby, I'm completely exhausted. The hurricane's hit too fast. Everything's spinning. Still, there's not much of a choice. Follow orders. Anything else is suspicious.

Sliding up to the teller booth that runs along the righthand wall, I grab a deposit slip and pretend to fill it out. It's the best way to watch the door, where the agent with the blond hair is still checking people off.

One by one they walk in and give their names. Not a single one of them pauses or thinks twice about it. I'm not surprised—the only one with the guilty conscience is me. But the more I sit there, the more the whole thing doesn't make sense. Sure, for me and Charlie, three million is a solid hunk of change, but around here . . . it's not a life-changer. And the way Shep asked me about it—about whether it was me—he wasn't just worried about being caught . . . he lost something too. And now that I finally stop to think about it . . . maybe . . . so did we.

Searching the always bustling front lobby, I check to see if anyone's watching. Secretaries, analysts, even the agent in charge—everyone's caught up in their day-to-day. The crowd comes in the revolving door and their names are checked off. I glide toward the same door, figuring it's my best way out—

"Have you signed in?" the agent with blond hair snaps.

"Y-Yeah," I say as the co-workers in line stare me down. "Oliver Caruso."

He checks his list, then looks up. "Go ahead."

I plow forward shoulder-first and push the door as hard as I can. As it gives, I'm thrown out on the frozen street, skidding full speed around the corner.

Racing up Park Avenue, I look around for a newsstand. I should know better. This neighborhood doesn't exactly attract the crowd who buys off the street. Except for payphones, the corners are empty. Ignoring the pain of running in dress shoes, I make a sharp left on 37th and take off toward the end of the block. The concrete's making me feel every step. The moment I hit Madison Avenue, I slam on the brakes and slide up to an outdoor newsstand.

"Do you have phone cards?" I ask the unshaven guy who's warming himself on a space heater behind the counter.

He motions Vanna-White-style at his world of wares. "Whattya *you* think?"

I look around, searching for—

"*Here*," he interrupts, pointing over his own shoulder. Next to the toilet-paper-rolls of scratch-off lottery tickets.

"I'll take the twenty-five-dollar one," I tell him.

"Beautiful," he says. He pulls the Statue of Liberty one from the clipboard, and I toss him two twenties.

Waiting for my change, I rip off the plastic wrapper right there. Sure, I could go back to the law firm, but after this morning, I don't want anything tracing me to yesterday. "Will these work to call out of the country?" I ask.

"You can call the Queen of France and tell her to shave her pits!"

"Great. Thanks." Gripping the card in a tight fist, I dart back toward Park Avenue, cross the six-lane street, and stop at a payphone diagonally down the block from the entrance to the bank. There're more inconspicuous places to call from, but this way, no one in the bank has a clear view of me. More important, since I'm only a few blocks from the subway, I have the best possible location for spotting Charlie.

I dial the 800 number on the back of the Lady Liberty calling card and punch in the pin code. When it asks for the number I want to dial, I pull out my wallet, slide my finger behind my driver's license, and pull out a tiny scrap of paper. I punch in the ten-digit number that I'd written on the paper in reverse order. I may carry the Antigua phone number on me, but if I get caught, it doesn't mean I have to make it easy.

"Thank you for calling Royal Bank of Antigua," a digital female voice answers. "For automated account balance and information, press one. To speak to a personal service representative, press two."

I press two. If someone stole it from us, I want to know where it went.

"This is Ms. Tang. How can I help you today?"

Before I can answer, I spot Charlie trailing a pack of people across the street.

"Hello . . . ?" the woman says.

"Hi, I just wanted to check the balance of my account." I wave to get Charlie's attention, but he doesn't see me.

"And your account number?" the woman asks.

"58943563," I tell her. When I memorized it, I didn't think I'd be using it this soon. Directly across, Charlie's by himself, but he's practically dancing up the street.

"And who am I speaking with?"

"Martin Duckworth," I say. "It's under Sunshine Distributors."

"Please hold while I check the account."

The moment the Muzak starts, I cover the receiver. *"Charlie!"* I scream. He's already too far past—and with the buzz of rush hour traffic between us . . . *"Charlie!"* I shout again. He still doesn't hear.

Making his way up the block, Charlie steps off the curb and gets his first good look at the bank. As always, his reaction is faster than mine. He spots the unmarked cars and freezes, right there in the middle of the street.

I expect him to run, but he's smarter than that. Instinctively, he glances around, searching for me. It's like my mom used to say: she never believed in ESP—but siblings . . . siblings were connected. Charlie knows I'm here.

"Mr. Duckworth . . . ?" the woman asks on the other line.

"Y-Yeah . . . right here." I wave my hand in the air, and this time, Charlie sees it. He looks my way, studying my body language. He wants to know if it's real, or if I'm just playing Chicken Little. Refusing to wait for the light, he hops into traffic, dodging and weaving through the onslaught of cars. A yellow cab lets loose with its horn, but Charlie shrugs it off, unbothered. Seeing me hit full panic means he doesn't have to.

"Mr. Duckworth, I'm going to need the password on the account," the woman from the bank says.

"*FroYo,*" I say to her.

"What happened?" Charlie asks the instant he hits the curb.

I ignore him, waiting for the bank teller.

"Tell me!" he challenges.

"Now what can I help you with today?" the woman on the other line finally says.

"I'd like the balance, as well as the most recent activity on the account," I reply.

Right there, Charlie lets out a belly laugh—the same patented little-brother taunt from when he was nine. "I knew it!" he shouts. "I knew you couldn't help yourself!"

I put a finger in front of my lips to quiet him down, but I don't have a prayer.

"You couldn't even hold out twenty-four hours, could you?" he asks, leaning in closer to the booth. "What'd it take? The cars outside? The federal plates? Have you even spoken to anyone or did you just see the cars and wet your pa—?"

"Can you please shut up! I'm not a moron!"

"Mr. Duckworth . . . ?" the original woman returns.

"Y-Yeah . . . I'm here," I say, turning back to the phone. "I'm right here."

"Sorry to keep you waiting, sir. I was hoping to get a supervisor on the line to—"

"Just tell me the balance. Is it zero?"

"Zero?" she says with a laugh. "No . . . not at all."

I let out a nervous laugh of my own. "Are you sure?"

"Our system's not perfect, sir, but this one's pretty clear. According to our records, there's only one transaction on the whole account—a wire transfer that was received yesterday at 12:21 P.M."

"So the money's still there?"

"Absolutely," the woman says. "I'm looking at it right now. A single transfer via wire—for a total of three hundred and thirteen million dollars."

11

W e've got *what!?*" Charlie shouts.

"I don't believe this," I stammer, my twitching
hand still resting on the hung-up receiver. "Do you have any
idea what this means?"

"It means we're rich," he shoots back. "And I'm not
talkin' filthy rich, or even extremely rich—I'm talkin'
obscenely, grotesquely, do-re-mi-fa-so-much-money-we-
got-a-gross-domestic-product rich. Or as my barber said
when I tipped him five bucks once: 'Dat's some major clam
action.'"

"We're dead," I blurt, my full body weight collapsing
against the frame of the payphone. That's what I get—all
from a stupid moment of anger. "There's no way to
explai—"

"We'll tell 'em we won it in the Super Bowl pool. They
might believe that."

"I'm serious, Charlie. This isn't just three million—
it's . . ."

"Three hundred and thirteen million. I heard you the first
three times." He counts on his fingers, from pinky to point-

er finger: "Three hundred and ten . . . three hundred and eleven . . . three hundred and twelve . . . three hundred and thirteen . . . Holy guacamole, I feel like the little old guy with the mustache in Monopoly—you know, with the monocle and the bald h—"

"How can you make jokes?"

"What else am I gonna do? Lean up against a payphone and cower for the rest of my life?"

Without a word, I stand up straight.

"Feels pretty good now, don't it?" he asks.

"It's not a game, Charlie. They'll kill us for this . . ."

"Only if they find it—and last I checked . . . all those fake companies—this bad boy's foolproof."

"Foolproof? Are you nuts? We're not—" I cut myself off and lower my voice. There're still plenty of people on the street. "We're way beyond petty cash," I whisper. "So stop with the Butch Cassidy bravado and—"

"No. Not a chance," he interrupts. "It's time to kiss a little reality, Ollie—this isn't another thing to run from—this is Candyland. All that money; all of it ours. What else do you want? No one knows how to find it . . . no one suspects it's us—if it was good before, it's doubly better now. Three hundred and thirteen times better. For once in our lives we can actually sit back and kick up our—"

"*Dammit, what's wrong with you!?*" I shout, flying from the booth and grabbing him by the collar of his coat. "Have you even been paying attention? You heard Shep—the only way it works is if no one knows it's gone. Three million fits in our pockets . . . but three hundred and thirteen . . . do you realize what they'll do to get that back?" I'm trying my best to whisper, but people are starting to stare. Looking around, I abruptly let go. "That's it," I mutter. "I'm done."

Charlie straightens his coat. I turn back to the payphone.

"Who're you calling?" Charlie asks.

I don't answer, but he watches my fingers pound the digits. Shep.

"I wouldn't do that," he warns.

"What're you talking about?"

"If they're smart, they're watching incoming calls. Maybe even listening. If you want information, go inside and talk to him face-to-face."

I stop mid-dial, glare at Charlie over my shoulder, and officially start the staring contest. He knows my look: the doubting Thomas. And I know his: the honest Injun. I also know it's just a trick . . . his favorite scheme for settling me down so he can get his way. It's what he always does. But even I can't argue with the logic. I slam down the phone and brush past him. "You better be right," I warn as I head back to the bank.

A quick stop at the local coffee shop gives me an eight-ounce cup of calm, and a perfect excuse for why I left the building in the first place. Still, it doesn't stop the Secret Service agent at the front door from putting another check mark next to my name—and one next to Charlie's.

"What's with the anal attendance taking?" Charlie asks the agent.

The agent jabs us with a look as if the check mark alone should bring us to our knees—but we both know the reality of this one: If they had a semblance of a clue, we'd be walking out in handcuffs. Instead, we're walking in.

On most days, I go straight for the elevator. Today is clearly different. Following Charlie as he slides past the marble-top teller window, I let him drag me toward the maze of rolltop desks. As always, it's packed with gossiping employees, but today, that's actually the payoff.

"Howya doin'?" Jeff from Jersey calls out, cutting us off and patting Charlie on the chest.

"There it is," Charlie sings. "My daily pat on the chest. Awkward to most—revered by a few."

Laughing, Jeff stops us just a few feet short of the elevator.

"You know I'm right," Charlie says, enjoying every moment. I'm tempted to drag him along, but it's clear what my brother's after. Jersey Jeff may violate just a bit too much of your personal space, but when it comes to office gossip, even I know he's king bee.

"What's the story with Mr. Attendance?" Charlie asks, elbowing toward the blond guy at the front door.

Jeff smiles wide. Finally, a chance to strut. "They say he's doing some security upgrade, but no one believes it. I mean, how stupid do they think we are?"

"Pretty stupid?" Charlie offers.

"Plenty stupid," Jeff agrees.

"What do you think it is?" I blurt with the patience of . . . well . . . with the patience of someone who just stole three hundred and thirteen million dollars.

"Hard to say, hard to say," Jeff replies. "But if I had to guess . . ." He leans in close, relishing the moment. "I'm betting on a pickpocket. Inside job."

"*What?*" Charlie whispers, playing up the outrage. From the strain on my face, he can tell I'm ready to lose it.

"It's just a theory," Jeff begins. "But you know how it goes—this place doesn't change the toilet paper without firing off a memo—but suddenly, they're redoing all of security without even a heads-up?"

"Maybe they wanted to see our normal routines," I offer.

"And maybe they didn't want to scream fire in the crowded movie theater. It's just like when they caught that woman embezzling from Accounts Payable—they try to keep everything quiet. They're not dumb. If it goes public, the clients'll panic and start taking back their cash."

"I wouldn't be so sure," I add, refusing to give in.

"Hey, believe what you want—but there's gotta be some reason all the bigshots are up on the fourth floor."

The fourth floor. Charlie stares my way. *That's where my desk is*, he glares.

"Excuse me?" Charlie blurts.

Jeff grins. That's what he was saving. "Oh, yeah," he says, walking back to his desk. "They've been up there all morning . . ."

I look at Charlie and he looks at me. Fourth floor it is.

The instant the elevator doors open, Charlie tears onto the gray carpet and takes a quick recon. From the copy room, to the coffee machine, to the cubicle canyon that fills the center of the room, nothing's out of place. Mailcarts are rolling, keyboards are clicking, and a few scattered groups are exchanging the first round of morning chitchat. Still, it doesn't take a genius to know where the action is—up here, there's only one place where the bigshots can hide. Weaving toward Charlie's desk as if it's just another day, we both focus on the office at the far end of the room. The Cage.

There's no way to tell if they're in there or if Jeff was blowing his usual smoke. The door's closed. It's always closed. But it doesn't stop us from staring—studying the grain of the wood, the shine of the doorknob, even the tiny black buttons on the punch-code lock. I could easily get us in, but . . . not today. Not until we—

"Call Shep—see where he is," I whisper as we slide into Charlie's cubicle. Charlie sits on one knee in his chair, his head just below the top of the cube. He picks up the phone and dials Shep's number. I lean in to listen, my eyes still on Mary's door. Paid to be paranoid, Shep usually picks up on the first ring. Not today. Today, the phone keeps ringing.

"I don't think he's—"

"Shhhhh," I interrupt. Something's happening.

Charlie jumps from his seat and studies The Cage. The door slowly opens and the room empties. Across the hall, Quincy's the first to leave, followed by Lapidus. I duck. Charlie stays up. It's his desk.

"Who else is there?" I whisper, my chin kissing his keyboard.

He keeps his eyes on the door and raises both hands in the air, pretending he's just stretching. "Behind Lapidus is Mary," he begins.

"Anyone else?"

"Yeah, but I don't know 'em . . ."

I pick my head up just enough for a peek. As Mary leaves the office, she's followed by a squatty guy in a poorly fitted suit. He walks with a slight limp and keeps scratching at the back of his buzz cut, right above his neck. Even with the limp, he's got the same meaty look as Shep. Secret Service. Behind Mr. Squat is another agent, much thinner in both hair and weight, carrying what looks like a black shoebox with a few dangling wires. FBI had the same thing when they prosecuted that woman in Accounts Payable. Hook it up to the computer and you get an instant copy of the person's hard drive. It's the easiest way to keep the place calm—don't let them see you confiscating computers—just take the evidence in a doggy bag.

Sure enough, as the door swings wide, I spot Mary's computer up on her desk. The disk drive slot is covered with evidence tape. Nothing goes in; nothing gets out.

It takes another second for the clown car to spit out its last passenger—the one person we've been waiting for. As he steps into the hallway, Shep's eyes lock on Charlie. I expect a grin, or maybe even a fiendish Elvis lip-curl. But all we get is wide-eyed anxiety. "Uh-oh," Charlie says. "My boy's looking crappy."

"Everything okay, Shep?" Mr. Squat calls out as he and the rest of the zoo crew wait for the elevator.

"Y-Yeah," Shep stammers. "I'll meet you up there in a second. I forgot something in my office." Heading to the other end of the hallway, he shoves open the metal door and ducks into the stairwell. Just before the door closes, he shoots us one last look. He's not running up the stairs. He's just standing there, waiting. For us.

As Mr. Squat turns our way, I duck back down. Charlie doesn't move.

"What're they doing?" I whisper, still trying to stay out of sight. I hear the elevator doors slide open.

"They're waving to us . . ." Charlie says. "Now Quincy's standing behind Lapidus, trying to give him the bunny ears . . . Oh, Lapidus is on to him. No bunny ears for anyone." He can make all the jokes he wants, it doesn't hide the fear.

I hear the elevator doors slowly slide shut.

"*C'mon . . .*" Charlie insists as he motions to my cup of coffee. "Let's go get some coffee."

Leaving my coffee cup on his desk, I follow him out of the cubicle and straight to the coffee machine—which just happens to be next to the stairs. Charlie plows forward. I check over my shoulder.

"Are you sure it's—?"

"Stop hesitating, Ollie—it's only gonna rot your brain."

Without looking back, he takes a swan dive into the abyss. But as he ducks into the stairwell, it's completely empty. Over the banisters, he looks up and down. No one's—

"Not exactly what we had in mind, now is it?" a deep voice asks as the door slams with a thunderclap. We spin around. Behind us is Shep.

"Not a bad day's work," Charlie whispers, extending the high-five.

Shep doesn't take him up on it. He's too focused on me. "So it's all in the account?"

"Forget the account. Why'd you call in the Service?" I insist.

"They were here when I got here," Shep snaps back. "I'm guessing it was Quincy or Lapidus—but believe me, when it comes to law enforcement, the Service is better than the FBI. At least we're dealing with friends."

"See . . ." Charlie interrupts. "Nothing to worry about."

We both shoot him looks that're meant to knock him on his ass. Me, he can handle. Shep's another story. Time to get serious.

"We'll catch the people and get the money back as quick as we can," Shep announces, leaning over the banister and eyeing the floors above us. He lowers his voice and mouths two words: "Not here." He's not taking any chances.

"So where do you want to go for lunch?" Charlie quickly adds. Smart. We need a place to talk. Someplace private. Simultaneously staring at the floor, the three of us fall silent. We're all on the same page, churning through the mental atlas.

"How about the Yale Club?" I suggest, going with Lapidus's favorite hideaway.

"I like it," Charlie says. "Quiet, secluded, and just snotty and repressed enough to know how to keep its mouth shut."

Shep shakes his head. Reading our confused looks, he

pulls out his wallet and gives us a quick flash of his driver's license. Good point. To get in there, we'll have to show ID.

"I got it," Charlie says. "How about Track 117?"

I smirk. Shep's lost. A quick whisper in his ear fills him in.

"You sure we can—?"

"Trust me," Charlie says. "No one even knows it exists." Watching us carefully, Shep doesn't have much of a choice.

"So I'll see you at noon?" Shep asks. The two of us nod our heads, and he takes off up the stairs. He disappears quickly, but we still hear his shoes clicking against the concrete steps.

The door slams above us, and I hit the stairs like Stallone in the first *Rocky*.

"Where're you going?" Charlie calls out.

I don't answer, but he already knows. I'm not waiting till lunch—I want the rest of the picture now.

Tearing up the corkscrewed stairs, I look back just enough to see Charlie trailing right behind me.

"They'll never let you in," he calls out.

"We'll see . . ."

Fifth floor . . . sixth floor . . . seventh floor . . . I shoot out into the hallway, heading straight for Lapidus's secretary. Charlie waits back, watching the rest through a crack in the stairwell door. That was his floor; this one's mine.

"They still in there?" I ask, blowing past her desk as if they're expecting me.

"Oliver, don't . . ."

She's not even close to being fast enough. I fling the door open and disappear.

Inside, the noisy chatter falls dead silent. Every single head turns my way. Lapidus, Quincy, Shep, Mary . . . even the two Secret Service agents who're crowded around

Lapidus's antique desk. They look at me like I crashed their funeral.

"Who the hell is this?" Mr. Squat barks.

I look to Lapidus for the save, but by now, I should know better.

"I'll take care of it," Lapidus says, rushing toward me. He reaches out for my elbow, and with the gracefulness of a ballroom dancer, glides past me, spins me around, and escorts me back to the door. It's so smooth, I barely realize what's happening. "We just need to take care of a few things first. You understand . . ." he adds as if it's no big deal. There's a loud creak and the door opens. Three seconds later, I'm out on my ass.

Across the hall, I catch Charlie watching from the stairwell. My eyes drop to the carpet. Behind me, Lapidus gives me the standard boss back-pat and sends me on my way.

"I'll call you when we have some news," Lapidus adds, his voice suddenly waning. At three hundred million, it's too big even for him. As I glance over my shoulder, he looks more ragged than both me and my brother—and the way he's clutching the doorknob, it's almost like he needs it to stand. Watching me leave, Lapidus slowly shuts the door. But in the last second . . . just as he turns away . . . just as he brushes his hand across his top lip . . . I swear, he's fighting back the slightest of grins.

"So he wouldn't give you anything?" Charlie asks as we race up Park Avenue, zigzagging in tandem through the lunchtime crowd.

"Can we please not talk about it?" I snap.

"What abou—"

"I said I don't want to talk about it!"

Charlie steps back, his palms facing me. "Listen, you

don't have to tell me twenty times—I got better stuff to do anyway. Now what d'you wanna buy first? I'm thinking something small, but easy to hide—like Delaware."

This time, I don't answer.

"What? You don't like Delaware? Fine—how 'bout a Carolina?"

I continue to stay quiet.

"Oh, c'mon, Ollie—throw me some love—a shrug . . . a yell . . . something." He knows I'm too opinionated to bite my lip—which means he also knows that when silence steps in, my mind's on something else.

"*Helloooooo*—Earth to Oliver! You speaka de Spanish?"

I step off the curb and cross 41st Street. Only one more block to go. "Do you think Shep would turn on us?" I blurt.

Charlie laughs out loud. That little-brother laugh. "Is that what's got you crapping your pants?"

"I'm serious, Charlie—for all we know, that's why he agreed to meet us. He'll tape our entire conversation, and then all he'll have to do is turn us over to the—"

"Whoa, whoa, whoa . . . it's time to jump on the trolley and get out of the Land of Make-Believe. This is Shep we're talking about. He's not in it to screw us over. He wants this money just as bad as we do."

"Speak for yourself," I shoot back. "I'm done with the money. I'm just worried that when push comes to shove, we're going to be knee-deep in *he said/we said.*"

"Well, let me tell you something, if we were, he'd be a moron. I mean, the way everything's set up, we couldn't have done this on our own. Even Shep knows that. So if he starts pointing the finger at us, it's clear we have plenty of his own fingerprints to point at him. Besides, it's not like we have a choice—he's our only man on the inside."

Once again, I fall silent. He's on the money with that one.

When it comes to the big picture, there's still a ton of information we're missing. And right now, as we cross 42nd Street and quickly approach the brass-and-glass doors of Grand Central Station, there's only one place we can get it.

"You ready?" Charlie asks, pulling open the door and bowing butler-style. He's watching me closely, checking to see if I'll hesitate.

I stop at the threshold, but only for a second. Before he can issue the challenge, I step inside without looking back.

"Now we're talking," he croons.

"C'mon," I call out, daring him to keep up. From the silence alone, I know what he's thinking. He can't tell if the bravery's real, or I'm just anxious to get some answers. Either way, as I turn around to check the look on his face, it's clear he's thrilled.

For the first few steps, we're running through a low-ceiling, claustrophobic subway tunnel. Then—like that moment when your car pulls out of the Brooklyn Battery Tunnel and all of Manhattan stands wide-open in front of you—we take our first step into the light . . . the ceiling rises up, up, up . . . and the enormous, marble-covered Main Concourse of Grand Central Station appears. Craning his neck up, Charlie can't help but stare at the seventy-five-foot arched windows along the left wall, and the blue-and-white zodiac mural that decorates the vaulted ceiling.

According to the clock at the center of the station, we only have about three minutes. I turn back to Charlie as I run. "What's the easiest way to—"

"Follow me," he interrupts, excitedly taking the lead. I may've heard of where we're going, but I've never been there myself. This place is all Charlie's. With me barely a step behind, he makes a sharp left, weaves through the bottlenecked crowd of commuters and tourists, and races full speed toward one of dozens of stairs that lead to the station's lower level.

"Nice and easy now," I say, tugging on his shirt to slow him down on the stairs. I don't want to make a scene.

Yeah, like anyone's watching, he says with a raised eyebrow.

Leaping down the last three steps, Charlie lands with a thwack, his shoes smacking against the concrete floor. His feet have to sting in his dress shoes, but he doesn't say a word. He hates I-told-you-so.

"Where now?" I ask, quickly catching up.

Without answering, Charlie takes off through the lower level of the station, which these days, is now just another food court. Charlie's nose follows the whiff of heat-lamped fries, but his eyes are glued to a left-pointing arrow at the base of a vintage-tiled sign: "To Tracks 100–117."

"And away we go," Charlie says.

Up the hallway, we've got the food court on our left and turn-of-the-old-century track entrances on our right. I count the doorways as we go. 108 . . . 109 . . . 110. At the far end of the hall, I quickly spot the rabbithole—Tracks 116 and 117.

Darting through a door, we're at the top of a tall staircase, looking down at the wide concrete platform. True to form, there's a train pulled into Track 116 on the right side of the platform. On the left, though—on 117—there's no chance that a train's coming. Not now. Not ever. Simply put, Track 117 doesn't officially exist. Sure, the space is there, but it's not an active track. Instead, for the past ten years, it's been filled with a long row of prefab construction trailers.

"This is where you used to play?" I ask as we stare at two construction workers through a lit window in the trailer.

"No . . ." he answers, cutting toward a short path on my left. "This is where we used to hide . . ."

Reading the confused look on my face, he explains, "Back when I was a junior in high school, me and Randy Boxer used to go track-to-track, playing music for Friday night commuters. His harmonica, my bass, and the biggest potential audience this side of Madison Square Garden. Naturally, the transit cops chased us at every opportunity, but in the labyrinth of staircases, the lower level always had the best places to disappear. And here—behind 117—this was where we'd reconvene so we could pick the fight all over again."

"Are you sure it's safe?" I ask as he rushes across the dirt-covered catwalk that runs perpendicular over Track 117. It's not the catwalk that's giving me pause—it's the metal door at the end—and the brown, faded words painted on it:

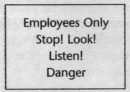

Employees Only
Stop! Look!
Listen!
Danger

Danger. That's where I hit the brakes. And, as always, where Charlie picks up speed.

"Charlie, maybe we shouldn't . . ."

"Don't be such a wuss," he calls out as he grabs the handle to the door. Eyeing the rusted metal frame, he gives it a hard yank, and just as the door swings open, a sandstorm of dust tumbles toward us. Charlie steps right into the whirlwind. And I realize I'm all alone.

As I follow him through to the adjoining room, we're in

a huge underground station, standing on the edge of an abandoned set of train tracks.

For Charlie, it's a homecoming. *"Where trains come to die*, Randy used to say."

Looking around, I can see why: The tunnel is wide enough for three sets of tracks, tall enough to fit the old diesel trains, and has ceilings black enough to show why they dropped the diesels in the first place. Next to the rusted tracks and between the even rustier I-beams, the floor is covered with condom wrappers, cigarette butts, and at least two used hypodermic needles. No question, it's a good place to hide.

"Close the door," Shep calls out from further up the platform.

"Nice to see you too," Charlie says. Pointing over his shoulder, he adds, "Don't worry about the door—you can't hear anything from back here."

Shep looks at him like he's not even there. "Oliver, shut the door," he demands. I don't hesitate. The door slams with a muffled thud, encasing us in silence. We've got fifteen minutes before someone realizes we're all gone at the same time. I'm not wasting a second.

"How bad is it?" I ask, wiping my soot-covered hands on the back of my pants.

"Ever heard of the *Titanic*?" Shep asks. "You should see it up there—every single one of them's a lit match away from exploding. Lapidus is tearing his ears off and threatening to unleash the ten plagues on anyone who leaks the info to the public. Across the table, Quincy's screaming through the phone at the insurance company and clicking his calculator to figure out just how much they're personally on the hook for."

"Have they told the other partners yet?"

"There's an emergency meeting tonight. In the meantime, they're waiting for the Service to dissect the computer system and possibly get a nibble on where the money went after London."

"So they still don't know where it is . . ." Charlie begins.

". . . and they still don't know it's us," Shep closes. "At least, not yet."

That's all I need to hear. "Fine," I say, my hands squarely on my hips.

Charlie glares my way. He hates this stance.

In no mood to listen, I turn to Shep. "Now how do you think we should turn ourselves in?" I ask.

"*What?*" Shep blurts.

"Whoa doggy," Charlie begs.

"Oliver, don't be hasty," Shep adds. "Even if it's a tornado now, it'll eventually slow down."

"Oh, so now you think we can outrun the Secret Service?"

"All I'm saying is it can still work out," Shep replies. "I know the Service's protocols. When it comes to the money, it'll take at least a week before they figure out if they can find it. If they do, we turn ourselves in with a full explanation. But if they don't . . . why walk away from the pot of gold? Forget the pocket change—three hundred and thirteen million means over a hundred and four million *each*."

Across Charlie's cheeks, the smile takes hold. Noticing the anger on my face, he pushes a bit further and starts to dance. Nothing big—just a little bounce in the shoulders and a stomp in the feet. It's purposely designed to annoy. "Mmmmm-mmm," he says, doing the full Stevie Wonder neck-sway. "Smells like rich!"

"I'm telling you, there's no reason to turn ourselves in," Shep adds, hoping to ram it home. "If we play it smart, we'll all be whistling a wealthy tune."

"Are you even listening to yourself?" I snap back. "We can't win. Think of what you said when we started—*it's a perfect crime when no one knows it's gone; it's only three million dollars*—that was your whole big speech. And where are we now? Three hundred and thirteen million missing . . . the Secret Service parked in our front yards . . . and when the press get ahold of it . . . plus whoever wanted this money in the first place . . . by the time this is done, the whole world's gonna be hunting our asses."

"I'm not disagreeing," Shep says. "But that doesn't mean we have to go for the hara-kiri on day one either. Besides, there's no way Lapidus is letting this get out. If he does, the other clients'll start hurtling for the exits. It's like when that guy hacked ten million out of Citibank a few years back— they did everything in their power to keep it out of the papers—"

"But eventually, it was on page one," I interrupt. "The word always gets out. There're no secrets anymore—this isn't the Fifties. Even if Lapidus can hold it back for a month . . . between reports, and insurance claims, and law-suits . . . it'll eventually worm its way free. And then we're back where we are right now . . . three dumb sitting ducks who—"

There's a loud thump, and we all stop. It's not like the random clangs that echo from the other tracks. Whatever just made that noise, it was in the room.

Shep jerks his head to the left and scans the crumbling concrete wall, but there's nothing in sight. Just a few long-abandoned electrical boxes and some faded graffiti.

"I thought it came from up *there*," Charlie whispers anxiously as he points toward the shadows of the arched ceiling. Between the lack of lighting and the stains from the soot, every arch is a dark floating cave.

"Were you followed?" Shep mouths.

I stop for a second. "No . . . I don't think so. Unless—"

Shep covers his lips in a Shhhh motion. Rotating his neck side to side, side to side, side to side, he scans the rest of the room with military precision. But it doesn't take years of Secret Service training to tell me what my gut already knows. We all get the same out-of-body feeling when we're being watched. And as Charlie nervously glances around, a pregnant silence settles on the room, and we can't help but feel like we no longer have this place to ourselves.

"Let's get out of here," Charlie says.

But just as he turns to the door, there's another noise. Not a thud. More like a creak. I instinctively look up, but it's not coming from the ceiling. Or the walls. It's lower.

There's another quiet creak and we all look down. "Behind you," Charlie motions to Shep. He spins around and checks out a section of flat wood planks that're built into the ground like a mini-life-raft.

"What're those?" I ask quietly.

"Vertical passageways. Underneath the planks, they lead down to the tracks below," Charlie explains. "That's how they move the big equipment and generators—they just take out the wood and lower them through the holes." He's trying to sound relaxed, but from the crinkle in his forehead— and the way he backs away from the planks—I can tell he's creeped out. He's not the only one.

"Can we please get out of here?" I ask.

Bending down toward the floor, Shep angles his head, trying to peer between the planks of wood. It's like staring into an underground air-conditioning vent. "You sure it's from here?" he asks. "Or is it echoing from somewhere else?" Changing course, Charlie moves in for a closer look.

"Charlie, get away from there," I plead.

There's another creak. Then another. Slow at first, but getting faster.

Shep looks up and re-scouts the entire tunnel. If it is an echo, it has to start somewhere.

I rush in and grab Charlie by the shoulder. "Let's go!" I say as I head for the door.

Stumbling to his feet, Charlie follows me, but keeps his eyes on Shep.

Through the planks, the pace of the noise gets even quicker. Like a soft scraping . . .

"C'mon!" I insist.

. . . or someone walking . . . no, more like running. The sound's not coming from in here. It's outside. I stop and slide to a halt along the dusty floor. "*Charlie, wait!*"

Passing me by, he turns around like I'm insane. "What're you t—"

There's a sharp crash in the corner, and the door we're headed for bursts open. "*Secret Service—nobody move!*" a beefy man shouts, rushing into the room with his gun pointed straight at my face.

Instinctively, I back up. He slows down, and I spot his limp. Mr. Squat. The lead investigator.

"He said *don't move!*" a blond-haired agent yells, racing in right behind him. Like his partner, he aims his gun straight at us—first at me, then at Charlie, then back to me. All I see is the black hole of the barrel.

12

W-We didn't . . ." Charlie tries to say something, but nothing comes out. My throat locks up and I feel like I swallowed my tongue.

"Back up!" the bull-necked agent shouts, moving deeper into the cavern.

My legs are jelly as we step back. I look to Charlie, but it only gets worse. His whole face is white . . . his mouth gapes open. Like me, all he can do is stare at the gun.

"Officer . . ." I stutter.

"Agent!" the man with the bull neck corrects me.

"I-I'm sorry . . . I just . . ."

"You must be Oliver."

"How'd you . . ."

"You really thought you could leave the bank twice without being followed?"

"What the hell're you doing, Gallo?" Shep calls out. "I was just about to bring them in. All I needed was—"

"Don't bullshit me!" Gallo barks as Shep falls silent. Before we can react, Gallo pushes between me and Charlie, shoving us back with his shoulders. Not too far. Just enough to aim his gun at Shep. "I'm not a moron," Gallo says. "I know what you're up to!"

Oh, God—he thinks we— "I-It's not how it looks," I blurt as Gallo turns back to me. "We were about to come in! I swear, that's where—"

"Enough," Gallo interrupts. He's got a heavy Boston accent that doesn't apologize for a single syllable. "It's over, Oliver. Y'understand?" He doesn't even wait for an answer. "The only thing that's gonna make your day better is if you spare us some headache and tell us where you hid the money."

It's a simple question. Spill the beans, hand over the money, and take the first step to getting our lives back. But the way Gallo asks it . . . the anger in his voice . . . the way he grits his teeth . . . you'd think he had a personal interest. I've seen enough divorce settlements to know something's up.

I look to Charlie, who slowly shakes his head. He sees it too.

"Oliver, this isn't the time to play hero," Gallo warns. "Now I'm gonna ask you again: Where'd you put the money?"

"Don't tell him!" Shep shouts.

"Shut up!" Gallo snaps.

"Once you give it up, we've got nothing left!" Shep continues. "It's our only bargaining chip!"

"*You want to see a bargaining chip!?*" Gallo explodes, his face a deep red rage. Standing between me and Charlie, he lifts his gun and points it directly at Shep.

"Oh, you gotta be kidding," Shep blurts.

"What're you doing?" Charlie asks, stepping forward.

"Plant your feet!" Gallo shouts, turning his gun to Charlie's face. My brother backs up, hands in the air.

"*DeSanctis* . . ." Gallo shouts to the lanky blond agent by the door.

"I got him," DeSanctis says, aiming his gun straight at Charlie's back.

Unable to turn around, Charlie looks my way to get the overview.

Don't move, I say with a glance.

Don't tell them, Charlie shoots back. He's trying to play strong, but I see the way he's breathing. Already short of breath.

"Last chance, Oliver," Gallo warns. "Tell me where the money is, or we start with Shep and work our way to your brother."

Charlie and I lock eyes. Neither of us says a word.

"He's bluffing," Shep says. "He'd never do it."

Gallo keeps his gun on Shep, but he's watching me. "You sure you're willing to take that chance, Oliver?"

"Please just put the gun down . . ." I plead.

"Don't fall for it," Shep says. "They're Secret Service, not hitmen. They're not gonna kill anyone." Turning to the blond agent by the door, he adds, "Isn't that right, DeSanctis? We all know the protocol."

Gallo looks back at DeSanctis, who gives him one of those imperceptible nods I usually save only for my brother. I know the look of that one. Storm clouds brewing. There's more riding on this than just some lost cash.

Without a word, Gallo pulls back the hammer of his gun.

"C'mon, Jim," Shep laughs. "The joke's over . . ."

But as we all quickly realize, Gallo isn't laughing. He tightens his grip, and his finger slithers across the trigger. "I'm waiting, Oliver."

Frozen in place, I feel like someone's standing on my chest. I can barely breathe. If I stay quiet, he pulls the trigger. But like Shep said . . . if I give up the cash, we lose our only chit. Big deal—it's better than gambling with our lives.

"Tell him!" Charlie shouts.

"*Don't say it!*" Shep warns. Turning back to Gallo, he adds, "Can we stop with this already? I mean, you've already caught us—what else are you hoping to—"

The two men stand face-to-face, and Gallo lets out the slightest of smirks.

Shep's expression falls. He's paste white. Like he just saw a ghost. Or a thief. "You want the money for yourself, don't you?" he stutters.

Gallo doesn't answer. He just steadies his aim.

"Don't do it!" I plead. "I'll tell you where it is!"

"So the big dollars were yours?" Shep asks. "Who brought you in? Lapidus? Quincy?"

The answer never comes. Gallo licks his lips. "Goodbye, Shep."

"Jimmy, please . . ." Shep begs as his voice cracks and shatters. "You d-d-d . . ." He can't get the words out. As big as he is, his whole body's shaking. His eyes flood with tears. "Not in the h-hea . . ."

"*No . . . !*" Charlie cries.

Gallo doesn't flinch. He just pulls the trigger.

13

*P*lease don't . . . !" I yell.

It's too late. The shot hisses like a dart from a blow-gun. Then another. And another. All three explode in Shep's chest, sending him crashing back into the concrete wall. He grabs at the wounds, but the blood's already everywhere. It covers his hands and bubbles up from his mouth. He tries to breathe, but all that comes out is an empty, wet wheeze. Still, he's on his feet . . . staring back at Gallo . . . at all of us . . . with a dead man's gray eyes. They're wide with fear—like a child who knows he's hurt, but hasn't yet decided to cry. He staggers, trying to take a step forward . . . struggling to keep his . . . c'mon, Shep . . . you can make it . . .

Gallo raises his gun again, but quickly realizes he doesn't have to.

Unable to hold his own weight, Shep's legs buckle, and like a giant oak, the big man falls forward, straight for the creaky wooden slats in the floor. But just as he hits—as the thud thunders through the tunnel—the wood shakes, but somehow, it holds.

"*Shep!*" Charlie screams, racing out and sliding knees-first next to Shep's facedown body. "Are you okay? Please, buddy . . . please be okay!" Squinting through a rush of tears, Charlie nudges the back of Shep's shoulder, searching for a reaction. Nothing—not even a twitch. "C'mon, Shep . . . I know you're there—please be there!" Ignoring the puddle of blood that's seeping out below Shep, Charlie shoves his hands under Shep's shoulder and waist, and tries to flip him on his back.

"Charlie, don't touch him!" I shout.

"*Both of you—nobody move!*" Gallo barks.

Charlie abruptly lets go, and Shep's body sinks face-first, back to the ground. The pool of blood is already seeping between the grooves in the wood planks. I look away and gag from the tinge of pre-vomit in my throat. That's when I spot the hypodermic needle right next to Shep's head. Charlie spots it too. His eyes are wide. He sees it as a break; I see it as a dumb way to get himself killed.

Don't do it, I warn with a glance.

Charlie doesn't care. Right there, a surge of adrenaline turns anguish to blood lust. He goes to grab it and . . .

"I said, *don't move!*" Gallo explodes, rushing in behind him. There's a quiet click and Charlie looks over his shoulder. Gallo's got his gun aimed at my brother's back. DeSanctis, who's still blocking the door, has his pointed at me.

"Charlie, listen to him!" I plead, my voice cracking.

"Finally, someone with some sense," Gallo says, turning his gun toward me. He steps in close and shoves the barrel into my cheek. "Now I'm going to ask you again, Oliver. You know what we're after. Just tell us where it is."

Unable to move, I stare over Gallo's shoulder. Behind him, Charlie's still down on his knees, primed to explode. Scouring the room, he searches for another out. But no matter where he looks, he still sees Shep. So do I—which is why I'm not letting it happen again.

"Don't be stupid, Oliver," Gallo warns. "Give it up and you can walk out of here."

"Don't tell him squat!" Charlie shouts. "You give him a dime and he'll leave us lying here with Shep."

"Shut your mouth!" Gallo snaps, pointing his gun at Charlie.

Stiffening with fear, I'm completely paralyzed. Charlie slaps me awake with a look. *Don't say it*, he warns. *Don't give him anything*. The problem is, no matter how good my poker face is, Gallo already knows my weakness.

With a ferret's grin and his gun still pointed at Charlie, Gallo pulls back the hammer and studies my response. "How much is he worth to you, Oliver?"

"Please don't . . . !" I beg, barely able to get the words out.

Leaving nothing to chance, DeSanctis moves in behind me, his gun digging into the back of my neck.

Behind Charlie, Gallo flicks his finger against the trigger. The gun's pointed at the back of Charlie's head, but Gallo's watching me. Still kneeling next to Shep's body, Charlie cranes his neck around and fights to get my attention. My eyes glaze and a hot spasm scratches up from my throat. We both know the outcome. No matter what we give Gallo, he's not letting us leave. Not after everything we've seen. Still, Charlie searches my face, looking for something . . . anything . . . to get out of here. It doesn't come.

Stubborn to his last breath, he turns away and stares back at Shep's broken body. But it's not until I notice Shep's blood seeping down through the wood in the floor that I actually see it—our one way out. Charlie has his back to me, but I spot the sudden pitch in his shoulders. He sees it too. Hunched over as if the pressure's too much, Charlie kneels in close to Shep's body . . . and carefully wedges his fingers around the edges of the loose wood plank that's in the floor.

"You know how to save him," Gallo warns, still focused on me. "Just tell us where the money is." From where Gallo's standing behind Charlie, he can't see a thing. Three feet away, I see it all. As quickly as I can, I angle my body so DeSanctis can't get a clear view.

"Please don't hurt him," I beg. "The information's all yours—I just need to get it from the bank—I don't have it on me."

It's all I can do. Keep trying to stall.

Pretending to brace himself for the gunshot, Charlie curls down even tighter—and curls his fingers around the sides of the wood. It wobbles slightly, but not enough. There's still a nail barely holding it in place. Focused on the thin gaps between the planks, Charlie wedges his fingers in as deep as they'll go. If he digs any deeper, his knuckles'll bleed. He doesn't care. He needs the leverage. With one final shove, his skin is rubbed raw. The tendons in his forearm twitch, and I can tell his fingers are wrapping around the bottom edges of the plank. Almost there—keep going, bro. He pulls as hard as he can without revealing himself. It quickly starts coming loose.

"Oliver, you're too smart not to've memorized it," Gallo warns as he takes aim at my brother. "Do better."

Behind Gallo, Charlie turns just enough to shoot me a look. *Don't say it,* he tells me. *The wood's about to give way.*

"Three seconds," Gallo says. "After that, you sweep up his brains yourself. One . . ."

Just give me another second, Ollie. That's all I need.

"Two . . ."

Just one more second . . .

Gallo's finger slips around the trigger. "Thr—"

"Please—don't do it! If you want it, it's in an account in An—"

Ollie, move! Charlie motions with nothing but a glance. There's a sharp crack as the wood comes loose.

Following the sound, Gallo turns away from me and spins toward my brother. He looks at the ground, but Charlie's already on his feet, swinging the wood plank like a baseball bat. The flat side catches Gallo square in the jaw, sending a mouthful of spit flying across the room. The sound alone is worth it . . . a sickeningly sweet crack that knocks him—and his gun—straight to the floor.

Before I even realize what's happening, I feel a sharp tug on the back of my shirt. DeSanctis tosses me backwards. He's trained to go after the threat. As I crash to the concrete, he turns to Charlie and aims his pistol for the killshot. Now my brother's in the black hole of the barrel. Instinctively, he holds up the plank as if it's a shield. Realizing what's happening, I scramble to my feet. I don't have a chance. Without hesitation, DeSanctis pulls the trigger. The shot explodes with an ear-splitting boom.

The wood thunders violently and something whizzes directly over Charlie's head. By the time he opens his eyes, the plank flies from his hands, cleaved in half by the gunshot. As the wood thunks against the ground, his palms are burning, stinging with dozens of splinters from the force of the impact. He looks up at DeSanctis, who's already readjusted his aim. Straight at him.

"*Don't!*" I yell, plowing into DeSanctis from behind. The gun jerks, and a shot goes off—tearing at the wall on my right and sending a storm cloud of loose concrete crumbling into the corner. The impact keeps DeSanctis off-balance enough for me to jump on his back and grab him in a quick choke-hold. Within seconds, though, training overtakes surprise. DeSanctis whips his head back, cracking me in the nose. The pain is ferocious. I don't let go.

"I'll kill you, you bastard!" DeSanctis shouts as I continue to hold on. Reaching backwards and clawing over his shoulder, DeSanctis still tries to get at me. That leaves his gut wide-open. It's all the distraction Charlie needs. Picking up the broken wood plank, he rushes forward . . . plants his feet . . . and swings away. As the plank collides with DeSanctis's stomach, he doubles over, and I swear his feet leave the ground. I fly off the bucking bull and tumble to the concrete—but DeSanctis clearly took the worst of it.

"You okay?" Charlie asks, offering me a hand.

I nod repeatedly, still unable to catch my breath.

Behind Charlie, there's a sharp scraping noise. He spins around and spots Gallo on the floor, crawling to reach his gun.

Scrambling next to him, Charlie scoops up Gallo's gun and stuffs it in the back of his pants.

"Charlie . . . !" I call out.

"Y-You're both dead," Gallo whispers, coughing up blood.

"You sure about that?" Charlie asks, winding up for another crack of the bat. I've never seen him like this. He lifts the plank over his head like a woodchopper and—

"Don't!" I shout, grabbing him by his shoulder. DeSanctis is already climbing to his feet. We're way out of our league. "C'mon—let's go!"

Charlie drops the wood, and we fly for the heavy metal door in the corner. Once I hear his shoes clicking behind me, I don't look back. All I want is out. With a quick shove, I'm through the door and across the catwalk. Just as Charlie's about to follow, he takes one last scan of the room. I can hear it from here. Gallo's already up and about, coughing uncontrollably. DeSanctis isn't far behind.

"We got trouble," Charlie calls out.

In full panic, I leave the construction trailers behind and leap out of the rabbithole, into the food court. Back in the hallway, we hear the metal door crash against the wall. They're faster than we thought.

"Check the trailers!" Gallo's voice bellows. That takes care of DeSanctis.

Right there, I make a sharp left and race back the way we originally came.

"Wrong way!" Charlie shouts.

"Are you . . . ?"

"Trust me," he calls out, heading to the right.

I pause, but it's a simple choice. We both know where we spent our Friday nights.

Checking to make sure I'm behind him, Charlie takes off up the hallway, and old instincts flood back into place. At the far end of the hall, he leaps for the nearby escalator and scrambles up the moving steps two at a time. Behind him, my shoes clack against the metal grooves. "They still behind us?" he asks.

"Just get us out of here," I say, refusing to look.

At the top of the escalator, which dead-ends into a cluster of magazine shops and newsstands, the only clear path veers to the left, back to the Main Concourse. Charlie keeps running straight—toward the beige service door in the corner.

"It looks locked," I say.

"It's not," he insists. "Or at least, it never used to be."

Praying that things don't change, I watch him plow into the door. It swings open and leads into an industrial beige hallway. Charlie's strides get longer. He's back on home turf. And I'm more lost than ever. Refusing to fall behind, I squeeze my fists tighter and pick up speed. My nails dig deep into the palms of my hands.

"You okay?" Charlie asks, feeling the instant vibe.

"Yeah," I tell him, still staring dead ahead.

In front of us are two automatic swinging doors. We stomp on the sensor-mat and the doors blink open. I immediately smell gas fumes. Through the doors, the lights dim and the cavern expands. Brick walls, no windows, and an old wooden teller booth with a punch clock on the outside. Charlie glances around at the fifty or so cars that're parked bumper-to-bumper in the underground garage.

"You got a ticket?" a man with a Puerto Rican accent shouts from the teller booth.

"No, thanks," Charlie says, catching his breath. Over his shoulder, he checks the automatic doors and searches for Gallo and DeSanctis. The doors mechanically close. No one's there. At least, not yet. But before we can relax, my stomach lurches and I heave uncontrollably. There's a violent splash against the pavement as I vomit up the milky-brown remainder of this morning's Raisin Bran. The smell alone makes me want to do it again. I clench my jaw to keep it in.

"You sure you're okay?" Charlie asks for the second time.

Bent over, with my hands pressed against my knees, I spit out the final chunks as a string of saliva dangles from my chin.

"Don't think I'm cleaning that up," the Puerto Rican guy warns from his booth.

Ignoring him, Charlie puts a hand on my shoulder. "They're gone," he promises. "We're fine." The words are nice, but he's missing the point.

"What?" Charlie asks, studying my green coloring. "What is it?"

My stomach's empty, and I'm about to pass out. But it's not until I backhand the spit from my bottom lip and slowly struggle to stand up that my brother gets his first good look at my eyes. They wander around the garage, dancing anxiously in every direction.

Without a word, he knows why I wouldn't look back while we were running. Sure, I was scared—but it wasn't just from what was chasing us. It was from what we left behind. Shep. I stare down at the splatter of throw-up by my feet. Forget fear—this is all guilt.

"It's not your fault, Ollie. Even when you were willing to hand them the account, Shep told you to stay quiet."

"But if we weren't— *Dammit, how could I be such a meathead? I'm smarter than that!* If we weren't there . . . If I wasn't so stupidly enraged about Lapidus . . ."

"If, if, if. Don't you get it yet?" he asks. "It doesn't matter what you were thinking—or why you talked yourself into it—Shep was stealing that money whether we were there or not. Period. End."

I pick my head up. "Y-You think?"

"Of course," he shoots back with a throatful of instant Charlie confidence. But as the words leave his lips, his expression falls. Reality hits hard. And fast. Now he's the one who's suddenly green.

"Are you alright?" I ask.

He doesn't say a word. Instead, he motions toward the steep ramp that leads up to the snow-lined street. "You ready to go?"

Before I can nod, Charlie takes off and runs straight up it. Behind him, I once again close my eyes and picture Shep's shattered body, twisted like a broken puppet across the floor. Unable to shake the image—or the rash decision that got us there—I chase my brother, racing as hard as I can to the top. Too bad for us, there're some things you can't outrun.

I'm still trailing Charlie as the parking ramp dumps us out onto 44th Street. We're quickly consumed by the lunchtime crowd, but in the distance, I already hear the sirens.

I look at Charlie; he studies me. We're not just thieves anymore. By the time Gallo and DeSanctis are done with us, we're murderers.

"Should we call mom . . . ?"

"No way," I counter, still tasting the vomit on my lips. "That's the first place they'll look."

The sirens get closer, and we step into the line that's curving out of a nearby pizza place. By now, the sound's almost deafening. At the end of the block, two police cars slam their brakes and screech toward Grand Central's Vanderbilt Avenue entrance. Our heads are lowered, but like everyone else in line, we're in full stare-mode. Within seconds, car doors slam shut and four uniformed officers race inside.

"C'mon," I say, jumping out of line.

You sure you want to run? Charlie asks with a glance.

I don't bother to answer. Like he said, this isn't about my anger anymore. Or some heated, knee-jerk revenge on Lapidus. It's about keeping us alive. And after almost fifteen years of freeze-tag, Charlie knows the value of a head start.

"You know where we're going?" he asks as he follows.

I'm already running toward the opposite end of the block. "Not really," I say. "But I have an idea."

14

Joey was the eighth to be called. Naturally, the first was the underwriter at KRG Insurance who wrote the policy. Lapidus chewed his head off in picoseconds and forced a fast transfer to a fidelity claims analyst, who, when he heard the amount, called the head of the fidelity claims unit, who called the president of claims, who then called the CEO himself. From there, the CEO made two calls: one to a forensic accounting firm, and one to Chuck Sheafe, head of Sheafe International, to personally request their top investigator. Sheafe didn't hesitate. He immediately recommended Joey.

"Fine," the CEO said. "When can he be here?"

"You mean *she*."

"What're you talking about?"

"Don't be a pig, Warren. Jo Ann Lemont," Sheafe explained. "Now do you want our best or do you want a boy scout?"

That's all it took. The eighth call went to Joey.

"So do you have any idea who stole it?" Joey asked from the seat opposite Lapidus's desk.

"Of course I don't know who stole it," Lapidus barked back. "What the hell kind of stupid question is that?"

Stupid, maybe, Joey thought—but she still had to ask it. If only to see his reaction. If he was lying, there'd be some sort of tell. A look-away, an uneasy grin, a hollow stare she could see in his eyes. As she brushed her short auburn hair from her forehead, she knew that was her gift—sharpening focus and finding the tell—she learned it playing poker with her dad, and honed it during law school. Sometimes it was in the body language. Sometimes it was . . . somewhere else.

When Joey first walked into Lapidus's office, the first thing she noticed was the intricate Victorian bronze oval doorknob. Embossed with an egg-and-dart motif, it was cold to the touch, difficult to turn, and it didn't match any other doorknob in the building. But as Joey knew—when it came to CEOs—that was the point. Anything to make an impression.

"Now is there anything else, Ms. Le—?"

"It's Joey," she interrupted, her chocolate eyes looking up from her yellow legal pad. Although she had a pen in her hand and the pad in her lap, she hadn't written a word—ever since her first notepad was subpoenaed, she knew better than that. Still, the pad helped people open up. So did using first names. "Please . . . call me Joey."

"Well, no offense, Joey, but as I remember it, you were hired to find our missing three hundred and thirteen million. So why don't you get back to it?"

"Actually, that's what I was about to ask . . ." she began as she pulled a digital camera from her briefcase. "Do you mind if I take some photos? Just for insurance purposes . . ."

Lapidus nodded, and she clicked off four quick shots. One in every direction. For Lapidus, it was a minor inconvenience. For Joey, it was the easiest way to document a potential crime scene. *Put it all on film*, she was taught early on. *It's the one thing that won't lie.*

Through the lens, Joey studied the cherry-paneled walls and Aubusson carpet that embraced the room with their deep burgundy hues. The room itself was filled with Asian artifacts: on her left, a framed calligraphy scroll containing a Japanese poem applauding spring; on her right, a pre–World War II step-tansu, which was a simple wood chest with small drawers; and straight ahead, behind Lapidus's desk, the obvious pride of his collection: a thirteenth-century Kamakura Period samurai helmet. Made of carved wood and layered with shiny black lacquer, it had a forged-silver crescent moon embedded in the forehead. As Joey knew from an old college history class, the shogun used to use the silver insignias to identify his samurais and see how they were doing in battle. *Just another boss who doesn't like to get too close*, she thought to herself.

"How do you get along with your employees, Mr. Lapidus?" Joey asked as she stuffed the camera back into her briefcase.

"How do I—" He stopped and watched her carefully. "Are you trying to accuse me of something?"

"Not at all," she quickly backed off. But she clearly found her first button. "I'm just trying to figure out if anyone had a motiv—"

Across the room, the door to Lapidus's office flew open. Quincy stepped in, but didn't say a word. He just held tight to the oval doorknob.

"What?" Lapidus asked. "What's wrong?"

Quincy glanced at Joey, then back to Lapidus. Some things were better said in private.

"Is he in there?" a hoarse voice shouted from the hallway.

Before Quincy could answer, Agents Gallo and DeSanctis shoved their way into the room. Joey grinned at the interruption. Baggy suit . . . barrel chest . . . cheap shoes scuffed up from running. These two weren't bankers. Which meant they were security or—

"Secret Service," Gallo blurted, flashing her the badge on his belt. "Can you excuse us for a moment?"

Joey couldn't help but stare at the swollen cut on Gallo's cheek. She didn't see it when he first walked in. His head was turned. "Actually, I think we're all on this together," Joey said, hoping to make nice. "I'm here from Chuck Sheafe's place." It wasn't often that she dropped her boss's name, but Joey was all too aware of how trust worked in law enforcement. Fifteen years ago, Chuck Sheafe was third in command of the Secret Service. To fellow agents, that meant he was family.

"So you're working for the insurance company?" Gallo asked.

It wasn't the reaction she was looking for, so Joey just nodded.

"Then that still makes you a civilian," Gallo shot back. "Now like I said: Please excuse us."

"But . . ."

"Goodbye, ma'am, it was n—"

"You can call me Joey."

Gallo cocked his head with a predatory glare and once again revealed the bruise on his cheek. He didn't like being interrupted. "Goodbye, Joey."

Too smart to push, Joey tucked her notepad under her arm and headed for the door. All four men watched her as she crossed the room, which wasn't something that happened often. With her relatively athletic build, she was attractive, but not gawking attractive. Still, she didn't acknowledge any of them. She made her living knee deep in male egos. There'd be plenty of time to fight later.

As the door slammed behind Joey, Lapidus rubbed his palm against his bald head. "Please tell me you have good news."

Quincy tried to answer, but nothing came out. He stuffed his hands in his pockets to stop them from shaking.

"Are you okay?" Lapidus asked.

"Shep's dead," DeSanctis blurted.

"*What?*" Lapidus asked, his eyes going wide. "Are you . . . How did he . . . ?"

"Shot in the chest three times. We rushed in when we heard the noise, but it was already too late."

Once again, the whole room was silent. Nobody moved. Not Lapidus. Not Quincy. No one.

"I'm sorry for your loss," Gallo added.

Grabbing at his own chest, Lapidus sank in his seat. "W-Was it for the money?"

"That's what we're still trying to figure out," Gallo explained. "We're not sure how they got it, but it looks like they may've had help from Shep."

Lapidus looked up. "What do you mean, *they?*"

"That's the other part . . ." DeSanctis said, jumping back in. He glanced at Gallo, almost like he was getting permission. When Gallo nodded, DeSanctis cut across the room and lowered his lanky frame into one of the two seats in front of Lapidus's desk. "As near as we can tell, Shep was killed by either Charlie or Oliver."

"Oliver?" Lapidus asked. "*Our* Oliver? That kid couldn't—"

"He *could*—and he *did*," Gallo insisted. "So don't talk to me about some bullshit little-boy innocence. Thanks to these two, I've got a man with three holes in his chest and a financial investigation that just flipped to a homicide. Add that to the missing three hundred and thirteen mil and we've got one of those cases that Congress holds hearings about."

Still collapsed in his chair, Lapidus just sat there—the consequences already settling heavy on his shoulders. Lost in thought and refusing to face anyone, he stared anxiously at the Japanese bronze letter opener on his desk. Then, out of nowhere, he shot up in his seat. His voice was racing. "On Friday, Oliver used my password to transfer money to Tanner Drew."

"See, now that's something we should know," Gallo said as he took a seat next to DeSanctis. "If there's a pattern of misapprop—" Cutting himself off, Gallo felt something on the cushion of the seat. Reaching under his thigh, he pulled out a blue-and-yellow pen emblazoned with the logo of the University of Michigan. *Michigan*, he thought. *The same place Joey's boss, Chuck Sheafe, went t—*

"Where'd you get this?" Gallo blurted, jamming the pen toward Lapidus. "Is it yours?"

"I don't think so," Lapidus stammered. "No, I've definitely never seen it . . ."

Gallo pulled off the cap, furiously unscrewed the barrel of the pen, and shook both pieces over the desk. Out popped a pen refill . . . a metal spring . . . and from the back part of the pen: a clear plastic tube filled with wires, a miniature battery, and a tiny transmitter. A pinhole in the base held the built-in microphone.

"Son of a bitch!" Gallo exploded. He winged the pen against the wall, where it barely missed the calligraphy scroll.

"Be careful!" Lapidus shouted as Gallo leapt out of his seat.

Knocking his chair to the floor, Gallo raged toward the

door, grabbed the oval doorknob, and tugged as hard as he could.

"Can I help you?" Lapidus's secretary asked from her usual spot behind her desk.

Gallo barreled past her and looked up the hallway . . . near the bathrooms . . . by the elevator. He was already too late. Joey was long gone.

15

The backseat of the black gypsy cab is covered with a stained brown towel that smells like feet. Under normal circumstances, I'd roll down the bubbling tinted windows for some air, but right now—after hearing those sirens—we're better off behind the tint. Ducking down so no one can see us, Charlie and I haven't said a word since I waved down the car. Obviously, neither of us will risk talking in front of the driver—but as I stare at Charlie, who's curled up against the door and staring vacantly out the window, I know it's not just because he wants privacy.

"Make a right up here," I call out, peeking above the headrest so I can get a better view of Park Avenue. The driver makes a sharp turn on 50th Street and gets about halfway up the block. "Perfect. Right here." As the car jerks to a halt, I toss a ten-dollar bill between the armrests, kick open the door, and make sure he never gets a good look. We're only a few blocks from Grand Central, but there was no way I was running on the open street.

"Let's go," I call to Charlie, who's already a few steps behind. I head straight for the front door of the Italian bakery right outside the cab. But the moment the driver speeds away, I turn around and walk out. This is no time to take chances. Not with myself—and certainly not with Charlie.

"C'mon," I say, rushing back toward Park Avenue. The sharp December wind tries to blow us back, but all it does is make the surrounding after-lunch crowd bundle up and hunch over. Good for us. As soon as we turn back onto Park Avenue, I bound up the concrete steps. Behind me, Charlie looks up at the ornate pink brick structure and finally understands. Nestled between the investment banks, the law firms, and the Waldorf, it's the one island of piety in what's otherwise an ocean of the ostentatious. More important, it's the nearest place I could think of that wouldn't kick us out—no matter how late we wanted to stay.

"Welcome to St. Bart's Church," a soft voice whispers as we step inside the arched stone foyer. On my left, from behind a card table covered with stacks of Bibles and other religious books, a pudgy grandmother nods hello, then quickly looks away.

I shove two dollars into the see-through donation box and head for the doors of the main sanctuary, where—the instant they open—I'm hit with that incense and old wood church smell. Inside, the ceiling rises to a golden dome, while the floor stretches out with forty rows of maple pews. The whole room is dark, lit only by a few hanging chandeliers and the natural light that filters through the stained glass along the walls.

Now that lunch is over, most of the pews are empty—but not all of them. A dozen or so worshipers are scattered throughout the rows, and even if they're praying, it only takes one random glance for one of them to be Crimestopper of the Week. Hoping for something a bit less crowded, I glance around the sanctuary. When a church is this big, there's usually . . . There we go. Three-quarters down the aisle—along the lefthand wall—a single unmarked door.

Trying not to be too quick or noticeable, Charlie and I keep the pace nice and smooth. There's a loud creak as the door opens. I cringe and give it a fast push to end the pain. We rush forward so quickly, I literally stumble into the stone room, which is just big enough to hold a few benches and a brass votive stand filled with burning candles. Otherwise, we're the only ones in the private chapel.

The door slams shut and Charlie's still silent.

"Please don't do this to yourself," I tell him. "Take your own advice: What happened with Shep . . . it's not my fault and it's not yours."

Collapsing on a wooden bench in the corner, Charlie doesn't answer. His posture sinks; his neck bobs lifelessly. He's still in shock. Less than a half-hour ago, I saw a co-worker get shot. Charlie watched someone he thought was a friend. And even if they barely knew each other—even if all they did was talk a few games of high school football— to Charlie, that's a lifetime. He leans forward, resting his elbows on his knees.

The sight alone makes me taste the lingering vomit in my throat. "Charlie, if you want to talk about it . . ."

"I know," he interrupts, his voice shaking. He's fighting to hold it together, but some things are too strong. This isn't just for Shep. On our left, the candles burn and our shadows flicker against the stone wall. "They're gonna kill us, Ollie—just like they killed him."

Moving in close, I palm the back of his neck and join him on the bench. Charlie's not a crier. He didn't shed a tear when he broke his collarbone trying to ride his bike down the stairs. Or when we had to say goodbye to Aunt Maddie in the hospital. But, today, as I open my arms, he falls right in.

"What're we gonna do?" he asks, his voice still a whisper.

"I have a few ideas," I tell him. It's an empty promise, but Charlie doesn't bother to challenge. He just keeps his head against my shoulder, searching for support. On the wall, we're one big shadow. Then my phone rings.

The shrill screech echoes through the room. I jerk back; Charlie doesn't move. Reaching into my suit pocket, I quickly shut off the ringer. When there's no answer, the person calls back. Whoever it is, they're not giving up. The phone vibrates against my chest. I reach back in and shut it off.

"You sure we shouldn't get it?" Charlie asks, reading my expression.

"I don't think so," I quickly reply.

He nods as if that'll keep us safe. We both know it's a lie. Along the back wall, the candles' tiny flames are dancing in place. And no matter how much we want to shut our eyes, from here on in, it's only getting worse.

16

W ell?" Gallo asked.

"No answer," Lapidus said as he hung up the receiver. "Not that I'm surprised—Oliver's too smart to pick up." Turning to the photocopied letter that Gallo left on his desk, Lapidus looked down and quickly skimmed it. "So this is how they did it?" Lapidus asked. "A fake letter signed by Duckworth?"

"According to the tech boys, that's the last document Oliver typed into his computer," Gallo explained as he limped across the vintage carpet. After what happened with Joey, he was in no mood to sit. "And from the hard copy we found hidden in the back of Shep's drawer, it looks like Shep was helping them along."

"So the three of them met this morning, and when things went sour, Oliver and Charlie took his head off," Quincy hypothesized from his usual spot by the door.

"That's the only thing that makes sense," DeSanctis said, shooting a cocky look at Gallo.

"And what about the investigation?" Lapidus asked. "As you know, we have a number of important clients who rely on our promise of privacy. Any chance of keeping it . . . how do you say . . . out of the papers?"

There it was—the one thing Gallo was waiting for. "I completely agree," he replied, seizing the opportunity. "If we throw this to the press, they'll broadcast our every move straight to Charlie and Oliver. When it gets this big, we're all better off on the quiet side."

"Exactly—that's exactly our point," Lapidus said, nodding vigorously at Quincy. "Isn't that right?"

Quincy didn't nod back. He'd had enough sucking up for one day.

"So you think you'll be able to find them?" Lapidus asked as Gallo picked up the phone on the corner of Lapidus's desk.

Gallo glanced at Quincy, then back to Lapidus. "Why don't you leave that to us." Quickly dialing a number, Gallo raised the receiver to his ear. "Hey, it's me," he said to the person on the other line. "I got a cell phone loose in the city—you ready to do some tracking?"

17

I don't turn the phone back on until I'm ten blocks away. And even as it flicks on, it takes me another block and a half to work up the nerve to dial. For strength, I think of Charlie. As I wait for someone to answer, I try to keep my balance in the back of the bus while it crawls uptown and crashes through the city's potholes. Sure, the subway is more inconspicuous, but last I checked, my phone didn't get a signal underground. And right now, I need to keep moving—anything to put distance between me and the church.

"Welcome to Greene & Greene Private Bank. How can I assist you?" a female voice sings through my cell phone. I'm not sure who it belongs to, but it's not any of the phonebankers I know. Good. That means she doesn't know me.

"Hi, this is Marty Duckworth," I say. "I had a quick question I was hoping you could help me with." As she checks my account and Social Security number, I can't help but wonder whether the bank's system is even going to be up and running. If the Secret Service were smart, they would've already shut it d—

"I have your account right in front of me. Now what can I help you with today, Mr. Duckworth?" She says the words so quickly . . . so eagerly . . . I can't help but smell a trap. Too bad for me, I need the cheese.

"Actually, I just wanted to check the most recent activity on my account," I tell her. "There was a large deposit that came in, and I need to know what day it posted." Clearly, it's a nonsense question, but if we plan on figuring out what's going on, we need to know how Duckworth's three million turned into three hundred and thirteen.

"I'm sorry, sir, but in the last week . . . I'm not showing any deposits."

"Excuse me?"

"I'm looking at it right now. According to our records, your current balance is zero, and the only activity on record is a three-hundred-and-thirteen-million-dollar withdrawal yesterday afternoon. Other than that, there were no deposits to—"

"What about the day before?" I ask, watching the passengers on the bus. No one turns around. "What was the balance on the day before?"

There's a short pause. "Not including interest, it's the same amount, sir—three hundred and thirteen million. And it's the same on the day before. I have no record of any recent deposits."

The bus bucks to a halt and I grab a metal pole for balance. "Are you sure the balance wasn't three million dollars?"

"I'm sorry, sir—I'm just telling you what's on my screen."

She says the words and my hand slides down around the pole. It can't be. It's not possible. How can we—?

"Mr. Duckworth . . . ?" the woman on the other line interrupts. "Can you hold on a second? I'll be right back."

"Of course," I agree. The line goes silent, and for thirty seconds I don't think much of it. After a minute, I can't help but wonder where my phonebanker went—it's the first rule they teach you—when you're dealing with rich people, you're never supposed to put them on hol . . . hold on. My chest twitches. This is still a company line. And the longer she keeps me on it, the easier it is for the Secret Service to tra—

I slap the phone shut, hoping I'm fast enough. There's no way they can do it that fast. Not when it's—

The phone vibrates in my hand, sending a frozen chill across the back of my neck. I check the number on Caller ID, but it's nothing I recognize. Last time, I ignored it. This time . . . if they're tracing it . . . I need to know.

"Hello?" I answer, keeping it confident.

"Where the hell are you?" Charlie asks. There's no phone in the chapel. If he's risking a call from the street, we've got problems.

"What's wrong? Are you—?"

"You better get back here," he demands.

"Just tell me what happened."

"Oliver, get back here. *Now!*"

I pound the bus's *Stop-Request* strip with the base of my fist. Goodbye frying pan—Hello, fire.

18

"Did we get him?" Lapidus asked, leaning over DeSanctis's shoulder.

"Hold on . . ." DeSanctis said, staring down at his laptop. Onscreen, courtesy of the cellular company's Mobile Telephone Switching Office, was the call log for Oliver Caruso's cellular phone.

"What's taking so long?" Gallo demanded.

"Hold on . . ."

"You already said—"

The screen of the laptop blinked and a grid of information suddenly appeared. Gallo, DeSanctis, and Lapidus all pulled in close, studying each entry: *Time, Date, Duration, Current Outgoing Call* . . .

"That's us!" Lapidus blurted, quickly recognizing the number for the customer service line. "He's on the phone with someone here!"

"In this building?" Gallo asked.

"Y-Yeah . . . on the first fl—"

"He's moving," DeSanctis interrupted. Onscreen were the cell sites that carried the call:

Initial Cell Site: 303C
Last Cell Site: 304A

"How do you . . . ?"

"Each number is a different tower," DeSanctis explained. "When you make a call, your phone finds the nearest cell tower with a signal—but here, his call started in one place and continues in another . . ." Next to his laptop, DeSanctis scoured the cellular map spread out across the desk. ". . . 303C is 79th and Madison; 304A is 83rd and Madison."

"So he's heading up Madison Avenue?"

DeSanctis rechecked the screen. "The call's only two minutes long. To get from 79th to 83rd . . . he's moving too fast to be on foot."

"Maybe he's on the subway," Lapidus suggested.

"Not up there. Subway doesn't run on Madison," Gallo said. "He's on wheels, though—either cab or bus." Rushing for the door and fighting his limp, Gallo looked back at Lapidus. "I need your customer service person to stall as long as she can. Make small talk . . . keep him on hold . . . whatever works."

"Do you want me to—"

"Don't even think of picking up—he hears your voice, he's gone."

"He's still in 304A," DeSanctis called out, madly tucking computer wires under his armpit. With his laptop balanced in his palm like a delivered pizza, he rushed to the door and out into the hallway. "That gives us about a four-block radius."

"So you think you can . . ."

"Good as dead," Gallo said as they darted for the private elevator. "He'll never see us coming."

19

As the bus pulls up to a pristine brownstone on the corner of 81st Street, I dial the number for the Kings Plaza Movie Theater in Brooklyn and hit *Send*. When the prerecorded voice picks up, I grab a newspaper from the seat next to me, wrap my cell phone in it, and slide the phone package under my seat. If they're tracing it, this should buy us at least an hour—and the infinite loop of movie times should give them a working signal that'll have them goosechasing all the way up to Harlem.

Before my fellow passengers realize what's going on, the bus bucks to a stop, the doors open, and I'm gone. My trip's over. Luckily, abandoned phones ride for free.

It takes ten more minutes for the bank teller at Citibank to empty the three thousand five hundred dollars that's left in my checking account, and it's one of the few times I'm glad that I can't afford the private bank minimums. With their access to Lapidus, the Service would've had an account at Greene shut down in no time.

Back at the church, I keep my head down and speedwalk through the main sanctuary, straight toward the private chapel. Up ahead, the glow of candlelight seeps out from the crack beneath the door. I grab the doorknob in a tight fist and check once over my shoulder, then again to be safe. No one looks up.

Shoving the door open, I rush into the candlelit room and scan the benches for Charlie. He's in the same one I left him in—in the corner—still hunched over. But now . . . there's something in his hands. His notepad. Once again, he's writing . . . no, not just writing. Scribbling. Furiously. The man who can't be stopped.

I nod to myself. He's finally coming back. "So what's the emergency?" I ask.

It's the only time he stops writing. "I can't find mom."

The words collide like a kidney-punch. No wonder he snapped out of his silence. "What're you talking about?"

"I called her before and—"

"I told you not to call her!"

"Just listen," Charlie begs. "I called her from a payphone seven blocks away . . . she never once picked up."

"So?"

"So, it's Tuesday, Oliver. Tuesday afternoon and she's not there?" Falling silent, he lets it sink in. As a seamstress, mom spends most of her time either in the house or at the fabric store—but Tuesdays and Thursdays are reserved for fittings. Out goes the coffee table; in come the clients. All day long.

"Maybe she was in the middle of measuring," I suggest.

"Maybe we should go check it out," he shoots back.

"Charlie, you know that's the first place they'll look. And if they nab us there, we're only putting mom at risk."

His eyes drop back to his notepad. Forget what I said. Everyone can be stopped.

"You okay?" I ask.

Charlie nods, which means it's a giant lie. Once he's wound up, he's allergic to quiet.

"Don't shut down again," I tell him. "She'll be okay. As soon as we get out of here, we'll figure out a way to get in touch."

"I'm sure we will," he says. "But let me tell you something—if they go near her . . ."

I look up, noticing the change in Charlie's voice. He doesn't joke about mom. "She'll be fine," I insist.

He nods to himself, trying his best to believe it. With his back to me, he adds, "Now tell me what happened with Duckworth. You find out where he got the money?"

"Not exactly," I say, carefully relaying my conversation with the woman at the bank. As always, Charlie's reaction is immediate.

"I don't get it," he says. "Even though when we checked, it said three million, Duckworth had the three hundred and thirteen all along . . . ?"

"Only if you believe what it says in the files."

"You think she was making it up?"

"Charlie, you know how many clients have over a hundred million in assets? Seventeen at last count . . . and I can name every one of them. Marty Duckworth isn't on that list."

Charlie stares at me, completely silent. "How's that possible?"

"That's the issue now, isn't it?" I ask. "Obviously, someone was doing a primo job of making it look like Duckworth only had three million to his name. The real question is, who did it, and how'd they hide it from the rest of the bank?"

"You really think someone can just hide all that cash?"

"Why not? That's what the bank's paid to do on a daily basis," I point out. "Think about it—it's the one thing every rich person loves: hiding their money. From the IRS . . . from ex-wives . . . from snotty kids . . ."

". . . that's why people come to us in the first place," Charlie adds, quickly catching on. "So with a specialty like that, there's gotta be someone here who's figured out how to make an account look like one thing and actually be another. *Yes, Mr. Duckworth, your balance is three million dollars—wink, wink, nudge, nudge.*"

"Stupid us, when Mary transferred the balance, we got the whole megillah."

Staring at the candles, we both kick our way through the logic. "It's not bad . . ." Charlie admits. "But for an insider to pull that off . . ."

"I don't think it was just an insider, Charlie—whoever it was, they were getting help . . ."

"Gallo and his buddy in the Service?"

"You heard what Shep said—he wasn't the one who called them in. They showed up the moment their money went poof."

We simultaneously nod our heads. It's not a bad theory. "So they were in on it from the start?" Charlie asks.

"You tell me: What's the likelihood that two Secret Service agents would wander into a case and then kill Shep just to turn a quick buck? I don't care how much money's at stake, Gallo and DeSanctis weren't randomly assigned. They came to protect their investment."

"Maybe they were on the take, selling their services . . ."

"Maybe they've been working with the bank all along."

"You mean like money laundering?" Charlie asks.

I shrug, still thinking it through. "Whatever it was, these guys had their hands in something bad, something big . . . and something that, if all went right, would've netted them three hundred and thirteen million George Washingtons."

"Not a bad day's work," Charlie agrees. "So who do you think they were scheming with?"

"Hard to say. All I know is, you can't spell Secret Service without *Secret*."

"Yeah, well, you can't spell *Asshole* without Lapidus or Quincy," Charlie says, pointing a finger.

"I don't know," I say doubtfully. "You saw their reactions—they were even more scared than we were."

"Yeah . . . because you, me, and everyone else were watching. Actors don't exist without an audience. Besides, if it wasn't Lapidus or Quincy, who could it possibly be?"

"Mary," I challenge.

Charlie stops, stroking an imagined goatee on his chin. "Not a bad call."

"I'm telling you, it could've been anyone. Though it still leaves us with the original question: Where'd Duckworth get three hundred and thirteen million?" The candles continue their dance. I stay quiet.

"Why don't you ask the man himself?" Charlie says.

"Duckworth? He's dead."

"You sure about that?" Charlie asks, cocking an eyebrow. "If everything else is a hall of mirrors, what makes you think this is the only wall?"

It's a good point. Actually, it's a great point. "Do you still have his . . ."

Charlie reaches into his back pocket and pulls out a folded-up sheet of paper. "That's the beauty of rewearing yesterday's slacks," he says. "I've got it right . . . here." Unfolding the paper, he reveals the Duckworth address that was on the Midland National Bank account: 405 Amsterdam Avenue. With his fuse lit, he takes off for the door.

"Charlie . . ." I whisper. "Maybe it's better to go to the police."

"Why—so they can turn us over to the Service, who'll put bullets in both our heads? No offense, Ollie, but the fact that we have the money . . . and the way they set us up with Shep—no one's gonna believe a word."

I close my eyes, trying to paint a different picture. But all I see is Shep's blood . . . all over our hands. It doesn't matter what we say. Even I wouldn't believe us. Stepping backwards, I take a seat on the bench. "We're dead, aren't we?"

"Don't say that," Charlie scolds. I'm not sure if it's denial or little-brother stubbornness, but I'll take it either way. "If we find Duckworth . . . that's our first step to finding answers," he insists. "This is our chance to shake the Magic Eight-Ball. I'm not giving that up." Yanking the door open, he disappears into the sanctuary.

Turning toward the votive stand, I watch the melted wax trickle down the necks of the candles. It doesn't take long for each one to burn down. Just a little time. That's all we have.

20

Turning onto Oliver's block and bundled up in an ankle-length olive green winter coat, Joey looked like any other pedestrian in Red Hook—head down, no time to talk, other places to be. Yet while her eyes stayed locked on Oliver's run-down brownstone, her fingers were far more busy: slowly kneading the empty black garbage bags stuffed in her left pocket, and the red nylon dog leash in her right.

Convinced she was close enough, she picked her head up and pulled out the leash, letting it dangle down toward her knees. Now she wasn't just an investigator, circling the block and checking windows for nosy neighbors. With the leash by her side, she was a member of the community, searching for her lost dog. Sure, it was a lame excuse, but in all her years using it, it never failed. Empty leashes took you anywhere: up driveways . . . across backyards . . . even into the narrow alleyway that ran along the side of the brownstone and held the three plastic garbage cans full of Oliver's and his neighbors' trash.

Slipping into the alley, Joey counted eleven windows that overlooked the garbage area: four in Oliver's brownstone,

four in the brownstone next door, and three in the one directly across the street. Without a doubt, it'd be better to do this
at night, but by then, the Service would have already picked
through it. That's always the race with Dumpster Dives.
First come, first served.

Wasting no time, she unzipped her coat and threw it aside.
A small microphone was clipped to the top button of her
shirt, and a tangle of wires ran down to a belt-attached cell
phone. She plugged an earpiece into her right ear, hit *Send*,
and as it rang, quickly flipped open the lids of all three
garbage cans.

"This is Noreen," a young female voice answered.

"It's me," Joey said, snapping on a pair of latex surgical
gloves. It was a lesson from her first Dumpster Dive, where
the suspect had a newborn baby—and Joey got a handful of
dirty diapers.

"How's the neighborhood?" Noreen asked.

"Past its prime," Joey said as she eyed the worn brick
walls and the cracked glass on the basement windows. "I
assumed young banking preppyville. This is blue-collar,
can't-afford-the-city first apartment."

"Maybe that's why he took the money—he's sick of being
second-class."

"Yeah . . . maybe," Joey said, happy to hear Noreen
participating.

A recent graduate of Georgetown Law's night school program, Noreen spent her first month after graduation getting
rejected by Washington, D.C.'s, largest law firms. The next
two months brought rejections from the medium and small
firms as well. In month four, her old Evidence professor
placed a call to his good friend at Sheafe International. *Top
night student . . . first impression's mousy, but hungry as can
be . . . just like Joey the day her dad dropped her off.* Those

were the magic words. One faxed résumé later, Noreen had a job and Joey had her newest assistant.

"You ready to dance?" Joey asked.

"Hit me . . ."

Reaching into the first garbage can, Joey ripped open the Hefty bag on top and the scent of ground coffee smacked her in the face. She angled the bag to get a good peek, searching for anything with a . . . There it was. Phone bill. Caked with wet coffee grinds, but right on top. She wiped away the grinds and checked the name on the first page. Frank Tusa. Same address. Apartment 1.

Next.

The bag below was a dark cinch-sack that, once opened, stank from rotted oranges. Hallmark card envelope was addressed to Vivian Leone. Apartment 2.

Next.

The middle garbage can was empty. That left the one on the far right, which had a cheap, almost see-through white bag with a thin red drawstring. Not Hefty . . . not GLAD . . . this was someone trying to save money.

"Anything yet?" Noreen asked.

Joey didn't answer. She tore open the bag, stared inside, and held her breath at the two-day-old banana smell. "Uh-oh."

"What?"

"He's a recycler."

"What do you mean, *he?*" Noreen asked. "How do you know it's Oliver's?"

"There're only three apartments—he's got the cheap one in the basement. Trust me, it's his." Once again checking the windows, Joey pulled a black garbage bag from her pocket, lined the empty garbage can, and quickly tossed Oliver's brown banana peels into the waiting bin. As a lawyer, she knew that what she was doing was perfectly legal—once you put your trash on the curb, it's anyone's to play with—but that didn't mean you should advertise your every move.

Item by item, Joey shoveled through the muck, grabbing and transferring fistfuls of old spaghetti, discarded rotini, and leftover mac and cheese. "Lots of pasta—not a lot of cash," she whispered to Noreen, whose job it was to catalogue. "There's onions and garlic . . . a wrapper for pre-cut portobello mushrooms—that's his baby-step to high society—otherwise, nothing expensive in the way of veggies—no asparagus or fru-fru exotic lettuce."

"Okay . . ."

"He's got a torn pair of old underwear—boxers, actually—which somehow seems impressive, though it's actually gross . . ."

"I'll make a note . . ."

"Some American cheese wrappers . . . a plastic Shop-Rite deli bag . . ." She pulled the deli label close to read it. ". . . a pound of turkey, the store-brand cheap stuff . . . empty bags of potato chips and pretzels . . . He's bringing lunch every day."

"How's take-out look?"

"No Styrofoam . . . no Chinese delivery containers . . . not even a pizza crust," Joey said, continuing to dig through the wet mess. "He doesn't spend a dollar ordering out. Except for the mushrooms, he's saving every dime."

"Packaging materials?"

"Nothing. No electronics . . . no batteries . . . just a plastic wrapper from a videotape. All within his means. The biggest splurges are high-tech Gillette razors and some double-ply toilet tissue. Ooop—he's also got a wrapper for some super-absorbent Tampax—looks like our boy's got a girlfriend."

"How many wrappers?"

"Just one," Joey answered. "She's not here every night—maybe she's new . . . or she likes him staying at her place." At the bottom of the bag, Joey shook out four filters of old coffee and used her fingers to rake through the sand dune of grinds. "That's it. A week in the life," Joey announced. "Of course, without the recycling, it's only half the picture."

"If you say so . . ."

"What's that supposed to mean?"

"I don't know . . . it's just . . . do you really think rummaging through garbage is going to help us find them?" Noreen asked sheepishly.

Joey shook her head to herself. Oh, to be that young. "Noreen, the only way to tell where someone's going is if you know where they've been."

There was a long pause on the other end. "Think we can get the recycling?" Noreen asked.

"You tell me. What day do they—?"

"Pickup's not till tomorrow," Noreen interrupted. "I got the web page up in front of me."

Joey nodded. Even the mouse had to sometimes roar.

"I bet it's still in his apartment," Noreen added.

"Only one way to find out . . ." Shoving the garbage cans back in place, Joey took her red leash on a walk toward the front of the house and down Oliver's shaky brick stairs. Next to the painted red door was a small four-pane window that held a single blue-and-white sticker: "Warning! Protected by Ameritech Alarms."

"My butt," Joey muttered. *This kid won't order Domino's; he's certainly not springing for an alarm.*

"What're you doing?" Noreen asked.

"Nothing," Joey said as she pressed her nose between the bars that covered the window. Squinting tight, she peered through the tiny apartment. That's when she saw it—on the floor in the corner of the kitchen—the royal blue plastic recycling bin filled with cans . . . and the bright green bin stuffed with paper.

"Please tell me you're not breaking in," Noreen asked, already panicking.

"I'm not breaking in," Joey said dryly. She reached into her purse and pulled out a zippered black leather case. From there, she removed a thin, wire-tipped instrument and shoved it straight into Oliver's top lock.

"You know what Mr. Sheafe said about that! If you get caught again . . . !"

With a quick flick of the wrist, the lock popped and the door swung open. Pulling her last garbage bag from her pocket, Joey took a quick scan and grinned. "Come to momma . . ."

"Why're you making such a big deal?" Joey asked, kneeling in front of and flipping through the two-drawer file cabinet that served as Oliver's nightstand. To keep it out of sight, and keep his papers safe, Oliver draped a piece of burgundy fabric over the entire cabinet. Joey went right for it.

"I'm not making a big deal," Noreen said. "I just think it's odd. I mean, Oliver's supposed to be the mastermind behind a three-hundred-million-dollar pie swipe—but according to what you just read me, he's writing monthly checks to cover mom's hospital bills and paying almost half her mortgage."

"Noreen, just because someone smiles at you, doesn't mean they won't shove a knife in your back. I've seen it fifty times before—welcome to your motive. Our boy Oliver spends four years at the bank thinking he's going to be a bigshot, then wakes up one day and realizes all he has to show for it is a stack of bills and a tan from the fluorescent lights. Then, to make things worse, his brother comes in and finds out he's in the same trap. The two of them have a particularly bad day . . . there's a moment of opportunity . . . and voilà . . . the dish runs away with the spoon."

"Yeah . . . no . . . I guess," Noreen added, anxious to get back on track. "What about the girlfriend? See anything with a phone number on it?"

"Forget digits—ready for the full address?" Flipping through the recycling bin, Joey quickly pulled out all the magazines. *Business Week* . . . *Forbes* . . . *SmartMoney* . . . "Here we go," she said, grabbing a *People* magazine and going straight for the subscription label. "Beth Manning. 201 East 87th Street, Apartment 23H. When the girlfriends come over, they always bring something to read."

"That's great—you're a genius," Noreen said sarcastically. "Now can you please get out of there before the Service comes in and whips your ass?"

"Actually, speaking of which . . ." Tossing the magazine back into the bin, Joey ran toward the bathroom and jerked open the medicine cabinet. Toothpaste . . . razor . . . shaving cream . . . deodorant . . . nothing special. In the trash was a crumpled-up white plastic bag with the words "Barney's Pharmacy" written in black letters. "Noreen, the place is called Barney's Pharmacy—we want a list of outstanding prescriptions for Oliver and his girlfriend."

"Fine. Can we go now?"

Moving back to the main room, Joey noticed a black laminate picture frame on top of the kitchen table. In the photo, two little boys—dressed exactly the same in tight-fitting red turtlenecks—were sitting on an oversized sofa, their feet dangling over the cushions. Oliver looked about six; Charlie looked two. Both were reading books . . . but as Joey looked closer . . . she realized Charlie's book was upside down.

"Joey, this isn't funny anymore," Noreen barked through the earpiece. "If they catch you breaking and entering . . ."

Joey couldn't help but nod at the challenge. Making a beeline for the TV, she reached around to the back of it, snared the electrical cord, and traced it down toward the wall socket. If the house was as old as she thought . . .

"What're you doing?" Noreen begged.

"Just a little electrical work," Joey teased. At the end of the cord, she saw the orange adapter that, once attached to the three-pronged TV plug, let it fit into the two-pronged wall socket. You gotta love old houses, she thought as she crouched down next to the outlet. Dragging her purse next to her, she again went for the small zipper case. Inside was an almost identical orange two-pronged adapter.

Unlike the battery-operated transmitter she'd left in Lapidus's office, this one was specially made for long-term use. Looks like a plug and acts like a plug, but transmits a solid four miles in residential neighborhoods. No one looks at it, no one questions it—and the best part is—as long as it's plugged in, it has an endless supply of juice.

"Are you done yet?" Noreen pleaded.

"Done?" Joey asked, yanking the plug from the wall. "I'm just getting started."

"Can you get it or not?" Gallo asked, standing over Andrew Nguyen's desk.

"Take it easy," Nguyen shot back. A lean, but muscular Asian man prematurely graying at the temples, Andrew Nguyen was in his fifth year at the United States Attorney's Office. In that time, he'd learned that although it was important to be tough on criminals, it was sometimes just as vital to be tough on law enforcement. "You want to lose another on appeal . . . ?"

"Spare me the Constitution. These two are dangerous."

"Yeah," Nguyen said with a laugh. "I hear they sent you and DeSanctis chasing buses all afternoon . . ."

Gallo ignored the joke. "You helping or not?"

Nguyen shook his head. "Don't give me crap, Gallo. What you're asking for is no small affair."

"Neither is stealing three hundred million dollars and killing a former agent," Gallo shot back.

"Yeah . . . I'm sorry to hear about that," Nguyen said, no longer willing to argue. He put away his legal pad, knowing better than to take notes. The last thing he needed was a judge making him hand them over to opposing counsel. "So getting back to your request," he added, "have you already exhausted the rest?"

"C'mon, Nguyen . . ."

"You know I have to ask it, Jimmy. When it comes to wiretaps and video, I can't pull out the big guns until you tell me you've gone through all your other investigative means—including all the credit card and phone records I subpoenaed for you this morning."

Gallo paused and forced his best grin. "I wouldn't lie to you, buddy—we're keeping this one on the complete up-and-up."

Nguyen nodded. That was all he needed. "You're really going after these two aren't you?"

"Like you wouldn't believe," Gallo said. "Like you wouldn't believe."

"Omnibank Fraud Department—this is Elena Ratner. How can I assist you?"

"Hi, Ms. Ratner," Gallo said into his cell phone as his navy Ford hugged the right lane of the Brooklyn Bridge. "This is Agent Gallo with the United States Secret Ser—"

"Of course, Agent Gallo—sorry to take so long getting back to you. We just got your paperwork . . ."

"So it's all taken care of?" he interrupted.

"Absolutely, sir. We've flagged and notated both accounts—an Omnibank MasterCard for a Mr. Oliver J. Caruso, and an Omnibank Visa for a Mr. Charles Caruso," she said, reading off both account numbers. "Now are you sure you don't want them shut down?"

"Ms. Ratner," Gallo scolded through gritted teeth, "if the cards get shut down, how'm I supposed to see what they're buying and where they're going?"

There was a pause on the other line. This was why she hated dealing with law enforcement. "I'm sorry, sir," she said dryly. "From here on in, we'll notify you as soon as either of them makes a purchase."

"And how long will that notification take?"

"By the time they get their approval code, our computer will have already dialed your number," she added. "It's instantaneous."

"Hi, this is Fudge," the answering machine whirred. "I'm not here right now, unless of course you're a telemarketer, in which case, I am here and I'm screening you because, quite honestly, your friendship means nothing to me. I have no time for hangers-on. Leave a message at the sound of the beep."

"Fudge, I know you're there," Joey shouted into the answering machine. "Pick up, pick up, pic—!"

"Ah, Lady Guenevere, thou doth sing the song of the enchantress," Fudge crooned, careful not to use Joey's name.

Joey rolled her eyes, refusing to get into it. When it came to cutouts, it was better not to get involved. And when it came to Fudge, well . . . it'd always been her policy not to get too close to men who still go by the name of their favorite Judy Blume character.

"So what can I do for you this evening? Business or pleasure?"

"Do you still know that guy at Omnibank?" Joey asked.

Fudge paused. "Maybe."

Joey nodded at the code. That was yes. It was always yes. Indeed, that's what the cutout business was all about: knowing people. And not just any people. Angry people. Bitter people. Passed-over-for-promotion people. In every office, there's someone who's miserable with their job. Those were the ones anxious to sell what they knew. And that's who Fudge could find.

"If I could, what would you be looking for?" Fudge asked. "Client records?"

"Yeah . . . but I also need monitors on two accounts."

"Uh-oh, big money talking here . . ."

"If you can't handle it," Joey warned.

"I can handle it just fine. I know a secretary in Fraud who's still pissed about a snotty comment at an office party with th—"

"Fudge!" Joey interrupted, turning a blind eye at the source. Sure, it made the lawyer in her cringe, but that's what the cutout was there for. Someone else does the dirty work; she gets the final work product. As long as she doesn't know where it comes from, she cuts out the liability. Besides, even if it is a legal fiction, it's worked for the CIA for years.

"A hundred for the records. A grand for the ears," Fudge said. "Anything else?"

"Phone company. Unlisted numbers and maybe a few taps on the line."

"What state?"

Joey shook her head. "Where do you find these people?"

"Honey, go to any chatroom in the world and type the words: *'Who hates their job?'* When you see a return e-mail address with AT&T.com on it, that's who you write back," Fudge said. "Think about that next time you're a jackass to the copy boy."

"What's this?" DeSanctis asked, flipping through a two-page document as he leaned on the trunk of his winter-worn Chevy.

"It's a mail cover," Gallo said, cupping his hands and breathing into them. "Bring it to their local post offices and they'll . . ."

". . . pull Oliver's and Charlie's mail and photocopy every return address," DeSanctis interrupted. "I know how it works."

"Good—then you also know who in the post office to hand it to. When you're done, take the search warrant to Oliver's. I've got one more stop to make."

"What's this?" the Hispanic woman in the dark blue post office sweater asked.

"It's a thank-you gift," Joey said as she held out a hundred-dollar bill.

Standing between two rickety metal bookshelves stacked with rubber-banded piles of mail, the woman leaned out of her makeshift cubicle and scanned the wide-open back room. Like the distribution area in most post offices, it was a human antfarm of activity: In every direction, bags of mail were dumped, separated, and sorted. Convinced that no one was looking, she studied the hundred dollars in Joey's hand. "You a cop?"

"Private," Joey said, turning on just enough lawyer calm to put the woman at ease. She hated doing this herself, but like Fudge said, when it came to mail, the scale was too large. If you wanted to build a real profile—and you needed every return address—you had to go in and find the local carrier yourself. "Private and willing to pay," she clarified.

"Drop it on the floor," the woman said.

Joey hesitated, searching the corners of the room for cameras.

"Just drop it," she repeated. "No harm done."

Lowering her arm, Joey let go, and the bill sailed to the floor. When it hit, the woman took a tiny step forward and covered it with her foot. "Now what can I help you with?"

Joey pulled a sheet of paper from her purse. "Just a little photocopy work on some friends in Brooklyn."

"Whattya mean it's gone?" Gallo growled into his cell phone as he pounded the elevator button for the fourth floor. There was a sharp lurch and the beat-up elevator slowly kicked into gear.

"Gone—as in, *no longer here*," DeSanctis shot back. "The garbage's been picked through, and the recycling bins are on the curb, completely cleaned out."

"Maybe they already got picked up. What day's recycling?"

"Tomorrow," he said dryly. "I'm telling you, she's been here. And if she figures out how we—"

"Don't be a moron. Just because she stole Oliver's garbage doesn't mean she knows what's going on." The elevator doors opened and Gallo followed the alphabet around to Apartment 4D. "Besides, in the grand scheme of things, we're about to get something a whole lot better than junk mail and some old newspapers . . ."

"What're you talking about?"

Ringing the doorbell, Gallo didn't answer.

"Who is it?" a soft female voice asked.

"United States Secret Service," Gallo said, lifting his badge so it could be seen through the door's eyehole.

There was a silent pause . . . then a fast thunking as a totem pole of locks unclicked. Slowly, the door creaked open, revealing a heavyset woman in a yellow cardigan. She pulled two pins from her mouth and stuck them into the red pin-cushion she wore around her left wrist. "Can I help you?" Maggie Caruso asked.

"Actually, Mrs. Caruso, I'm here about your sons . . ."

Her mouth opened and her shoulders dropped. "What's wrong? Are they okay?"

"Of course they're okay," Gallo promised, reaching out and putting a hand on her shoulder. "They just got into a little trouble at work, and, well . . . we were hoping you could come downtown and answer a few questions."

Instinctively, she hesitated. The phone started ringing in the kitchen, but she didn't answer it.

"I promise, it's nothing bad, Mrs. Caruso. We just thought you might be able to help us clear it up. You know . . . for the boys."

"S-Sure . . ." she stammered. "Let me get my purse."

Watching her scurry back into her apartment, Gallo stepped inside and slammed the door. Like he was always taught, if you want the rats to come running, you have to start messing with their rathole.

21

Is this even right?" Charlie asks.

"That's what it says," I point out. I recheck the address, then look up at the numbers stickered to the filthy glass door: 405 Amsterdam. Apartment 2B. Duckworth's last known address.

"No. There's no way," Charlie insists.

"Why? What's wrong?"

"Open an eyeball, Ollie. This guy's got a three-hundred-million-dollar piggy bank. This should be some Upper West Side, snooty doorman snazzfest. Instead, he's living in a scrubby bachelor pad that's tucked above a bad Indian restaurant and a Chinese laundromat? Forget three hundred million . . . this isn't even three hundred thousand."

"Looks can still be a liar," I counter.

"Yeah, like when three million turns out to be three hundred?"

Ignoring the comment, I point to the unlabeled button for Apartment 2B. "Should I ring it or not?"

"Sure—what else we got to lose?"

It's not a question I'm ready to answer. The gray sky's

getting dark. In a few hours, mom'll start to panic. Unless, of course, the Service has already been in touch.

I ring the buzzer.

"Yeah?" a man's voice shouts back.

Charlie spots an empty brown box in front of the laundromat. "I got a delivery here for 2B," he says.

For a moment, there's nothing but silence. Then, the raspy buzzer explodes, and Charlie pulls on the door. He holds it open; I grab the brown box. Duckworth, here we come.

As we climb the stairs, the poorly lit hallway is haunted by the potent smell of Indian curry and laundromat bleach. The paint on the walls is cracked and mildewy. The old tile floor is missing pieces in every direction. Charlie lobs me another glance. Bank customers don't live in places like this. He expects it to slow me down, but all it does is make me pick up the pace.

"That's it . . ." Charlie says.

At 2B, I stop and hold the brown box up to the eyehole. "Delivery," I announce, banging on the door.

Locks crackle and the door swings open. I'm ready for a fifty-year-old man on the verge of tears—just dying to tell us the full story. Instead, we get a frat boy with a perfectly curved Syracuse baseball cap and oversized lacrosse shorts.

"You got a delivery, yo?" he asks in full white-boy accent.

I shoot a glance at Charlie. Even in his Brooklyn-rapper phase, my brother wasn't this cliché.

"Actually, it's for Marty Duckworth," I say. "Does he live here?"

"You mean that freaky little guy? Kinda looked like the moleman?" he laughs.

Flustered, I don't answer.

"That's him," Charlie jumps in just to keep him talking. "Any idea where he went?"

"Florida, baby. Ocean retirement."

Retirement, I nod. Charlie's got the same thought. *That means he's got money. The only thing that doesn't make sense is this dump.*

"What about a forwarding address?" Charlie asks. "Did he leave one for you to—"

"What country do you think this is?" Frat Boy teases. "Everybody loves their mail . . ." Crossing back through the studio apartment, he grabs his electronic organizer from the top of his TV. "I keep it under 'M,' for *M*oleman," he sings, plenty amused.

Charlie nods appreciatively. "Sweet, dude."

From my back pocket, I pull out the letter where we wrote down Duckworth's other address.

"Here you go," Frat Boy announces, reading from his organizer. "1004 Tenth Street. Sun-shining Miami Beach. 33139."

Charlie reads over my shoulder, checking to see if it matches. "Same Bat-time. Same Bat-channel," he whispers.

Saying our goodbyes, we leave the apartment. Neither of us says a word until we hit the stairs.

"What'd you think?" I ask.

"About Duckworth's life state? I got no idea—though the walking Abercrombie catalogue up there didn't act like he was dead," Charlie says.

"That's who you're putting your faith in?"

"All I'm saying is, that's two people confirming a Miami address."

"And not just any address—a retirement address."

Still sniffing the bleached curry, Charlie knows what I'm getting at. People don't live in apartments like this to save for retirement—they live here because they have to. "Which means if Duckworth's retiring to Florida . . ."

". . . it's because he suddenly came into some money," Charlie agrees.

"Only problem is, according to the bank's records, he's had plenty of money for years. So why's the prince dressing like a pauper?"

At the bottom of the stairs, Charlie pulls open the door to the street. "Maybe he's trying to keep his money hidden . . ."

"Or maybe *someone else* is trying to keep his money hidden," I point out, my voice getting quicker. "Either way, it's not just the hallway that's starting to reek." I speed outside, man on a mission. "Until we talk to Duckworth, we'll never know for sure."

Tossing the cardboard box back to its home, I head straight for the payphone on the corner, reach for my phone card, and quickly dial the number for Florida information.

"In Miami . . . I'm looking for a Marty or Martin Duckworth at 1004 Tenth Street," I tell the computerized voice that answers. There's a short pause as we wait in silence. It's only five o'clock, but the sky's almost completely black, and a night wind whips down Amsterdam Avenue. As my teeth start to chatter, I step back from the booth and pull Charlie in toward the phone, hoping to keep him warm. And hidden. I search over my shoulder, checking to make sure we're safe.

Charlie nods a thank-you and . . .

"You said *Duckworth?*" a female operator interrupts on the other line.

"Duckworth," I repeat. "First name Marty or Martin. On Tenth Street."

Once again, we're back in silence.

"I'm sorry," she finally says. "That's a nonpublished number."

"Are you sure?"

"M. Duckworth on Tenth Street. Nonpublished. Now is there anything else I can help you with?"

"No . . . that's it," I say, my voice completely losing steam. "Thanks for the help."

"Well?" Charlie asks as I hang up.

"Unlisted."

"But not disconnected," he challenges, stepping out of the booth. "Wherever Duckworth is, he's still got an active number."

I look up, unconvinced . . . and quickly notice that we're standing on an open street. Motioning with my chin, I point us back toward the recessed alcove that shields the entrance to Frat Boy's building. We take a fast scan of the street and head straight for the alcove. Sliding inside, I add, "Enough with the Sherlock Holmes, Charlie. For all we know, the phone company hasn't updated their database since Duckworth died."

"Maybe," he admits as he joins me in the alcove. "Though he can just as easily be tucked away in Florida, waiting for us to come visit." Before I can argue, he flicks his finger against the Duckworth address sheet in my hands. "Like you said: Unless we talk to him, we'll never know for sure."

"I don't know . . . why don't we check to see if there's a death certificate first?"

"Ollie, yesterday the bank said this guy only had three million dollars. You really trust records anymore?"

Leaning back against the concrete wall, I weigh it all carefully.

"Don't make it all analytical, bro. Go with your gut."

It's a fair point. Even coming from Charlie. "You really think we should go to Miami?"

"Hard to say," he answers. "How long you think we can hide in the church?"

Watching a throng of commuters flood off a nearby bus, I'm completely silent.

"C'mon, Ollie—even parents know when their kids are right. Unless we can prove what really happened, Gallo and DeSanctis have a complete hold on reality. And on us. *We* stole the money . . . *we* killed Shep . . . and *we're* the ones who'll pay for it."

Once again, I give him nothing but silence. "You sure we're not chasing rainbows?" I finally ask.

"And what's wrong with that?"

"Charlie . . ."

"Fine, even if we are, it's gotta be better than hiding here."

I nod my head at that one. When I first started at the bank, Lapidus told me I should never argue with facts. Without another word, I stand up straight and turn to my brother. "You know they're going to be watching the airports . . ."

"Don't even give yourself a tummy ache," Charlie says. "I've already got a way around it."

22

Ready to go two-for-two?" Joey whispered into the collar of her shirt as she strolled quietly down Avenue U. Surrounded by commuters returning home from work, she didn't need the red dog leash. For now, she was one of the crowd.

"You never learn, do you?" Noreen asked.

"Not until we get caught," Joey said, rounding the corner onto Bedford Avenue and picking up the pace. "Besides, if they invite you inside, it's not breaking and entering." Up the block, she eyed the six-story building that Charlie and his mom called home.

"Any doorman?" Noreen asked.

"Not in this neighborhood," Joey said, already plotting her way in. It wouldn't take much. As long as mom was still in the dark, any old story would do. *Hi, I'm a Realtor . . . Hi, I'm one of Charlie's friends from work . . . Hi, I'm here to sneak into your apartment and hopefully plug some of these creatively designed transmitters into your outlets.* Laughing at her own joke, Joey continued to scan the block. Two kids skateboarding on the sidewalk. A navy blue sedan parked illegally across the street. And out front, a broad-chested man holding the door open for a heavyset woman. Joey recognized Gallo instantly.

"I don't believe it . . ."

"What?" Noreen asked.

"Guess who's here?" she growled, lowering her head, but refusing to turn away. Slowly backing up toward the used bookstore on the corner, Joey ducked into the doorway and poked her neck out just enough to steal a good look.

"Who is it?" Noreen pleaded. "What's going on?"

Up the block, Gallo opened the passenger seat to his car and escorted Mrs. Caruso into place. She clutched her purse close to her chest, completely in shock. Paying no attention, Gallo slammed the door in her face.

"What a gentleman," Joey muttered. But as Gallo crossed around to the driver's side, he stared up the block, almost like he was searching for someone. Someone who wasn't there. But would be soon.

"Oh, crap," Joey added, reading the cocky look on his face.

"Can you please tell me what's going on!?" Noreen demanded.

Gunning his engine, Gallo sped up the block. Joey took off instantly, darting back toward the building. "He's got a crew coming," Joey warned.

"Right now?"

"That's what I'm guessing . . . in the next two to ten minutes . . ."

"They're putting ears on her already? How'd they get warrants so fast?"

"I have no idea," Joey said as she jerked open the building's front door. As an elderly woman came out from the lobby, Joey caught the interior door, cut inside, and flew for the elevator.

There was a short pause on the other line. "Please tell me you're not running toward the building . . ."

"I'm not running toward the building," Joey said, attacking the elevator call button like a Morse code operator.

"Dammit, Joey, this is stupid."

"No, what's stupid is trying to do this after the Service have their eyes and ears in place."

"Then maybe you shouldn't do it at all."

"Noreen, remember what I told you about the tug of home? I don't care how hardened these kids are, once they're on the run, they'll eventually feel it. And in this case . . . when one of them's paying mom's bills and the other's still living with her . . . When the ties are that tight, it's like a magnet in their chest. They may only call in for two seconds, but when it happens, I plan to hear it. And trace it."

Once again, Noreen was silent. For about half a second. "Just tell me what you need me to d—"

Joey stepped into the elevator, and the line went dead. That's the way it was with cell phones and old buildings. She checked the lobby one last time, but there was nothing to see. As the doors slid shut, Joey was on her own.

23

"You sure this is a good idea?" I ask, keeping lookout as Charlie punches the number into the Excelsior Hotel's payphone. It may not be the best hotel in the city, but it is the closest one with the best selection of phonebooks.

"Oliver, how else do you plan on getting on a plane?" he counters as he puts the receiver to his ear. "If we use our real IDs, we're fools; if we use our credit cards, they track us."

"Then maybe we should check out some other forms of transportation."

"Like what? Renting a car and driving? You still need a credit card and ID . . ."

"What about the train?"

"Oh, please—you really wanna spend two days riding Amtrak? Every second we waste lets the Secret Service tighten the thumbscrews. Trust me, if we want to get out of town, this is our best option."

Unconvinced, I lean in and make him share the receiver. In my ear, the phone rings for the third time. "C'mon . . ."

Charlie grumbles, staring down at the New Jersey Yellow Pages. "Where the hell are y—"

"Law offices," Bendini answers without the slightest stutter. "Whattya need?"

24

The first fifteen minutes were supposed to calm her down. No one to yell at . . . no one to speak to—just her—alone in a room, with nothing to stare at but a single wooden desk and four mismatched office chairs. All around her, the walls were stark white—no pictures, nothing to distract—except for the enormous mirror that ran along the righthand wall. Obviously, the mirror was the first thing Maggie Caruso noticed. It was supposed to be. As the Secret Service well knew, with today's miniaturized video technology, there was no practical reason to still use two-way mirrors. But that didn't mean that, even when there was no one behind them, they didn't have their own psychological effect. Indeed, the sight alone had Maggie twisting uncomfortably in her seat. And that's what the next fifteen minutes were all about.

Trying to block it out, Maggie used her right hand to shield her eyes. In her head, she reminded herself that everything was okay. Her sons were fine. That's what Gallo told her. He said it right to her face. But if that were the case, what was she doing downtown, at the New York headquarters of the Secret Service? The answer came with a sharp rattle and a twist of the doorknob. She turned to her left, and the door swung wide.

"Maggie Caruso?" DeSanctis asked as he stepped inside. With a file folder swinging at his side, he was dressed in a navy suit, but without the jacket. Sleeves rolled up to his elbows. Serious, but hardly threatening. Behind him, Gallo followed, nodding a fast hello. Forever the seamstress, Maggie couldn't help but notice his poorly fitted suit—a clear sign of either bad taste, vast impatience, or an oversized ego (men always thought they were bigger than they were). Despite the forty-minute car ride from Brooklyn, she still didn't know which. But she did know what she wanted. Her voice cracked as she said the words.

"*Please* . . . when can I see my boys?"

"Actually, that's what we were hoping you could help us with," DeSanctis said. He took the seat on her left; Gallo took the one on her right. Neither of them sat straight across, she noticed. Both were on her side.

"I don't understand . . ." she began.

Gallo looked at DeSanctis, who slowly slid the file folder on the table. "Mrs. Caruso, sometime last night, someone stole a . . . well . . . a significant amount of money from Greene Private Bank. This morning, when the thieves were confronted, gunfire was exchanged and—"

"Gunfire?" she interrupted, her voice shaking. "Was anyone . . ."

"Oliver and Charlie are fine," he reassured her, cupping his hands over her own. "But in the process, a man named Shep Graves was shot and killed by the two suspects, who managed to escape."

Maggie turned to Gallo, who was biting at a blood-red cut on his lip. "What does this have to do with my sons?" she asked hesitantly.

Still holding her hands, DeSanctis leaned in close. "Mrs. Caruso, have you heard from Charlie or Oliver in the past few hours?"

"Excuse me?"

"If they were hiding somewhere, do you know where that might be?"

Maggie yanked her hands free and shot out of her seat. "What're you talking about?"

Just as fast, Gallo was on his feet. "Ma'am, can you please sit down?"

"Not until you tell me what's going on! Are you accusing them of something!?"

"Ma'am, *sit down!*"

"Oh, God—you're serious, aren't you?"

"Ma'am . . . !"

DeSanctis grabbed Gallo by the wrist and pulled him back into place. Facing Maggie, he added, "Please, Mrs. Caruso, there's no need to—"

"They'd never do something like that! *Never!*" she insisted.

"I'm not saying they would," DeSanctis offered, keeping his voice slow and smooth. "I'm just trying to protect them . . ."

"That's funny—because you sound like someone who's dying to pin them down."

"Call it whatever you want," Gallo jumped in. "But the longer they stay out there, the more they're in danger."

Right there, Maggie stopped. "What?"

Taking a deep breath, Gallo rubbed the back of his buzz cut. Maggie studied him carefully, unsure if it was frustration . . . or real concern. "We're only trying to help you, Mrs. Caruso. It's just that, you know how these things go . . . you watch the news. When was the last time a fugitive made a safe getaway? Or lived happily ever after?" Gallo asked. "It doesn't happen, Maggie. And the longer you keep your mouth shut, the more likely some law enforcement hotshot is going to put a bullet in one of your sons' necks."

Unable to move, Maggie just stood there, letting the logic sink in.

"I know you want to protect them—and I understand your hesitation," Gallo added. "But ask yourself this: Do you really want to bury your own children? Because from here on in, Maggie, the choice is up to you."

Still frozen, Maggie Caruso watched the world blur in a flood of tears.

Outside of Maggie's apartment building, the Verizon van pulled into an open spot right behind a dented black car. There was no running, or scrambling, or screeching of brakes. Instead, the side door of the van slid open and three men in Verizon uniforms got out. All three carried telephone company IDs in their right pocket, and Secret Service badges in their left. Their pace stayed calm and steady as they unloaded their toolboxes. Part of the training. Telephone repairmen never rushed.

As physical security specialists in the Technical Security Division, all they needed was twenty minutes to turn any home into a perfect soundstage. Gallo said they'd have at least two hours. They'd still be done in twenty minutes. Heading inside, the tallest of the three shoved a tiny three-pronged tweezer toward the lock. In four seconds, the door was open.

"Phone box in the basement," the one with black hair called out.

"I got it," the third said, heading for the stairwell in the corner of the lobby. Only novices put wiretaps in the actual phone. Thanks to Hollywood, it's the first place everyone looked.

In the elevator, the other two noticed the rusty metal door and the outdated callbox. Old buildings usually took an extra step or two. Thicker walls; deeper drilling. Eventually, the elevator hiccuped to a halt on the fourth floor. The door rolled open and Joey was waiting. She took one look at the Verizon uniforms and lowered her head.

"Have a good night," the taller one said as he stepped out.

"You too," Joey replied, sliding around him to get in. As they passed each other, Joey's chest brushed against his arm. He smiled. She smiled right back. And just like that, she was gone.

"I swear, I haven't heard from them once," Maggie stammered, wiping her eyes with the edge of her sleeve. "I was home all day . . . all my clients . . . but they never . . ."

"We believe you," Gallo said. "But the longer Charlie and Oliver are out there, the more likely they are to check in. And when they do, I want your promise that you'll keep them talking as long as possible. Are you listening, Maggie? That's all you have to do. We'll take care of the rest."

Catching her breath, Maggie tried to picture the moment in her head. So much of it still didn't make sense. "I don't know . . ."

"I realize it's hard," DeSanctis added. "Believe me, I have two little girls myself—no parent should ever be put in this situation. But if you want to save them, this is truly the best . . . for everyone."

"Now whattya say?" Gallo asked. "Can we count on you?"

25

It takes us almost a full hour to get from Duckworth's to Hoboken, New Jersey, and as the PATH train pulls into the station, I carefully nod to the opposite end of the subway car, where Charlie's hidden amongst the after-work yuppified crowd. No reason to be stupid.

In one giant push, the human wave of commuters flush from the train and flood the stairwells, shoving their way toward the street. As always, Charlie's at the front, body-surfing his way through the crowd. He moves with ease. Hitting the street, he continues to pick up the pace. I stay a good twenty steps behind, never letting him out of my sight.

Following Bendini's instructions, Charlie blows past the New York–wannabe bars and restaurants that line Washington Avenue and takes a sharp left on Fourth. Right there, the neighborhood morphs. Coffee shops become townhouses . . . bakeries become brownstones . . . and uber-trendy clothing stores become five-story walk-ups. Charlie takes one look and stops dead in his tracks.

"This can't be right," he calls out.

Moving in close, I have to agree. We're looking for a

storefront; this is all residential. Still, when it comes to Bendini, nothing surprises. "Just follow the address," I whisper as an old Italian man stares curiously down at us from a nearby window. His TV flickers behind him. "Hurry," I insist.

Sure enough, three blocks later, we see it: Smack in between a string of row houses is a one-story square brick building with a home-painted *Mumford Travel* sign right above it. The letters on the sign are thin and gray—and like the brass plaque outside the bank—it's clearly meant to be overlooked. Inside, the lights are on, but the only one there is a sixty-year-old woman sitting behind an old metal desk and flipping through a thumb-worn copy of *Soap Opera Digest*.

Charlie goes straight for the doorbell. *Please ring for service.*

"It's open," the woman calls out without looking up. A push on the door lets us in.

"Hi," I say to the woman, who still won't face us. "I'm here to see—"

"I got it . . . !" a screechy voice calls out in a heavy Jersey accent. From the back room, a wiry man in a white golf shirt pushes aside a red curtain and steps out to greet us. He's got slightly bulging eyes and a brushed-back receding hairline. "You got an emergency?" he asks.

"Actually, we were sent by—"

"I know who sent you," he interrupts, staring over our shoulders and checking out the street through the plate glass window. In his line of work, it's pure instinct. Safety first. Convinced we're alone, he motions us to join him in the back.

As we follow, I notice the faded and outdated travel posters that cover the walls. Bahamas . . . Hawaii . . . Florida—every ad is filled with big-haired women and mustache-wearing men. The bubble font dates it as late-Eighties, though I'm sure the place hasn't been touched in years. Travel agency, my ass.

"Let's get you started," the man calls out, holding open the drape that leads to the back room.

"Pay no attention to the man behind the curtain," Charlie says, already trying to make nice.

"You got that right," the man agrees. "But if I'm Oz, who're you—the Cowardly Lion?"

"Nah, *he's* the Cowardly Lion," Charlie says, pointing my way. "Me? I see myself more as Toto . . . or maybe a flying monkey—the lead one, of course—not one of those simpleton primate lackeys who stand in the background."

Oz fights his smile, but it's still there.

"So I hear you need to get to Miami," he says, moving toward his desk, which sits in the direct center of the dingy back room. It's the same size as the room out front, but back here, there's a copier, a shredder, and a computer hooked up to a high-tech printer. All around us, the walls are stacked high with dozens of unmarked brown boxes. I don't even want to know what's inside.

"Um . . . can we get started?" I ask.

"That depends on you," Oz says, rubbing his thumb against his pointer and middle finger.

Charlie shoots me a look, and I reach for the wad of money stuffed into my wallet. "Three thousand, right?"

"That's what they say," Oz replies, once again serious.

"I really appreciate you helping us out," Charlie adds, hoping to keep it light.

"It's not a favor, kid. It's just a job." Leaning over, he reaches down to the bottom drawer of his desk, pulls two items out, and wings them our way. I catch one; Charlie catches the other.

"Clairol Nice 'n Easy Hair Color," Charlie reads out loud. On the front of his box is a woman with silky blond hair. On the cover of mine, the model's hair is jet black.

Oz immediately points us to the bathroom in the corner. "If you really want to get lost," he explains, "you gotta start up top."

Twenty minutes later, I'm staring in a filthy mirror, amazed at the magic of a cheap dye job. "How's it look?" I ask, brushing my newly black hair into place.

"Like Buddy Holly," Charlie says, peering over my shoulder. "Only nerdier."

"Thank you, Carol Channing."

"Bullet-head."

"Aquaman."

"Hey, at least I don't look like all of mom's friends," Charlie shoots back.

I check myself in the mirror. "Who're you—?"

"You two ready yet?" Oz interrupts. "Let's go!"

Snapped back to reality, we head out of the bathroom. I'm still playing with my hair. Charlie hasn't touched his. He's already used to it. After all, this isn't the first time he's changed color. Blond in tenth grade, dark purple in twelfth. Back then, mom knew he had to get it out of his system. I wonder what she'd say now.

"Stand over there and pull the shade," Oz says, pointing to the window at the back of the room. On the floor, there's a small X taped on the carpet. Charlie leaps for it and jerks down the shade's cord.

"Blue?" he asks, noticing the pale blue color on the inside of the shade.

On Oz's computer, the screen blinks on and a digital image of a blank New Jersey driver's license blooms into focus. The background for the photo is pale blue. Just like the shade. Grinning at the technology, Oz steps in front of Charlie, digital camera in hand.

"On three, say *'Department of Motor Vehicles . . .'*"

Charlie says the words, and I squint at the bright white flash.

26

Craning her neck skyward, Joey stared up at the thirty-story building on Manhattan's Upper East Side. "You sure she's home?" Joey asked, almost dizzied by the height.

"I just spoke to her ten minutes ago pretending to be a telemarketer," Noreen said. "It's past dinner. She's not going anywhere."

Nodding to herself, Joey turned under the awning and peered through the double glass doors that led to the lobby. Inside, a doorman was hunched against the front desk, flipping through the newspaper. No uniform; no tie; no problem. Just another daddy's little girl's first apartment.

Painting on a wide grin, Joey unclipped her cell phone from her belt, held it to her ear, and pulled open the door. "Uch, I hate it when they do that!" she whined into the phone. "Panty hose are *so* middle-class."

"What're you talking about?" Noreen asked.

"You heard me!" Joey shouted. She blew by the doorman without a wave and stormed straight for the elevator. The doorman shook his head. Typical.

Twenty-three floors later, Joey rang the bell for Apartment 23H.

"Who is it?" a female voice answered.

"Teri Gerlach—from the National Association of Securities Dealers," Joey explained. "Oliver Caruso recently applied for his Series-7 license, and since he listed you as one of his references, we were wondering if we could ask you a few questions." As she said the words, Joey knew there was no reference check for the Series-7, but it never slowed her down before.

There was a quiet clink and Joey could feel herself being studied through the eyehole. Once it got dark outside, women in New York had plenty of reasons to not open their doors to strangers.

"Who else did he list?" the voice challenged.

For effect, Joey pulled a small notepad from her purse. "Let's see . . . a mother by the name of Margaret . . . a brother, Charles . . . Henry Lapidus from Greene Bank . . . and a girlfriend named Beth Manning."

Chains whirred and locks thunked. As the door opened, Beth stuck her head out. "Didn't Oliver already take his Series-7?"

"This is for the renewal, Miss Manning," Joey said matter-of-factly. "But we still like to check the references." She motioned back to the notepad and offered a perfectly pleasant smile. "I promise, it's just a few simple questions—painless as can be."

Shrugging at no one in particular, Beth moved back from the door. "You'll just have to excuse the mess . . ."

"Don't worry," Joey laughed as she stepped inside and waved a hand against Beth's forearm. "My place is fifty times worse."

* * * *

Francis Quincy wasn't a pacer. Or even a worrier. In fact, when the lid on the pressure cooker clamped down, while everyone else was anxiously roving back and forth across the carpet, Quincy was the one stuck to his seat, quietly calculating the odds. Even when his fourth daughter was born three months premature, Quincy stepped back and took silent solace in the fact that eighty percent of similarly aged babies turn out just fine. Back then, the numbers were in his favor. Today, they were out of his control. He still didn't pace.

"Did he say anything else?" Quincy asked dryly.

"Nothing . . . less than nothing," Lapidus said, rapping his middle knuckle over and over against the desk. "They just want us to keep a tight lip."

Quincy nodded, standing alone by the window in the corner. Staring out at the electric skyline, he reached up and gripped the top of the butterfly-covered shoji screen for support. "Maybe we should wait a day before telling the partners."

"Are you crazy? If they found out we were holding back . . . Quincy, they'd drink our blood for breakfast."

"Well, I hate to break it to you, Henry, but they'll be screaming for blood no matter what—and until we find Oliver and that money, there's nothing we can do."

Lapidus's knuckle rapped even harder. "I already called twice. Gallo hasn't called back."

"If it'll make it easier, Henry, I'm happy to take a stab at it."

"I don't understand . . ."

"Maybe Gallo needs to hear it in both ears," Quincy suggested. "Just to tip the scales a little."

Lapidus paused, studying his partner. "Yeah . . . no . . . that'd be great."

Almost immediately, Quincy headed for the door.

"Just don't forget whose side Gallo and DeSanctis are on," Lapidus called out. "When it comes right down to it, law enforcement is just like any other client—out for their own peanut."

"You don't have to tell me," Quincy said as he left the room. "I know all about it."

"So how're we looking?" DeSanctis asked, cradling the phone with his chin.

"Hard to say. Obviously, we hit a few speedbumps, but I think it's all about to smooth out," his associate explained. "What about there? How's Gallo doing with the mom?"

Peering through the one-way glass, DeSanctis watched as Gallo helped Mrs. Caruso thread her arms into her coat. "We've got it covered," DeSanctis said dryly.

"You don't sound too confident . . ."

"I'll be confident when we have them," he insisted. Charlie and Oliver may've gotten away once, but it wasn't going to happen again. Not with stakes like this.

"Have you thought about calling in other agents?"

"No—no way," DeSanctis shot back. "Believe me, we don't want that headache."

"So you really think you and Gallo can keep it quiet?"

"Personally, I don't see much of a choice—for any of us."

"What's that supposed to mean?"

"Nothing," DeSanctis said coldly. Through the glass, Gallo led Mrs. Caruso out of the interrogation room. "You just do your job, and we'll do ours. As long as that's taken care of, they don't have a chance."

27

"Here you go," Oz says, slapping a blue-and-white Continental Airlines envelope against Charlie's chest. I rip mine open; Charlie does the same. Flight 201—9:50 tonight, nonstop to Miami.

"You didn't put us next to each other, did you?" I ask.

Oz stings me with the same do-I-look-like-a-schmuck look I usually get from Charlie. Still, this is no time to take chances. "25C," I tell my brother.

He studies his ticket. "7B." Turning to Oz, Charlie adds, "You stuck me in a middle seat, didn't you?"

Oz rolls his eyes. It's always been Charlie's best magic trick. Keep 'em talking. Reaching down to the laminating machine that's balanced on a stack of boxes, Oz picks up the iron-on wrapper and peels it open. "Remember that crappy fake ID that helped you buy beer in high school?" he brags. "Well, say hello to the real thing . . ." Like a cop flashing his badge, Oz shoves the laminated card straight at us. Without question, it's a perfect New Jersey license, complete with my picture and brand-new black hair.

"Spiffy," Charlie adds.

Oz told us to pick easy-to-remember names. Charlie's says Sonny Rollins, jazz master and legend. Mine says Walter Harvey, dad's first and middle names. Physically and in name, we're no longer brothers.

Charlie kisses the picture of himself. "Mmmmm, mmmm—this baby's gold . . ."

"But it ain't foolproof," Oz warns in full Hoboken accent. "Like I tell everyone, don't put all your eggs on the ID. It may get you on the plane . . . and maybe into a motel . . . but it only gets you so far . . ."

"What do you mean?" I interrupt.

"It's just the way the world spins," Oz explains. "No matter how fast you think you are, three things always pull the rug out: ego, greed, and sex." Knowing he has our attention, his high voice gets quicker. "Ego—you mouth off to your waiter; you're a jerk to the maître d'—that's how the guy at the restaurant remembers you and picks you out for the cops. Greed—you buy a big watch; you bite off five lobster dinners in a row—that's how the bartender recognizes your photo. And sex—baby, that's why all the clichés are true. Ain't nothing like a woman scorned."

"Do you see this streaky blond hair?" Charlie asks, pointing to himself. "And his nasty black bird's nest?" he adds, pointing to me. "From here on in, women are the least of our worries."

"So when you add in the travel and everything else," I interrupt, "how long you think we have before people realize we're gone?"

Oz turns to his computer and studies Charlie's fake driver's license, which is still staring back at us from the screen. "Hard to say," Oz replies as his voice gets shaky. "Depends who you're running from."

28

"Whattya mean, *Wonder Bread*?" Noreen asked through the cell phone.

"Wonder Bread," Joey repeated as she drove back through Brooklyn. "As in *yawn* . . . as in *boring* . . . as in *whiter than white*. I'm telling you, whatever Oliver sees in her—this girl's as exciting as a speedbump. I knew the moment I walked in: flower-patterned sofa, with matching throw pillows, with matching carpet, with matching coasters, and a matching Monet poster on the wall . . ."

"Hey, don't bust on Monet—"

"It was *Water Lilies*," Joey interrupted.

There was a pause. "Well then, you should've killed her right there."

"You're missing the point," Joey insisted. "It's not like there's anything wrong with her—she's nice, and she smiles, and she's pretty . . . but, that's it. Every once in a while, she blinks. There's nothing else."

"Maybe she's just an introvert."

"I asked her for a funny story about Oliver, and all she

could come up with was '*He's nice*' and '*He's sweet*.' That's as excited as she gets."

"Okay, so she's probably not in on it with the brothers. Did she give you anything else about Oliver?"

"See, that's the tickle," Joey said as her car bounced across the potholes of Avenue U. "Oliver may be a nice guy, but if he's dating Beth, he can't be much of a daredevil."

"So?"

"So think about how that fits with the other pieces: Here's a twenty-six-year-old kid scrimping and saving with the age-old dream of getting out of Brooklyn. He gets his kid brother a job, pays for mom's mortgage, and basically plays dad full-time. At work, he spends four years as boy Friday to Lapidus, hoping it's an inside track to stardom. Clearly, he's got bigger aspirations—but does he break out and start his own company? Not a chance. Instead, he applies to business school and decides to take the safe road to riches . . ."

"Maybe Lapidus wanted him to go to business school."

"It's not just B-school, Noreen. Pay attention to the details. In Oliver's recycling bin was a subscription to SpeedRead. Y'know what that is?" When Noreen didn't answer, Joey explained, "They put out a monthly pamphlet summarizing all the top business books so you can have something smart to say at cocktail parties. In Oliver's world, he actually thinks that matters. He thinks the system works. That's why he waits in line—and that's why he goes out with Beth."

"I'm not sure I'm following . . ."

"And I'm not sure there's anything to follow," Joey admits. "I can't describe it . . . it's just that . . . people who date the Beths of the world . . . they're the last ones to plan a three-hundred-million-dollar heist."

"Wait a minute," Noreen blurted, "so now you think they're—"

"They're not innocent," Joey insisted. "If they were, they wouldn't be running. But for Oliver to leave his happy little comfort zone . . . there's clearly something else we're not seeing. People don't change their spots without a damn good reason."

"If it makes you feel better, Fudge told me we should have most of the research tomorrow."

"Perfect," Joey said as she turned onto Bedford Avenue. Unlike the last time she was here, the light gray sky was now pitch black, making it look less like a neighborhood and more like a dark alley. Still, even in the darkness, one thing stood out: the telephone company truck parked in front of Maggie Caruso's building. Pulling in close, Joey glided by the van and studied her rearview. Two agents were in the front bucket seats.

"Everything okay?" Noreen asked through the cell phone.

"I'll tell you in a second." Heading halfway up the block, Joey ducked the car into a private driveway diagonally across from the building and cut the engine. Close enough to see, but still far enough not to be noticed. Squinting toward the van, she knew it didn't make sense. Black bag jobs were supposed to be in and out. If they were still here, something was up. Maybe they found something, Joey thought. Or maybe they were waiting for—

Before she could finish the thought, tires screeched and a car turned onto the block.

"What's going on?" Noreen asked.

"Shhhh," Joey whispered even though Noreen's voice only came through the earpiece. The car was moving fast—but it wasn't someone passing through. Coasting past the van, the car bucked to a halt right in front of a fire hydrant. Joey shook her head. She should've known.

The doors swung wide, and Gallo and DeSanctis stepped

into the night air. Without a word, DeSanctis opened the back door and extended a hand to Maggie Caruso. As she stepped out, her shoulders were slumped, her chin quivered, and her coat hung open clumsily. DeSanctis led her toward the building, but even in silhouette, it was easy to see she was a mess. She wasn't getting upstairs without help. They must've torn her apart, Joey thought.

"I'll be up in a second," Gallo called out as he crossed around to the trunk. But the instant Maggie and DeSanctis disappeared, he headed down the block, straight for the van.

The driver rolled down his window, and Gallo reached in to shake his hand. At first, it looked like nothing more than a thank-you between friends—quick nodding; head back laughing—then just like that, Gallo stopped. His posture tensed and the driver handed him something. "Since *when?*" Gallo asked in a quiet roar. The driver stuck his hand out the window and pointed up the block. Straight at Joey.

"Aw, crap," she whispered.

Gallo whirled around and their eyes locked. Joey's throat locked up. Gallo's dark glare sliced through her. "What the hell do you think you're doing?" Gallo thundered, storming straight at her car.

"Joey, are you okay?" Noreen asked.

There was no time to answer. Joey thought about starting her car, but it was too late. He was already there. Thick knuckles rapped against her window. "Open up," Gallo demanded.

Knowing the drill, Joey rolled down her window. "I'm not breaking the law," she insisted. "I have full credentials . . ."

"Screw credentials—what the hell were you doing inside that apartment?"

Staring straight at Gallo, Joey ran her tongue against the

back of her teeth. "I'm sorry, I don't know what you're talking about."

"Don't play stupid!" Gallo warned. "You know you have no jurisdiction!"

"I'm just doing my job," Joey shot back. She pulled a leather ID case from her pocket and flashed her investigator's license. "And last I checked, there's no law against—"

In a blur, Gallo whipped his hand forward, slapped the ID from her fingertips, and sent it flying against the opposite window. "*Listen to me!*" he exploded in Joey's face. "*I don't care about your learner's permit—if you interfere with this investigation again, I'll personally drag your ass back across the Brooklyn Bridge!*"

Stunned by the outburst, Joey stayed silent. Law enforcement was always territorial about jurisdiction . . . but in the Secret Service . . . they didn't lose their temper like that. Not without a reason.

"Anything else?" Joey asked.

Gallo tightened his gaze, shoved a closed fist into the car, and dumped a Ziploc bag of shattered electronics into Joey's lap. All her bugs and transmitters, wrecked beyond repair. "Take it from me, Ms. Lemont—this isn't a game you want to play."

29

My eye twitches when I'm nervous. Just slightly—a light flutter that's strong enough to tell me my body's in complete revolt. Most of the time, I can turn it off by humming the theme song to *Market Wrap* or saying the alphabet backwards—but as I stand at the end of the line in Newark International Airport, I'm too focused on every thing in my way: the fidgety brown-haired woman in fron' of me, the fifteen people ahead of her, and most important, the metal detectors at the front of the line and the half dozen security officials I'm thirty seconds away from facing.

If the Service put the word out, this'll be the shortest trip we've ever taken, but as the line shuffles forward, nothing seems out of pla—

Damn.

I didn't even notice him at first. Back beyond the conveyor belt. The broad-shouldered guy in the airport security uniform. He's got a metal detector in his hand, but the way he's gripping it like a bat, it's like he's never held one before in his life. His posture alone . . . only the Service grows them that big.

As he looks my way, I lower my head, refusing eye contact. Ten people in front of me, Charlie's craning his neck in every direction, anxious for interaction.

"Long day, huh?" he asks the woman running the X-ray machine.

"Never ends," the woman says with an appreciative grin.

On a normal day, I'd say it was typical Charlie small talk. But today . . . He may be yapping with the woman, but I see where he's looking. Straight at the broad-shouldered man. And the way Charlie's bouncing on the heels of his feet— it's the same as the twitch in my eye. We both know what happens if we're caught.

"No bags?" the woman asks as Charlie gets closer to the machine.

"Checked it," he brags, holding up his ticket and pointing to the single claim check.

In Hoboken, a quick stop at the army-navy store got us a blue gym bag filled with underwear, shirts, and a few toiletries. It also got us a miniature lead-lined box that—when stuffed in the bottom of the gym bag—became the perfect hiding spot for Gallo's gun.

No doubt, it's a bad idea—the last thing we need is to be caught with the murder weapon—but as Charlie pointed out, these guys are leaping for our throats. Unless we want to wind up like Shep, we need the protection.

"Keep it moving," a black guard calls out, motioning Charlie through the detector.

I hold my breath and once again lower my head. Nothing to worry about . . . nothing to worry about . . . Two seconds later, a high-pitched beep rips through the air. Oh, no. I look up just in time to see Charlie forcing a laugh. "Must be that erector set I ate this morning . . ."

Please, God, don't let him blow it . . .

"Man, I used to *hate* those erector sets," the guard laughs, waving a handheld detector up Charlie's chest and down his shoulders. "Couldn't build jack with 'em." In the background, the guard with the square shoulders slowly turns our way.

"That's why you gotta go with Lego," Charlie adds, unable to stop himself. Spreading his arms, he waves hi to the guard with square shoulders. The guard nods awkwardly and looks away. He wants two brown-haired brothers—not a flaky blond kid traveling alone.

Finding nothing, the black guard lowers his detector. "Have a safe trip," he tells Charlie.

"You too," Charlie adds. It's a great act, but there's not a single ounce of color left in his face. Stumbling forward, he can't get out of there fast enough.

One by one, the rest of the line takes their turn. As I step through the detector, Charlie turns around and glances back. Just to make sure I'm okay. Passing the two guards, I keep my mouth shut and glide by. And just like that, we're in. Nowhere to go but south. Nonstop to Miami.

30

Glaring at the back of Gallo's thick neck, Joey watched him walk across the street, back toward the apartment building. Halfway there, he shot a wave to his buddies in the van, who flashed their lights back. With a punch of the pedal, the van pulled out of its spot and hummed past Joey's car.

"Nice seeing you!" the driver shouted to Joey.

She forced a grin, pretending it didn't matter. Typical tech losers, she thought as they disappeared up the block. Within seconds, the black bag guys were gone. And as Gallo stepped inside the apartment building, so was her biggest obstacle.

"What was that about?" Noreen asked in her ear.

"Nothing," Joey shot back. She kicked the car door open and crossed around to the trunk.

"Maybe you should call the boss—he's got some buddies in the Service."

"Noreen, not now," Joey said, her voice echoing as she leaned down into the trunk. She pulled out a shiny metal suitcase and balanced it on the edge of the trunk. Locks popped and flipped open. Inside, it looked like a high-tech tackle box, with folding stackable trays filled with wires, mikes, and small metal gizmos that resembled miniature cellular phones. At the base of the box was a bulky radio receiver and collapsible headphones.

"What're you doing?" Noreen asked anxiously. "Where are you?"

Joey didn't answer. She stuffed what she needed in her pockets and crossed the street.

"You're not going back in the apartment are you?"

"Nope," Joey said, picking up speed.

"I heard you fidgeting with the goody box—just tell me where you're going."

Joey stopped in front of Gallo and DeSanctis's car.

"They took all my taps, Noreen—and you know what it's like getting back in while they're listening . . ."

"Wait a minute . . . you're not—" The slam of a car door cut Noreen off. "Joey, please tell me you're not in the Secret Service's car."

"Fine, I'm not in their car." Joey eyed her watch. There wasn't much time. It may've looked like they were helping Maggie back upstairs, but it was probably just Gallo's way of getting another peek around the apartment. Over her shoulder, Joey took one last glance at the building. Two minutes at the most.

"Joey, they can shoot you for this . . ."

Right next to the moon roof, Joey reached up for the dome light that lit the inside of the car, snapped off its plastic covering, and quickly undid the two screws that held the tiny bulb in place. "They started it, Noreen."

"*They* started it? You're bugging the United States Secret Service! That car's federal property."

"It's also the only place these bastards are too cocky to

look," Joey pointed out. "Hell, they're so sure of themselves, they even left the doors unlocked." She connected a tiny microphone to the red wire that dangled down toward the bulb. It was a trick she learned years ago. The dome light was one of the few places that always had power—even when the car was off. Hooked in there, you could spy on someone for months. All it took was a little risk.

"Please, Joey—they're gonna come any minute . . ."

"Almost done . . ." Snapping the dome back into place, she ducked down in the back of the car and reached under the driver's seat. There was one other easy-to-reach place that always had power. And thanks to an upgrade in law enforcement vehicles, Gallo's car was fully stocked with power seats.

Feeling around for the wiring that ran up from the floorboard, she clipped onto a red wire and quickly plugged the other end into the black box that looked like an outdated cell phone, but without the keypad.

"Joey, they won't hesitate to throw you in jail . . ."

She lifted her head to glance out the side window, and a bright light caught her eye. Inside the building. The elevator doors slid open. Here they come. Less than thirty seconds. Fighting her hands from shaking, she pulled one last item from her pocket. It was a shiny extendable pointer with a slight hook at the end of it. Opening it to its full three feet, she attached it to the wiry antenna that ran out of the black box and tucked it under the base of the cloth-covered seat.

"Joey, get out of there . . ."

With a sharp shove, she threaded the pointer—and the antenna—straight up the back of the seat. Completely out of sight, but still perfectly angled to send a signal through the moon roof. One homemade global positioning system coming up.

"Joey . . . !"

"Call him," she whispered.

"What?" Noreen asked.

"Call him."

Frantically stuffing the black box under the seat, Joey locked it in place with a magnetic thunk. That was it. Time to get out.

From the back window, she could see Gallo and DeSanctis walking up the block. Less than fifty feet away. It was too late . . .

A high-pitched ring screamed through the night and Gallo stopped in his tracks. So did DeSanctis. "This is Gallo," he answered, flipping open his cell phone. The two agents turned back toward the building. That was all Joey needed. In one fluid movement, she ducked out the back door and scuttled across the street.

"Sorry, wrong number," Noreen said in Joey's ear.

Gallo shut his phone and headed back to his car. As he pulled the door open, he squinted up the dark block. Joey was sitting on the hood of her car.

"Any luck up there?" she called out.

Gallo ignored her, dumping himself in the driver's seat and slamming the door shut. In a blink, the dome light clicked off. Joey sat back and grinned.

31

Stepping off the plane at Miami International Airport, I stick to the crowd and lose myself in the mass of recently arrived passengers being smothered by loved ones. It's not hard to tell the difference between natives and guests—we're in long sleeves and jackets; they're in shorts and tank tops. As the group fans out toward baggage claim, I scan the terminal, searching for Charlie. He's nowhere in sight.

All around us, the airport shops and last-minute newsstands are closed. Metal bars cover every storefront; lights are off. It's past midnight and the whole place is nothing but a traveler's ghost town. Spotting the sign for the men's bathroom—and knowing Charlie's tiny bladder—I make a sharp right and weave my way toward the urinals. The only one there is an overweight man in an aqua Florida Marlins jersey. I keep going and check the stalls. All empty.

Racing back into the terminal, past the Christmas tree and menorah that're on display, I double my pace and fly down the escalator. Charlie knows he was supposed to wait for me when we got off the plane. If he didn't . . . I stop myself. There's no reason to think the worst.

With a leap from the escalator, I'm down in baggage claim, checking every corner. Past the rental cars . . . around the conveyor belts . . . still no Charlie. On my right is a phone bank, where a Hispanic woman is laughing into the receiver. Beyond the phones, there's an e-mail and fax stand, where a man in dark sunglasses—

Dark sunglasses?

I slow down, tempted to turn the other way. If he's with the Service, I'm not serving myself up on a platter. But just as I'm about to switch direction . . . just as I get close . . . he turns away like I'm not even there. I pass right by him. He doesn't even look up. And that's when I realize—this is Miami—sunglasses are just part of the landscape. As long as no one knows who we are, there's no reason to—

"Excuse me . . . sir?" a raspy voice asks. He puts a strong hand on my shoulder.

Wheeling around, I spot a black man in a skycap uniform. He looks me dead in the eye and slowly hands me a folded-up sheet of paper. His voice is dry and cold. "This is for you . . ." he says.

I take the paper and unfold it in a frenzy. Inside are three words written in black pen: "Wait for me." No signature at the bottom.

The block print handwriting reminds me of Charlie's, but it's a little off. Like someone was trying to copy it.

I look over my shoulder. The man with the sunglasses is gone.

"Who gave you this?" I ask the skycap.

"Can't say," he tells me. "They said it'd ruin the surprise."

"*They?*" I ask anxiously. "Who's *they?*"

The skycap turns and walks away. "Merry Christmas . . ."

A loud buzzer rips through the room. *An alarm.* A second

later, the conveyor belt starts to whir. Our luggage is finally here.

Catching my breath, I stare at the skycap, who rolls his luggage cart right up to the belt. All around him, fellow passengers angle into place. A college kid with a "Capitalism Rocks" T-shirt. A lawyer with a pen stain on the pocket of his suit. An angry-looking mom with a New York City fake-tan. I swear, everyone glances up and studies me.

I look down at the note, which is shaking in my hand. What the hell is going on? We had a plan—in and out together. There's no way he'd go off on his own . . . not unless someone made him . . .

My whole chest caves. I rush to the closest door, angling my way through the crowd—but the moment I step outside, I'm pummeled by a wave of Florida heat that reaches straight into my lungs. As a puddle of sweat soaks the small of my back, I realize for the first time I'm still wearing my overcoat. Throwing my arms back, I fight furiously to get it off. All I want to do is find Charlie.

Behind me, someone else grabs my shoulder. I tighten my fist, ready to swing. Then I hear the voice.

"Y'okay there, Ahab?" Charlie asks.

I spin around, checking for myself. There he is—dimples and his goofy grin. I don't know whether to kill him or hug him, so I settle on a hard shove in the shoulder. "What the h—" A woman by the taxi stand glances our way, and I drop it down to a whisper. "What the hell is wrong with you? Where were you?"

"Didn't you get my note?" he whispers back.

"So you . . ." I steer him aside, down the taxi line and out of earshot. "Were you even listening to what Oz said? No contact with anyone! That includes skycaps!" I hiss.

"Well, no offense, but this was an emergency."

"What kind of emergency?"

He looks up, but won't answer.

"What?" I ask. "What'd you do?"

Again, no answer.

"Oh, jeez, Charlie, you didn't . . ."

"I don't wanna get into it, Oliver."

"You called her, didn't you?"

His voice is so low, it almost disappears. "Don't worry about it—I got it under control."

"We said we weren't going to call her!" I insist.

"She's our mother, Ollie—and more important, one of us still lives with her. If I didn't check in, she would've been grabbing her chest in a heart attack."

"Yeah, well what do you think'll upset her more—missing us for a few nights, or setting up our funerals after the Service hunts us down and buries us? They'll be tracing every call."

"Really? I didn't even think about that—even though it's in, like, every *single* man-on-the-run movie that's ever been done." Losing the sarcasm, he adds, "Can you please trust me for once? Believe me, I did it smart. Whoever's listening . . . they're not gonna hear a word."

32

"How we doin'?" Gallo asked.

"Just gimme a sec," DeSanctis said from the passenger seat. In his lap, his fingers pounded the keyboard of what looked like a standard laptop. A closer examination, however, revealed that the only working keys were the numbers along the top, which DeSanctis used to adjust the receiver that was perfectly hidden inside. It was just like tuning a radio: Find the right frequency and you'll hear your favorite song. Hunting and pecking across the row, he typed in the numbers the Technical Security Division guys gave him: 3.8 gigahertz . . . 4.3 gigahertz . . . The closer they got to microwave frequencies, the harder it'd be for outside parties to intercept. Add some encryption with a frequency-hopping signal and it was next to impossible. With the signal always moving across the dial—it was now a radio station built for two.

Stabbing the keys, he punched in the final digits. Onscreen, a window in the bottom left corner blinked to life. As it faded in and the colors became crisp, they had a perfect digital feed of Maggie Caruso bent over the coffee table in the living room, looking like she was about to throw up on it. Her tight fists rubbed against the table. Her legs buckled and she slowly sank to her knees.

"What's wrong?" Gallo asked. "Is she sick?"

"Just another second . . ." DeSanctis keyed in one final number and Mrs. Caruso's voice echoed from the built-in speakers.

". . . ank you . . . thank you, God!" she shouted as the tears flooded. She shook her head and unleashed a pained, but unmistakable smile. "Just take care of them . . . please take care of them . . ."

"What the hell is going on?" Gallo barked.

DeSanctis's mouth dropped open.

"They called her!" Gallo blurted. "The bastards just called her!"

Furiously clicking at the keyboard, DeSanctis opened another window on the laptop. *Caruso, Margaret—Platform: Telephony.* "That's impossible," DeSanctis said, reading from the screen. "I got everything right here—it's blank—nothing incoming; nothing outgoing."

"Fax? E-mail?"

"Not for the seamstress. Doesn't even have a computer."

"Maybe the brothers called it in to a neighbor."

DeSanctis pointed to the video picture on the screen. In the background, behind Mrs. Caruso, was a clear view of her front door. "Tech boys were watching since we got here. Even for the two minutes it took to set this up, we'd see someone coming and going . . ."

"Then how the hell did they get to her?"

"I have no idea—maybe—"

"Don't give me *maybes!* This isn't time for guessing games!" Gallo shouted. "She's clearly got something in there that's letting her talk to her boys—now I don't care if a neighbor's tapping the radiator in Morse code, I want to know what it is!"

"She's clearly got something in there that's letting her talk to her boys—now I don't care if a neighbor's tapping the radiator in Morse code, I want to know what it is!"

Staring up the block at Gallo and DeSanctis's car, Joey sat back in her seat and lowered the volume on her walkie-talkie-sized receiver. For a single mike stuffed in a dome light, it did the job just fine.

On her lap, she flipped up the screen of her laptop computer and opened up the photos of the offices she had downloaded from her digital camera. Oliver's, Charlie's, Shep's, Lapidus's, Quincy's, and Mary's. Six in all, plus the common areas. One by one, she studied each room, raking through the details. The cheap reproduction banker's lamp on Oliver's desk . . . the Kermit the Frog poster in Charlie's cubicle . . . the photos on Shep's wall . . . even the lack of personal artifacts on Lapidus's desk.

"Sounds like you were right," Noreen interrupted through the earpiece. "They're already calling in to mom."

"Yeah . . . I guess."

Noreen knew that tone on her boss. "What's wrong?"

"Nothing," Joey said, still digitally flipping through the photos. "It's just . . . if Gallo and DeSanctis are treating this like a real manhunt, why're they the only two people doing surveillance?"

"What do you mean?"

"It's just protocol, Noreen. The FBI may bumble it, but when it comes to surveillance, Secret Service is top dog. When they sit on a house, they send four people at a minimum. Why's it suddenly two guys sitting alone in a car?"

"Who knows? They could be shorthanded . . . or over budget . . . maybe the rest are coming tomorrow . . ."

"Or maybe they don't want anyone else around," Joey challenged.

"C'mon, now—you really believe that?"

Joey stopped to think. Through the receiver, she could hear Gallo and DeSanctis arguing.

"When Shep was killed, they lost a former agent," Noreen pointed out. "Ten bucks says that's why they're keeping it personal."

"I hope you're right," Joey said, pulling the receiver in close. "But if I were Charlie and Oliver, I'd be praying we're the ones who find them first."

33

Lying on my stomach and hiding from the morning sun, I hug my pillow like a best friend and refuse to open my eyes. The futon's about as comfortable as a sack of doorknobs, but it's still not as bad as the garbage truck outside, which is scraping against my eardrums like broken glass.

"Clear!" a garbage man shouts as the truck churns up the block.

I roll over. My left arm's asleep. And just as I blink myself into the day, I swear . . . for the tiniest of seconds . . . I have no idea where I am. That's when I open my eyes.

Rank beige carpet. Stale bug-spray smell. Rotting vinyl floor in the filthy kitchenette. Damn. The sight alone floods it back. Shep . . . the money . . . Duckworth. I was hoping it was a bad dream. It's not. It's our life.

Next to me, Charlie's still asleep, cuddling with his own pillow and content in his drool pool. I pull the tattered blanket up to his chin and make my way to the shower.

Ten minutes later, it's time for Charlie to do the same.

"Charlie! Get up!" I call from the bathroom.

No response.

"C'mon, Charlie! Get up!"

He shrugs it off and finally rolls over to face me. Rubbing the crust from his eyes, he doesn't remember where he is either. Then he looks around and realizes we're in the same bad dream. "Crap," he mutters.

"There's no hot water," I tell him, drying my Johnny Cash hair with a fistful of left-behind paper towels.

"I'll be sure to drop a note in the landlord's suggestion box."

In New York, they call it a studio. Here, it's an efficiency. To me, it's a no-bedroom rathole. But last night, when we were searching through the neighborhood at two in the morning, it was exactly what we needed: located on a side street, a "For Rent" sign out front, and a light on in the apartment marked "Manager." Anywhere else, they would've been suspicious and called the cops. But on the sketchy outskirts of Miami's beyond-trendy South Beach, we're business as usual. Between the drug dealers and the illegal foreigners, they're well accustomed to tenants who show up at two A.M.

"C'mon, we should get going," I say, pulling on a pair of fresh underwear. "I want to get there early."

He sits up in bed and rolls his eyes. "What else is new?"

Stepping back into the main room, I finish getting dressed. Outside, the sun is shining, but we can barely see through the papers that cover the windows. Last night, in the dark, Charlie thought they were broken vertical blinds. Today, we see reality. Ripped pages from a free Budweiser girls-in-bikinis calendar Scotch-taped to every window. Whoever was here last didn't want to be seen. Neither do we. The calendar stays where it is.

"Let's go, Charlie—you're up," I say as I move back to the bathroom. I turn on the shower. That's what mom used to do to get us moving.

"Those tricks don't work anymore," he warns me.

Ten minutes later, he paper-towels himself dry and jumps into his own new pair of boxers.

"All set?" I ask.

"Almost . . ." He reaches back into the gym bag and feels around for something inside.

"What're you looking for?" I ask even though I know the answer. The metal box with Gallo's gun.

"Nothing," Charlie tells me, digging even deeper. Unable to find it, he starts yanking clothes from the bag. Within seconds, the bag's empty. "Ollie—the box . . . it's not here . . ."

"Relax," I say. He looks over his shoulder, and I pull up the edge of my untucked shirt. I've got the gun stuffed in the waist of my pants.

"Since when're you—?"

"Can we go now?" I interrupt.

Charlie cocks his head at my tone. "Let me guess," he says. "There's a new sheriff in town."

I don't bother to answer. Turning around, I head outside. Charlie's a few steps behind. Ready or not, Duckworth—here we come.

"What're you doing?" Charlie calls out, chasing me as I make a sharp right on Sixth Street and accelerate up the block. Straight ahead, early-rising holiday tourists and late-to-work locals crisscross along Washington Avenue. Here on the side streets, we're safe. Half a block up, we're out in the open. Even Charlie wouldn't take that risk, which is why he grabs the back of my shirt and tugs me to a sudden halt. "Are you drinking suntan lotion?" he asks. "I thought we were going to Duckwor—?"

"Don't say it," I cut him off, scanning the block around us. "Trust me, this is just as important."

Wriggling my arm free, I hustle to the corner, where a long row of newspaper vending machines stretches up the block. *Miami Herald*, *el Herald*, *USA Today* . . . and the one I fly toward—the *New York Times*. I shove four coins in the machine's throat, pull down on the door, and reach for a paper from the middle of the stack.

"Why don't you ever take the top one?" Charlie asks.

Ignoring the little-brother challenge, I grab my middle paper.

"No, you're absolutely right," he continues. "The top one's got cooties." As the newspaper machine slams shut, he shakes his head.

"Let's go," I call out, rushing back down Sixth Street. As we walk, I open the paper and flip through the front section.

"Are we in there?" Charlie asks.

I keep flipping, scouring for any mention of yesterday's events. No money; no embezzlement; no murder. To be honest, I'm not surprised. Lapidus is keeping this on lockdown from the press. Still, some things run every day. I stop on the side street and fold the paper back. Right at Obituaries.

"Lemme see," Charlie says, stepping next to me.

Standing under a dried-out palm tree, I hold the left half of the page; Charlie holds the right. We both find it alphabetically. On most days, I read and he skims. Today it's reverse. "Graves—Shepard . . . 37 . . . of Brooklyn . . . Vice President of Security . . . Greene & Greene . . . survived by wife, Sherry . . . mother, Bonnie . . . sister, Claire . . . memorial service to be announced . . ."

"I didn't know he was married," Charlie says, already lost in Shep's life. But the more he reads on . . . "Those revisionist bastards," he blurts. "It doesn't even say he was in the Service."

"Charlie . . ."

"Don't *Charlie* me! You didn't know him, Ollie—that was his life!"

"I'm not saying it wasn't—I'm just asking you to pay attention for once! This isn't about his résumé . . . it's about what's missing from the picture." Catching myself, I turn it down to a whisper. *"Three hundred million gets lifted, and it doesn't even make the gossip columns? A former Secret Service agent is shot in the chest and no one reports a word!?* Don't you see what they're doing? For these guys, a fake obit is the easy part. Whatever they say, people believe it. And whatever really happened . . . it's all being erased. That's what they're gonna do with us, Charlie. They shake the Etch-A-Sketch and the whole picture disappears. Then they write in whatever they want. *Suspects found with millions—investigation points to murder.* That's the new reality, Charlie. And by the time they're done scribbling, there'll be no way for us to change it."

I stare Charlie down and let it burrow into his brain. At the exact same moment, we both head toward Tenth Street. Duckworth's only a few blocks away.

With three hundred million in his account and retirement on his mind, Marty Duckworth could've picked anything. I predicted Art Deco townhouse; Charlie said Mediterranean bungalow. We couldn't be more wrong if it were a contest.

"I don't believe it," Charlie says, staring across the street at the one-story 1960s rambler. Beaten by weather and covered in peeling light pink paint, the building is clearly past its prime.

"It's definitely the right address," I confirm as I check it for the third and fourth time.

Charlie nods, but stays silent. After everything it took to get here—just the sight of it . . . this is finally it.

"Maybe we should come back later," he suggests.

"Come back later? Charlie, this is the guy with all the answers. Now c'mon, all we have to do is ring the doorbell . . ." I step off the curb and cross the street. When Charlie doesn't follow, I stop mid-step and look back over my shoulder. "Are you okay?"

"Of course," he says. But he still refuses to cross the street.

"You sure?"

This time, he takes slightly longer to answer. Charlie doesn't like fear on me—and he hates it on himself. "I'm fine," he insists. "Just ring the bell."

Weaving past the overgrown shrubbery and around the classic blue Beetle that's parked out front, I race up the front walk, open the humidity-rusted screen door, and jam an anxious finger at the doorbell.

No answer.

I ring it again, leaning against the open screen door and trying to look relaxed.

Still no answer.

Hiking myself up on my tiptoes, I crane my neck, struggling to peek through the diamond-shaped windowpane that's set into the door.

"What's in there?" Charlie asks.

I press my nose against the pollen on the glass, trying to get a better view . . . and then from inside . . . locks clunk open. The doorknob turns. I jump back. It's already too late.

"Can I *help* you?" a young woman asks, opening the door. She's got black ringlet hair, thin lips, and a tiny, pointed nose. My eyes go straight to her beat-up jeans and spaghetti-strap white tank top.

"I-I'm sorry," I begin. "I wasn't trying to . . . we were just looking for a friend . . ."

"We're trying to find Marty Duckworth," Charlie blurts.

I thank him for the save as the woman's body language shifts—her brow unfurrows; her shoulders sag. "You're friends of his?"

"Yeah," I say cautiously. "Why?"

She pauses a moment, choosing the words carefully. "Marty Duckworth died six months ago."

The statement floats in the air, and I stare up at it, mesmerized. It's almost like I'm waiting for Duckworth himself to jump out and scream, *"April Fool's—I'm right here!"* Needless to say, it never happens. I look around, but nothing's in focus. I-It can't be. Not after all this . . .

"So he's really dead?" Charlie asks, already starting to panic.

"I'm sorry," she offers, reading his expression. "I didn't mean to . . ."

"It's okay," he says. "You couldn't have—"

"Did you know him?" I interrupt.

"Excuse me?"

"Duckworth—did you know him?"

"No," she stammers. "But—"

"Then how do you know he's dead?"

"I-I just remember his name from the deed," she adds. "It was an estate sale."

"What about a forwarding address? Is there somewhere we can contact him?"

Unsure of what to say, the woman shakes her head, clearly overwhelmed. I don't care—we didn't come this far to not get answers. "I'm sorry," she repeats. "There's no forwarding address . . . he's dead."

The words don't make sense. "It's impossible," I tell her as my voice cracks. "What abou—"

"He's just upset," Charlie says. He leans in and pinches

the skin on my back. "We should get going," he adds through gritted teeth. Fake-smiling at the woman, he gives her a quick wave. "Thanks again for all the help . . ."

"I'm really sorry," she calls out as we walk away. "I'm sorry for your loss."

"Yeah," Charlie whispers as he shoves me up the block. "That makes three of us."

"What's wrong with you?" Charlie asks as we cut back through our courtyard. He steps over the sprawling hose and ducks past the rotating sprinkler that's spraying everything in sight. Checking to see that no one's around, he makes a quick beeline for our new apartment. "Why'd you go after her like that?"

"She might've known something."

"Are you really that delusional?" Charlie asks, racing inside. He watches uncomfortably as I pace back and forth between the living room and kitchenette. "Didn't you see her reaction, Ollie—she was floored. Newsflash at eleven: Duckworth's dead. End of story."

"It can't be," I insist. As I say the words, I hear my own voice stuttering.

Charlie hears it too. "Ollie, I know you've always had more to lose, but—"

"What if there's something we're missing?"

"What could we possibly miss? They told us he was dead in New York . . . we came down here to see for ourselves . . . and she tells us the same thing. Duckworth's gone, bro. Show's over—time to find a new drummer."

Still pacing, I stare down at the ground. "Maybe we should go back and talk to her again . . ."

"Ollie . . ."

"Duckworth could be hiding somewhere else . . ."

"Are you even listening? The man's dead!"

"Don't say that!" I explode.

"Then stop acting like a lunatic!" he shoots back. "The sun doesn't rise and set on Marty Duckworth!"

"You think that's all it's about? Marty Duckworth!? I could give a crap about Duckworth—I just want my old life back! I want my apartment, and my job, and my clothes, and my old hair . . ." I grip a fistful of black follicles from the back of my head. "I want my life back, Charlie! And unless we figure out what's going on, Gallo and DeSanctis are going t—"

A loud splat smacks against the window. We both duck down. The noise stays loud—rat-a-tat-tatting against the glass—like someone breaking in. I look up to see who, but the only thing there is a starburst of water. It pummels the calendar-covered glass and quickly drips down the pane. Sprinkler . . . just the sprinkler.

"Someone probably tripped on the hose . . ." Charlie says.

I'm not taking any chances. "Check outside," I insist.

I run to the small window in the kitchenette; he goes for the one near the door. The sprinkler's still barreling against the glass. I peel back a piece of the calendar and peek outside . . . just as a blurred figure darts below the windowsill. I jump back, almost falling over.

"What? What is it?" Charlie asks.

"Someone's out there!"

"Are you sure?"

"*I just saw him!*"

Staggering backwards, Charlie does his best to fight fear, but even he's not that good.

"Do you have the—?"

"Right here," I answer, reaching down and grabbing the

gun from my pants. I cock back the pin and put a finger on the trigger.

Stuck in the kitchen, Charlie rummages through the drawers, looking for a weapon. Knives, scissors, anything. Top to bottom, he rips open each drawer. Empty. Empty. Empty. The last one slides out and his eyes go wide. Inside is a rusted machete, broken in half so it fits perfectly in the drawer.

"Blessed are the drug dealers," he says, yanking it out.

As he takes off, I follow him through the main room and into the bathroom. Just like we worked out last night. Tiny efficiencies may be too small for back doors . . . but they still have back windows. Leaping on the toilet, he cranks open the cheap window and punches out the screen. I hop up next to him.

"You go first," Charlie says, cupping his hands to boost me up.

"No, you."

He won't budge.

"*Charlie* . . ." The tone and my scolding eyes are all mom. He knows it's been ingrained since birth—protect your little brother.

Realizing it's a fight he'll never win, he tosses out the machete and steps into my boost. Up and out—he's gone in an instant. Another perfect landing. I follow, though I almost kill myself on the landing.

"Ready to run?" he asks, rechecking the narrow concrete alley created by the building ours backs up to. On our left is a swinging metal gate that leads back to the street; on our right is an open path that snakes around to the main courtyard—right where they're hiding. With a shared glance, we scramble toward the gate . . . and quickly spot the metal chain and padlock that keeps it shut tight.

"Damn," Charlie whispers, smacking the lock.

I motion with the gun. *I can shoot it open.*

He shakes his head. *Are you crazed? They'll hear in a second!* Without thinking, he takes off toward the other end of the alley, and I grab him by the arm.

"You're gonna run right into them," I whisper.

"Not if they're already inside . . . besides, you got a better way out?"

I look around, but there's no arguing with impossibility.

C'mon, Charlie motions. He speeds down the alley, sticking to the patches of dried-out grass to keep quiet. At the edge of the building, he stops and turns my way. *Ready?*

I nod, and he peeks around the first corner. *All clear,* he signals, waving me forward.

Like burglars in our own backyard, we slip down behind the building, ducking under the windowsills. Around the next corner is where we saw him. I hear the stream from the sprinkler still gushing against the glass. The sound drowns out our own footsteps . . . and whoever's waiting for us there.

"Let me go first," I whisper.

He shakes his head and shoves me back. He's done letting me play protector. I don't care. Squeezing in next to him, I check the ground for stray shadows and slowly stick my head out. Around the corner, a discarded jump rope sits on the lawn, right next to a deflated beach ball. I scan the courtyard from tree to tree, but I can barely hear myself think. The sprinkler still pounds against the window. Charlie's breathing heavy next to me. No one's in sight, but I can't shake the feeling that something isn't right. Still, there's no choice. It's the only way out. Charlie licks a puddle of sweat from the dimple above his lip and puts up his fist. Counting by fingers, he nods my way. *One . . . two . . .*

We tear out of there at full speed, ducking under the sprinkler. My heart's thundering . . . all I see is the street . . . almost there . . . the metal gate's in sight . . .

"Where you off to, Cinderella—late for the ball?" a voice asks from our front steps.

Whirling around, we stop in our tracks. I lift the gun; Charlie raises the machete.

"Easy there, cowboy," she says, hands already in the air. Forget the Service. It's the woman from Duckworth's.

"What're you doing here?" Charlie challenges.

She doesn't answer. Her eyes are fixed on my gun. "You want to tell me who you really are?" she asks.

"This isn't about you," I warn.

"Why were you asking about him?"

"So you *do* know Duckworth?" I blurt.

"I asked you a question . . ."

"So did I," I shoot back. I wave the gun to get her attention. She doesn't know us well enough to decide if she should call the bluff.

"How did you know him?" Charlie demands.

She lowers her hands, but never stops staring at me. "You really don't know?" she asks. "Marty Duckworth was my father."

34

Maggie Caruso was never a good sleeper. Even when things were going well—during her honeymoon in the Poconos—Maggie had trouble mustering five hours of continuous sleep. As she got older—when the credit card companies started calling at the end of the month—she'd be lucky to get three hours straight. And last night, with her sons gone, she sat up in bed, clawed at the sheets, and barely made two—which was exactly what Gallo was counting on when he brought her in this morning.

"Thought you'd like some coffee," Gallo said as he entered the bright white interrogation room. Unlike yesterday, DeSanctis wasn't by his side. Today it was just Gallo, wearing his standard ill-fitting gray suit and a surprisingly warm grin. He handed Maggie the coffee with both hands. "Careful, it's hot," he said, actually sounding concerned.

"Thanks," Maggie replied, watching him carefully and studying his new attitude.

"So how're you feeling?" Gallo asked as he pulled up a chair. Like before, he sat right next to her.

"I'm fine," Maggie said, hoping to keep it short. "Now is there something I can help you with?"

"Actually, there is . . ." He let the words dangle in the air. It was a tactic he learned right when he started in the Service. When it came to getting people to talk, there was no better weapon than silence.

"Agent Gallo, if you're looking for Charlie and Oliver, you should know that neither of them came home last night."

"Really?" Gallo asked. "So you still don't know where they are?"

Maggie nodded.

"And you still don't know if they're okay?"

"Not a clue," she said quickly.

Crossing his arms, Gallo once again embraced the silence.

"What?" Maggie asked. "You don't believe me?"

"Maggie, did Oliver and Charlie contact you last night?"

For the slightest of seconds, Maggie paused. "I don't know what you're—"

"Don't lie to me," Gallo warned. His eyes narrowed and the nice guy disappeared. "If you lie to me, we'll only take it out on them."

Clenching her jaw, she ignored the threat. "I swear to you, I don't know anything."

For the third time, Gallo let silence do its work. Thirty seconds of nothing. "Maggie, do you have any idea what you're up against?" he finally asked.

"I already told you—"

"Let me catch you up on a case we worked on last year," he interrupted, cutting her off. "We had a target who was using a typewriter to stay in contact with another suspect. It's pretty ingenious—destroy the ribbon, fax it from an untraceable location—nothing for us to pick up on, right? Too bad for the target, all electric typewriters emit their own electromagnetic emanations. It may not be as easy to read as a computer, but our tech boys had no problem picking it up. And once we told them the make and model number of the typewriter, it took less than three hours to re-create the message from the sound that each key makes. He hit *A*, we saw *A*. We had 'em both locked up within the week."

Maggie squared her shoulders, struggling to hold it together.

"They can't outrun us," Gallo added. "It's only a matter of time." Refusing to let up, he added, "If you help us find them, we can work out a deal, Maggie—but if I have to do this myself . . . the only way you'll ever see your boys is through two-inch-thick glass. That is, assuming they make it that far." In one smooth motion, Gallo slowly scratched at the back of his neck, and the front of his jacket spread open. Right there, Maggie caught a glimpse of Gallo's gun in its leather holster. Staring straight down at her, Gallo didn't have to say a word.

Her chin was trembling. She tried to get up, but her legs were dead.

"It's over, Maggie—just tell us where they are."

She turned away and pressed her lips together. The tears streamed down her cheeks.

"It's the only way to help them," Gallo pushed. "Otherwise, their blood's on your hands."

Wiping her eyes with her palm, Maggie searched desperately for something—anything—to focus on. But the stark whiteness of the walls kept leading back to Gallo.

"It's okay," he added, leaning in close. "Just say the words, and we'll make sure they're safe." He put a hand on her shoulder and slowly lifted her chin. "Be the good mother, Maggie. It's the only way to help them. Now where are Charlie and Oliver?"

Staring up, Maggie felt the world melt in front of her. All that was left were her sons. They were all she had. And all she'd ever needed. Sitting up straight, Maggie Caruso jerked her shoulder out of Gallo's reach and finally opened her mouth. "I don't know what you're talking about," she said, her voice measured and smooth. "I haven't heard from them at all."

"Don't be such a momma's boy," Joey scolded through the phone. She sat back in her car and stared across the street at Maggie's building. "Just tell me what's in the files."

"You know I can't do that," Randall Adenauer said in his native Virginian accent. "Ask again though."

"Oh, c'mon," Joey moaned, rolling her eyes. Still, if she wanted a law-enforcement-level search of Charlie's and Oliver's records, there was only one way to play the game: "Are these the type of people I want to hire?" Joey asked.

There was a pause on the other line. As the Special Agent in Charge of the FBI's Violent Crimes Unit, Adenauer had access to the FBI's best files and databases. And as an old friend of Joey's father, he also had a few chits that were long overdue for payback. "Absolutely," he said. "I'd hire both of them today."

"Really?" Joey asked, surprised, but hardly shocked. "So everything's clean?"

"Squeaky," he answered. "The younger one had a few snags for loitering, but there's nothing after that. According to our records, these two are angels. Why, what were you expecting?"

This time, Joey was the one who paused. "No . . . nothing," she replied. Before she could say another word, there was a beep on the other line. Caller ID showed Noreen. "Listen, I should run," Joey added. "I'll speak to you later. Thanks, Poochie."

With a click, she was on with her assistant. "Gallo and mom back yet?" Noreen asked.

Joey glanced down at her passenger seat, where a digital screen showed a blinking blue triangle moving across an electronic map toward the Brooklyn Bridge. "They're on their way back now," she relayed. "What about you? Anything interesting?"

"Just some old college records from the bank's personnel office. Academically, Oliver's grades were good, but not great . . ."

"Little fish, big pond . . . new level of competition . . ."

". . . but according to his résumé, he was working two different jobs at the time, one of them his own business. He sold T-shirts one semester, set up limo rides another, even had his own moving business at the end of each year. You know the type."

"Forever the young entrepreneur. What about Charlie?"

"Two years at art school, then he dropped out and finished up at City College. In both, though, the worst kind of C student: Straight As in the subjects he cared about; Cs and Ds in the rest."

"And why'd he leave? Fear of success, or fear of failure?"

"No idea—but he's clearly the wild card."

"Actually, Oliver's the wild card," Joey pointed out.

"You think?"

"Take another glance at the details. Charlie may be better on a date, but when it comes to taking risks, Oliver's the one who stepped further into a world that wasn't his." Joey waited, but Noreen didn't argue. "Now what else did you find besides the transcripts?"

"That was it," Noreen said. "Zip, zada, zilch. Except for mom's apartment, all Charlie and Oliver have are some overdue credit cards and a now empty bank account."

"And you checked everywhere?"

"Do I listen when you speak? Driver's license, Social Security, insurance records, corporate records, property records, and every other piece of our private lives that the government's been selling to the credit agencies for years, but only now—as they blame it on the Internet—is finally getting some press play. Otherwise, nothing fishy. How'd the FBI go?"

"Same dance—no convictions, no warrants, no recent arrests."

"So that's it?" Noreen asked.

"Are you kidding? This is just the first mile. Now when did Fudge say we'd have credit card and phone details?"

"Any minute," Noreen answered, her voice quickening. "Oh, and there is one thing you might find interesting. Remember that pharmacy you wanted me to check out? Well, I called up, said I was from Oliver's insurance company, and asked if they had any outstanding prescriptions for a Mr. Caruso."

"And?"

"Nothing for Oliver . . ."

"Damn . . ."

"Though they did have one for a Caruso named Charles." Joey stopped. "Please tell me you . . ."

"Oh, I'm sorry—did I say *Oliver?* I meant *Charles*. That's right—Charlie Caruso."

"Beautiful, beautiful," Joey sang. "So what'd you find?"

"Well, he's got a prescription for something called mexiletine."

"Mexiletine?"

"That's exactly what I said—then I called the office of the prescribing physician, who was only too happy to help out with an ongoing insurance investigation . . ."

"You're really getting good at this, aren't you?" Joey asked. "And the final result?"

"Charlie has a ventricular tachycardia."

"A what?"

"A heart arrhythmia. He's had it since he was fourteen," Noreen explained. "That's where all the hospital bills came from. All this time, we thought they were mom's. They're not. They're all Charlie's. The only reason they're in mom's name is because he was a minor at the time. Too bad for them, when the first attack hit, it took a hundred-and-ten-thousand-dollar operation to fix him up. Apparently, he's got some bad electrical wiring in his heart that doesn't let the blood pump correctly."

"So it's serious?"

"Only if he misses his medication."

"Aw, crap," Joey said, shaking her head. "You think he has it with him?"

"They took off straight from Grand Central—I don't think he has a second pair of socks, much less his daily dose of mexiletine."

"And how long can he go without taking it?"

"Hard to say—the doctor guessed three or four days under perfect conditions—less if he's running around or under any stress."

"You mean like taking off and scrambling for your life?"

"Exactly," Noreen said. "From here on in, Charlie's clock is ticking. And if we don't find him soon—forget the money and the murder—those'll be the least of this kid's problems."

35

He's your father?" Charlie blurts.

"So he's alive?" I add.

The woman looks at both of us, but stays with me. "He's been dead for six months," she says almost a bit too calmly. "Now what'd you want with him?" Her voice is high-pitched, but strong—not a bit intimidated. I step forward; she doesn't step back.

"Why'd you lie about who you were?" I ask.

To our surprise, she lets out an amused grin and runs her foot against the top of the grass. It's the first time I realize she's barefoot. "Funny, I was about to ask you the same thing."

"You could've said you were his daughter," Charlie accuses.

"And you could've said why you were looking for him in the first place."

Biting my bottom lip, I know a stalemate when I see one. If we want information, we need to give it. "Walter Harvey," I say, extending a handshake and my fake name.

"Gillian Duckworth," she says, shaking back.

Across the street and up the block, the mailman's making his morning rounds. Charlie hides his machete behind his back and motions my way. "Uh . . . maybe we should take this inside . . ."

"Yeah . . . that's not a bad idea," I say, stuffing the gun back in my pants. "Why don't you come in for some coffee?"

"With you two? After you pull a gun and a pirate's knife? Do I look like I want my photo on a milk carton?" She turns to leave and Charlie glares at me. *She's all we've got.*

"Please just wait," I say, reaching out for her arm.

She pulls away, but never raises her voice. "Nice meeting you, Walter. Have a good life."

"Gillian . . ."

"We can explain," Charlie calls out.

She doesn't even slow down. The mailman disappears into the apartment next door. Last chance. Knowing we need the info, Charlie goes nuclear.

"We think your father may've been murdered."

Gillian stops dead in her tracks and turns around, head cocked. She brushes three black ringlets from her face.

"Just give us five minutes," I plead. "After that, you can wave us goodbye." Ripping a page from the Lapidus Book of Pigheaded Negotiations, I charge for our front door and never give her a chance to say no. Gillian's right behind me.

As I step into our efficiency, I wait for her to make a crack or some backhanded remark. The barren walls . . . the paper-covered windows . . . she's gotta say something. But she doesn't. Like a cat exploring, she takes a quick lap around the main room. Her thin arms sway at her side; her fingers pick at the frayed pockets of her faded jeans. I offer her the foldable chair next to me in the kitchen. Charlie offers the futon. She heads toward me. But instead of sitting in the seat, she props herself up on the white Formica countertop. Her bare feet dangle off the edge. My gaze lingers a second too long, and Charlie abruptly clears his throat. *Oh, please,* he says with a glance. *Like you've never been in a girls' locker room.*

I shake my head and turn back to Gillian. "So you were telling us about your dad . . ." I begin.

"Actually, I wasn't telling you anything," she responds. "I just want to know why you think he was murdered."

I look to Charlie. *Be careful,* he warns with a nod. But even he realizes we have to start somewhere.

"Up until yesterday, the two of us were living in New York, working at a bank," I begin hesitantly. "Then this past Friday, we're going through these old accounts—"

"—and we came across one registered to a Marty Duckworth," Charlie interrupts, already flying. I'm about to cut him off, but decide against it. We both know who's the better liar. "Anyway, as far as we can tell, your father's account was past its heyday—it was an old abandoned account in the system. But once we found it, and once we reported it to the head of Security, well . . . yesterday there were three of us on the run. Today there're only two." Barely able to finish, Charlie turns away and falls silent. He's still haunted by what happened. And as he retells the story, it's clear he still hears Shep . . . falling as he crashed into the wooden slats. My brother's eyes say it all. *God, why'd we do something so stupid?*

Charlie looks up at Gillian, who's staring straight at him. I hadn't really noticed it before—she rarely turns away; she's always watching. Their eyes connect, and just then, she pulls back. Her feet are no longer swinging. She sits on her hands, perfectly still. Whatever she saw in my brother, it's something she knows all too well.

"You okay?" I ask her.

Gillian nods, unable to get the words out. "I knew . . . I-I knew it . . ."

"Knew what?"

At first she hesitates, refusing to answer. We're still complete strangers. But the longer we sit there . . . the more she realizes we're as desperate as she is.

"What did you know?" I persist.

"That something was wrong. I knew it the moment I got the report." Reading the confusion on our faces, she explains, "Six months ago, it's like any other morning. I'm pouring myself some Cheerios, then suddenly the phone rings. They tell me my dad died in a bicycle accident—that he was riding over the Rickenbacker Causeway when a car veered out of its lane . . ." She shifts in her seat as she relives the memory. Burying it back down, she adds, "Have you ever seen the Rickenbacker?"

We shake our heads simultaneously.

"It's a bridge that's as steep as a small mountain. When I was sixteen, it was a tough ride. My dad was sixty-two. He had trouble tackling the paved road along the beach. There's no way he was biking the Rickenbacker."

We're all silent. Charlie's the first to react. "Did the cops—?"

"The day after the accident, I drove to his house to pick out the suit he was going to be buried in. When I opened the door, the place looked like it was hit by a hurricane. Closets ripped apart . . . drawers overturned . . . but as far as I could tell, nothing was taken except his computer. The best part is, instead of sending the police, the break-in was investigated by—"

"The Secret Service," I say.

Gillian turns with a sideways glance. "How'd you know that?"

"Who do you think's chasing us?"

That's all it takes. Like she did with Charlie, Gillian locks her gaze on me. I can't tell if she's looking for the truth, or just a connection. Either way, she's found it. Her soft blue eyes stare straight through me.

Charlie lets out a loud, fake cough. "So what do you think they were looking for?" he asks.

"Who? The Service?" I ask.

"Of course, the Service."

"I never found out," Gillian explains, her voice still soft and lost. "When I called their Miami office, they had no record of an investigation. I told them I met the agents, but without their names, there was nothing they could do."

"So that's it? You just gave up?" Charlie asks. "Didn't you think that was a weensy bit odd?"

"Charlie . . . !"

"No, he's right," Gillian says. "But you have to understand, when it came to my dad's business, secrets were just part of the game. That's just . . . that's just how he was."

Charlie watches her closely, but I give her a reassuring nod. When it comes to our own jackass dad, I've been able to forgive. Charlie never forgets. "It's okay," I say. "I know what it's like." As I reach out to touch her arm, Gillian's bra strap falls from under her tank top and sinks to her shoulder. She lifts it back into place with perfect grace.

"Okay, hold on," Charlie interrupts. "I'm still having trouble with the timeline: Your dad died six months ago, right? So was that right after he moved from New York?"

"New York?" Gillian asks, confused. "He never lived in New York."

He glances at me and studies Gillian. "You sure about that? He's never had an apartment in Manhattan?"

"Not that I know of," she says, never one to insist. "He took a few business trips there every once in a while. I know he was scraping cash together for one of them this past summer—but otherwise, he's lived in Florida his entire life."

His entire life. The words ricochet through my brain like pinballs off a bumper. It doesn't make sense. All this time, we thought we were looking for a New Yorker who made some cash and moved to Florida. Now we find out he's a Floridian who could barely afford the few trips he'd taken to New York. Marty Duckworth, what the hell were you up to?

"Can someone please tell me what's going on?" Gillian asks as her eyes shift nervously between us.

I nod to Charlie; he nods to me. Time to give her another piece of the puzzle. It takes Charlie ten minutes to tell her everything we know about her father's run-down New York apartment.

"I don't understand," she says, once again sitting on her hands. "He owns a place in New York?"

"Actually, if I had to guess, I'd bet he was renting," I clarify.

"How long did you say he was away last summer?" Charlie jumps in.

"I-I don't know," Gillian sputters. "Two and a half . . . maybe three weeks. I never really paid much . . . I barely even saw him when he was here . . ." Her voice fades, and it looks like she's been stabbed in the stomach. Her fair skin goes albino white. "How much did you say was in that account you found?" she asks.

"Gillian, you don't have to get involved wi—"

"Just tell me how much!"

Charlie takes a deep breath. "Three million dollars."

Her mouth almost hits the floor. "*What?* In my dad's? There's no way. How could he possibly—?" She cuts herself off and the cogs quickly start spinning . . . whirling through the possibilities. All the while, even though Charlie told her the news, she's locked on to me. "You think that's why they killed him, don't you?" she eventually asks. "Because of something that happened with the money . . ."

"That's what we're trying to figure out," I explain, hoping to keep her moving.

"Did your dad know anyone in the Secret Service?" Charlie adds.

"I-I don't know," she replies, still clearly overwhelmed. "We weren't that close, but . . . but I still thought I knew him better than that."

"Do you still have any of his stuff in the house?" he asks.

"Some of it . . . yeah."

"And have you ever gone through it?"

"Just a little," she says, her voice slowly starting to highstep. "But wouldn't the Service have—"

"Maybe they overlooked it," he tells her. "Maybe there's something they missed."

"Why don't we take a look together?" I add. It's the perfect offer. Safety in numbers.

Nice, Charlie grins.

I turn away from the compliment, already feeling guilty. Regardless of how much it helps us, it's still her dead father's house. I saw it in her eyes before. The pain doesn't go away.

With Gillian's hesitant nod, Charlie hops out of his seat, and I follow him to the door. Behind us, Gillian lingers on the countertop.

"You okay?" I ask.

"Just tell me one thing," she interrupts. "Do you really think they killed my dad?"

"Honestly, I don't know what to think," I say. "But twenty-four hours ago, I watched these guys murder one of our friends. I saw them pull the trigger, and I saw them turn their guns on us—all because we found an account with your dad's name on it."

"That doesn't mean . . ."

"You're right—it doesn't mean they killed him," Charlie agrees. "But if they didn't, then why aren't they here, trying to find him?"

Sometimes I forget how aggressively sharp Charlie is. She doesn't have an answer for that one.

She takes a final look around the apartment and studies every detail. The lack of furniture, the papered windows, even the machete. If we were the bad guys, she'd already be dead.

Gillian tentatively slides off the counter, smacks the linoleum with her bare feet, and pauses a moment just as she's about to open the door. She's trying not to look distressed, but as her hand holds the doorknob, she still needs to take it all in. Without turning around, she says six words: "This better not be a trick."

Charlie and I scramble forward. She steps outside. The sun's not shining, but it's close.

"Gillian, you're not gonna regret this," Charlie says.

36

Clutching the sides of the computer screen in his callused hands, Gallo glared down at the laptop that he balanced between his gut and the base of the steering wheel. For two hours, he watched Maggie Caruso make her lunch, clean her dishes, readjust the hems on two pairs of pants, and hang three silk shirts on the clothesline outside her window. In that time, she got two phone calls: one from a client, and one wrong number. *Can you have it ready by Thursday?* and *I'm sorry, there's no one here by that name*. That's it. Nothing more.

Gallo cranked the volume up and opened the feeds from all four digital cameras. Thanks to their most recent interrogation, as well as her recent contact with her sons, they were able to expand the warrant and add one to her bedroom, one to Charlie's room, and another in the kitchen. Onscreen, Gallo had views of every major room in the apartment. But the only person there was Maggie— hunched over the sewing machine on the dining room table. In the corner, an old TV blared midday talk shows. Up close, the sewing machine pounded like a jackhammer. For a full two hours. That's it.

"Ready for some relief?" DeSanctis asked as the passenger door popped open.

"What the hell took so long?" Gallo asked, never taking his eyes off the laptop.

"Patience—haven't you ever heard of patience?"

"Just tell me what you got. Anything useful?"

"Of course it's useful . . ." Still standing outside, DeSanctis swung two silver aluminum attaché cases into the front seat, stacking them one on top of the other. Sliding in next to them, he pulled the top one onto his lap.

"They give you a hard time?" Gallo asked.

DeSanctis answered with a sarcastic smirk and a flip of the attaché locks. "You know how it is with a Delta Dash— tell 'em what you need, tell 'em it's an emergency, and bing-bang-bing, the James Bond gadgets are on the next shuttle. All you have to do is pick 'em up at baggage claim."

Inside the silver case, set into a black foam mold, DeSanctis found what looked like a pudgy, round camcorder with a wide oversized lens. A sticker on the bottom read "DEA Property." Typical, DeSanctis nodded. When it came to high-tech surveillance, Drug Enforcement and the Border Patrol always got the top toys.

"What is it?" Gallo asked.

"Germanium lens . . . indium antimonide detector—"

"English!"

"Handheld infrared videocamera with complete thermal imaging," DeSanctis explained as he peered through the viewfinder. "If she's sneaking out late at night, it'll home in on her body heat and spot her down the darkest alley."

Gallo looked up at the bright winter sky. "What else did you get?"

"Don't give me that look," DeSanctis warned. Resting the infrared camera on his lap, he tossed the first case into the backseat and flipped open the second. Inside was a high-tech radar gun with a long barrel that looked like a police flashlight. "This one's just a prototype," DeSanctis explained. "It measures motion—from running water, to the blood flowing through your veins."

"Which means what?"

"Which means it lets you see straight through nonmoving objects. Like walls."

Gallo crossed his arms skeptically. "No friggin' . . ."

"It works. I saw it myself," DeSanctis insisted. "The computer inside lets you know if it's a ceiling fan or a kid spinning around in circles. So if she's meeting someone in the hallway, or stepping out of camera range . . ."

"We'll catch her," Gallo said, grabbing the radar gun and pointing it up toward Maggie's apartment. "All we have to do is wait."

37

So where do you want to start?" Gillian asks as we step into her dad's faded pink house.

"Wherever you want," Charlie says as I survey my way through the overcrowded living room. Set up like an indoor garage sale, the room is filled with . . . well . . . a little bit of everything. Overstuffed bookshelves that're crammed with engineering and science fiction books cover two of the four white stuccoed walls, stacks of papers bury an old wicker chair, and at least seven different throw pillows—including one shaped like a pink flamingo and another shaped like a laptop—are tossed haphazardly across the stained leather couch.

In the center of the room, a mod Woodstock-era coffee table is lost under remote controls, faded photographs, an electric screwdriver, random loose change, plastic squeezable figures of Happy and Bashful from *Snow White and the Seven Dwarfs*, a stack of Sun Microsystems coasters, and at least two dozen rabbits' feet that're dyed in impossibly bright colors.

"I'm impressed," Charlie blurts. "This room's an even bigger wreck than mine."

"Wait'll you see the rest," Gillian says. "He was purely function over form."

"So all this stuff is his?"

"Pretty much," Gillian replies. "I've been meaning to go through it, but . . . it's not that easy to throw away someone's life."

She hits it right on the head with that one. It took my mom almost a year to toss dad's toothbrush. And that's when she hated him.

"Why don't we start back here," she suggests, leading us into the spare bedroom her dad used as an office. Inside, we find an L-shaped black Formica countertop jutting out from the back wall and continuing down the righthand side of the room. Half of it's covered in paperwork; the other half with tools and electronics—wires, transistors, a miniature soldering iron, needle-nose pliers, a set of jeweler's screwdrivers, and even some dental tools to work with small wiring. Above the desk is a framed picture of Geppetto, from Disney's *Pinocchio*.

"What's with the Disney fetish?" Charlie asks.

"That's where he used to work—fifteen years as an Imagineer in Orlando."

"Really? So did he ever design any cool rides?" Charlie asks.

"To be honest, I don't even know—I barely knew him growing up. He used to send a stuffed Minnie doll every year for my birthday, but that was really it. That's why my mom left—we were just his second job."

"When did he move back to Miami?"

"I think it was five years ago—said goodbye to Disney and found a job at a local computer game company. The pay was barely half, but luckily, he had a pocketful of Disney stock options. That's how he bought the house."

"And maybe that's how he opened the account at Greene," Charlie says, adding the rest with a glance. But we both know that even Disney stock options don't add up to three hundred million.

I nod in agreement. "He wasn't a bigshot at Disney, was he?"

"Dad?" she asks in that completely disarming laugh. "Naw, even with the engineering degree, he was pure worker bee. The closest he got to the action was linking the computer systems so when Disney's central weather station sees rain coming, all the gift shops in the park get immediate messages to put out umbrellas and Mickey ponchos. The shelves get stocked before a single drop hits."

"That's still pretty cool."

"Yeah . . . maybe—though knowing my dad, his role might be a bit . . . overstated."

"Join the club," I say with a nod. "Our dad was a—"

"*Our* dad?" she stops. "You two are brothers?"

Charlie pummels me with a look, and I bite my tongue.

"What?" Gillian asks. "What's the big deal?"

"Nothing," I tell her. "It's just . . . after yesterday . . . we're just trying to keep a low profile." As I say the words, I watch her weigh each one. But like Charlie on his best day, Gillian lets it roll away. "It's okay," she says. "I'd never say a word."

"I know you wouldn't," I smile back.

"Can we get on with this?" Charlie interrupts. "We've still got a house to search."

Twenty minutes later, we're lost in paper. Charlie has the piles on the top of the desk, I've got the drawers below, and Gillian's working the file cabinet in the corner. As far as we can tell, most of it's useless. "Listen to this one," Charlie says, wading through a stack of science newsletters. "*The Institute of Electrical and Electronics Engineers' Lasers and Electro-Optics Society Journal.*"

"Ready to be shamed?" I ask. "Dear Martin, If Abby lived across the sea, what a great swimmer you would be. Happy Valentine's Day. Your friend, Stacey B."

"You think that beats the Lasers and Electro-Optics Society?"

"It's a Valentine's card from the 1950s!" I shout, waving the musty card through the air. In front of me, the bottom drawer of the cabinet is packed tight with thousands of others. "He's got every postcard, thank-you note, and birthday card he's ever been sent. Since birth!"

"These are all magazines and old newspapers," Gillian says, slamming her own file drawer shut. "Everything from *Engineering Management Review* to the Disney employee newsletter—but nothing that's actually useful."

"I don't get it," Charlie says. "He keeps everything he ever touched, but doesn't have a single bank statement or phone bill?"

"I'm guessing that's what he kept *here* . . ." I say, pulling open the file drawer above the birthday cards. Inside, a dozen empty file folders sway on metal brackets.

"They must've grabbed them when they grabbed the computer," Gillian says.

"Then that's it—we're dead," Charlie blurts.

"Don't say that," I tell him.

"But if the Service already picked through this—"

"Then what? We should give up and walk away? We should assume they took everything?"

"They *did* take everything!" Charlie shouts.

"No, they didn't!" I snap. "Look around—Duckworth's got junk stuffed everywhere—fifteen colors of rabbits' feet.

And since we have no idea what the Service left behind, I'm not leaving this place until I flip over every coaster, pick apart every drawer, and tear off Happy and Bashful's plastic squeaky heads just to see what might be hidden inside. Now if you have any better options, I'm happy to hear them, but like you said before, we've got a whole house to search!"

Charlie steps back, surprised by the outburst—but just as quickly shrugs and moves on. "You take the kitchen; I'll take the bathroom."

38

S he knows," Gallo said.

"How could she possibly know?" DeSanctis asked.

"Just look at her," he said, jabbing a fat finger at the computer that rested on the seat between them. "Her sons are
missing . . . it's another night alone . . . but does she report
it? Does she cry on the phone, sobbing to a friend? No—she
just sits there, sewing away and watching the Food
Channel."

"It's better than watching soaps," DeSanctis said, pointing the thermal imager up the dark block.

"That's not the point, ass-face. If she knows we're watching, she's less likely to—"

The chime of a doorbell blared through the laptop's
speakers. Gallo and DeSanctis shot up in their seats.

"She's got a visitor," DeSanctis said.

"Was that from downstairs?"

DeSanctis aimed the imager at the glass windows of the
lobby. In the camera, a muddy dark green image of the lobby
came into focus. Green was cold; white was hot. But as he
scanned between the buzzer area and the lobby, the only

thing he saw were two white rectangular starbursts along the ceiling. No people—just fluorescent lights. "No one's down there."

"Coming . . . !" Maggie shouted toward her door.

"How'd they get past us? Is there a back door?" Gallo shouted.

"Could be a neighbor," DeSanctis pointed out.

"Who is it?" Maggie asked.

The answer was a mumble. Microphones didn't work through doors.

"Just a minute . . ." Maggie said as she shut off the TV. Undoing the locks with one hand, she straightened her hair and her shirt with the other.

"She's making an impression," DeSanctis whispered. "I'm betting a client."

"At this time of ni—?"

"Sophie! So nice to see you," Maggie sang as she opened the door. Over Maggie's shoulder they saw a gray-haired woman wearing a cable-knit brown cardigan, but no coat.

"Neighbor," DeSanctis said.

"*Sophie* . . ." Gallo repeated. "She said *Sophie*."

DeSanctis tore open the glove compartment and yanked out a stack of paper. *4190 Bedford Avenue—Residents— Real Property.*

"Sophie . . . Sofia . . . Sonja . . ." Gallo suggested as DeSanctis frantically ran his finger down the printed list.

"I got a Sonia Coady in 3A and a Sofia Rostonov in 2F," DeSanctis said.

"How have you been?" Sophie asked in a thick Russian accent.

"Rostonov it is."

"Fine . . . just fine," Maggie replied, inviting her inside.

"Watch her hands!" Gallo barked as Maggie reached out and touched Sophie's shoulder.

"You think she's passing something?" DeSanctis asked.

"She doesn't have a choice. No fax, no e-mail, no cell phone—not even an electronic organizer—her only hope is getting something from outside. I'm guessing a pager or something small that can do text-messaging."

DeSanctis nodded. "You take mom; I got Sofia." Crouching down toward the laptop, the two agents were silent. In the darkness, their faces glowed with the pale light from the screen.

"I took almost an inch off all the sleeves—let me get them off the line . . ." Maggie said as she walked toward the kitchen window. From his bird's-eye view in the smoke detector, Gallo only saw her back, but he studied everything she touched. Hands at her side. Opening the kitchen window. Pulling in the clothesline. Unhooking two women's blouses and angling each onto a hanger.

"You put them out in this weather?" Sophie asked.

"The cold's good for it—makes them crisper than the day you bought them." Maggie hooked both hangers on one of the three coat racks that lined the living room wall.

"Watch the money change . . ." Gallo warned.

"Uck, where's my head?" Sophie began, searching for a purse that wasn't there. "I left my . . ."

"No harm done," Maggie said. Even in the pixelized digital image, Gallo could see her strained grin. "Bring it by whenever. I'm not going anywhere."

"Dammit!" Gallo shouted.

"You're a nice person," Sophie insisted. "You're a nice person, and good things are going to happen for you."

"Yeah," Maggie said, glancing up toward the smoke detector. "I should be so lucky."

* * * *

Shutting the door behind Sophie, Maggie took a silent breath and made her way back to the window in the kitchen. Along the wall, the old radiator hiccuped with a sharp clang, but Maggie barely noticed it. She was too focused on everything else—her sons . . . and Gallo . . . and even her routine. Especially her routine.

Jamming her palms under the top of the window frame, she gave it two hard pushes and finally forced it open. A blast of cold air shoved its way inside, but again, Maggie didn't care. With Sophie's shirts gone, there was an open spot on the clothesline. An open spot she couldn't wait to fill.

Grabbing the damp white sheet that was draped over the nearby ironing board, she leaned outside the window, took a clothespin from the pouch in her apron, and clipped the corner into place. Inch by inch, she scrolled the sheet out over the alley, slowly pinning more of it to the line. At the edge, she pulled the sheet taut. A gust of wind did its best to send it flying, but Maggie held it down with a tight fist. Just another normal night. All that was left was the hard part.

As the wind passed, she stuffed both hands back into the apron's pouch. Her left hand felt around for a clothespin; her right searched for something more. Within seconds, her fingers skimmed along the edge of the note she had written earlier in the night. Careful to keep her back to the kitchen, she palmed the folded-up sheet of paper in her already shaking hand. Out of the corner of her eye, she saw the faint glow in Gallo and DeSanctis's car. It didn't slow her down.

Fighting off tears, she clamped her jaw shut and planted her feet. Then, in one fluid motion, she leaned out the window, tucked her right hand under the sheet, and clipped the note in place. Directly across the way, the window in the

building next door was dark—but Maggie could still make
out the inky silhouette of Saundra Finkelstein. Hiding in the
corner of her window, The Fink carefully nodded. And for
the third time since yesterday—under the glare of four digital videocameras, six voice-activated microphones, two
encrypted transmitters, and over fifty thousand dollars'
worth of the government's best military-strength surveillance equipment, Maggie Caruso tugged at the two-dollar
clothesline and, under a cheap, overused, wet sheet, passed
a handwritten note to her next-door neighbor.

39

You can learn a lot about a man by going through his bathroom. A toothbrush with frazzled bristles . . . baking soda toothpaste . . . no Q-Tips anywhere. You can even learn more than you want to know. Down on my knees under the sink, I snake my arm past the rusted pipes and rummage through random, long-expired toiletries.

"What about the medicine chest?" Charlie asks, squeezing past me and hopping up on the edge of the bathtub.

"I already went through it."

There's a magnetic click as the medicine cabinet door opens. I lift up my head. Charlie's picking it apart.

"I told you—I already went through it."

"I know—just double-checking," he says, quickly scanning the stash of brown prescription vials. "Lopressor for blood pressure, Glyburide for diabetes, Lipitor for high cholesterol, Allopurinol for gout . . ."

"Charlie, what're you doing?"

"What's it look like, Hawkeye? I want to know what medication he was on."

"What for?"

"Just to see—I want to find out who this guy was—get into his brain—see what he's made of . . ."

The rambling goes on a beat too long. I give him another look. He quickly starts putting the brown vials back in place.

"Want to tell me what you're really doing?" I ask.

"See, now you're smoking too many Twinkies," he says, forcing a laugh. "I'm telling you, I'm just looking for his—"

"You forgot your medication, didn't you?"

"What're you—?"

"The mexiletine—you haven't been taking it."

He rolls his eyes like a pouty teenager. "Can you please not overreact—this isn't *General Hospital* . . ."

"Dammit, I knew something was—" I hear a noise in the hallway and cut myself off.

"Saved by the bella," Charlie whispers.

"What's going on?" Gillian asks, stopping by the door.

"Nothing," Charlie says. "Just raiding your dad's medicine chest. Didja know he's got tampons in there?"

"Those're mine, Einstein."

"That's what I meant . . . I meant, those're yours." Dancing around me, he slides out of the bathroom—but right now, my eyes are on Gillian as she walks down the hallway.

"Careful, you've got some drool on your lip," he whispers as he passes. "I mean, not that I blame you—with all that hippiechick voodoo she's got going, I'm getting all sweaty myself."

"We'll talk about this later," I growl.

"I'm sure we will," he says. "But if I were you, I'd slow down on buying her a corsage, and focus more on the problem at hand."

* * * *

By seven o'clock, all we've got left are the kitchen, the garage, and the two hall closets. "I got the kitchen," Gillian says. That leaves the final two. Charlie grins at me. I squint right back. Only a fool would take the garage.

"On three . . ." he challenges. "Two takes it."

I grin this time—and tuck my right hand behind my back.

"One, two, three, *shoot* . . ." His rock beats scissors.

"*Shoot* . . ." My scissors beats paper.

"*Shoot* . . ." Rock beats scissors . . . again.

"*Damn!*" I say, annoyed.

"I'm telling you, you're a sucker for those scissors . . ."

I turn my scissors into a middle finger and storm to the garage.

Smiling ear to ear, he pivots and heads up the hallway.

As I'm about to turn the corner, I spin around, ready to issue a double-or-nothing challenge. Charlie should be at the hall closets. Instead, he's at the closed door at the far end of the hall. Duckworth's bedroom. The only place we haven't been. In truth, it shouldn't matter—Gillian already said she went through it—but I know my brother better than that. I see the skulk in his walk. He stares at the door like he's got X-ray vision. After nine hours of picking through this dead man's life, he wants to know what's inside.

"Where're you going?" I ask.

He glances over his shoulder and gives me nothing but a mischievous arched eyebrow. With a twist of the doorknob, he disappears into Duckworth's bedroom. I stop right there, well aware of his reindeer game. It may've worked when I was ten, but I'm not letting him goad me into this one. Turning back to the garage, I hear the bedroom door close behind me. I take a full three steps before I once again stop.

Who'm I kidding? Spinning back toward the bedroom, I rush toward the closed door.

"Charlie?" I whisper, knowing he won't answer.

Sure enough, nothing comes back. Searching over my shoulder, I check the hallway just to be safe. All clear. Trying not to make a sound, I twist the doorknob and step inside. As the door shuts behind me, the lights are off, but thanks to some cheap vertical blinds on the window, the room still gets a bath of fading dusk light.

"Pretty spooky, huh?" Charlie asks. "Welcome to the sanctum sanctorum . . ."

It takes about four seconds for my eyes to adjust, but when they do, it's clear why Gillian checked this room herself. Like the living room and the office, Duckworth's bedroom has the same unapologetic engineer's fashion sense: a plain bed shoved against the dingy off-white wall, an unpainted wood nightstand holding a ratty old alarm clock, and to make sure every single piece seems randomly selected, an almond Formica dresser that looks like it was plucked from the back of a truck. But the closer I look, the more I realize there's something else: A cream-colored comforter softens the bed, a vase of burgundy eucalyptus flourishes on top of the dresser, and in the corner, a Mondrian-styled painting leans against the wall, waiting to be hung. This room may've started as Duckworth's—but now it's all Gillian's. So this is where she lives. A pang of guilt swirls through my gut. This is still her private space.

"C'mon, Charlie, let's go . . ."

"Yeah . . . no . . . you're absolutely right," he says. "We're only trusting her with our lives. Why would we ever want to learn anything more about her?"

I go to grab his arm, but as always, he's too fast. "I'm serious, Charlie."

"So am I," he says, sidestepping around me. Moving in further, he searches the floor, the bed, and the rest of the furniture, hunting for context clues. Ten steps in, he stops, suddenly confused.

"What? What's wrong?" I ask.

"You tell me. Where's her life?"

"What're you talking about?"

"Her life, Ollie—clothes, photos, books, magazines—anything to fill in the picture. Take a look around. Besides the flowers and the art, there's nothing else out."

"Maybe she likes to keep things neat."

"Maybe," he agrees. "Or maybe she's—"

There's a loud clunk as a door slams behind us. I spin around and realize it came from the hallway. Still, we know when we've overstayed our welcome. I glance at the alarm clock on the nightstand to check the time—and quickly cock my head to the side. That's not an alarm clock. It's an old—

"Eight-track player!" Charlie blurts, already excited. But as he squints through the darkness of the room, he notices that the slot that usually holds the 8-track looks a little wider than normal. At the edges, the silver-colored plastic is chipped away. Like someone cut it open, or made it bigger. Curious, he moves in, squatting down in front of it.

"Sombitch," he whispers.

"What now?" Stepping behind him and trying to make the best of the fading light, I lean over his shoulder. He points down at the 8-track.

"I don't get it," I tell him.

"Not the 8-track, Ollie. Here . . ." He points again. But what he points at isn't the player. It's the nightstand underneath. "Check out the dust," he explains.

I angle my head just enough to see the thick layer of dust that blankets the top of the nightstand.

"It's so perfect, you barely notice it," Charlie says. "Like no one's put anything on it, or even touched it . . . in months, even though it's right next to her bed." He turns back to me and tightens his gaze.

"What?"

"You tell me, Ollie. How could she not—"

"What's this, a panty raid?" a female voice asks behind us.

Charlie whips around to face Gillian.

She flicks on the lights, making us squint to compensate. "What're you doing in my room?"

40

Oh, this is yours?" Charlie asks. "We were just . . . just checking out this awesome 8-track." He jabs a thumb over his shoulder to point, but she doesn't bother to look. Her dark eyes lock on his and don't let go. She just stands there, arms crossed against her chest. I don't blame her. We shouldn't have been snooping through her stuff.

"Listen, I'm really sorry," I offer. "I swear, we didn't touch anything." Locking on me, she puts me through the exact same test. But unlike Charlie, I don't lie, fumble, or condescend. I give her the absolute truth and hope it's enough. "I . . . I just wanted to learn more about you," I add.

Perfect, Charlie smirks.

He thinks it's an act, but in many ways, it's the most honest thing I've said today. With everyone else after us, Gillian's the only one who's offered to help. As she stares me down, her arms are still crossed in front of her chest. The free spirit's gone. And then . . . just like that . . . it's back again.

"It *is* pretty cool, isn't it?" she asks as her shoulders bounce.

I smile a thank-you. Suspicious of the kindness, Charlie looks around like she's talking to someone else.

"The 8-track," she explains, moving excitedly toward the nightstand.

With a shove, she pushes my brother aside and sits on the bed, right next to me. She scoots back, then forward, then back a little more. "Wait'll you see what he did to it," she tells me eagerly. "Hit the *Pause* button."

She's got that same singsong laugh as before. Next to her, though, Charlie motions down low, where her bare toes are balled up like fists against the carpet.

See? Charlie scowls with that I-told-you-so look he usually reserves for Beth. But we both know Gillian's no Beth.

Gillian flicks the power switch on and leans back on her hands. "Just hit *Pause*," she adds.

Following instructions, I reach down and press the *Pause* button. The ancient machine hums with a mechanical whir. It's such a familiar sound . . . and just as I place it, a plastic CD tray—complete with a shiny compact disc—slides out of the widened opening where you'd normally put the 8-track.

"Pretty cool, huh?" Gillian asks.

"Where're you from again?" Charlie blurts.

"Excuse me?"

"Where're you from? Where'd you grow up?"

"Right here," Gillian replies. "Just outside Miami."

"Oh, that's so weird," Charlie says. "Because when you just said *Pretty cool*, I coulda sworn I smelled a hint of New York accent."

Clearly amused, Gillian shakes her head, but she won't

take her eyes off my brother. "Nope, just Florida," she sings without a care. It's the best way to take him on—don't take him on at all. She turns back to me and the CD/8-track. "Check out the disc," she offers.

I reach down and spear it with a finger: *The Collected Speeches of Adlai E. Stevenson.* "I take it your dad did this?"

"I'm telling you, after he left Disney, he had way too much time—he used to always—"

"And when did you move in here again?" Charlie interrupts.

"I'm sorry?" she asks. If she's annoyed, she's not showing it.

"Your dad died six months ago—when did you move in here?"

Playfully grinning, she hops up from the bed and crosses around to the foot of the mattress.

See that? Charlie glares my way. *That's the same trick I use on you. Distance to avoid confrontation.*

"I don't know," she begins. "I guess a month or so ago . . . it's hard to say. It took a while to do the paperwork . . . and then to get my stuff over here . . ." She turns toward the window, but never gets flustered. I listen for a New York accent, but all I hear is her short-O Flooorida tone. "It's still not that easy sleeping in his old bed, which is why most nights I'm curled up on the couch," she adds, watching Charlie. "Of course, the mortgage is paid, so I got no reason to moan."

"What about a job?" Charlie asks. "Are you still working?"

"What do I look like, some trust fund beach bunny?" she teases. "Thursday, Friday, and Saturday nights at Waterbed."

"Waterbed?"

"It's a club over on Washington. Velvet rope, guys looking for supermodels who'll never show . . . the whole sad story."

"Let me guess: You bartend in a tight black T-shirt."

"Charlie . . ." I scold.

She shrugs it off without a care. "Do I seem like that much of a cliché to you? I'm a manager, cutie-pie." She's trying to make nice, but Charlie's not biting. "The good part is, it leaves the days free for the paintings, which're really the best release," she adds.

Paintings? I scan the canvas in the corner and search for a signature. *G.D.* Gillian Duckworth. "So this *is* yours," I say. "I was wondering if—"

"You painted that?" Charlie asks skeptically.

"Why so surprised?" she asks.

"He's not surprised," I interrupt, trying to keep it light. "He just doesn't like the competition." Pointing to Charlie, I add, "Guess who used to go to art school—and is still a wannabe musician?"

"Really?" Gillian asks. "So we're both artists."

"Yeah. We're both artists," he says flatly. He quickly checks her fingers—if I had to guess, I'd bet he's looking to see if there's any paint trapped under her nails. *Strike two*, he warns as if it means anything. "You ever sell any of these?" he continues.

"Only to friends," she says softly. "Though I'm trying to get them in a gallery . . ."

"*You* ever sold any songs?" I jump in. I'm not letting him hit below the belt. Besides, whatever else his imagination comes up with, Gillian is letting us pick through the whole place. Of course, Charlie can't stop staring at the dust that blankets the nightstand.

"Did I say something wrong?" Gillian asks.

"No, you've been great," Charlie says as he takes off for the door.

"Where're you going?" I call out.

"Back to work," he tells me. "I've got a closet to rummage through."

41

At midnight, Maggie Caruso sat at her dining room table with the newspaper spread out in front of her and a hot cup of tea by her side. For fifteen minutes, she didn't touch either. *Give it time*, she told herself as she glanced up at Charlie's painting of the Brooklyn Bridge. *Better to wait the full two hours.* That's how they passed it at nine o'clock, and that's how they did it at eleven. Anxious to get up, but unwilling to reveal her expression, she subtly angled her wrist and watched the seconds tick away on the plastic *Wizard of Oz* Wicked Witch watch Charlie gave her for Mother's Day. All it took was a little patience.

"I hate it when she does this," DeSanctis said, glaring at the laptop. "It's the same as last night—she stares down at the crossword, but never puts in an answer."

"It's not the puzzle," Gallo began. "I've seen it before—when people know they're in the fire, they freeze. They're so scared of making the wrong move, they're completely paralyzed."

"So go to bed," DeSanctis yelled at Maggie on the screen. "Make it easy on yourself!"

"We all have our habits," Gallo said. "This one's clearly hers."

Fifty minutes later, Maggie's eyes continued to tick-tock between her watch and the newspaper. On any other night, the waiting alone would've put her to sleep. Tonight, her feet tapped against the floor to keep her awake. *Two more minutes*, she counted to herself.

Annoyed and impossibly antsy, DeSanctis flicked on the thermal imager and aimed it up the block. Through the viewfinder, the world had a dark green tint. Street lamps and house lights glowed bright white. So did the hood of Joey's car, which was now impossible to miss even though it was tucked into an alley. If she wanted the heat to work, the engine had to be at least partially on.

"Guess who's still watching us?" DeSanctis asked.

"I don't wanna hear it," Gallo rumbled. Pointing to the laptop, he added, "Meanwhile, look who's finally ready for bed . . ."

Battling exhaustion, Maggie shuffled toward the kitchen and pretended to take a final gulp of tea. But as she tilted her head back, she reached into the pouch of her apron and felt around for her newest note. That was it. Time to get moving. With a twist of her wrist, she poured out the full mug of tea. But instead of marching off to her bedroom, she turned back toward the kitchen window.

"What's she doing now?" Gallo asked.

"Same thing she's been doing all day—being cheap about dry cleaning."

Leaning out toward the clothesline, Maggie tugged hand over fist to rein in the night's final load. Halfway through, she stopped to stretch her fingers, which were suddenly burning with pain. Forget the arthritis and the hours hunched over the sewing machine—the stress alone was finally taking its toll.

"She's ready to break," Gallo said, studying the small screen and reading her body language from behind. "She can't take another night like this."

"Check it out—you can see her arms," DeSanctis gloated, still looking through the thermal imager. He flipped open the LCD screen on the side of the camera so Gallo could get a look. Sure enough, sticking out of the green-tinted building were two pasty white arms that glowed like incandescent snakes slithering through the night.

"What's that stuff over here?" Gallo asked as he pointed to tiny white splotches on the rope of the clothesline.

"That's the residue from her touch," DeSanctis explained. "The rope's so cold, every time she grabs it, it holds the warmth and gives us a thermal afterglow."

Gallo's eyes narrowed as he studied the white spots on the glowing conveyor belt. As they scrolled away from Maggie, each spot faded and disappeared.

One by one, Maggie inspected each piece of clothing on the line. Dry came in; wet stayed out. By the time she was done, the only thing left was the still damp white sheet. Keeping her head down, Maggie eyed the dark window across the alley. In the shadows, as before, Saundra Finkelstein nodded.

On the LCD screen, Gallo and DeSanctis watched Maggie unclip the clothespins, reach under the sheet, and rotate it a half-turn. Thanks to the low temperature of the wet fabric, her arms glowed faintly underneath. Clipping the pins back in place, she gave the rope a final tug and sent the sheet on its way. Once again, the thermal white splotches on the rope faded in a horizontal blur—but this time, something else remained: Just below the rope—where the clothespin hit the sheet—a white golfball-sized comet streaked across the alleyway. And disappeared.

"What the hell was that?" Gallo asked.

"What're you talking about?"

"On the sheet! Play that back!"

"Hold on a second . . ."

"*Now!*" Gallo roared.

Frantically pressing buttons on the camera, DeSanctis froze the picture and punched *Rewind*. Onscreen, it scrolled in reverse, and Maggie's sheet zoomed back toward her window.

"Right there!" Gallo shouted. "Hit *Play!*"

The tape whirred back to normal speed. With the camera on the dashboard, Gallo and DeSanctis leaned in close. For the second time, they watched as Maggie readjusted the sheet. Her left hand clipped on the clothespin. Her right was underneath, holding it all in place. In one quick movement, Maggie pulled her hand out and sent the sheet across the alley—and just like before, there was a fuzzy white dot right below where the clothespin was clipped.

"There!" Gallo said, pausing the picture. He pointed right at the white dot. "What's that?"

"I-I have no idea," DeSanctis said. "Maybe her arm touched the blanket . . ."

"Of course her arm touched the blanket—she had it under there for a full minute, moron—but that dot's still the only thing that's lit up!"

DeSanctis leaned in even closer. "You think she had something under there?"

"You tell me—you're the expert in this nonsense—what could possibly hold a heat signature for that long?"

Squinting at the screen, he shook his head. "If she was hiding it in her hand . . . if her palms were sweaty . . . it could be anything—plastic . . . a piece of clothing . . . even some folded-up paper would—"

DeSanctis stopped.

Gallo looked skyward. Four stories up, Maggie Caruso's white sheet flapped in the night air. Across the alley, the window directly opposite Maggie's was black. Without a word, DeSanctis stopped the tape and raised the thermal imager. And as the dark green picture came into focus, there was something new inside the window—a faint, milky gray silhouette of an older woman staring out at the clothesline. Watching. And patiently waiting.

"*Son of a bitch!*" Gallo shouted, punching the roof of the car. The dome light blinked on and off at the impact. "*How the hell did we miss that?*"

"Should I—?"

"Find the neighbor!" he continued to yell. "I want to know who she is, how long she's known them, and most important, I want a list of every call that's gone in and out of that house in the last forty-eight hours!"

* * * *

"If she was hiding it in her hand . . . if her palms were sweaty . . . it could be anything—plastic . . . a piece of clothing . . . even some folded-up paper would—"

There was a long pause as DeSanctis's voice faded. Joey glanced up the block, where both agents were staring up at—

"Son of a bitch!" Gallo thundered as a high-pitched feedback screech squealed through Joey's receiver. Wincing from the sound, she turned the volume down. As she turned it back up, the only thing left was static.

"Oh, c'mon," she moaned, slapping the side of the receiver. Nothing but static. She hit the *Power* button and restarted the system. Static and more static. "No, no, no . . ." she begged, madly twisting knobs to retune the frequency. "Please . . . not now . . ." Reaching the end of the dial, she looked back up the block. Gallo pounded the steering wheel with his fist, screaming something at DeSanctis. Red brake lights lit up and Gallo abruptly started the car.

"You gotta be kidding me," Joey mumbled.

Tires groaned as they spun angrily against a patch of filthy snow. Finding traction, the car swerved wildly into the street, almost smacking into a brown Plymouth halfway up the block. And as Joey watched the red brake lights turn the corner and disappear, she knew right there and then that it was just the start of an even longer night.

42

Welcome to Suckville—Population: Two," Charlie says dryly, knee-deep in the sea of cardboard file boxes.

"Can you please stop complaining and just check that one over there?"

"I already checked it."

"Are you s—?"

"Yes, Oliver, I'm sure," he says, carefully pronouncing every syllable. "For the ninety-fifth time, I'm absolutely sure."

It's been three hours since Charlie joined me in the Warehouse of Useless Garbage doubling as Duckworth's garage. In hour one, we were hopeful. By hour two, we got impatient. Now we're just annoyed.

"What about those over there?"

Charlie glances at a stack of brown boxes stuffed between a heap of rusty lawn chairs and a broken, rotted-out barbecue. "I. Checked. Them," he growls.

"And what was inside?" I challenge.

His ears burn fiery red. "Let me think . . . Oh yeah, now I remember—it was *yet another* carton of thumbed-through sci-fi novels and outdated-as-the-dinosaurs computer texts . . ." Ripping the lid off the top box, he pulls out two books: a water-damaged paperback copy of *Fahrenheit 451*, and a faded handbook titled *The Commodore 64—Welcome to the Future.*

I stare him down and point to the other boxes in the stack. "What about the ones underneath?"

"That's it . . . I'm gone," Charlie announces, flying toward the door. He trips and stumbles over one of Gillian's over-sized canvases, but for once he doesn't land right back on his feet. Smacking into a separate stack of boxes, he regains his balance, but only after knocking the entire pile to the ground. Dozens of books scatter across the floor.

"Charlie, wait up!"

Chasing him into the living room, I quickly spot Gillian, who's hunched over on the armrest of her dad's wicker chair. Her head's down and her elbows are resting on her knees. As she looks up, her eyes are all red—like she's been crying.

Charlie blows right by her and disappears into the kitchen. I can't help but stop.

"What's wrong?" I ask. "Are you okay?"

She nods silently, but that's all she'll give. In her hands, she's holding a blue wooden picture frame with a tiny Mickey Mouse painted in the bottom right corner. The picture inside is an old photograph of an overweight man standing in a swimming pool—and proudly showing off his tiny one-year-old girl. He's got a crooked-but-beaming smile; she's got a floppy beach hat and bright pink bathing suit. Even the mole-man had his day in the sun. With the little girl frozen in mid-clap, he holds her close to his chest, arms wrapped snugly around her. Like he'll never let go.

I don't know Gillian Duckworth all that well—but I do know what it's like to lose a parent.

Kneeling down next to her, I do my best to get her attention. "I'm sorry we're rummaging through his life like this . . ."

"It's not your fault."

"Actually, it is. If we didn't get you all riled up, we wouldn't be—"

"Listen, if I didn't go through his stuff now, I would've done it in six months. Besides," she adds, looking down at the photo, "you never promised me anything." She goes to say something else, but it never comes out. She just stares at the photo, shaking her head slightly. "I know it sounds pathetic, but it just makes me realize how little I knew him." Her head stays low and her curly black hair cascades down the side of her neck.

"Gillian, if it makes you feel any better, we've got the exact same photo in our house—I haven't seen my dad in eight years."

She looks up and our eyes finally connect. She wipes the tears away with the back of her hand. There's a tiny gap between her lips. I reach out and palm her shoulder, but she's already turned away. She buries her face in her hands, and as the tears start flowing, she cries to herself. Even with me kneeling next to her, Gillian's doing her best to keep it private. But eventually . . . as I'm learning . . . we all need to open up. Sagging sideways, she leans her head against my shoulder, wraps her arms around my neck, and lets the rest out. With each breathless weep, she barely makes a noise, but I feel her tears soak my shirt. "It's okay," I tell her as her breathing slows. "It's okay to miss him."

Over her shoulder, I spy Charlie watching us from the kitchen. He's searching for the glint in her eye . . . the flicker in her voice . . . anything to prove it's an act. But it never shows. And as he watches her crumble, even he can't look away.

Realizing I see him, my brother spins around and pretends to recheck the kitchen cabinets. As Gillian's sobs subside, he circles back toward us in the room.

"Who's up for some TV?" Charlie interrupts. "We can—" He stops and suddenly acts surprised. "I'm sorry—I didn't mean to—"

"No, it's okay," Gillian says, sitting up straight and pulling herself together.

What're you doing? I ask with a glance. I'm not sure if he's jealous or just trying to calm her down, but even I have to admit, she can use the distraction.

"C'mon," Charlie adds, putting on his nice-guy voice and waving us over to the TV. "No more heartache—time to relax with some mindless entertainment."

She glances my way to check my reaction.

"Actually, it's probably not a bad idea," I agree. "Just to clean the mental palate . . ."

"Now you're talkin'," Charlie says as he cruises past us. Springboarding off the carpet, he lands on the couch with his feet already crossed on the coffee table. Gillian follows me to the living room, her fingers holding on to my hand.

"That's it—there's room for everyone—one big happy family," Charlie teases as he grabs the remote. He clicks it at the TV, but nothing happens. Again, he clicks. Again, nothing.

"Did you hit *Power*?" I ask.

"No, I hit *Mute*—the sad thing is, I can still hear you." Flipping the remote over, Charlie presses his thumb against the back and shoves open the battery compartment.

Raising an eyebrow, he looks up at Gillian. The party's over. "It's empty."

"Oh, that's right," she says. "I meant to put some new ones in."

"Don't worry," I say. "Charlie, didn't you say there were some in the closet?"

"Yeah," he says coldly, still locked on Gillian. "There's a whole toolbox of 'em. Every size imaginable."

Running back and forth to the closet, I return with a handful of fresh double-As. Gillian's already manually turned on the TV, but Charlie's focused on the remote. He slides the batteries in and gives it another shot. Nothing happens.

"Maybe it's broken."

"In this house?" Gillian asks. "Dad fixed everything."

"Here, give it here," I say to Charlie as I sit on the edge of the coffee table. Time for the trick I used to use on my old Walkman. Pulling the batteries out of the back, I bring the remote up to my lips and blow a quick puff of air into the empty battery area. To my surprise, I hear a fast, fluttering sound—like when you blow hard against a blade of grass . . . or the edge of a sheet of paper.

Charlie's head slowly cocks off-center. I know what he's thinking.

"Maybe it *is* broken," Gillian admits.

"No way," Charlie insists. His eyes are wide with that hungry look on his face. In any other house, a broken remote is just that. But here . . . like Gillian said, Duckworth fixed everything. "Let me have it," Charlie demands.

I'm already one step ahead. Cramming two fingers into the battery compartment, I start feeling around for whatever made that noise. Nothing there.

Charlie's out of his seat, anxiously standing over me. "Break it open."

Gillian shakes her head. "You really think he . . ."

"Break it!" he repeats.

With my fingers still inside, I yank hard on the back of the remote. It doesn't give. Not enough leverage.

"Here," Charlie says, tossing me a nearby pencil. I jam it into the battery area, and pull hard on the lever. There's a loud crack . . . plastic snaps . . . and the entire back of the remote breaks off, flying straight into Gillian's lap.

"Well blow me down," Charlie says.

I'm not sure what he's talking about. Then I look down. Inside the remote, tacked down by two thick staples, is a sheet of paper folded up so small and tight, it has the length and width of a flattened cigarette. The Secret Service may've ripped through every other nook and cranny, but they certainly didn't come to watch TV.

Gillian's mouth gapes open.

"What is it?" Charlie asks.

I wedge the staples out with the tip of the pencil. With a yawn, the folded-up paper slowly fans open. The excitement hits so fast, I can barely . . .

"Open it!" Charlie shouts.

I unfold it in a blur of fingertips—and from inside the first sheet of paper—a glossy, much shorter piece of paper falls to the floor. Charlie dives for it.

At first, it looks like a bookmark, but there's a confused squint on Charlie's face.

"What's it say?" I ask.

"I have no idea." Flipping it around, Charlie turns the bookmark sideways and reveals four photos—headshots, all in a row. A salt-and-pepper-haired older man, next to a pale mid-forties banker type, next to a freckled woman with frizzy red hair, next to a tired-looking black man with a cleft chin. It's like one of those photo-booth strips, but since it runs horizontally, it looks more like a lineup.

"What's yours say?" Charlie asks.

I almost forgot. Gripping the legal-looking document, I skim as fast as I can: *Confidentiality . . . Limits on Disclosure . . . Shall not be limited to formulae, drawings, designs . . .* "I may've never gone to law school, but after four years of dealing with paranoid rich people, I know an NDA when I see one."

"A what?" Charlie asks.

"NDA—a nondisclosure agreement. You sign them during business deals so both sides'll keep their mouths shut. It's how you prevent a new idea from leaking out."

"And this one . . . ?"

I hold up the document and point to the signature at the bottom. It's a mad scribble in muddy black ink. But there's no mistaking the name. Martin Duckworth.

43

I don't get it," Gillian says. "You think dad invented something?"

"Oh, he definitely invented something," I say, my voice already racing down the mountain. "And from the looks of it, he was up to something big."

"What're you talking about?" Charlie asks.

I once again wave the creased paper through the air. "Read the other signature on the contract."

He grabs my wrist to hold it steady. *Agreed to and signed—Brandt T. Katkin—Chief Strategist, Five Points Capital.* "Who's Brandt Katkin?" Charlie asks.

"Forget Katkin—I'm talking about Five Points Capital. With a name like that and a letter like this, I'll bet you my boxers it's a VC."

"VC?" Gillian asks.

"Venture capital," I explain. "They lend money to new companies . . . get entrepreneurs rolling by investing in their ideas. Anyway, when a venture capital firm signs a nondisclosure agreement—trust me on this one—we're talking pocketfuls of cash on the line."

"How do you know?"

"That's how the business works—these VCs see hundreds of new ideas every day—one guy invents Widget A; another guy invents Widget B. Both widget guys want to get nondisclosure agreements before they go in and lift their skirts. But the VCs—they hate nondisclosures. They want to see up every skirt they can lay their eyes on. More important, if a VC signs a nondisclosure, it opens itself up to liability. When we took a client to Deardorff Capital in New York last year, one of the partners said the only way they'd sign an NDA was if Bill Gates himself walked in and said, 'I have a great idea—sign this and I'll tell you about it.'"

"So the fact that Duckworth got them to sign . . ."

". . . means that he's got a Bill Gates–sized idea," I agree. Turning to Gillian, I ask, "Do you have any clue what he was working on?"

"No, I . . . I didn't know he was building anything. All his other inventions were tiny—like the 8-track."

"Not anymore," I say. "If this is right, he came up with something that makes the 8-track look like, well . . . like an 8-track."

"It had to be something with computers," Charlie adds.

"Really? You think?" Gillian asks sarcastically.

"No. Just a guess," he shoots back.

"Both of you—stop," I warn. "Gillian, are you sure there's nothing you can think of? Anything at all that he might've been trying to sell?"

"What makes you think he was selling it?"

"You don't go to a VC unless you need some cash. Either he got them to invest, or he made the sale outright."

"So that's where he got the money?" Charlie asks. "You think the idea was that good?"

"If they're giving him three million dollars," Gillian adds, "it's gotta be major good."

Charlie wings me a look. *If it's three hundred mil, it's King Kong good.*

"What about the photos?" Gillian blurts out of nowhere. She sounds incredibly excited, but as Charlie immediately points out, her bare feet are once again fists on the carpet. What does he expect? We're all anxious.

"So they're not relatives or anything?" Charlie asks her.

"Never seen 'em before in my life."

"What about friends?" I ask.

"I bet one of them's Brandt Katkin," Charlie says, motioning with his chin at the nondisclosure agreement.

"They could be anyone," I add, unable to slow down. With the taste of hope on my tongue, I stare down at the four headshots. "I'm betting they were his contacts at the VC."

"Maybe they were people he was working with," Charlie adds. "Maybe they were the people he trusted."

"Or maybe they were the ones who killed him," Gillian says. "They could all be Secret Service."

All three of us fall silent. At this point, anything's possible.

"So what do we do now?" she adds.

"We should call up this guy Brandt Katkin and ask him about Five Points Capital," Charlie suggests.

"At two in the morning?" Gillian asks.

"The later the better," he glares back at her, refusing to give a centimeter. "We should go down there and bust through a window. In high school, Joel Westman once taught me how to take out an alarm with a kitchen magnet. We can rummage through the files Watergate-style."

"No, that's a great idea," I chime in. "Then you two can lower me on a rope from the airvents, where I'll try to stop a single drop of sweat from falling to the ridiculously over-protected floor and simultaneously grab the NOC list."

Charlie's eyes narrow. "Are you being sarcastic?"

"Stay focused," I tell him. "Why risk it all sneaking through the back when we can walk right in the front?"

"Say what?"

"Work with what you have," I say, pointing to Gillian. "If they made that kind of investment in Duckworth's future, don't you think they'll want to meet his next of kin . . . ?"

"So you really want to go down there?" Charlie asks.

"First thing tomorrow morning," I say, still feeling the sugar rush. "Me, you, Gillian . . . and all our new friends at Five Points Capital."

44

You're not going to like it," DeSanctis warned as he entered Gallo's office in the downtown Field Office of the Secret Service. It was almost two in the morning and the halls were dead-empty, but DeSanctis still shut the door.

"Just tell me what it says," Gallo demanded.

"Her name's Saundra Finkelstein, fifty-seven years old . . ." DeSanctis began, reading from the top sheet of the stack. "Tax returns say she's been renting there for almost twenty-four years—plenty of time to become best friends."

"And the phone records?"

"We went back six months. On average, she spends at least fifteen minutes a day on the horn with Maggie. Since last night, though, not a single call."

"What about long distance?"

"See, that's where it starts getting ugly. At one A.M. last night, she accepted her first-ever collect call—from a number we identified as—ready for this?—a payphone in Miami International Airport."

Biting at the knuckle of his thumb, Gallo stopped. *"What?"*

"Don't look at me . . ."

"*Who the hell else am I supposed to look at!?*" he asked, slamming the desk with his fist. "*If they're at Duckworth's—*"

"Believe me, I'm well aware of the consequences."

"Have you looked into flights?"

"Two tickets. They're booking them as we speak."

Ramming his chair backwards as he stood up, Gallo let it crash into his credenza. The impact shook the half a dozen Secret Service plaques and photographs that decorated his wall. "There's nothing to find there," he insisted.

"No one said there was."

"We should still call—"

"Already did," DeSanctis said.

Nodding to himself, Gallo stormed toward the door. "When did you say we leave?"

"Next flight out—six A.M. into Miami," DeSanctis added, chasing behind him. "We'll be standing on their necks by breakfast."

"Fudge, I know you're there!" Joey yelled into the answering machine. "Don't act like you're sleeping—I know you can hear me! Pick up, pick up, pick up . . ." She waited, but no one answered. "Are you there, God, it's me, Joey." Still nothing. "Okay, that's it—now you can deal with my niece's alphabet song—A is for *Acrobat*, B is for *Bubbles*, C is for *Charley Horse*, D is for—"

"D is for *Death*, my dear," Fudge answered, his voice hoarse with sleep. "It's also for Destruction, Dismemberment, Disemboweling . . ."

"So you know the song?" Joey asked, working hard to keep it light.

"Mommie dearest, it's currently two-fourteen in the bloody morning. You are, indeed, the devil herself."

"Listen, I'll make it up to you tomorrow—no playing around—I need you to speed up that phone trace on Margaret Caruso."

"It's now two-*fifteen* in the bloody morning . . ."

"I'm serious, Fudge! I've got a crisis!"

"So what do you want me to do?"

"Can't you get your people at the phone company?"

"Now?" he asked, still groggy. "My people don't work these hours—these hours are for deviants, and rock stars, and . . . and deviants."

"Please, Fudge . . ."

"Call me tomorrow, sweetie-pie—I'll have my baby-fresh scent after nine." With a click, he disappeared.

Pulling the earpiece from her ear, Joey glanced down at the digital map on her global positioning system. Fifteen minutes ago, a blue blinking triangle slowly made its way toward downtown. Whatever Gallo and DeSanctis had seen, they were taking it back to headquarters. As they entered the Service's garage, though, the blue blinking triangle disappeared and a high-pitched beep screamed through Joey's car. *System Error*, the screen flashed. *Transfer interrupted*. Joey didn't bat an eye. When it came to locking down external transmitters, there was no messing with the Secret Service.

45

When Charlie was in high school he used to love walking down empty streets at two in the morning. The vacuum of silence. The undertow of darkness around every corner. The noble power of being the last man standing. He used to thrive on it. Now he hates it.

Speedwalking back to our apartment, he sticks to the sidewalks, loses himself under the rows of palm trees, and every few steps, checks anxiously over his shoulder.

"Who're you looking for?" I ask.

"How about lowering your voice?" he hisses. "No offense, but I want to see if she's following."

"Who, Gillian? She already knows where we're staying."

"Okay, then I guess we have nothing to worry about . . ."

"See, now you're being paranoid."

"Listen, Ollie, just 'cause you've got a new kick in your walk doesn't mean you can shut your brain."

"Is that what I'm doing? Shutting my brain?" Crossing into the street, I'm sick of the arguing. And the jealousy.

"Get back here," he scolds, motioning toward the sidewalk.

"Who made you mom?" I ask. He makes a face; I love the dig. There's a near-full moon up above, but he doesn't bother to look. "Why're you giving Gillian such a hard time anyway?"

"Why do you think?" Charlie asks, once again checking over his shoulder. "Didn't you see that layer of dust in her bedroom?"

"And that's what's got the ants in your undies? She doesn't touch her nightstand?"

"It's not just the nightstand—it's the bathroom and the closets and the drawers and everything else we went through. . . . If you moved into your dead father's house, would you still keep his stuff everywhere?"

"Didn't you hear what she said about sleeping on her couch? Besides, it took mom a year to—"

"Don't talk to me about mom. Gillian's been living there for a month, and the place looks like she moved in last week."

"Oh, so now she's working against us?" I ask.

"All I'm saying is, she's got some random clothes and a dozen modern art, neoplastic rip-off paintings. Where's the rest of her life? Her furniture, her CD collection—after all this time, you're telling me she doesn't have her own TV?"

"I'm not saying she doesn't have her quirks—but that's what happens when you're dealing with an artist . . ."

Right there, he's ready to lose it. "Do me a favor—don't call her an artist. Putting tracing paper on an old Mondrian does not an artist make. Besides, have you even looked at her fingernails? That girl hasn't painted a day in her life."

"Oh, and suddenly you're the authority on all things artistic? It's called washing your hands, Charlie—it's an amazing concept. And you're just mad because she's out-Charlie-ing you at your own game."

"What're you talking about?"

"You saw how she lives . . . the fact that she's happy with the bare essentials . . . that she doesn't need to be in the race. . . . Starting to sound familiar? Rhymes with barley. . . . Even when she came after us—she doesn't get mad—she just kinda looks through you—like she's not afraid of anything."

"Ax murderers also aren't afraid of anything."

"Can you please give it a rest?" I beg as we turn onto our block. "You're the one always saying I have no sense of adventure. Would you rather I date someone like Beth?"

"*Date?* You're not *dating* Gillian . . . you're not even courting her. You're just two people in an extreme situation who happen to be standing next to each other. It's like falling in love on a teen tour—but without the James Taylor songs."

"You can make all the fun you want, but we both know you hate it when anyone challenges your role as Mr. Nonconformity. It's the same reason you never join a band—you feel threatened anytime you spot some competition."

"Oh, now I get it—is that what you think this is? A competition? You can have her, Ollie. She's all yours. But just so you know, it's not about competition anymore—it's about one thing: divide and conquer. That's what she's gonna do."

"How can you say that?"

Checking the block one last time, he scrambles across the street, pushes open the cheap metal gate, and races through the courtyard that leads to our apartment. We're both silent until I turn the key and let us inside. The bug spray smell hits first. "It's still better than staying at Gillian's," Charlie says, taking his own whiff.

"You don't even know her," I challenge.

"That doesn't mean she doesn't have a vibe," Charlie shoots back, kicking his shoes off and undressing for bed.

"Oh, pardon me—I didn't realize you were in the midst of channeling your inner Buddha—you're like one of those water-divining rods when it comes to people's vibes."

"You're saying I'm not?"

"All I'm saying is I'm not the one who *lent* his favorite amp to a complete stranger, and then watched it get traded to some crappy pawn shop in Staten Island."

"First of all, it was old and I needed a new one anyway. B) I've got one Grand Canyon–sized proper noun for you: Ernie. Della. Costa."

"Ernie Dellacosta?" I ask. "Mom's old boyfriend?"

"For an interminable seven and a half months," Charlie adds. "Remember what happened the first time mom brought him to meet us? He was respectful and nice and he even successfully bought my love by bringing us Chicken Delight for dinner. But the instant I snatched that chicken bucket out of his hands, I hated him. I hated his comb-over . . . I hated his fake designer shoes . . . and the entire time they dated, I hated that man like poison. And y'know what? I was right."

Shoving my way next to him at the sink, I cup my hands and soak my face. There's a quick skirmish over space, but Charlie dodges around me and storms back to the futon. Chasing behind him, I add, "Well, if you want to remember the rest of reality—while you were strumming your guitar—"

"It's a bass."

"Whatever—while you were strumming your bass and living in Fantasyland, Ernie Dellacosta was also the guy who got me that job at Moe Ginsburg during my freshman year. If it wasn't for him, I wouldn't have had the money to stay at NYU."

"Y'know, I forgot all about that sales job. You're right—he really was an inspiration to us all," he says with an extra scoop of sarcasm.

"What's that supposed to mean?" I ask.

"Nothing. Forget it."

"Oh, no—don't play your passive-aggressive headgames with me. Say what you're thinking."

Charlie stays quiet, which means he's holding something back. "Just drop it," he eventually says.

"Drop it? But you're so close to making your all-important point. C'mon, Charlie, we're all eating pins and needles—you obviously brought Dellacosta up for a reason—so what's your problem? That I sucked up to him so he'd help me get a job? That I laughed uncontrollably at his dumb-ass jokes? That I acted like everyone else in working-class America and busted my ass so I could someday stop worrying about debt collectors calling the house and harassing me for the last forty dollars in my bank account? Tell me what's got your socks all wet?"

"*You do!* You and your self-obsessed, woe-is-me-and-my-poor-lifestyle whine-fest!" Charlie explodes. "This isn't about you, Oliver—and if you ever stopped to realize that, you might actually notice the things that're going on under your own damn roof!"

"What're you talking about?"

"The guy was an asshole, Ollie. A complete asshole. Doesn't that make you wonder why mom dated him for so long?"

"What're you saying?"

"Did you know she was terrified you'd lose your job? Or that she hated him after month two, but was worried that without the paycheck you wouldn't make it through the semester? You can bury your past under all the résumé paper you want, but back home, she was the one putting up with the abuse."

I stop, completely lost. "W-Whattya mean abuse?" I ask.

"Uh-oh, someone's using his old Brooklyn accent . . ."

"What abuse, Charlie? He hit her?"

"She never said it, but I heard their arguments—you know how thin our walls are."

"That's not the question," I insist. "Did you ever see him hit her?"

For once, Charlie doesn't fight back. "I walked in, and they were in the kitchen," he begins. "She was crying; he was using a tone that was more heated than anything you'd want directed at your mother. He spun around to see if I'd back off. I told him if he didn't get out, I'd use his larynx as my own personal jump rope. Mom started crying even harder, but she didn't stop him from leaving. We never saw him again. And that was your buddy Mr. Dellacosta."

Teetering in place, I feel like my chest's about to shatter. My chin quivers and I look at Charlie like I've never seen him before. All this time, I thought I had the hard part. All this time, I had it wrong. "Charlie, I didn't know . . ."

"Don't say it," he warns, in no mood to listen. Hopping into bed, he turns away and pulls the mangy fuzzy blanket we found in the closet up over his head. The cigarette smell on the fuzz has to be worse than the bug spray, but for Charlie, it's clearly a lot better than dealing with me. "Just remember what I said about Gillian," he calls out as he disappears under the covers. "Divide and conquer—that's always how it works."

46

I can't sleep. I'm not good at it. Even when we were little—when Charlie and I used to take turns telling each other horror stories about Old Man Kelly and the creepy people who lived in our building—Charlie was always the first one snoring. It's no different tonight.

Staring up at the jagged black fissure in our popcorn-stucco ceiling, I still hear the echoes of my mom crying. And Dellacosta leaving. Why the hell didn't anyone tell me? Still wrestling with the answer, I listen to the rise and fall of Charlie's labored breathing. When he was sick, it was much worse—a wet hacking wheeze that used to have me watching over him like a human heart monitor. It's a sound that'll forever haunt—like the sound of my mom's sobs—but as I turn over and face Charlie—as the minutes tick by and his breathing falls into its steady rhythm, I try to take comfort in the feeling that we're finally getting a break. Between the photos and the nondisclosure agreement and the leads at Five Points Capital, there's actually a pinhole at the end of the tunnel. And then, out of nowhere, it's stolen away by a slight tapping against the front window.

I bolt up in bed.

The tapping stops. I don't move. And then it starts again. The persistent rap of a knuckle hitting glass.

"Charlie, get up," I whisper.

He doesn't budge.

"*Oliver,*" a voice comes from outside.

I jump out of bed, struggling to be silent. If I yell, they'll know we're awake. I reach back to pull the covers off my brother—

"*Oliver, are you there?*" the voice asks.

Spinning around, I let go of the blanket. That's not just any voice . . .

"*Oliver, it's me.*"

. . . that's a voice I know. Racing to the door, I ram my eye toward the peephole, just to be safe.

"*Open up . . .*"

I twist and unclick the locks. Cracking the door open, I peek outside.

"I'm sorry—did I wake you?" Gillian asks with a soft grin. As always, she can't stand still. She stuffs her hands in her back pockets, then shifts her weight from one foot, to the other, then back again. Swaying like a folk singer.

"What're you doing here?" I whisper.

"I don't know . . . I just kept thinking about the remote . . . and the photos and . . . and there's no way I was falling asleep, so I figured—" She cuts herself off and takes a fast glance down at my boxers. I blush; she laughs. "Listen, I know you have your own reasons, but I appreciate what you're doing with my dad. He'd . . . he'd thank you for it."

My face only gets redder.

"I'm serious," she says.

"I know you are."

Enjoying the moment, she adds, "When's your birthday?"

"What?"

"What're you, an Aries or Leo? Melville and Hitchcock were Leos, but . . ." She pauses, absorbing my reaction. "You're an Aries, aren't you?"

"How can you—? How'd you know?"

"C'mon, Stiffy, it's spray-painted on your forehead—the perfection posture, the scolding dad tone when you talk to your brother, even the spotless white boxers . . ."

"These boxers are brand-new."

"They definitely are," she says, staring down at them. Once again, I blush and she laughs. "C'mon," she adds. "Put on some clothes—I'll let you buy me some cheap coffee."

Over her shoulder, I check the empty street. Even at this hour, it's not smart to be strolling in public. "How 'bout a raincheck?"

Slinking back, she looks like a hurt puppy.

"It doesn't mean you have to go, though . . ." I offer.

She stops and quickly turns back. "So you want me to stay?"

It's a tease and we both know it. Charlie would tell me to shut the door. But that would just leave me lying awake in the dark. "All I'm saying is, I have to be careful."

"Oh, because of the . . . I didn't even think . . ." She stumbles in the sweetest way possible. It's one of those moments that no one could fake. "Of course I want you to be careful. In fact . . ." A playful smile lights her face.

"What?"

"Grab some sneakers," she says, already beaming. "I've got an idea."

"To go out? I don't think that's—"

"Trust me, handsome-pants, this is gonna be one you thank me for. No one'll even know we're there."

She says something else, but I'm still munching on *handsome*. "Are you sure it's safe?"

"I wouldn't ask you if it wasn't," she says, suddenly serious. "Especially when we're in it together."

That's the shove that puts me over the mountain. If she wanted to hurt us, Gallo and DeSanctis would've been here hours ago. Instead, we had a whole day of peace. From here on in, the longer she stays with us, the more she puts herself at risk. She doesn't care. She wants the truth about her dad. So do we. I leave a quick note for my brother, then look back at him to make sure he's still asleep.

"Don't worry," Gillian says. "He'll never know you're gone."

Racing down the dock, I have to hand it to her. In a town that prides itself on being seen, she's found the one cool place where no one's watching.

"Abandoned enough for you?" she asks as our shoes clunk along the wooden planks of the Miami Beach Marina. All around us, the docks are dead silent. Back on shore, there's a security guard making his nightly rounds, but a friendly wave from Gillian keeps him at bay.

"You come out here often?" I ask.

"Wouldn't you?" she replies as she hits the brakes.

I'm not sure what she means—that is, until she points down to the small, weather-scorched, white fishing boat that's bobbing up and down against the dock. Barely big enough to seat six, it's got frayed Miami Dolphins seat cushions and a windshield with a crooked crack down the center. With a flick of her foot, Gillian kicks her sandals down into the boat.

"This is yours?" I ask.

"Dad's last gift," she says proudly. "Even godless engineers still appreciate the majesty of catching a fish at sunset."

As she undoes the ropes from the dock, I watch her thin arms swoop and glow gracefully in the moonlight. I hop in the boat without hesitating. She starts the engine and grabs the steering wheel in a soft but assured grip. It may be four in the morning, but there are still majestic sights at sea.

Making a sharp left as we leave the marina and ignoring the "No Wake" signs, Gillian shoves the throttle forward, guns the engine, and sends us skipping across the water. The bouncing ride is enough to knock us to our seats, but both of us grab the dashboard and fight to stay on our feet. "*If you don't stand above the windshield, you can't taste the ocean!*" she shouts over the engine. I nod and lick the salty air from my lips. When I first started at Greene, Lapidus private-jetted me to St. Bart's and took me out on one of our client's personal yachts. They had wine-tasting classes, Thai massage, and two full-time butlers. It sucked compared to this.

Thanks to a foglight on the front of the boat, we can see a few feet through the darkness, but with the moon hidden by a pack of clouds, it's like driving with your brights on through an abandoned field. In the distance, the ocean fades and the whole world turns black. The only things in sight are the parallel jetties that run along our right- and lefthand sides—a natural guardrail that leads us out toward the ocean.

"Ready to get on the magic bus?" she calls out as we hit the open water. I expect her to punch the engine. Instead, she slows down. At the end of the jetty, she pulls a hard left around the rocks and cuts the engine.

"What're you doing?"

"You'll see," she teases, rushing toward the front of the boat.

We're a good hundred and fifty yards from shore, but I still hear the faint crashing of the waves against the beach.

"Can people see us?" I ask, squinting toward a barely visible lifeguard stand.

"Not anymore," she says as she cuts our foglight. The darkness hits quick, swallowing us whole.

Searching for safety, my eyes go straight for the hot pink, sky blue, and lime green neon signs that trace the tops of Ocean Drive's Art Deco hotels. This far away, they're like Day-Glo landing lights. Everything else is gone.

"You sure this is smart?"

There's a loud plop of water and a slight jerk from the front of the boat. There goes the anchor.

"Gillian . . ."

Flipping toward the back of the boat, she yanks the Dolphin seat cushions from the bench, lifts up the wooden seat, and reveals a storage locker underneath. From the locker, she pulls out two wet suits, masks, flippers . . .

"Give me a hand here," she calls out, struggling with something heavier.

I race next to her and help her lift a cold metal canister from the locker. Then another. Scuba tanks.

"Is there something you're trying to tell me?" I ask her, struggling to sound unintimidated.

She pulls out a flashlight and shines it in my face. "I thought you were up for some adventure . . ."

"I am," I say, blocking the light with my hand. "That's why we came on the boat."

"No, we came on the boat to get under. The adventure starts here." Flushed with adrenaline, she props the flashlight on the bench and pounces for the pile of equipment.

Reading the gauges, adjusting knobs, untangling a knot of hoses. . . . "Just wait till you see it," she says, her voice whizzing with excitement.

"Gillian . . ."

"It's gonna overload your senses—sight, touch, sound—boom—blown like a giant speaker."

"Maybe we should . . ."

"And the best part is, only the locals know about it. Forget the tourist parade gawking on South Beach—this is just for the home-growns. Here, put this on." She tosses me a wet suit, which hits me in the chest.

Even if I lose cool-points, it's no time to hold back. "Gillian, I don't know how to scuba-dive."

"Don't worry—you'll be fine."

"But isn't it dangerou—"

She unzips her jeans and slides them down to her ankles. As she steps out of them, she unbuttons her shirt and tosses it aside. "Relax," she says, standing there in her sheer bra and white cotton panties. "I'll teach you." Right above the thin waistband of her underwear is a tiny purple butterfly tattoo. I can't take my eyes off it.

"Careful, you might go blind," she teases, wiggling into her wet suit.

"Have I ever told you how much I love scuba-diving?" I ask, still staring at the butterfly.

Grinning, she motions to my pants. I strip down to my boxers and tug my way into my wet suit, which is more tight-fitting than I expected. Especially in the crotch.

"Don't worry," Gillian says, reading my expression. "It'll loosen up when it gets wet."

"Me or the suit?"

"Hopefully, both."

Shoving my arms in, I practically run to catch up with her.

In the back of the boat, she props up both scuba tanks and opens each with the twist of a knob. "This is your regulator," she says as she points to the top of the tank, where she attaches a small black gizmo that has four hoses snaking out in every direction. "And here's your mouthpiece," she adds, handing me the short black hose on the right.

Following her lead, I put it in my mouth and take a long deep breath. There's a slow Darth Vader hiss as a cold rush of air plows down my throat and fills my lungs.

"That's it . . . there you go," she says as I exhale and do it again. "Nice and slow—you're a total natural."

It's easy praise, but as my breath wheezes through the tube, the testosterone starts wearing thin. "What're all these other hoses for?" I ask nervously.

"Don't get freaked by the minutiae," she says as she zips the front of my wet suit and pats me on the chest. "When you scuba, there's only one life-or-death rule: keep breathing."

"But what about the regulator and these tubes—"

"All the equipment runs automatically. As long as you're breathing, it keeps the air flowing and regulates the pressure. After that, it's like driving a car—you don't need to know how the engine and combustion and everything else works—you just need to know how to drive."

"But I've never driven before . . ."

Ignoring my comment, she motions for me to raise my hands in the air, hooks a thick yellow belt around my waist, and buckles it with what looks like a plastic version of an airline seat belt. "How much do you weigh?" she adds as she loads the belt's Velcro pouches with square lead weights.

"About one-sixty. Why?"

"Perfect," she says, sealing the last pouch. "That'll sink you like a mob stoolie." Refusing to slow down, she cuts behind me. I spin around to follow, but the extra weight on my waist and the bobbing of the boat send me slightly off-balance.

"Don't I need to be certified for this?" I ask.

"You love rules, don't you?" she shoots back, putting on her own weight belt. "The only thing those classes teach you is how not to panic." With that, she angles my arms into an inflatable red vest. Strapped to the back of the vest is the scuba tank and its tentacles of hoses. As I squat down, she lifts the vest onto my shoulders and I almost fall over backwards from the thirty pounds of extra weight. Gillian's right there to catch me.

"I'm telling you," she promises, making sure my vest is clipped in place. "I wouldn't take you down there if it weren't safe."

"What about the bends? I don't want to wind up in some sci-fi decompression chamber."

"We're only going down twenty feet. The bends aren't a risk until you hit at least sixty."

"And this is only twenty?"

"Only twenty," she repeats. "Thirty at the most." Squatting down, she hoists her own vest and scuba tank onto her shoulders. "Not much more than the length of this boat." When she's done adjusting her vest, she reaches for one of my four hoses and pushes a button on the end. There's a sharp hiss. The vest fills with air and tightens around my ribs. "If all else fails, you even have a life jacket," she points out, making it sound like I'm afraid of drowning in the kiddie pool.

Inflating her own vest, she grabs a mask and flashlight, slips into her flippers, and steps up on the cooler at the back of the boat.

"Gillian, wait . . ."

She doesn't even turn around. There's a splash and the boat rocks from the loss of weight. Off the back, she sinks out of sight, then bobs right back up again. "Ooooh, you gotta feel this!" she shouts.

"It's warm?"

"It's freezing! We're talking iceberg in my pants!" She laughs out loud, like it's the party of the year. And the more I watch her, the more I realize it is.

"C'mon," she calls out. "You have to at least come in. If you hate it, you'll float around up here."

It's not fair, but I try to imagine Beth in the same position. She hates the cold. And at this hour? She'd never even get in the boat.

"There you go!" Gillian shouts as I reach for a mask and flippers. "No whammies on this one—just stand up on the cooler and leap out!"

I pull the mask over my face and grip all the hoses in an anxious fist. "Are you sure this is the best way to get in?"

"Jacques Cousteau himself couldn't do better—one giant step for all manki—"

Shutting my eyes, I leap out and plummet fast. The extra weight sends me straight under, but thanks to my vest, I bob right back up to the top. The temperature hits first. Without the sun on the water . . . even with my wet suit . . . iceberg in my pants is right.

"Cold enough for you?" Gillian asks.

"Naw, this is good—I like it when I absolutely, positively can't feel my penis."

It's an easy joke, but she knows it's not just the cold that's got me shaking. The water's dark and deserted, the mask is tight around my face, and all I hear is the *Jaws* theme.

"So you ready to go under?" she asks.

"Right now?"

Watching me carefully through her own mask, she kicks forward and grabs me by both shoulders. "You're gonna be great—no doubt."

"Are you—?"

"I'm positive," she promises.

As she floats back, I reach over my right shoulder and grab the hose with the mouthpiece. "All I have to do is breathe through this?"

"That's the entire instruction book. Breathe and breathe and breathe. In fact, why don't you take a lap around the block . . ."

Like before, I slide the mouthpiece between my teeth, and Darth Vader returns. After three or four breaths, Gillian points down to the water. Biting hard on the rubber prongs that hold the mouthpiece in place, I bend over and put my face in the ocean.

There's a slight pause before I take my next breath, but my brain flips right back to Gillian's crash course. Breathe, breathe, breathe. Opening my lungs, I suck in a puff of air . . . and quickly blow it out. A burst of tiny bubbles shoots from the regulator. From there, each breath is short and tentative, but it still works.

Gillian taps me hard on the shoulder. Picking my head up, I take out the mouthpiece.

"Ready for the pop quiz?" she challenges.

I nod, hoping it'll slow her down. It only speeds her up.

"Okay, here's what I'd put on the cheat sheet. First, if you get disoriented, follow the bubbles—they'll always lead you up to the surface."

"Follow the bubbles. Check."

"Second, as we go down, don't forget to pop your ears— you don't want to blow out an eardrum."

I pinch my nose and take myself through a dry run.

"And third—which is actually the most important—as you come back up to the surface, keep breathing. You'll be tempted to hold your breath, but you have to fight the urge."

"What do you mean?"

"It's human instinct. You're underwater . . . you start to panic. The first thing you'll do—guaranteed—is hold your breath. But if you come up to the surface like that—and you're not breathing in and out—your lungs'll pop like a balloon." Readjusting her mask, she gives me the quick once-over. "All set to go?"

Once again, I nod—but I'm still focused on a single image. *My lungs popping like a balloon.* Down under the waves, I kick my feet in a backpaddle.

"What?" she asks. "Now you're scared?"

"You telling me I shouldn't be?"

"I'm not telling you anything. If you want to back out, that's your choice."

"It's not about backing out—"

"Really?" she interrupts, annoyed. "Then why're you suddenly acting like the first rat off the ship?"

The question stings like a corkscrew in my chest. I've never heard that tone in her voice.

"Listen," I tell her, "I'm doing my best here. Anyone else would've let you sink alone."

"Oh, I'm sure . . ."

"You think I'm kidding? Name one other person who would put on a wet suit, jump into the freezing ocean, and risk their life for a cheap thrill at four in the morning?"

"Your brother," she shoots back, staring me down to drive it home. Before I can react, she puts in her mouthpiece and grabs the hose that's resting on her left shoulder. Raising it above her head, she presses a button on the end. A hiss of air tears through the silence. As her vest deflates, she slowly starts sinking.

I shove in my own mouthpiece, lift my hose, and jam my thumb against the button. The vest loosens around my ribs. The water's already up to my chin.

"You won't regret it, Oliver," she calls out, removing the mouthpiece for one last breath. As she's about to go under, she adds, "You'll thank me later."

I shake my head, pretending to ignore the sudden enthusiasm. But as I sink down—as the black water licks my cheeks and fills my ears—it suddenly hits me that I never told her my real name was Oliver.

47

At three in the morning, her car now blocking the fire hydrant in front of Maggie Caruso's building, Joey promised herself she wouldn't fall asleep. At three-thirty, she rolled down her window, so the cold would keep her awake. By four, her head sagged. By four-thirty, it flopped back into the headrest. Then, at exactly ten minutes to five, a sharp, shrill beep jolted her awake.

Blinking herself back to the waking world, she chased the sound down to the lit-up screen of her global positioning system. The bright blue triangle was once again moving across the digital map, straight down the West Side Highway. Pulling the screen onto her lap, she watched as Gallo's car weaved its way toward the tip of the city. It was like a primitive videogame she had no control of. At first, she thought they were headed back to Brooklyn, but when they blew past the entrance to the bridge and instead shot up the FDR Drive, she felt a flame blaze at the back of her neck. There were only a few things open this late. Or this early. *Aw, don't tell me they're . . .*

The tiny triangle turned onto the 59th Street Bridge, and

when Joey saw it make its way toward the Grand Central Parkway, she cranked the ignition and took off. At the top of the digital map, the blue triangle veered straight toward it. The most popular five A.M. destination in Queens: La Guardia Airport.

48

Sinking under the waves, I float like an astronaut and plummet into darkness. Bubbles rise all around me, bouncing against the front of my mask. I crane my neck up at the only source of light, but the deeper I fall, the faster it fades. Sea green becomes dark blue becomes a cloud of pitch black. Just breathe, I tell myself as I force a raspy puff of air through the mouthpiece. I suck in again and it sounds like a respirator. No waves, no wind, no background noise. Just the gurgling echo of my own breath. And Gillian saying my name.

Don't even think about it—not now. But some things can't be ignored. She probably heard it from Charlie. He said my name at least a dozen times in the garage. Struggling to remain calm, I search around for reassurance, but everything—in every direction—it's all dark. I grab my nose to pop my ears and a wave of tiny fluorescent fish zip by my face. I duck to the left and they're gone. Back to black. It's like swimming through ink. And then—a white lightsaber slices through the dark. Gillian's flashlight. She shines it at me, then back on herself. She was right next to me the entire time.

C'mon, she motions, trying to get me to follow. I hesitate, but quickly realize she has the only light. Besides, after what she said about Charlie—there's no way I'm proving her right.

She kicks her legs, and her flippers whip through the water. The way she moves—the graceful stretch of her arms—it's like she's flying. Behind her, I fight to keep up, thrashing my arms in a violent breaststroke. It's harder than I thought. For every few inches I swim forward, the underwater current seems to push me back. She looks over her shoulder to see if I'm following, then quickly picks up speed. Whatever she wanted me to see, we're getting close.

Swimming forward, she shines the light outward and it hits a beige wall. Then I notice the way her air bubbles slide down her back. That's not a wall. It's the floor. We're at the bottom.

Instinctively, I spin myself upright. My breathing quickens; I'm not sure why.

I look to my right, but the mask blocks my peripheral vision. I quickly turn my head to both sides. There's nothing to see. No one's there. That is, until something slithers up against the left side of my neck.

Jerking wildly, I spin back and grab it by the throat. In front of me, Gillian whips around and shines the light my way. There it is. My attacker: the inanimate inflation hose that's supposed to float next to me while I swim. Assaulted by my own octopus.

You okay there? Gillian motions with a sarcastic hand on her hip.

Floating helplessly, I just nod.

Once again, she dives toward the darkness. Once again, I follow.

She shines the light to survey the ocean floor, but all

we've got are some swaying green plants, loose shells, and what looks like a rusty, abandoned lobster trap. Turning herself rightside-up, Gillian snaps her flippers and a snowglobe of sand swirls around her.

Not much further, she motions by holding her pointer finger only a few inches from her thumb. She lets out a huge breath of air and the bubbles rise between us. Tracing the slant of the ground downward, she swims out even deeper. As I breaststroke behind her, she just keeps going. From where I'm watching—the way she holds the light against her chest—the outline of her body glows with a shimmering halo. It's like chasing a firefly through an underwater forest.

A convex black wall rises up from the sand and comes to a point right above our heads. To the left, it continues on further than the flashlight lets us see. With her hand sliding across its chipped metal surface, Gillian swims to the right and quickly turns the corner. Above a broken rudder and missing propeller, the words *Mon Dieu II—Les Cayes, Haiti* run perpendicular toward the ocean floor. Even when it's turned on its side, there's no mistaking a sunken ship.

The moment I see it, my breathing again starts to quicken. It's like standing outside an abandoned house. Freaky and cool, but there's no reason to go in. Gillian, of course, sees it differently. Wasting no time, she swims around to the back deck, leaving me in a blur of bubbles. By the time I catch up, she's already investigating—shining the light up and down the barely rotted deck. There's a bit of greenish brown moss, but not much—it hasn't been down here long.

Straight above us, a silver flash catches my eye. At first, I assume it's the metal railing that surrounds the deck, but as Gillian lifts the light, I quickly realize that's just part of it. Bolted to the deck and perpendicular to the ground, a red-and-white Coca-Cola machine sways open above our heads.

Inside, all the cans are gone. No doubt about it—the rust-bucket little ship hit a rock and got picked clean. Haiti steals sodas from us; we steal 'em right back. Only in Miami.

I turn to share the joke with Gillian, but to my surprise, the only thing there is the flashlight—sitting on the ocean floor, pointed up at the Coke machine. Confused, I glance around the ship. No one's there. Above my head, the door of the machine continues to swing with the tide.

"Illian . . . ?" I whisper through the mouthpiece, though I know she can't hear me. Spinning around, I crane my neck in every direction. A cold wave of water shoves me in the chest. I don't understand. Gillian's gone.

Reaching down, I grab the flashlight and shine it out across the horizontal plane. In front of me, a trail of bubbles leads straight to the boat's two-story cabin. The door's missing from the doorframe and the glass has been pulled from the porthole windows, but even from here I can see how dark it is. I shake my head to myself. No way I'm going in there.

A minute later, the trail of bubbles is long gone. And still no Gillian. I shine the light at the doorframe of the cabin. No movement. No puffs of air. Slowly, I swim closer, mentally replaying every teenage slasher flick I ever laid eyes on. At the door, I hammer the flashlight against the metal hull. It clangs with a low vibration. There's no way she'd miss it. Not unless she was stuck . . . or needed help.

I kick my flippers and glide through the door. The light flicks around, but it's still hard to get my bearings. It's a small galley—big enough for three or four people—and the sink, the stove, even the countertops are all on their side. In the corner, a ladder that usually runs up to the second floor now runs horizontally. Same with the stairs that go down to the cargo hold. The ceiling's on my right; the floor's on my left. When I look up, two empty wood cabinets sway open like the Coke machine. In between them is an open porthole window. Weightlessness hits hard and the room starts to spin.

I do my best to follow the bubbles, but the confined space is getting the best of me. The walls ripple like they're made of mercury. It's like looking through melted glass. My stomach cartwheels and the taste of vomit bites me in the back of the throat. Oh, God—if I puke in the airhose ... Frantically, I spin to my left, searching for the door. Instead, I'm face-to-face with the linoleum floor. It doesn't make sense. I wheel around, but nothing's familiar. The whole world kaleidoscopes as light-headedness sets in. I grab my chest, panting like a rabid dog. I swear, the room's getting smaller. And darker. Everything—in every direction—it all goes gray.

A sharp jab hits me in the back and two arms lock around my chest. We flip sideways and I'm not sure which way's up. The impact knocks the flashlight from my hands and it tumbles in slow motion toward the bottom. As it falls, the whole room flickers like a disco. Fighting free, I spin back and face Gillian. I can barely see her through all the bubbles. Her arms thrash wildly, gripping and grabbing at the front lower part of my vest. It's the only thing holding my air in place. Why's she trying to unhook it? Panicking, I hold her by the wrists. She digs in her nails. Refusing to give up, she comes at me again, clawing in a mad rage. But this time, I get a look at her eyes.

"*Please . . . trust me*," she begs with a glance.

Desperately, her hand charges out. A plastic hook flips open, and my weight belt falls away. In a blur, Gillian grabs me by the lapels and shoves me backwards. Following her gaze, I look straight up—and just as I see the open porthole window—she finally lets me go. Without the weight belt, I rise like a human cork. She gives me a final tug to make sure I don't bang the tank on the way out, but after that, I've got a clear shot to the surface.

Swimming madly to catch up, Gillian points to her mouth, reminding me to breathe. I let out a huge puff of air and stare up through the water. Black becomes dark blue becomes sea green. She grabs my hand to make sure I don't rise too fast. Don't blow it now, Oliver. Breathe, breathe, breathe.

We crack the surface and the cool night air whips against my face. Next to me, Gillian's already inflating her vest.

"You okay? Can you breathe?" she asks frantically as she swims to my side. Holding me up, she hits the button on my inflation tube and the vest starts to hiss. It hugs my ribs and squeezes my stomach. Right there, I dry-heave, but the vomit never comes.

"Is that better? Are you okay?" she asks again.

Bobbing in the water, I barely hear the question. Slowly, the color in my vision locks into focus. "Wh-Why'd you leave me?" I ask her.

"Leave you?"

"On the ship—I turned around and you were gone."

"I thought you saw me—I waved as I left . . ."

"Then why didn't you take me with you?"

"For the exact reason I had to pull you out—going down is one thing—navigating *inside* a wreck . . . the disorientation . . . that's not something you try on your first dive."

"And that's the *real* reason?"

"What other reason would th—?" Her eyes go wide like I jammed a scalpel in her ribs. "Y-you think I . . . I'd never abandon you . . . I wouldn't leave *anyone* like that." Her voice cracks as she says the words. It's like she can't comprehend it. Letting go of me, she slowly floats away.

"Gillian . . ."

"I'd never hurt you . . ."

"I'm not saying you would, it's just . . . when you said my real name—"

"In the house—your brother said it."

"I figured . . . but when I turned around—when you were gone—I just got scared."

"But to think I'd . . . God! This is . . . this is where I come before I paint . . . growing up—even now—this is home. If I thought you didn't trust me, I . . . I never would've invited you."

Stretching across the water, I grab the shoulder of her vest. "If I didn't trust you, Gillian, I never would've come."

She shoots me a lasting glance, digesting each word.

"I'm serious," I quickly add. "I wouldn't be here if I—"

Her hand flies out like a dart, grabs me by the back of my neck, and reels me in for a soft, smooth kiss. The salty taste on her tongue stings in the best way possible. Underneath, her fingers flick the zipper on my chest.

As we bob in the ocean, the wind's cold, it's completely dark, and it's going to be a bitch of a swim to get back to the boat. But right now, with the neon lights behind us, I'm just enjoying my kiss.

49

Please tell me you're joking," Joey pleaded through her
cell phone as her car tore around the corner in the USAir
parking lot.

"How many different ways you need me to say it?"
Debbie asked. As a USAir ticket counter agent, Debbie was
used to dealing with short-tempered customers. But as
Joey's oldest high school friend, she knew this was one who
couldn't be ignored and sent to the back of the line. "The
computers froze—the whole system's down. Stop giving me
heartache. They'll have it back up in ten minutes."

"I don't have ten minutes," Joey said as she screeched
into an open spot. "I need it now."

"Yeah, well, I need a push-up bra that works minor mira-
cles and a husband who remembers how to make my toes
curl in bed, but sometimes you're stuck with what you've
got."

"What about frequent-flier miles? Can't you track them
by that?"

"Joey, the computers are down—it's all on the same system. Besides, how do you even know they're on USAir?"

"Why else would you leave your car in the USAir parking lot?" Joey asked as she cut the engine. Taking one last look at the blue triangle on the electronic screen, she hopped outside, squinted in the slowly rising sun, and feverishly scanned the packed-to-capacity lot. According to this, the car should be right—

There.

In the corner . . . close in toward the terminal—Gallo's government-issued navy Ford—parked illegally in a handicapped spot.

"Crap," Joey whispered as she turned back and yanked her bags from the trunk. Tacklebox under one arm; duffel bag under the other. With the earpiece still dangling from her ear, she ran off-balance toward the terminal. Dashing across the crosswalk, she cut off two honking taxicabs. "What about searching by government-issued tickets? Or on the manifest list?" she called to Debbie. "Isn't that how you found out who Marsha's lowlife husband was sitting next to?"

"How many different ways can I say it? It's all on the same—"

"What about the LEO list?" Joey asked, referring to the airline's list of law enforcement officers. "Don't they have to file special paperwork if they want to travel with their guns?"

There was a pause on the other line. "Y'know what . . ." Debbie began. "Hold on a sec. Lemme call the gate . . ."

Shoving her way through the automatic doors and ignoring the baggage claim carousels, Joey made a sharp right and flew up the escalator stairs two at a time. At the top, along the ticket counters, she surveyed the sparse early morning crowd. Businessman in a rumpled suit, high school student in an oversized sweatshirt, old lady in a pale yellow turtleneck—but no one who resembled Gallo or DeSanctis.

"You better thank the Lord for useless government paperwork," a familiar voice sang in her ear.

"You found them?" she asked Debbie.

"I swear to you, sometimes I think some of this stuff was invented by the CIA to keep track of us . . ."

"So what'd you—"

"According to our records, Agent James Gallo and Agent Paul DeSanctis just hit the LEO list on our 6:27 A.M. flight to Miami."

Joey went right for her watch. 6:31. "Are they—?"

"Long gone."

"When's the next—?"

"Hour and a half. I already told them to book you a seat as soon as the system goes up."

Shaking her head, Joey checked the TV screen. *Miami—Flight 412—Departed.* "How the hell did I miss them?"

"Don't wet your eyes," Debbie said. "All they have is a head start."

50

"What floor?" Charlie asks early Thursday morning as we step into the elevator.

"Seven," I say as he pushes the button. I straighten my tie; Charlie licks his hand and flattens his matted blond hair. If we're going to reprise our roles as bankers, we have to look the part. Next to us, Gillian does the female equivalent with her long flowered skirt. When she's done smoothing it out, she looks my way. Letting my eyes linger on her legs, I can't help but stare—that is, until I notice Charlie watching me. I glance at the floor; he shakes his head. You can't fool little brothers.

The elevator jerks to a stop and the doors slip open. In the hallway, a tasteful and understated (for Miami) silver-and-gold logo hangs on the wall: shaped like a star, but with a circle at the end of each point. The silver letters across the bottom tell us we've reached our destination: Five Points Capital—where Duckworth made his deal.

Gillian bounces off the brass railing of the elevator and glides out. Before I can follow, Charlie grabs me by the arm. "You touched her cookies, didn't you?" he whispers.

"What're you talking about?" I ask, annoyed as I step out of the elevator.

"That's the best you can muster? Anger, but no denial?"

This time, I don't answer.

"When was it? Last night? When you went to get the clothes this morning?"

Pulling out of his grip, I make a hard left and head for the glass doors of the reception area. Charlie's right behind me. He doesn't have to say it. From here on in, he's not letting me out of his sight.

"You sure you're ready?" Gillian asks, reading what she thinks is fear on my face.

"I'm fine," I say, still eyeing Charlie. But as I take a deep breath, reality collides. He sees it on my face. It's one thing to call up and ask for an appointment. It's quite another to pull it off.

To the right of the doors, a small sign says *Ring Bell for Reception.* But it's what's above the bell that gets our attention—a gray keypad that looks like the one we have at the bank. Next to the numbers, though, there's also a flat space just big enough for a thumbprint. *Biometric ID* it says across the top.

I ring the bell, and Charlie raises an eyebrow. "Fingerprint recognition?" he asks. "Someone's taking themselves a bit too seriously."

A receptionist with teased brown hair looks up and buzzes us in. Charlie's first in line, ambassador of smiles. Every bigshot needs an assistant. "Hi, we called this morning . . ." he says, copying my salesman voice and pointing my way. "From Greene Bank—I have Henry Lapidus here to see Mr. Katkin."

"Of course," she says as she nods at me. "I'll page him for you, Mr. Lapidus."

Charlie grinds his teeth as she says the name. *You sure this is right?* he asks with a glance.

Trust me, I insist. Over the past four years, I've taken tons of clients on the venture capital roadshow. And even in Florida, it takes a big name to open a big door.

Fidgeting with the tie he borrowed from Duckworth, Charlie sits back on the cream-colored sofa. The instant Gillian sits next to him, he gets up and paces. I scowl, but he doesn't care. Ignoring me, he pretends to check out the view of Brickell Avenue from the enormous plate glass windows.

"Mr. Lapidus, can you please sign in for me?" the receptionist asks me. She points to a free-standing computer kiosk right next to her desk. Onscreen, there's a blank for your name. I type in *Henry Lapidus* and hit *Enter.* Behind the receptionist, a high-tech laser printer hums and spits out an ID sticker. *Henry Lapidus—Visitor.* But unlike a normal guest pass, the front of this one has a liquid, almost translucent quality to it. Underneath, if you angle it in the light, the word *Expired* appears in faint red letters.

"What's this made of?" I ask, rubbing my thumb against the smooth pass.

"Aren't they wild?" the receptionist croons. "After eight hours, the ink on the front dissolves and the *Expired* part becomes bright red."

I nod, impressed.

"You guys take security pretty seriously, don't you?" Charlie adds.

"We don't have a choice," the receptionist says with a laugh. "I mean . . . considering who we're partners with . . ."

"Totally," Charlie says, forcing his own fake laugh.

"Absolutely," I agree.

We stare at the woman. She stares right back. We're clueless.

"So what's it like working with them?" Charlie asks, searching for details.

"Honestly? It's not that big a deal. I thought they'd show up in dark suits and sunglasses—but they're like everyone else—they put on their tank tops one armhole at a time."

Charlie eyes me; I eye Gillian.

"The only difference is, we now get government tank tops," she adds with a laugh.

My whole face freezes. "You're part of the government?"

"Not directly, but—" Cutting herself off, she adds, "Oh, I'm sorry—I thought you knew. It's in all our clippings . . ." She hands me a press kit in a forest green folder.

I flip it open as Charlie and Gillian read over my shoulder. It's right there on the front page: *Welcome to Five Points Capital, the venture fund of the United States Secret Service.*

Behind us, a door swings open. "Mr. Lapidus?" a baritone voice asks. We turn around and a tall man with military shoulders and thick forearms extends a handshake. His watch has a gold presidential seal. "Brandt Katkin," he introduces himself. "Please . . . c'mon in."

51

"Secret Service—this is Marta."

"Hi, Marta," Quincy said calmly into his speaker-phone. "I'm looking for Agent Jim Gallo . . ."

"One moment and I'll transfer you to a supervis—"

"I don't want to be transferred—I've already been transferred twice." Sitting with his hands folded tightly on his desk, Quincy was determined to keep his cool. After last night's partner meeting . . . there'd already been enough yelling. Even threatening. Now, though—now was the time for calm. "The supervisor I spoke to transferred me back to Agent Gallo's voicemail. It doesn't do me any good," he explained. "Now can you please find him for me? It's an emergency."

"Is someone in physical danger, sir?"

"No, but he—"

"Then Agent Gallo will get back to you as soon as he returns."

Tightening his grip on the phone, Quincy drummed his fingers against the crystal bowl of caramels on the corner of his desk. The candy was just for clients. Made grown men feel like boys. Beyond the crystal bowl—through the glass paneling next to his door—Quincy eyed the flurry of people who swarmed back and forth across the seventh floor. On the opposite end, the door to Lapidus's office suddenly flew open and his partner stormed out. When Lapidus was walking that fast, there was only one place he was headed.

"Ma'am, you don't understand," Quincy insisted. "I need to find Agent Gallo. *Now*."

"I'm sorry, sir—the supervisor transferred you back, and Agent Gallo isn't at his desk."

"Clearly he's not at his desk. That's why I want to know where he is."

"Even so, sir, we don't give out that information."

"But he's supposed to—"

"I'm sorry, sir—there's nothing I can do."

"But—"

"I'm sorry, sir. Have a good day." There was a click on the line and a knock at the door. Quincy kept the receiver close as Lapidus stepped inside.

"Yeah . . . no . . . don't worry—everyone's sitting tight," Quincy said into the phone. "Okay . . . Thanks, Jim . . . I'll speak to you later."

"You found Gallo?" Lapidus asked as Quincy hung up.

"Ask and thou shalt receive."

"So what'd he say?" Lapidus asked.

"Nothing really—he won't get into specifics."

"Does he know where they are?"

"Hard to tell," Quincy said as he reached for a caramel. "But if I had to guess, I'd say it won't be long now—it's just a matter of waiting it out."

52

"Brandt Katkin—nice to meet you," he says as he shakes each of our hands.

"Jeff Liszt," I say, using another name from the bank. Katkin looks down at my nametag, which says *Lapidus*.

"Sorry . . ." Charlie jumps in, exactly how we practiced. "Mr. Lapidus was running late, so we asked Mr. Liszt to join us instead . . ."

"No, of course," Katkin says, too polished to show even a hint of annoyance. In the VC world of name-dropping and instant impressions, he's well accustomed to the bait-and-switch. Leading us back to his office, he weaves through the corporate gray hallways. I'm in front, followed by Gillian. Charlie's in back.

The further we move from reception, the quieter it gets. Scanning around, I try to check out individual offices, but quickly realize every door is closed.

"So has this always been a division of the Secret Service?" Charlie asks. He's got his usual playful tone, but there's no mistaking the anxiousness in his voice.

"I wouldn't call us a division," Katkin clarifies as we

make a sharp left into his office. He's wearing khakis, loafers, and a Doral golf shirt. The Miami three-piece suit. But the flat twang of his Minnesota accent makes him seem out of place. "It's more of a partnership."

Gillian and I take the two seats in front of Katkin's enormous glass-top desk. Charlie steals a space on the contemporary black leather couch. The office is high-tech wannabe on a government-issue budget. In the corner, a black-lacquered credenza is covered with dozens of deal toys—the thank-you trinkets a company gives out when a big deal closes: a toy fire-engine, a fake syringe, a bookend shaped like a microchip. Typical business jockey. Directly above, there's a framed certificate commemorating Katkin's appointment as a Special Agent in the Secret Service. Charlie's staring straight at it.

Partnership, my big fat behind, he signals.

I nod in agreement. Secret Service is Secret Service. Still, Katkin doesn't seem to know us—which means, wherever they are, Gallo and DeSanctis are still keeping quiet.

"So how exactly does the fund work?" I stammer, trying not to panic.

"Don't let the Secret Service part fool you," Katkin says. "This is just the next step in R&D. With technology whizzing along at lightspeed, government agencies couldn't keep up. As soon as we figured out one security system, another popped up in its place. CIA . . . FBI . . . everyone was at least five years behind the private market. The CIA opened In-Q-Tel to close the gap. Two years ago, we opened Five Points.

"It's simple when you think about it," he continues. "Why kill yourself trying to sprint against Silicon Valley, when you can let them line up at your door? It's the beauty of the ballgame—every new idea needs money, even the illegal ones. And this way, we make it all work in our favor. For example, if a guy invents a bullet that slices through Kevlar, instead of letting him go to the black market, we buy it ourselves, figure out what makes it tick, and then outfit our agents with the appropriate countermeasures. It's the best of both worlds—we can use it ourselves, or beat it if it's used against us. By the time we're done, our entrepreneurs get their funding—and we get a first-look at the best blueprints."

"So the government keeps the profits?" I ask.

"What profits?" Katkin teases. "We're a 501(c)(3). Nonprofit is our middle name. That way, the politicians are happy, competitors don't see us as a threat, and we're still allowed to jump into the world of business. Welcome to the future. Government, Inc."

"If you can't beat 'em . . ." Charlie begins.

"Eat 'em," Katkin jokes. Too bad he's the only one laughing. "Now what can I help you with today?"

"It's about my dad," Gillian says, finally speaking up. "Marty Duckworth . . ."

"Duckworth was your father?" Katkin asks, sounding amused. "I really liked that guy. How's he doing these days?"

Gillian's gaze drops away. "Actually, he passed away recently."

"Oh, I'm . . . I'm sorry," Katkin offers. I watch closely for his reaction. Eyes wide. Chest sunk. Not overly shocked, but clearly concerned. I look over my shoulder and peek at Charlie for the confirmation. He sees it too.

If this guy's acting, he's getting this year's Emmy, Charlie agrees.

"I didn't realize . . ." Katkin continues.

"It's okay," I interrupt, turning on my inner banker. "As you might've guessed, we're representing Mr. Duckworth's estate and thought there might be a few things you could help us with. You see, when we were going through his effects, we found this . . ." Reaching into my jacket pocket, I pull out the nondisclosure agreement and hand it to Katkin.

Nodding to himself, Katkin fights a grin. "There it is—the one that got away . . ."

"Excuse me?"

"He was brilliant, but he was a real character. Purebred entrepreneur. I mean, we were once at the airport on a moving walkway and I jokingly said, 'How long do you think it would take to walk around the world on something like this?' He thinks about it for a second, then turns to me and says, '2,633.3 hours—assuming you're using the Earth's polar diameter and not the equatorial one.'"

Gillian wants to laugh, but can't go through with it.

"So you remember dealing with him?" Charlie asks.

"How could I forget? He was a cold call, I tell ya. Just found our name in the phonebook. To be honest, they opened this office to cast lines to Latin America . . . Who would've ever thought someone like him would stumble in?"

Leaning forward, Gillian crosses her arms and holds her own stomach. "What did he say?" she asks, sounding pained.

"He just walked in. Laptop under one hand, rusty old clipboard in the other. We sent an intern to talk to him—we don't take unsolicited submissions in the office. Ten minutes later, they took him to the commercialization folks. Ten minutes after that, they brought him straight to me." Waving the NDA in front of him, Katkin added, "We used to joke that he downloaded this off some law firm's website. But to his credit, he wouldn't show us how it worked until we signed it."

"It was that good?"

"Y'know how many NDAs we signed last year?" Katkin asks. "Two," he answers. "And the other one was for the guy from—" He cuts himself off. "Let's just say . . . it's someone you've heard of."

Charlie sits up straight, knowing we're close. "So you signed it?"

"He left the paperwork with us. We hemmed . . . we hawed . . . eventually, we signed. But after the first few appointments—I'm guessing it was about eight months ago—we never heard from him again."

"Wha?" Charlie and I say simultaneously.

"That's exactly what we thought. We were all set to go—we had our team . . . it was in the budget—we even flew in our financial crimes expert from New York."

The instant he mentions our hometown, a sharp pain swoops in between my shoulders. It's like a vulture gnawing at the back of my neck.

"New York?" I ask.

"We actually have some friends in the New York office," Charlie adds. "What's his name?"

Gillian scowls, but it does the trick.

"Oh, he's one of our best," Katkin says as the vulture's claws dig deeper. I stare blankly through the glass desk while his feet rest easily on the carpet. "Really nice guy," Katkin explains. "His name's Jim Gallo."

53

E verything okay?" Katkin asks, confused by our silence.

"Of course," Charlie insists as we try to pull it together. "That's just . . . Jim Gallo isn't the guy we know . . ."

"It's a big office," Katkin admits.

"So my dad took the idea with him when he left?" Gillian asks, anxious to get back to the invention.

"Happens all the time," Katkin answers. "Entrepreneurs come in, they talk it up, and when a better offer gets slapped in front of them, we never hear from them again. That's the business. And with a moneymaker like this—I mean, some of those things he was working on . . . I don't know how he pulled it off, but—I just assumed he found a new partner and moved on."

"See, that's what we're hoping you could help us with," I interrupt. "With the lack of documentation in Mr. Duckworth's estate, we're having a hard time putting a valuation on his inventions . . ."

"We just want to know what he made," Gillian jumps in.

Charlie twists in his seat. *Goodbye patience; hello desperation*, he glares.

"I'm sorry," Katkin begins. "I'm not permitted to give out that information."

"But she's Mr. Duckworth's only heir," I insist.

"And that's a nondisclosure agreement," Katkin shoots back.

"We're not asking for schematics . . ."

"No, you're asking me to violate a binding legal contract—and in the process, open our company up to a mess of liability."

"Can you at least tell us what it has to do with the photos?" Gillian pleads.

"The what?"

"These . . ." From my jacket pocket, I pull out the strip with the four side-by-side headshots.

Katkin's face is blank. He has no idea what he's looking at.

"We found it with the agreement," Charlie explains.

"Do you know who they are?" Gillian asks.

"Not a one," he says in full Minnesota drawl. "Never seen them before in my life."

"So it doesn't have to do with the invention?" I ask.

"I already told you . . ."

"I know—but this is far more important than a dead man's gag order," I push. It's one push too many.

Katkin stands from his seat and stares down at all of us. "I think we're done here."

"Please . . . you don't understand . . ." I beg.

"It was nice meeting all of you," Katkin says coldly.

Hopping up, Charlie heads for the door. Gillian follows. "Let's go," Charlie calls.

"But it's extremely urgent that we—"

"*Oliver, let's go!*"

Katkin looks my way and the oxygen is sucked from the room. Crap. Fake names.

I freeze. Gillian and Charlie just stand there. Katkin drills us with a stare that's so bitter, it actually burns.

"Son, I don't know who you think you are, but let me give you a nugget of advice—you don't want to pick this fight."

Charlie puts a hand on my shoulder and pulls me toward the door. In four seconds, we're gone.

"What did he make? What did he make?" Charlie moans from the backseat of Gillian's vintage blue Beetle. "Why'd you have to start blabbing like that?"

"I blabbed?" Gillian blasts as she stares him down through the rearview mirror. "Who's this? *Oliver . . . Oliver— Oops, did I just get us escorted out of the building? I'm sorry—I wasn't thinking. In fact, I wasn't using a single brain cell."*

"Can both of you please stop?" I beg, sitting shotgun as we ride back across the causeway. "We're lucky we got as much as we did."

"What're you talking about?" Charlie asks.

"You heard Katkin—the story about Duckworth . . . bringing in Gallo—at least now we know what we're looking at."

"So you think Gallo came in and made dad a better offer?" Gillian asks.

"You tell me," I begin. "Act One: Your dad scrounges around for VC money to help with his invention. Act Two: He brings the idea to Five Points Capital, arm of the Secret Service. Act Three: Gallo is brought in. Act Four: Your dad suddenly changes his mind, falls off the face of the earth, and rents a crappy place in Gallo's hometown. What do you think is most likely, Miss Marple?"

"So Gallo was called into Five Points Capital to consult, but when he saw the invention . . ."

". . . he realized he could take it to the black market and sell it on his own. From there, he approaches Duckworth: *Why split it with the VC, when we can keep it for ourselves?*"

Charlie leans forward between the bucket seats. "But if they were working together, why would Gallo turn on him?"

"Because keeping the profits for himself is better than splitting it in two: *Sure, Marty, we'll help you build the prototype . . . Yeah, Marty, it'll be better if you work directly with us . . . Thanks for the help, Marty, now we'll take your idea, stuff all our cash in an account with your name on it, and you can play fall guy.* The moment Duckworth realized what was going on was the same moment they took him out. Only by then, they already had their hands on his baby."

Gillian stares out the window, completely silent.

"You know what I mean," I add.

She doesn't respond.

"What about the money itself?" Charlie asks. "Even if the theory's right, it doesn't tell us how they hid it in the bank."

"That's why I think they had an inside man," I say.

"Maybe that's where the photos come in," Gillian says, suddenly bouncing back. I pull down the mirror in the sun visor just in time to see Charlie make a face.

"Maybe that's who's in the photos—that's who helped Gallo hide it," Gillian adds.

"I don't know," I say, grabbing the strip of photos from my jacket. "I've never seen these people in my life."

"Could they be from another office? Don't you have branches around the country?"

"A few . . . but the partners are all in New York. And the

way that account was hidden . . . it takes a bigshot to pull that off."

Charlie angles his head, once again worming his way into my mirror. He thinks I'm hiding something. He's right. "You thinking of anyone in particular?" he asks, reading the Lapidus-look on my face. As usual, Charlie nails it. Gallo didn't just show up to investigate—he came searching for his own cash. And from what we saw back at the bank, Lapidus and Quincy were the only ones he was working with.

"So Duckworth invented it, Gallo and DeSanctis took it over, and somewhere along the way, they found an inside man who helped them bury it in the bank," Charlie adds. "It's your call, Ollie—who's the bigger lowlife, Lapidus or Quincy?"

I shake my head and replay my two seconds in Lapidus's office. There was one other person there. "It makes sense, but . . . How do you know it wasn't Shep? I mean, he *is* former Secret Serv—"

"It wasn't Shep," Charlie interrupts. "Trust me, he wouldn't do that."

"But if he—"

"It wasn't Shep!" he insists.

I stare at Charlie in the backseat. Gillian watches from her mirror. Better not to argue. Still, Duckworth had to have had some help.

"Maybe that's where the photos come in," I continue. "Maybe they were the other people who were in on it . . . from the black market . . . or other rogue agents from the Secret Service—Duckworth could've been keeping their pictures as insurance."

"Then why didn't he have photos of Gallo and DeSanctis?" Gillian asks.

It's a good question. Jerking the wheel toward the exit, Gillian leaves the causeway behind and curves onto Alton Road. I stare back down at the photos. They're not glossy, like an actual print. They're flat—like they came from a color printer.

"Any ideas?" Gillian asks.

"Not really. But when you look at them side by side . . . the stiff poses . . . don't they look like ID photos?"

"Y'mean like a driver's license?" Gillian asks.

"Or a passport," Charlie says.

"Or maybe a company ID card . . ." I add.

"At least we saw Katkin's reaction," she says. "That alone tells us they weren't people from the VC."

"I still think they're people your dad trusted," Charlie says. "It's like the nondisclosure agreement—you don't safekeep things that'll get you in trouble—you keep what you want to protect."

The car bucks at a red light and Gillian nods at Charlie in the rearview. She knows a good theory when she hears it. "What if they're people who helped him with the original idea?"

"Or people he confided in," Charlie blurts.

"What's that game company he worked at after Disney?" I ask, suddenly feeling the pump of excitement.

"Neowerks—I think they're in Broward . . ."

"I saw the address on an old pay stub," Charlie jumps in. "In the file cabinet." There's a pregnant pause. All three of us trade glances and taste the adrenaline in the air.

Gillian pulls a hard right down Tenth Street and lurches to a halt in front of her house.

"How far are we from Broward?" Charlie asks.

"Forty minutes at the most," Gillian replies.

"I'll make some phone calls—set up an appointment," I

offer, kicking open the car door and helping Charlie squeeze out from the back. Gillian stays put.

"Aren't you coming?" I ask.

"I should check in and make sure I still have a job—I'll be back in ten minutes." She tosses me the house keys, and with a wave, she's gone.

"Oh, I miss her already," Charlie says. Swiping the keys, he charges up the concrete path and bolts through the front door. Inside, he goes for the files; I slam the door and head for the phone. But when we hear the locks slide behind us, we follow the sound and spin around. That's when we notice all the shades are closed. The whole place is dark. And then . . . in the corner . . . we hear a click. A lamp flicks on in the living room. Every ounce of air leaves my chest.

"Nice to see you, Oliver," Gallo says from his seat on the sofa. "Now here's the part that hurts . . ."

Back by the door, a shadow arches, pouncing toward us. Charlie turns and tries to run, but it's too late. An arm slices the air toward him. Behind me, Gallo grabs me around the neck. And the last thing I see is DeSanctis's fist as it collides with my brother's face.

54

Welcome to Miami Airport—how can I help you?"

"Hi, I'm here to pick up a car," Joey said to the petite blond woman at the National car rental counter. "It should be under the name Gallo."

"Gallo . . ." the woman repeated as she typed it into the computer. "Nothing under Gallo . . ."

"Actually, he probably put it under DeSanctis," Joey added, forcing the bluff. The Formica counters for the other car companies stretched out across the terminal, but when she got off the escalator, Joey went straight for National. After all, when it came to government discounts, there were only three companies the Secret Service travel office listed as "preferred providers." National was number one.

"Any luck?" Joey asked.

Squinting at her screen, the rental agent looked confused. "I'm sorry . . . but it says here that someone already picked it up."

"Oh, those enthusiastic *bastards*," Joey laughed. "I *knew* they'd jump on the early flight—anything to catch a bad guy." Flipping open her wallet, she whispered "United

States Secret Service," and flashed a gold badge. Sure, she covered the words "Fairfax County Police" with the tips of her fingers, but as Joey learned over the years, a badge was more than a badge. Especially when it was her dad's. "We were supposed to meet in Miami and . . . Can I borrow your phone?" she asked. "I'll try their cell."

Stretching the cord over the counter, the rental agent punched in the number Joey gave her. Through the receiver, Joey heard her own answering machine pick up. Suddenly serious, she looked up at the rental agent. "All I'm getting is voicemail . . ."

"I-Is that bad?"

"Do you have any idea where they went?" Joey asked nervously.

"Actually, we're not supposed to—"

"They're my partners," Joey pushed. "If something happens . . ."

The rental agent was about to say something, but hesitated.

"It's an emergency," Joey pleaded. "Please . . ."

The agent ripped a paper map from the stack and anxiously slid it on the counter. "They wanted directions to South Beach . . . That's what I gave them . . ."

"Anywhere in particular?"

"Tenth Street—they didn't give an address—but it's a small area . . ."

"I'll find it," Joey said, grabbing the map. "How fast can you get me a car?"

55

The third punch pummels my jaw, and the sour-sweet taste of blood floods across my tongue.

"Leave him alone—!" Charlie screams, though he barely gets the words out. Whipping his arm forward, DeSanctis pounds the butt of his gun against Charlie's jaw.

"*Where is it!?*" Gallo roars in my face, winding up for another blow. He grips my tie and swings me back toward the couch. "Tell us where it is, Oliver! Say the words and we're out of your life!"

It's a simple promise and an absolute lie. The only reason we're still breathing is because we have what they want.

"Don't tell 'em shit!" Charlie yells, blood dripping down his chin. DeSanctis cranks his arm back and this time plows Charlie in the ear. Crumbling to his knees, Charlie screams and cups the side of his head.

"*Charlie!*"

"*Don't move!*" Gallo warns, tugging me back by the neck.

"Hit him again and you'll get nothing!" I shout.

"You think we're *negotiating?*" Gallo barks, still holding me by my tie. He smashes me into the bookcase, where a dozen engineering texts tumble to the floor. Refusing to let me catch my breath, he grabs me by the lapels and wings me back toward the endtable. The lamp shatters and picture frames go flying. I'm stumbling . . . fighting to stay on my feet . . . but I can't get my balance—or the gun that's in the back of my pants. *"Y'know how much of my time you wasted?"* he continues to rage. *"You have any idea what this cost me?"*

Like a wrestler in the ring, he regrabs the knot on my tie, whips me around, and tosses me back into the bookcase. On impact, the edge of the shelf stabs me in the back of the neck, and my head snaps back. For a second, I can't see. Pulling me forward, Gallo winds up and shoves me back again. Then again. Each time I collide, a stack of books rains down on me. *"Where's the money, Oliver! Where'd you fuckin' put it?"*

Spit flies from his mouth. There's a small gap between his yellowing teeth. On each impact, the world blinks on and off. I'm about to pass out, but Gallo won't let up. Eventually, he wraps his claws around my throat and pins me back against the bookcase. I can't breathe. As he tightens his grip, I fight for air. Nothing comes but an empty gasp. "P-Please . . ."

Over Gallo's shoulder, Charlie's still on the ground, holding his ear. DeSanctis stands over him with a cocky grin. And behind them all . . . I swear, something moves in the kitchen. Before I can react, the whole room fades and spins sideways. It's like being underwater, sucked down by the tide. Gallo squeezes tight and I float back to last night. Back to Gillian. She's all I see—which is why, when I open my eyes—I almost don't believe she's actually there.

Gillian tears into the living room swinging the glass blender straight at the back of DeSanctis's head.

There's a loud, haunting thunk as it ricochets against his skull. The impact sends a zigzagging fracture down the side of the jar, even as it sends DeSanctis staggering forward and tripping over Charlie.

As Gallo turns to follow the sound, I grab a stray hardcover book from the shelf and crack him in the back of the head. It knocks him off-balance, which is all Gillian needs to rush in close. Gallo reaches for his gun, but he doesn't have a chance. Already in mid-swing, Gillian wheels the blender jar through the air and catches Gallo on the side of the head. But just as the jar collides with his skull, there's a loud crash . . . the fracture gives way . . . and the glass shatters into hundreds of tiny shards which flick against my chest. In Gillian's hand, all that's left is the solid glass handle. On the carpet, Gallo's dazed, but not out.

"*Let's go!*" Gillian shouts as she grabs me by the hand. Coughing and fighting to catch my breath, I step over Gallo and go straight for Charlie, who's just now picking his head up from the carpet. His eyes flit back and forth—first at Gillian, then to me, then back to Gillian. He's in shock. Gillian takes one arm; I take the other. We scoop him up by the armpits and pull him to his feet.

"You okay? Can you hear me?" I ask.

He nods, quickly finding his equilibrium. "Get us out of here," he demands. There's no fear in his voice. Just anger.

Gillian leads the way. Not to the front door—to the bedrooms in the back. Where she snuck in. She's first . . . then Charlie . . . then me. But just as I fly forward, something grabs me by the ankle. And twists. Hard. An electric shock of pain shoots up my leg and I crash to the floor. Behind me, DeSanctis grips my ankle, refusing to let go. He's on his stomach, clawing his way closer. A trickle of blood drips from his hairline, down the side of his forehead, to his cheek.

Scurrying backwards on my elbows, I kick wildly, fighting to get free. His nails dig deep into my ankle. I can't get him off. *"Charlie!"*

I look back frantically, but he's already there. My brother's thick black shoe stomps down on DeSanctis's wrist. Howling in pain, DeSanctis lets go and looks up at Gillian.

"What're you—?"

Before DeSanctis can finish, Gillian lets loose with a whirlwind kick that crashes into the side of his head. His neck snaps to the side with an unearthly crack. It doesn't slow Gillian down. Lashing out, she kicks him again. And again. Her clunky shoe hits like a brick. Over and over.

"Enough," Charlie says, pulling her back. From my place on the carpet, he's twenty feet tall. The new big brother. *"Let's go!"* Charlie shouts, reaching down and tugging me to my feet.

Unsure of what's waiting out front, he rushes toward the back of the house. Ignoring the pain in my ankle, I follow as fast as I can, hobbling down the hallway. Behind me, Gillian has a hand on my shoulder. "Just keep going," she whispers. We cut through the bedroom, where the sliding glass door that leads to the backyard is wide open.

"Go right!" Gillian yells.

Spotting his own way out, Charlie goes left.

Bursting outside, we're on a cement patio. Straight ahead, the wall's too high. On the left, the path runs through the neighbors' backyards—each patio connecting with the one next to it. Charlie's already at the end—leapfrogging off someone's rusted, sun-bleached lounge chair to help him over the concrete wall.

"*Hurry!*" Charlie calls out, one leg already straddled on the other side the wall.

"The car's this way," Gillian says, yanking me back to the right.

I look both ways, but the answer's simple. "Charlie, wait!" I shout as I race toward my brother.

"Are you crazy—this way's safer!" Gillian insists, refusing to give in.

I don't even pause.

"I'm serious," she adds. "You leave now, you're on your own." It's a great threat, but even Gillian doesn't want to run by herself. Shaking her head as she pounds the cement, she falls in right behind me.

"C'mon, they'll be up in a second!" Charlie yells, sliding his other leg over. Shifting his weight to his arms, he pushes off from the wall and disappears.

"Just wait a—" It's too late. He's already gone.

Hopping on the lounge chair, I crane my neck over the wall to make sure he's okay. But just as I spot Charlie on the other side, a single shot explodes down the block. Two inches to my left, the top of the wall shatters in a violent burst, spraying concrete shards in every direction. It's like a kick of sand in the face. Squinting, I try to see through the storm. Over the wall and down the street, Gallo limps as quick as he can around the corner, his gun aimed right at me.

"*Get down!*" Charlie screams.

A second shot rings out.

I duck below the ledge completely off-balance and tumble from the lounge chair to the ground. Flat on my ass, I stare straight at the wall that separates me from my brother.

"Oliver!?" Charlie calls.

"*Run!*" I shout back. "Get out of there!"

"Not until you're—"

"Go, Charlie! *Now!*"

No time to debate. I hear the rumbling of his shoes against the grass as he takes off. Gallo can't be far behind him.

Scrambling to my feet, I pull the gun from the back of my pants and study the wall as if I could see through it. Gillian lightly touches my back. "Is he—?"

A third shot rings out, cutting her off. Then a fourth. My heart contracts and I stare at the wall. Holding my breath, I shut my eyes, trying to hear footsteps. There's a muffled tapping in the distance. Please, God, let it be Charlie.

I scratch to look up over the wall, but Gillian tugs me in the opposite direction. "We should get out of here," she insists, pulling me back. When I don't move, she adds, "Please, Oliver . . ."

"I'm not leaving him."

"Listen to me—you go back up there, you might as well paint a target on your forehead. Charlie'll be fine—he's got ten times the speed of Gallo."

"I'm not leaving him," I repeat.

"No one said anything about leaving—but if we don't get out of here—"

A fifth shot thunders up the block. Jolted by the sound, we both crouch down.

"How far is your car?" I ask.

"Follow me." She grabs my hand and we run back across the open patios. Halfway there, we race past the sliding glass door to Gillian's bedroom—which is exactly when DeSanctis's hand flies out and latches on to Gillian's curly black hair.

"Ready for Round Two?" DeSanctis asks, looking way too wobbly.

The right side of his face is covered in blood—and before

he can even step outside, Gillian wheels around and pounds her knee into his testicles. He drops to the ground, I pound him with the butt of the gun, and we continue running to the far end of the backyard. As we reach the wall, it looks like a mirror image of the one Charlie went over—that is, until I glance to my left and see the black metal gate that's cut into the wall. Taped to the bars is an index card stuffed into a sealed plastic Baggie: *Do Not Lock—For Fire,* it says in handwritten chicken scrawl.

Grabbing the bars, Gillian yanks open the gate. It slams with a clang behind us and dumps us in the parking lot of a low-rise apartment complex. We make a sharp left the instant we hit the street.

"Over here," she says, hopping inside her blue Beetle, which is parked under a tree.

With a flick of her wrist, she starts the car. I'm looking over my shoulder for DeSanctis. "Go, go, *go* . . ."

"Which way?" she asks.

"Straight ahead. We'll find him."

Tires shriek, wheels kick in, and we buck back in our seats. We keep our heads low, just in case we spot Gallo. But as we reach the end of the block—the corner where Charlie was headed—there's no one in sight. Not Gallo . . . not Charlie . . . not anyone. In the distance, there's a faint howl of sirens. Gunshots bring police.

"Oliver, we really should . . ."

"Keep looking," I insist, scouring every alley next to every pink house we pass. "He's here somewhere." But as the car crawls up the block, there's nothing but empty driveways, ratty overgrown lawns, and a few swaying palm trees. Behind us, the sirens scream even louder.

If I were the one running, I'd make a right at the next stop sign. "Make a left," I tell Gillian. I still know my brother.

Yet when we curve around the corner, the only person there is an old man with shoe-leather brown skin and a 1950s sky blue cabana shirt. He's sitting on his stoop, peeling a grapefruit with a pocketknife.

"Have you seen anyone run by?" I call out as I lower my window and hide the gun.

He looks at me like I'm speaking . . .

"Spanish," Gillian clarifies.

"Oh, uh . . . have you veras un muchacho?"

Still no response. He goes back to peeling his grapefruit. The siren's almost on us.

Gillian stares in the rearview, knowing it's close. She needs a decision. "Oliver . . ."

"Hold on," I tell her. "Por favor—es muy importante. Es mi hermano!"

He won't even look up.

"Oliver, please . . ."

Behind us, tires screech around the corner.

"Go—get us out of here," I finally give in.

She pumps the gas, and the wheels once again search for traction. A quick right and an ignored speed limit turns the neighborhood into a pink-and-green blur. I stare out the window, waiting for Charlie to jump out from the bushes and shout that he's safe. But he never does. I don't stop looking.

Next to me, Gillian reaches out and cups her hand softly on the back of my neck. "I'm sure he's okay," she promises.

"Yeah," I reply as South Beach—and my brother—fade behind us. "I hope you're right."

56

If she'd been ten minutes earlier, Joey would've seen the whole thing: the ruby red lights of the police car, the uniformed cops as they ran out, even Gallo and DeSanctis as they gave their hastily prepared explanation: Yes, that was us; yes, they got away; no, we can handle it fine by ourselves, thanks all the same. But even with everyone gone—even with Gallo's rental car nowhere in sight—it was still impossible to miss the bright yellow-and-black police tape that covered Duckworth's front door.

Jumping out of the car, Joey headed straight for the door and knocked as hard as she could. "It's me—anyone there?" she shouted, making sure she was alone.

A glance over her shoulder and a flick on the lock's pins did the rest. As the door swung open, she ducked and slid under the police tape limbo stick. Inside, the kitchen was untouched, but the living room was wrecked. Lamp shattered, coffee table overturned, books thrown from their shelves. The struggle was short—all confined to one space. At the bottom of the bookcase was a stack of old *Wired* magazines. Joey went right for them, grabbing the one on top and scanning the subscription label. *Martin Duckworth?* she read to herself, clearly confused. On a nearby shelf, she noticed the cracked picture frame with the photo of Gillian and her dad. Finally, something physical. Joey pulled out the photo and stuffed it in her purse.

Down low, glass blender shards sparkled against the pale carpet, which had a blotted dark stain by the door. Joey bent down to look closer, but the blood was already dry. Up the hallway, the blood continued—tiny drops trailing out like planets from a dark sun. The further she went, the smaller they got, eventually leading her toward the bedroom. And the sliding glass door.

Through the glass, a four-year-old Cuban boy in red underwear and a blue Superman T-shirt stared back, his hands stuffed down his pants. Joey smiled and slid the door open slowly, careful not to scare him. "Have you seen my brother?" she asked playfully.

"Bang-bang!" he shouted, pointing a finger-gun at the far wall on her left. Turning to follow, Joey noticed the jagged divot at the top of the concrete. At the base, the lounge chair was propped into place. Up and over, Joey thought.

Grabbing her cell phone from her purse, she went right for speed-dial.

"How was your flight? You get free peanuts?" Noreen answered.

"Ever hear of a guy named Martin Duckworth?" Joey asked, staring down at the rolled-up *Wired*.

"Isn't that the guy whose name is on the bank account?"

"That's the one. According to Lapidus and the records at Greene, he's living in New York—but I'll bet if we put him through the meat grinder, we'll get something more."

"Give me five minutes. Anything else?"

"I also need you to find their relatives for me," Joey

explained as she walked closer to the wall. "Charlie and Oliver—anyone and everyone they might know in Florida."

"C'mon, boss—you think I didn't do that the moment you stepped on a plane for Miami?"

"Can you send me the list?"

"There's only one name on it," Noreen said. "But I thought you said they were too smart to hide with relatives."

"Not anymore—from the look of things here, they had a little surprise visit from Gallo and DeSanctis."

"You think they got nabbed?"

Still picturing the stain on the carpet, Joey stood up on the lounge chair and ran her fingertips against the missing chunk of the concrete wall. No blood anywhere. "I can't speak for both of them, but something tells me at least one got away—and if he's on the run . . ."

". . . he'll be desperate," Noreen agreed. "Give me ten minutes—you'll have everything."

57

When I was twelve years old, I lost Charlie in the mall at Kings Plaza. Mom was in one of the old discount stores, deciding what to put on layaway; Charlie was sneaking through Spencer Gifts, trying his best to sniff the "Adults Only" erotic candles; and I . . . I was supposed to have him right by my side. But when I turned around to show him their selection of nudie playing cards, I realized he was gone. I knew it instantly—he wasn't hiding or wandering off in a corner of the store. He was missing.

For twenty-five minutes, I frantically ran from store to store, shouting his name. Until the moment we found him—licking the glass at JoAnn's Nut House—there was a stabbing pain that burrowed into my chest. It's nothing compared to what I'm feeling right now.

"Can I help you?" the security guard at the front desk asks. He's an older man with a *Kalo Security* uniform and white orthopedic shoes. Welcome to the Wilshire Condominium in North Miami Beach, Florida. The one place to go in an emergency.

"I'm here to see my grandma," I say, using my nice-boy voice.

"Write your name," he says, pointing to the sign-in book. Scribbling something illegible, I scan every signature above mine. None of them is Charlie's. Still, we went over this a dozen times. If we ever got lost, go to what's safe. Under *Resident*, I add the words "Grandma Miller."

"So you're Dotty's?" he asks, suddenly warming up.

"Y-Yeah, Dotty's," I say, stepping into the lobby. Sure, it's a lie, but it's not like I'm a stranger. For almost fifteen years, my grandmother, Pauline Balducci, lived in this building. Three years ago, she died here—which is precisely why I use the name of her old neighbor to get us in.

"Dotty's grandson!" the security guy boasts to passing residents in the lobby. "He's got the same nose, no?"

Dragging Gillian by the arm, I cut through the lobby, pass the bank of elevators, and follow the exit signs down the twisting, peeling-wallpapered hallway that reeks of chlorine. Pool area, straight ahead. Mom used to send us here for some quality time with the *good* side of the family. Instead, it was two weeks of splash fights, breath-holding contests, and the Condo Commandos complaining that we were diving too loud, whatever that meant. Even now, as I step outside, a brother and sister are knee-deep in a ruthless game of Marco Polo. The boy closes his eyes and yells, "Marco!" The girl shouts, "Polo!" When he gets close, she darts up the stairs, runs around the pool, and jumps back in. Blatant cheating. Just like Charlie used to do to me.

"Oliver, where're we—?"

"Wait here," I say, pointing Gillian to an open lounge chair.

Next to the pool, a grandfather with a white shirt, white shorts, and pulled-up-to-his-knees black socks is studying a betting sheet from the racetrack. "I'm sorry to bother you, sir—but can I borrow your clubhouse key?" I ask him. "My grandmother took ours upstairs."

He looks up from the betting sheet with black button eyes. "Who you belong to?"

"Dotty Miller."

Giving me the once-over, he pulls the key from his pocket. "Bring it right back," he warns.

"Of course—right away." I nod to Gillian, and she follows me past the shuffleboard court and around the tree-shaded footpath that hides the one-story clubhouse. Once she's inside, I return the key to Mr. Black Socks and head right back to her.

Inside, the "clubhouse" is exactly as we left it years ago: two cruddy bathrooms, a broken sauna, and a rusty, universal weight set that predates Jack LaLane. It was designed to be a social setting where the elderly residents could interact and make new friends. It's never been used. We could stay here for days and no one would interrupt.

Gillian takes a seat on the red vinyl of the bench press. I look at the mirror-covered walls and sink down to the floor.

"Oliver, are you sure he knows this place?"

"We talked about it a thousand times. When we were little, we used to hide back here in the sauna. I'd jump inside and pretend I was Han Solo getting frozen in carbonite. Then he'd swing to my rescue and . . . and . . ." My voice trails off and I once again stare in the mirror. Half a person.

"Please don't do this to yourself," Gillian begs. "It took us forty minutes to get here, and we have a car. If he's in a cab or a bus—it'll take him a bit longer—it doesn't mean anything. I'm sure he's fine."

I don't even bother to reply.

"You have to be positive," she adds. "You think the worst; you'll get the worst. But if you think the best—"

"Then everything will blow up in your face anyway! Don't you get the punch line yet? It's the great cosmic practical joke. Knock, knock. Who's there? Big kick in the ass. That's it—end of joke. Isn't it a riot?"

"Oliver . . ."

"It's like running the Boston Marathon: You train forever . . . you pour your life into it—and then, just as you're about to hit the finish line, some jerk-off sticks his leg out and you limp home on two broken ankles, wondering where all that hard work disappeared to. Before you know it, it's all gone—your life, your work . . . and your brother . . ."

Watching me carefully, Gillian raises her head. Like she's seen something she's never seen before.

"Maybe we should just go to the police," she interrupts. "I mean, finding out about my dad is one thing, but when they start shooting at us . . . I don't know . . . maybe it's time to wave the white flag."

"I can't."

"What're you talking about? All we have to do is dial 911. If you tell them the truth, there's no way they'll turn you over to the Service."

"*I can't*," I insist.

"Sure you can," she shoots back. "All you did was see a bank account on a computer screen—it's not like you did anything wrong . . ."

I turn away as the silence wipes the pulse from the air.

"What?" she asks. "What're you not saying?"

Again, I don't respond.

"Oliver—"

Nothing but silence.

"Oliver, you can tell m—"

"We stole it," I blurt.

"Excuse me?"

"We didn't think it belonged to anyone—we looked up your dad, but he was dead . . . and the state couldn't find any relatives, so we thought it was a victimless—"

"You *stole* it?"

"I knew we shouldn't—I *told* Charlie that—but when I found out Lapidus was screwing me . . . and Shep said we could pull it off . . . It all seemed to make sense back then. But the next thing we knew, we were sitting with three hundred million of the Secret Service's money."

Gillian coughs like she's about to choke. "How many million?"

I look her dead in the eye. If she were working against us, there's no way she'd attack Gallo and DeSanctis. Instead, she did. She saved us. Just like she saved me diving last night. It's time I returned the favor. "Three hundred and thirteen."

"Three hundred and thirteen *million?*"

I nod.

"You stole three hundred and thirteen million dollars?"

"Not on purpose—not that amount." I expect her to scream, or slap me, or slice at my neck, but she doesn't. She just sits there. Perfect Indian position. Perfect silence. "Gillian, I know what you're thinking—I know it's your money—"

"It's not *my* money!"

"But your dad . . ."

"That money got him killed, Oliver! All it's good for now is lining his casket." She looks up and her eyes are filled with tears. "How could you not tell me?"

"What was I supposed to say? *Hi, I'm Oliver—I just stole three hundred and thirteen million dollars of your dad's money—want to come and get shot at?* We just wanted to know if he was alive. But after meeting you . . . and spending time—I never meant to hurt you, Gillian—especially after all this."

"You could've told me last night . . ."

"I wanted to—I swear."

"Then why didn't you?"

"I just . . . I knew it would hurt."

"And you think this doesn't?"

"Gillian, I didn't want to lie—"

"But you did. You did," she insists as her voice shakes.

I look away, unable to face her. "If I could do it all over, I wouldn't do it again," I whisper.

She sniffles at the statement, but it doesn't do much good.

"Gillian, I swear to you—"

"It's not even about the lie," she cuts me off. "And it certainly isn't about some truckload of dirty cash," she adds, wiping her eyes with the palm of her hand. She's still stunned, but deep down I hear the first tinge of anger. "Don't you get it yet, Oliver? I just want to know why they killed my dad!"

As she says the words, the quiver in the back of her throat shakes me by the shoulders and once again reminds me what we're doing here in the first place. I lift my chin and stare in the mirror. Bags under my eyes. Black hair on my head. And my brother still missing.

Please, Charlie—wherever you are—come home.

58

W hat're you doing in there?" an elderly woman asked, tapping Joey on the shoulder.

"Sorry—just searching for a lost sock," Joey replied as she backed her way out of the laundry room. Turning around in the hallway to face the woman, Joey eyed the *Trash Room* sign on the nearby metal door.

"Do you even live here?" the woman challenged with her plastic laundry basket and her gold-plated Medic-Alert bracelet.

"Absolutely," Joey said, stepping around the woman and peeking her head in the trash room. Smell of rotting oranges. Trash chute in the corner. No Oliver or Charlie.

"Listen to me—I'm talking to you," the woman threatened.

"I'm sorry," Joey said. "It's just that it's my mother's favorite sock. She made me do the laundry down here because the dryers are better on the lower floors . . ."

"They *are* better."

". . . I completely agree, but now the sock is gone, and, well . . . it was her favorite sock." Rushing away from the woman, Joey pressed the button for the elevator, ran to the doors as they opened, and quickly hopped inside.

"I'll keep an eye out for it!" the woman shouted. But before she could finish, the doors slammed shut.

"*It was her favorite sock?*" Noreen teased through the earpiece.

"Oh, bite yourself," Joey said. "It got the job done."

"Yessiree, you've once again outsmarted the ninety-year-old retirees in that hotbed of spydom—the Wilshire Condominium & Communist Lodge."

"What's your point?"

"All I'm saying is, I don't see the use in scouring some condo—much less the third floor and its laundry room—just because Charlie and Oliver's grandmother once lived there."

"First of all, if grandma lived on the third floor, that's the one they'll know best. Second, never underestimate a laundry room as a hiding place. And third, when it comes to human behavior, there's only one thing in the whole world that you can absolutely, unquestionably count on . . ."

"*Habit*," Joey and Noreen said simultaneously.

"Don't mock," Joey warned as the elevator doors opened in the lobby. "Habit's the only thing all human animals share. We can't help ourselves. It's why we drive home by the same route; and get our morning coffee from the same place; and brush our teeth and wash our face in the same order." Sidestepping a group of old ladies in matching lavender sweatsuits and headbands, Joey followed the sign for the pool area and pushed her way outside. "It's the same reason my dad only enters his house through the back door. Never the front. I call it insanity—he thinks it makes his life easier—"

"And that's where all habits are born," Noreen interrupted. "Slight moments of control in a world of black chaos.

We're all afraid of death, so we all put on our underwear before we slide on our socks."

"Actually, some people put on their socks first," Joey pointed out as she eyed the old man by the swimming pool with the racing form and the black knee-grabbers. "But when we're in trouble, we run to what's familiar. And that's the most basic habit of all." Strolling past the pool, Joey studied Oliver and Charlie's favorite old playground. For the two kids currently in the Marco Polo Super Bowl, there was no place better. But as she watched the brother and sister chase each other back and forth across the shuffleboard court, she knew that the best games always keep moving. On her left was a path that led around to the condo sales office. On her right was the clubhouse. One was filled with condo employees. The other was obscured by bushes and trees. Joey didn't hesitate.

"They have a clubhouse," she said to Noreen as she passed the hot tub and threaded down the tree-lined path. A right and left turn later, the pool area was out of sight. Checking over her shoulder, Joey slowly approached the door.

She put her ear up against it, but heard nothing from inside. Trying not to scare, she tapped lightly with her knuckle, then listened again. Still nothing. "Hello! Anyone there?" she called out, banging a bit harder. Again, no one answered.

Reaching into her purse, she unzipped her black leather lockpick case. A branch snapped behind her and her purse slipped off her shoulder.

"Everything okay?" Noreen asked.

Spinning around, Joey scanned the bushes and trees on the path. Nothing there. At least nothing she could see. Beyond a thick hibiscus, another twig snapped. Joey boosted herself up on her tiptoes while craning her neck. The bush was too tall. Reaching out, she shoved the branches aside, hopped the metal chain that ran alongside the path, and ducked through the landscaping.

"Joey, is everything okay?" Noreen repeated.

Sneaking quietly under a stray branch, Joey crouched and leaned in toward the bush where the noise came from. There was a hushed tapping on the opposite side of it. Someone being impatient. Lowering her head toward the mulch-covered earth, Joey tried to get a better look, but the underbrush was too thick. Only one way around it.

She reached back into her purse and pulled out a highly polished revolver. Miniature five-shot .38. Her dad's gun. *On three*, Joey counted to herself as she slid her finger around the trigger. Her legs coiled, humming with anticipation. *Uno . . . dos . . .*

Charging out at full speed, she sped to the other side of the bush and aimed her gun at the source of the noise—the stark white egret with wide, flapping wings. As Joey turned the corner, the bird took off toward the sky—once again leaving Joey all alone.

"What is it? What happened?" Noreen asked through the earpiece.

Refusing to answer, Joey stuffed her gun into her purse and hopped back onto the concrete path outside the clubhouse.

"Excuse me, ma'am . . ." a man's voice called out behind her.

Caught off-guard, Joey flipped around and faced the young man with the bleached blond hair.

"I'm sorry to bother you," Charlie said, using his hand to block the cut on his lip. "But can I borrow your clubhouse key? My grandma took ours upstairs."

59

Charlie stared at the redhead, knowing something was up. You'd think I asked for the key to her diary, he thought.

"Y-You want what?" the woman stammered.

"The clubhouse," he said as he pointed to his and Oliver's old hideout. "I just wanna use the bathroom." Hoping to make nice—and noticing that she was a solid fifty years below the average age range around there—he added, "Unless, of course, you want to let me use the one in *your* grandmother's place."

"Yeah, she'd love that," the woman said, giving Charlie the up and down. She smirked to herself, and Charlie wondered if he was getting the I-love-you vibe. She's cute too, he realized. Older, but with red hair—somehow it evened itself out. Too bad this wasn't the time or place.

"So you're down here visiting grandparents too?" she asked.

"Actually, just my grandmother."

"What apartment?"

"317," he said, pointing up at the third-floor balcony that overlooked the pool. She didn't even give it a glance. She's clearly still stuck on me, he thought—that is, until he noticed the blood that was all over the back of his hand. Crap. His lip was still bleeding.

"You okay?" she asked.

"Yeah . . . of course . . . I'm golden."

"You sure?" she asked, reaching out. "Because I can—"

"I'm fine," he insisted, pulling away. Realizing he'd creeped her out, he quickly forced a laugh. "It was a bad chewing gum accident. Cherry Bubblicious—a poorly timed bite—we're talking colossal inner-lip damage. I think I'm still having flashbacks." Looking around in a pretend dream-state, he added, "Momma? Is that you?"

Charlie kept laughing, but the woman was dead silent. That's it. Show's over. "Listen, if I can just get that key . . ."

"Of course, of course," she said, diving back in her purse. "I have it right here . . ." She paused like she was about to say something else. "Let me just get it for you . . . Charlie."

Shit.

Her hand came out of her purse and she was holding a gun.

"W-What're you doing?" Charlie asked, hands in the air.

"Don't panic—it's okay," she said calmly. Her voice was all velvet—which was exactly why Charlie wasn't buying a word.

"Are you with Gallo?" he asked.

"I'm not here to hurt you," she promised.

"Yeah . . . that seems to be the theme lately," he said, wiping his still bleeding lip. He tried to whip out the comebacks, but all he saw was the barrel of her gun.

"I swear to you, Charlie, I'm not Secret Service; I'm not law enforcement. All I care about is getting the money back and getting you home safe." Reading the doubt on his face, she steadied her gun hand, slid her free hand back into her purse, and whipped out a white business card, which she flashed like a badge.

Squinting, Charlie read the words *Attorney at Law*.

"I can't see it," he lied.

She didn't budge—she was too smart to let him get close. With a flick of her wrist, she winged the business card straight at him. It fluttered down at Charlie's feet, where he scraped it up and read the rest. *Jo Ann Lemont—Attorney at Law—Sheafe International.* On the bottom right, it said, "Virginia P.I. License #17-4127." A lawyer *and* a private eye. As if one weren't bad enough. "What're you, like Columbo or something?" he asked her.

"You always use humor as a defense mechanism?"

Watching her carefully, he knew she was trying to dig around his head. For that alone, he didn't like her. Over her shoulder, the pool sat calmly in the distance. Charlie prayed for a distraction, but they were too well hidden by the trees for anyone to notice. "What do you want, lady?"

"Please," she offered, "call me Joey."

He sneered at the fake pleasantries. "What do you want, *Joey?*" he asked through gritted teeth.

"I assume you know Henry Lapidus . . . ?"

Charlie didn't bother to answer.

"I'm just trying to do my job, Charlie. Now do you want to tell me where Oliver's hiding, or do you want me to kick down the door to the clubhouse myself?"

It took everything Charlie had to avoid glancing at the clubhouse. He was standing right next to it. "You have no idea what you're talking about."

"You can keep telling yourself that, but I saw how you left Duckworth's place. I saw the blood on the carpet. And on your lip." Her gun was still up, but her voice was back to velvet. "I also know you don't have your medication,

Charlie. So why don't you tell me what's really going on—maybe I can help."

Again, he didn't answer.

"Believe me, I know I have no business asking for your trust. But I also know it's not easy to toss your life in the garbage. I did the same thing when I dropped out of college—it took me three months before I realized I had to go back." Charlie'd seen this one before. She was trying to make peace by finding common ground. Letting the thought grind in, she added, "I know what you're throwing away, Charlie. Forget the job and that other nonsense—there's your music . . . and your mom . . . and let's not forget your health—"

"I get the picture."

"Then tell me what happened. Was it something with Duckworth? Is that why you took the money?"

"We're not thieves," he told her. She arched an eyebrow. "All I'm saying is, we didn't mean to hurt anyone."

"What about Shep?" she challenged.

"Shep was my friend! You ask anyone—all the snots at the bank—*I'm* the one who grabbed coffee with him, and talked football with him, and made fun of the fact that he thought the front section of the paper was just there to keep the sports section from getting wet."

She studied his face, his hands, even his shoes. Charlie knew she was looking for the tell—trying to figure if it was a lie. Still, if she didn't believe him, they wouldn't be talking. "Okay, Charlie, so if you're innocent, who killed him?" she finally asked.

He expected her to lower the gun, but she didn't. His hands were still in the air. "Why don't you try turning your psych profiles on Gallo and DeSanctis?"

She didn't seem surprised as Charlie said the names. "You have proof of that?" Joey asked.

"I know what I saw."

"But do you have proof?"

It was exactly like Oliver said—their word against the Service. "We're working on it," he shot back.

"Charlie, you're gonna have to do better than that."

He stopped and paused. He didn't want to say it, but— Actually, that was a lie. He did. "While you're at it, you should take a look at Gillian as well."

Her forehead crinkled. "Gillian who?"

Charlie wasn't sure if she was bluffing or fishing, but by now, he had nothing to lose. "Duckworth's daughter. It's her house now."

Around the corner, there was a shuffling noise on the other side of the clubhouse. Charlie assumed it was some-one's grandmother. So did Joey, who lowered her gun to make sure it was out of sight. With one eye on Charlie, she stepped backwards, carefully trying to get a peek around the edge of the building. But just as she poked her head around the threshold, there was a familiar click. Joey's hands went straight toward the clouds. She took a step back from the corner, and Charlie finally saw what had her so distressed: a small black gun was pressed against the side of her head.

"I swear I'll use it," Oliver promised as he turned the cor-ner of the clubhouse and stepped into sight. With Gallo's pistol in his hand, he pulled back on the hammer. "Now drop your gun and get the hell away from my brother."

60

Oliver, this isn't the time to be stupid," Joey warned as Oliver moved forward, gun cocked straight at her.

"I'm serious—I'll use it," Oliver said, his finger flickering against the trigger.

Joey watched the way his hands were shaking. Then she studied his eyes. Unwavering. Frozen and dark. He wasn't joking.

"Joey, what's happening?" Noreen begged through the earpiece. "Is that them? You want me to call it in?"

"Don't do it . . ." Joey warned. Oliver turned, and Noreen stopped talking.

"You're only going to infect the wound," Joey added.

"Charlie, step back!" Oliver demanded.

Charlie jumped.

Joey watched the whole scene carefully. She knew which one she had to work on.

"Oliver . . ." she began. "Let me help you get out of th—"

"Lose the gun!" Oliver interrupted. "Throw it on the roof."

This time, Joey didn't budge.

"I said, *throw it on the roof!*" he insisted, his hand finally steadying.

Watching his brother, Charlie was speechless. So was Joey. Two days ago, she didn't think Oliver Caruso had it in him. Today, she wasn't so sure. Joey glanced up at the roof of the clubhouse and prepared to toss her gun. "I'm just warning you, it'll probably go off."

"I'll take my chances," Oliver replied.

With a soft toss, Joey lobbed her pistol up toward the edge of the roof. It landed with a thud, but didn't explode.

Behind Oliver, a car horn beeped twice. Through the slats in the wood fence that surrounded the entire pool area, Joey spotted Gillian's sky blue Beetle pull up to the swinging gate that led out to the parking lot.

Oliver didn't have to say a word. Charlie started running.

Joey studied Oliver, looking for his weakness. But after all the time chasing him, she already knew it. "The more you run, the less likely you'll ever get your old life back."

To her surprise, Oliver didn't flinch. He just watched Charlie. The instant his brother cut through the fence, Oliver took another look at Joey. "Stay the hell away from us," he warned.

His gun was still on her as he ran backwards toward the car. And before Joey could react, the car door slammed, tires spun, and Oliver, Charlie, and Gillian were gone.

"Joey, are you okay?" Noreen interrupted through the earpiece.

Ignoring the question, Joey ran toward the opening in the fence. "Damn!" she shouted as she watched Gillian's car bounce over the speedbumps and make its way out onto the street. Like a bullet, Joey took off for her own car, which was double-parked in front of the building. But just as she turned the corner, she spotted the new flat tires on her two rear wheels.

"Oh, screw me," she mumbled to herself. "Noreen, call triple-A."

"You got it."

"And the millisecond you hang up, I want you to start checking . . ."

". . . Gallo and DeSanctis. Already on it," Noreen explained. "I started the instant Charlie said the words."

"And what'd you think of his reaction when I mentioned Lapidus?" Joey asked.

"All I got was silence."

"You should've seen the look on his face."

"Okay, I'll take a peek at Lapidus too. By the way, did you know the offices of Duckworth's last job are only twenty minutes away?"

"Beautiful—that's what I want to hear," Joey said as she ran back to get her gun off the roof. "And what about his daughter? Any gossip on her?"

"See, that's what doesn't make sense," Noreen answered. "While you were dealing with the Wonder Twins, I've been digging through birth certificates, driver's licenses, even tax records of Duckworth's family. I'm not sure what Charlie was talking about, but according to everything I can find—Marty Duckworth doesn't have a daughter."

"Pardon?"

"I'm telling you, Joey—I checked it a dozen times— according to every government and private database, Gillian Duckworth doesn't exist."

61

Brandt! How you feeling, you old fart?" Gallo announced, his wide grin highlighting the brand-new chip in his front tooth.

"Jimmy-boy!" Katkin said, enveloping Gallo in a back-patting bear hug. Pulling him into his office at Five Points Capital, Katkin asked, "What brings your fat ass back this far south?"

Gallo glanced at DeSanctis, then back to Katkin. "You mind if I shut the door, Brandt?"

Watching his friend, Katkin stopped. "If this is about Duckworth . . ."

"So they were already here?"

"The two kids with the dye jobs? First thing this morning. I'll tell ya, I *knew* something wasn't right. Then when I got the call from you—"

"Was there anyone else with them?" DeSanctis interrupted.

"You mean besides the daughter?"

Once again, Gallo shot a quick look at his partner. "What did she say?" he asked Brandt.

"Not much. The kid with the dark hair spent most of the time fishing. All the daughter did was sit there. She was cute, though—kinky hair, understated, but also real fire in her eyes. She watched me like a cat—know what I'm saying? Nothing like her dad. Why, you think she's got something going?"

"That's what we're trying to figure out," Gallo explained. "Three days ago, an account with Duckworth's name on it disappeared from New York. Today, this . . . this *daughter* won't sit still for a single question."

"Any idea where they were headed?" DeSanctis asked. "Any other contacts you may have for Duckworth?"

Katkin crossed around to his desk and clicked through the electronic database on his computer. "All I have here is his home, and some old work address—"

"Neowerks," Gallo interrupted. "That's right—I almost forgot about that one . . ."

62

The pre-rush-hour traffic is easy and the midday sun is shining bright as Charlie, Gillian, and I cruise up the wide-open lanes of I-95. But even with the engine revving, and the radio humming the local pop station, the car itself is way too quiet. For the entire twenty minutes it takes to get from grandma's old condo to Broward Boulevard, no one—not me, not Charlie, not Gillian—says a single syllable.

From my jacket pocket, I pull out the strip of photos. The white edges of the paper are starting to curl, and for the first time, I wonder if the people are even real. Maybe that's why it came from a color printer. Maybe the photos are doctored. Fake IDs to help with a disguise. I stare down at the four faces in my lap. I change the redhead to blond; the black man to white. To me, they're still complete strangers. To Duckworth, they were important enough to sock away in his best hiding spot. And while we're still not sure if they're friends or enemies, one thing's absolutely clear: If we don't figure out who they are and how they knew Duckworth, this trip is about to get even more uncomfortable.

"Here we go," Gillian says, eventually breaking the silence as she points to the exit ramp. "Almost there."

I flip down the passenger seat sun visor and use the mirror to check on Charlie.

In the backseat, he doesn't even look up. Three days ago, he'd be scribbling in his notebook, feeding on adrenaline, and turning every awkward moment into stanza, verse and, if he were lucky, maybe even a full-fledged ballad. *Rob from reality*, he used to say with full adolescent swagger. But for all his bravado, Charlie doesn't like danger. Or risk. And the problem right now is that he's finally realizing it.

"It's okay to be scared," I tell him.

"I'm not scared," he barks back. But I see his reflection in the visor. His eyes drop to his lap. For twenty-three years, he's set his sights low—living at home, leaving art school, refusing to join a band . . . even taking the filing job at the bank. He's always played it off on being carefree. But, as we learned from dad, there's a fine line between a carefree spirit and a fear of failure.

"It should only be a few more blocks," Gillian says, quickly clamming back up.

Like Charlie, she'll only give me a quick, short sentence. I'm not sure if it's our lying about the money, the loss of her dad, or just the simple shock from the attack, but whatever it is—as she grips the steering wheel in two tight fists, her childlike aura is finally starting to fade. Like us, she knows she's jumped on yet another sinking ship—and unless we get a break soon, we're all going down with it.

"There it is," she announces as she makes a right turn into the parking lot. The sun ricochets off the glass-front, four-story building, but the purple-and-yellow sign above the front door says it all: *Neowerks Software*.

* * * *

"So you're Ducky's daughter?" a bushy-haired man with tight wire-rimmed glasses sings as he grabs Gillian in an overexcited both-hands handshake. Dressed in a schlumpy blue button-down, high-tech wrinkle-free khakis, and leather sandals with socks, he's exactly what you get when you cross a fifty-year-old Palm Beach millionaire with a Berkeley teaching assistant. But he's also the only guy who came out to the lobby when we asked if we could speak to one of Duckworth's old colleagues. "So, it's Gillian, right?" he asks for the third time. "God, I didn't even realize he *had* a daughter."

Gillian nods sheepishly, while Charlie slingshots me a look. I raise my shield and let it bounce off my armor. After everything she's done—everything she risked—I'm not getting into his petty mindgames.

If she wanted to turn us in, she would've narced on us at the condo and at the house, I say with a glare.

Not until she gets her money, Charlie stares back.

"And you're friends as well?" Bushy Hair interrupts.

"Yeah . . . yeah," I say extending a hand as he once again shakes with both of his. "W-Walter Harvey," I say, almost forgetting my fake name. I lower my voice to keep it down, but can't help but notice the dark-haired secretary who's staring me down from the *Star Trek* black shiny reception desk. She lowers her eyes back to whatever magazine she's flipping through, but it doesn't make me feel any better. The whole lobby—with its space-age chrome chairs and silver amoeba-shaped coffee table—is so cold it can't help but pump up the fear factor. "And this is Sonny Rollins," I add, pointing to Charlie.

"Alec Truman," he announces, clearly excited to introduce himself. "Sonny Rollins, huh? Like the jazz guy."

"Exactly," Charlie says, already unnerved. "Just like the jazz guy."

"Listen, Mr. Truman," Gillian jumps in. "I appreciate you taking the time to come out and—"

"My honor . . . it's my honor," he insists. "I'm telling you, we still miss him here. I'm just sorry I can't stay long—I'm right in the middle of this bug hunt, and—"

"Actually, we just had one quick question we were hoping you could help us with," I interrupt. Reaching into my jacket pocket, I take out the horizontal photo strip. If these headshots belong to people who helped with Duckworth's original invention, we're hoping this is the guy who'll know. "Do any of these faces look familiar to you?" I ask Truman.

His face lights up like a kid eating crayons. "I know *that one*," he blurts, pointing to the salt-and-pepper-haired older man in the first photo. "Arthur Stoughton." Reading our confused looks, he adds, "He used to be with us over at Imagineering—now he runs their Internet group."

"So you were at Disney too?" Gillian asks.

"How'd you think I met your pop?" Truman says playfully. "When your dad left and came here, I followed two years later. He was the front line—first in; least paid."

"And what about this guy Stoughton?" I ask, pointing to the picture. "Did you guys all work together?"

"With Stoughton?" Truman laughs. "We should be so lucky . . . No, he was the old VP of Imagineering—even before he went to Disney.com, he didn't have time for grunts like us." As he says the words, he catches himself and looks at Gillian. "I'm sorry . . . I didn't mean to . . . your dad was great, but they never gave us a chance to—"

"It's okay—it's fine," Gillian offers, refusing to get off-subject.

"What about the other people in the photos?" Charlie leaps in.

Truman takes a long look. "Sorry, they're strangers to me."

"Are they even Disney people?" I ask.

"Or someone from here?" Charlie adds.

"Or are they just people he used to be friends with?" Gillian pushes.

Stepping back at the onslaught of questions, Truman goes to say something . . . then hesitates. Pulling away, he adds, "I really should get going . . ."

"Wait!" Gillian and I shout simultaneously.

Truman freezes. None of us moves. That's it. He's officially wigged out. "Nice meeting you," he says as he hands me the photos.

"Please," Gillian begs. Her voice cracks; her hand reaches out to hold his wrist. "We found the photos in dad's drawer . . . and now that he's gone . . . we just want to know who they are . . ." Letting the thought dig deep, she adds, "It's all we have."

Glancing over at Charlie, then back to me, Truman's dying to walk away. But as he looks down at Gillian's hand holding his wrist . . . as his eyes lock with hers . . . even he can't help himself. "If you wait out here, maybe I can take the photos inside and see if anyone knows the other three."

"Perfect—that'd be perfect," Gillian sings.

Holding the photos and promising to bring them right back, Truman heads for the main entrance behind the receptionist. I'm tempted to follow—that is, until I see the security keypad that's clearly designed to keep us out. It's the same as the one they had at Five Points, except here, there's a digital screen—like a small TV—built into the wall above the keypad. Just as Truman approaches, the screen blinks on, and nine blue square boxes appear like a telephone touch-pad. But instead of numbers, each of the boxes fills with one human face, making it look like the opening credits of *The Brady Bunch*. Even with Truman's shoulder blocking our view, we still see the reflection off the polished black walls.

Touching his pointer finger to the screen, Truman selects the face on the bottom right. The box lights up, all nine faces disappear, and just as quickly, nine brand-new head-shots take their place. Like he's entering the password on an alarm, Truman presses the touch-screen and selects the face of the Asian woman on the top left. Once again, the faces disappear; once again, nine new ones take their place.

"You guys really got the whole Buck Rogers thing going, don't you?" Charlie asks.

"This?" Truman laughs, motioning to the screen. "You'll see Passfaces everywhere in the next few years."

"Passfaces?"

"Ever forget your PIN code at the ATM?" he asks. "Not anymore. There's a reason people don't forget a face—it's embedded in us at birth. It lets us know mommy and daddy, and even friends we haven't seen for over a dozen years. Now, instead of random numbers, they give you random stranger's faces. Combine that with a graphical overlay, and you've got the one password that cuts across every age, language, and educational level. *Global authentication*, they call it. Let's see your PIN code do that."

Tapping the center square, Truman selects one last face. The box with a blond woman blinks on and off. Magnetic locks hum, the door clicks open, and Truman heads for the back with our pho—

A rush of adrenaline flushes my face. I don't believe it. That's it.

"Did you say Stoughton still works at Disney.com?" I call out as he leaves.

"I think so," Truman says. "You may want to check the website, though. Why do you ask?"

"No . . . nothing," I tell him. "Just curious."

The door slams shut and Truman disappears. Charlie's still lost, but the longer I eye the touch-screen . . .

"Sombitch," Charlie mutters.

Gillian's mouth drops open and we're officially on the three-person bike. "You think that's—?"

"Abso-friggin-lutely," Charlie whispers.

I can't help but smile.

All this time, we've been staring at the inkblot upside down. Like Charlie said on the way back from Five Points: You don't safekeep what'll get you in trouble—you keep what you want to protect. Like the combination to your bike lock. When I was in eighth grade and Charlie was in fourth, I used to keep my combo in his knapsack; he used to keep his in my Velcro wallet. It's no different now. We thought the key was to figure out the faces; but now . . . it's clear that the faces are the key. Literally. Forget random strangers; Duckworth used people he knew.

Charlie's so excited, he's even stopped staring at Gillian. He's bouncing on the balls of his feet. *Let's go*, he says with a nod.

As soon as Truman brings back the photos, I nod back. "I'm sorry to interrupt," I say to the receptionist as she looks up from her magazine. "But do you have any idea where we can get some Internet access?"

63

There're thirty spanking new computers on the fifth floor of the Broward County Library. All we need is one. One computer, some Internet access, and a little bit of privacy, which comes courtesy of the *Out of Order* signs that Charlie just drew up and taped to the screens of the three computers closest to ours.

"Anyone mind if I type?" he asks, sliding his chair up to the keyboard.

I'm about to object, but decide against it. It's a simple concession—and the busier I keep him, the less he'll catfight with Gillian. Naturally, he's still annoyed I invited her along, but between his typing responsibilities and figuring out the photos, he's distracted enough that he almost doesn't mind.

"All set?" Charlie asks as Gillian and I scoot our chairs next to his.

I nod, practically bursting with energy. Finally, a can't-miss.

"Go to www.disney.com," Gillian says, equally excited.

He shoots her a glare that would carve diamonds. "Really? I wasn't sure," he says sarcastically.

I lean in and pinch his back.

Shaking his head, he types the address. The computer chugs to the front page of the Disney website. "Fun for Families," it says in gold letters, which are right next to our first pair of mouse ears—Mickey and Pluto sitting outside a cartoon house. "Where the Magic Lives Online," it says at the top of the screen. "It better," Charlie warns.

Scrolling down, there're three buttons on the Disney Directory: *Entertainment*, *Parks & Resorts*, and one labeled *Inside the Company*.

Gillian's about to open her mouth. Charlie pounds her with a "duh" glare, hits *Inside the Company*, and takes far too much joy in watching her shut up. I pinch him again.

Y'know, she saved our asses back at the house, I motion.

She's also the one who dropped us there, he glares as he turns back to the monitor and clicks the button for *Disney Online*.

As the newest page fills in, there's a box marked *Search*. And even though we came up short when we showed the photos to Duckworth's Neowerks buddy, he was still able to pick out the first of the four.

"Put Stoughton in there," I blurt, already out of my seat and regretting the typing concession.

Charlie hunts and pecks the words *Arthur Stoughton* into the *Search* box and hits *Enter*.

Seconds pass and all three of us glance around, making sure no one's watching. Four computers down, there's a teenage boy testing the limits of the library's porn-screening software, but he hasn't looked up once.

> Results for 'Arthur Stoughton': 139
> documents
> 1. Executive Bio for Arthur Stoughton
> 2. Executive Biographies for Disney.com

The list goes on. Charlie clicks on *Executive Bio* and the computer pulls up Stoughton's overpadded résumé. Right next to it, though, is the thing that makes our eyes widen: the official corporate headshot—identical to the one on the photo strip. Arthur Stoughton. Salt-and-pepper hair, fancy suit, Disney smile.

"Executive vice president and managing director of Disney Online," Charlie reads from the bio. "Zip-A-Dee-Doo-Dah." He goes straight for the photo.

"Press it," I agree as he slides the cursor over Stoughton's face. But as he clicks on the digital photo, nothing happens. He tries again. Still nothing.

"Are you sure you're doing it right?" Gillian asks.

"You want to try it yourself?" he growls.

"Relax," I warn.

He gives me his death stare. "Maybe I don't want to relax, *Ollie* . . ."

The porn kid looks our way and all three of us fall silent. The first to recover, Gillian winks at the kid like she's flirting. His eyes go back to his screen.

"Just let me try," she tells Charlie as she attempts to grab control of the mouse. A week ago, Charlie was carefree enough to share with the world. But after these past few days—as his tongue flicks the beginnings of the scab on his lip—control is the last thing he's got left. Especially when it comes to Gillian.

"I've. Got. It," he tells her.

Knowing we need more faces, he clicks back one screen and hits the button for *Executive Biographies for Disney.com*. Once again, the computer pulls up the same photo of Arthur Stoughton. Damn.

"What do we do now?" he asks.

"Scroll down," Gillian insists.

She taps her fingernail against the bottom of the screen,
pointing at what looks like the top of another photo.
Stoughton's not alone. As Charlie anxiously scrolls down
the screen, a pyramid of pictures rolls into place. It's the full
organizational chart for Disney.com, with Arthur Stoughton
in the top spot and the rest spread out below. The pyramid
expands to a total of about two dozen photos: vice presidents and other associates in Marketing, Entertainment, and
Lifestyles Content Development, whatever that is.

"There's photo number two," I blurt, bringing it to a
whisper for the last few syllables. "Banker guy."

Sure enough, as I hand Duckworth's photo strip to Charlie,
he matches it up with the picture onscreen. There's the second
guy . . .

"Can you say pale, tired, middle-management pencil-
gnawer?" Charlie asks.

"Jeez," I agree. "If I ever get that sad and pasty, put a
stake in my heart and kill me with some garlic."

"There's the third," Gillian points out, pecking her fingernail against the company photo of the frizzy redhead. But as
we look back through the Polaroid hierarchy, none of us see
photo number four: the black man with the cleft chin.

"Are you sure that's all there are?" Gillian asks.

Charlie scrolls to the bottom, but that's it. All we have are
the two dozen photos.

"Maybe he left the company," I say.

"Maybe there's an even bigger list somewhere else,"
Gillian offers.

"Or maybe this one's just right," Charlie says as he heads
back to the top. Moving the cursor onto Stoughton's photo,
he clicks the face and prays for some of his usual magic.
Amazingly, he gets it. The border of the box moves just
slightly

I shoot out of my seat. "Did that just—?"

"Don't say it," he warns. "No jinxes."

"It's not going to do any good without the last face," Gillian points out.

Ignoring her, Charlie puts the cursor on the pale banker and presses the button. Onscreen, the box once again flinches. The last one there is the redhead.

"Miss Scarlett . . . in the library . . . with the lead pipe," he announces. Staying with the order on the photo-strip, he clicks on the company photo of the frizzy redhead. The box blinks and I put a hand on Charlie's shoulder, tightly grabbing the back of his shirt. Gillian and I lean in close, our bodies draped on the armrests. All three of us hold our breath. The copter's on the helipad and gassed to go. But nothing happens.

"What's wrong?" I ask.

"I'm telling you," Gillian says. "You need all four photos for the keys to work."

Sinking in his chair, Charlie stares blankly at the screen. He won't admit it, but this time, she's right. Nothing's happening. And then . . . out of nowhere . . . something does.

The screen flickers and goes black, like it's clicking to another web page.

"What're you doing?" I ask.

"It's not me," Charlie says, taking both hands off the keyboard. "This bad boy's on autopilot."

Unconvinced, Gillian reaches for the mouse, but before she gets there, the screen once again hiccups . . . and the Seven Dwarfs appear in front of us. Doc, Sneezy, Grumpy— they're all there—each one standing over a different button, from *Community* to *Library*.

Gillian and Charlie scour the page. I go for the web

address at the top of the screen. There's no *www*. Instead, the prefix is *dis-web1*.

"Any idea what we're looking at?" Charlie asks.

"If it's like at the bank, I think we're on their *Intranet*," I say. "Somehow, the pictures tunneled us into Disney's internal network."

"So what happened to the website?"

"Forget the website—that's for the public," I tell him. "From here on in, we're officially snooping in the private computer network for Disney employees."

"Welcome Cast Members!" it says toward the top of the screen.

"What about the guy with the cleft chin?" Gillian asks.

"I don't think we're going to have to wait that much longer," Charlie says as he raps a knuckle against the screen. Directly below the Seven Dwarfs, there's a red button at the bottom of the screen: *Company Directory*. "If we're looking for employees . . ."

"Reel it in," Gillian sings.

Cringing at her enthusiasm, Charlie tightens his jaw and pretends not to notice. Even he knows now's not the time to stop.

A flick of his wrist and another mouse-click take us to a place marked *Employee Locator*. From there, a new screen pops up and we're staring at dozens of brand-new faces. CEO . . . Board of Directors . . . Executive Vice Presidents . . . the list keeps going—tons of photos under each category heading. Forget the few dozen people who run the website—we're talking the full organizational hierarchy here—from the CEO, all the way down to background animators.

"There's gotta be two thousand photos here," Gillian says, sounding overwhelmed.

"Go to Stoughton's Internet group," I interrupt, my voice

surging as I let go of Charlie's shirt. "If I'm Duckworth, I'm keeping it on the home team."

"Guess who's back in boy-wonder mode?" Charlie asks. He loves the tease, but I can tell he's excited. Nodding, he scrolls down through the various groups until he gets to *Disney Online*. Set up in the exact same pyramid as before, it doesn't take us long to find Stoughton's salt-and-pepper portrait. Below him, we once again spot the pale accounting guy, followed by the redhead. But once again, that's where the Online group ends. Just like before. No black man; no cleft chin. Right back where we started.

"Didn't your dad ever do anything easy?" Charlie asks.

"It's in here somewhere," I insist, eyes locked on the screen.

Gillian's silent, but the way she fidgets with her skirt, it's like she sees something familiar. Something she knows. Her voice is slow in its deliberation. "Go to *Imagineering,*" she eventually suggests.

Charlie looks at me; I nod a quick approval. Duckworth's old stomping ground.

He scrolls back up as quickly as he can. Imagineers. At the top, the VP of Imagineering is a handsome middle-aged man with a restrained, taunting grin. Underneath, his first lieutenant is about the same age, with a collection of double-chins that makes him look almost jolly. And below the two of them . . . is Marcus Dayal, a dark-skinned black man with an unmistakable cleft chin.

Charlie presses the photo strip against the screen to match up the pictures. The static electricity on the monitor holds it in place. Perfect match.

"I'm telling you, we'd whup the Hardy Boys' asses any-day," he says.

"Press the button," I insist, barely able to contain myself.

Moving the cursor over Marcus's digital photo, Charlie clicks it once and starts the countdown.

Once again, nothing happens. And then—once again—something does.

"They're heeeere . . ." Charlie whispers as the screen fades to black.

This time, though, it's different than before—a cascade of images appear, and just as quickly vanish. Web page after web page opens at whirlwind speed, their words and logos fading immediately after they appear: *Team Disney Online . . . Company Directory . . . Employee Locator*—the cursor's moving and clicking in every direction, like it's surfing through the site on fast-forward. The rush of images fly at us, faster and faster, deeper into the website and further down the wormhole. The pages are skimming past us at such high speeds that they merge in a dark purple blur. I'm almost dizzy from staring at it, but only a fool would look away.

And then the brakes kick in. A single, final image slaps the screen. I actually jump back as it stops. So does Charlie. To her credit, Gillian doesn't flinch.

"Here we go . . ." Charlie says.

He's right about that one. Wherever we are, this is it. Duckworth's three-hundred-and-thirteen-million-dollar idea.

64

Practically blocking my view, Charlie's leaning so close to the screen, his chest presses against the keyboard. As I pull him back, it takes me all of two seconds to recognize what he's gaping at. The midnight blue *Greene & Greene* logo on the top left. The *est. 1870* sign on the top right.

"A bank statement?" Charlie asks.

I nod, checking it myself. At first glance, that's all it is—just a regular, end-of-the-month bank statement. Except for the Greene logo, it doesn't look any different from the monthly statement at any bank: deposits, withdrawals, account number—all the pieces are there. The only difference is the name of the account holder . . .

"Martin Duckworth," Charlie reads from the screen.

"This is dad's account?" Gillian asks.

". . . 72741342388," I read out loud as my finger brailles the numbers on the screen. "This is definitely his—the same as the one we—" I cut myself off as soon as Gillian glances my way. "The same as the original one we looked at," I tell her.

Smooth, Charlie says with a look.

I turn back to Gillian, but her eyes are now glued to the screen . . . and to the box that's labeled *Account Balance:* $4,769,277.44.

"Four million?" Gillian asks, confused. "I thought you said the account was empty?"

"It was . . . it's supposed to be," I insist defensively. She thinks I'm lying. "I'm telling you, when I called from the bus, they said the balance was zer—"

There's an audible click and all three of us turn to the monitor.

"What was . . . ?"

"*There*," I say, once again stabbing a finger at the screen. I point to the *Account Balance:* $4,832,949.55.

"Please tell me that just went up," Charlie says.

"Does anyone remember what it said before it—"

Click.

Account Balance: $4,925,204.29.

None of us says a word.

Click.

Account Balance: $5,012,746.41.

"If my mouth opens any wider, my chin's gonna hit the carpet," Charlie blurts. "I don't believe it."

"Lemme see," I say as I shove Charlie out of his seat. For once, he doesn't fight. Right now, he's better off riding shotgun.

Moving the cursor up toward the *Deposits* section, I study the three newest entries to the account:

$63,672.11—wire transfer from Account 225751116.

$92,254.74—wire transfer from Account 11000571210.

$87,542.12—internal transfer from Account 9008410321.

My eyes narrow and I press my lips together.

"It's the same way he studies mom's bills," Charlie says to Gillian.

Reaching forward, I palm the top corner of the monitor. I'm not letting this one go. "Oh, don't tell me he—" I cut myself off and recheck the numbers.

"What?" Gillian asks.

I don't answer. I shake my head, lost in the screen. Searching for more, I click on the box marked *Deposits*. A smaller window opens, and I'm staring at Duckworth's full account history. Every deposit on record from start to—

"How the hell did he . . . I-It's not possible . . ." I stumble, scrolling down the digital pages of the account. The more I scroll, the longer it goes. Deposit after deposit. Sixty thousand, eighty thousand, ninety-seven thousand. They don't seem to stop. I've got that gnawing pit in my stomach. It doesn't make sense . . .

"Just say it!" Charlie begs.

Startled, I turn around.

"What? You forgot we were here?" Gillian asks, surprisingly curt.

Letting go of the monitor, I move back from the screen so they can squeeze in. "See this right here?" I ask, pointing to the box for *Deposits*.

Charlie rolls his eyes. "Even I know how a deposit works, Ollie."

"It's not the deposit," I say. "It's where it came from."

"I don't understand . . ."

Behind us, the elevator dings and Charlie angles his neck back toward its opening doors. Two elderly women holding each other's hands come out. Nothing to worry about. At least, not yet.

"Check out each of the deposits," I say as Charlie turns back to the screen. "Sixty-three thousand . . . ninety-two thousand . . . eighty-seven thousand." I motion to the other deposits before them. "See the trend?"

He squints toward the monitor. "You mean, besides being buckets of cash?"

"Look at the amounts, Charlie. Duckworth's account has over two million dollars moving in every day—but there's not a single deposit that's over a hundred thousand dollars."

"So?"

"So, one hundred thousand is also the threshold amount where the bank's automatic auditing system kicks into place—which means . . ."

". . . anything under a hundred grand doesn't get audited," Gillian says.

"That's the game," I reply. "It's called smurfing—you pick the amount that's just small enough to squeeze under the monitoring threshold. People do it all the time—especially when clients don't want us questioning their cash transactions."

"I don't get what the big deal is. So, he's a smurf."

"He's not a smurf. He's smurfing. *Smurfing*," I say. "And the big deal is that it's the number one way to keep it below the radar."

"Keep *what* below the radar?"

"That's what we're about to find out," I say, turning back to the screen.

65

Stuck in a strangle of traffic on Broward Boulevard, Joey reached over to the passenger seat, fished through her purse, and pulled out the photo of Duckworth and Gillian. At first glance, it was dad and daughter, happy as could be. But now that she had it in the light—now that she knew . . .

Damn, that's a rookie mistake, she told herself as she slammed the steering wheel. Holding the photo up close, she didn't know how she missed it before. It wasn't just the bad proportions—even the shadows were skewed. Duckworth had the shade on the left side of his face; Gillian had it on the right. Total rush job, she decided. Rushed, but still decent enough to pass.

Pulling into a strip mall parking lot, she flipped open her laptop and went back to the digital photos of the Greene Bank offices she took the first day. Oliver's, Charlie's, Shep's, Lapidus's, Quincy's, and even Mary's. One by one, she took another pass, flipping through the . . .

"Rat bastards," she muttered as soon as she saw it. She leaned down toward the screen, just to make sure she was right. The hair was a different color and straightened, but there was no mistaking it. There it was. A single headshot. Right in front of her the entire time.

Joey pumped the gas, and a whirlwind of dust blew behind her. Her hand went right for the phone. Speed-dial.

"This is Noreen."

"I need you to run a name for me," Joey announced.

"You got something new?"

"Actually, something old," Joey said as the car flew toward the offices for Neowerks. "But if the dominoes tip right, I think I finally have the real story on Gillian Duckworth."

66

See this deposit right here? The eighty-seven thousand?"
I ask, pointing Charlie and Gillian to the most recent
addition to Duckworth's account. Before they can answer, I
explain, "That's from Sylvia Rosenbaum's account. But for
as long as I can remember, she's had it set up as a trust with
specific beneficiaries."

"Which means?"

"Which means once every quarter, the computer automatically makes two internal transfers: a quarter-million-dollar
transfer to her son, and a quarter-million-dollar transfer to
her daughter."

"So why is this wealthy old woman transferring money to
my dad?"

"That's just it," I say. "Besides her family and the once-a-
year payment to her advisors, Sylvia Rosenbaum doesn't
transfer money to *anyone*. Not your dad, not the IRS, no one.
That's the whole purpose of the trust account—it runs on its
own and makes the same exact payments every quarter. But
when you look here . . ." I scroll up through Duckworth's
records and point to one of the first deposits—another eighty-

thousand-dollar transfer from Sylvia's account. This one's dated June. Six months ago. "See, this shouldn't be here either," I explain. "It doesn't make sense. How the hell could he—?"

"Can you please slow down a second? Whattya mean, *it shouldn't be here?*" Charlie asks. "How could you possibly know?"

"Because *I'm* the one who handles her account," I say, struggling to keep my voice down. "I've been checking this woman's statements since the first day I started at the bank. And when I checked it last month—I'm telling you—these transfers to Duckworth weren't there."

"You sure you didn't just miss them?" Gillian asks.

"That's what I was wondering when I first saw it," I admit. "But then I saw this one . . ." I highlight another internal transfer that recently came into Duckworth's account. $82,624.00 transferred from Account 23274990007.

"007," Charlie blurts, reading the last three digits. He doesn't miss a beat.

"That's the one," I shoot back. Seeing that Gillian's lost, I explain, "007 belongs to Tanner Drew."

"*The* Tanner Drew?"

"The man himself—newest member of the Forbes 400. Anyway, last week, he threatened our lives until we transferred forty million dollars into one of his other accounts. All of that happened on Friday at exactly 3:59 P.M. Now check out the time that Tanner Drew made this transfer to Duckworth . . ."

Gillian and Charlie lean toward the screen. Friday—December 13—3:59:47 P.M.

I see a single teardrop of sweat run down from my brother's sideburns. "I don't get it," Charlie says. "We were the only people accessing the account. How could he possibly be transferring his cash to Duckworth?"

"That's what I'm saying . . . I don't think he did," I suggest. "In fact, I *know* he didn't. Once we transferred the money, I checked Tanner Drew's account half a dozen times, just to make sure it was on its way. Know what the last transfer was? Forty mil."

"Then where did this eighty-two thousand come from?" he asks.

"That's what I'm trying to figure out. But whatever hat Duckworth pulled it out of, it's clear that he had his hand in almost everyone else's business. I mean, half these accounts—here, and here, and here . . ." I point one by one to all the different account numbers that're listed under *Deposits*. "Every one of them is a client of the bank—007 is Tanner Drew. 609 is Thomas Wayne. 727 is Mark Wexler. And 209 . . . I'm pretty sure that's the Lawrence Lamb Foundation."

"Wait . . . so dad was getting cash from all of them?" Gillian interrupts.

"That's what it looks like," I say, once again studying the blue glare of the monitor. "And the money never stopped flowing."

Gillian looks around, making sure no one's nearby. Charlie steps away from her, just to be safe. He can't help himself. "You think dad was blackmailing them?" she asks.

"I don't know—but when you look at what he did in the trust account—and then with Tanner Drew—it's like the transfers shouldn't exist. Forget what it says here. On the bank's system, not a single dollar left any of these accounts. I mean, it's almost like this ticking program is convincing the computer to see what's not really—" My chest tightens and I freeze.

"What? What's wrong?" Gillian asks.

"You okay?" Charlie adds, shoving her aside and putting a hand on the back of my neck.

"Oh, crap . . ." I stutter, pointing to the screen. "That's what he invented." My voice rattles down the runway, slowly taking off. "It's like a funhouse mirror—it shows you a reality that's not really there."

"What're you talking about?"

"I mean, how else do you get a credit to match the corresponding debit? That's what the Secret Service wanted to invest in . . . and that's what Gallo wanted for himself. The next step in financial crime. Virtual counterfeiting. Why steal money when you can just create it?"

"What do you mean, *create it?*" my brother asks.

"Electronically make it. Convince the computer it exists. Build it out of thin air."

Charlie goes back to the screen. "Sombitch . . ."

"Wait a minute," Gillian says. "You think my dad *created* all that cash?"

"It's the only thing that makes sense. That would explain why the Service is on it, instead of the FBI. It's like Shep said—they're the ones with jurisdiction over counterfeiting."

"But to build money out of nothing . . ." Gillian begins.

". . . would make a VC place like Five Points Capital wet itself. Think about how it played out: Six days ago, Martin Duckworth had three million dollars in his account. Three days ago, the computer said it was three hundred and thirteen million. But when you look at these records, it's clear that that didn't just happen overnight. These transactions go back six months. Hundreds of deposits. It's like keeping two sets of books. The regular system always said he had three million, but below the surface, his little invention was quietly creating the full three hundred. Then, when the gold-plated nest egg got big enough—wham!—they went to grab it. But we nabbed it first—and as it was sent on its way, the second set of books merged with the first, and every one of his fake deposits now somehow correlated with a real transaction at the bank."

"Maybe that's how the program works," Charlie jumps in. "Like the forty million we transferred to Tanner Drew—it waits for a real transaction to take place, then takes a random amount that's under the audit criteria. By the end, you've got a whole new reality."

"It's the same thing happening now," I agree. "The bank thinks Duckworth's account is empty, but according to this, there's a new five million in there. The crazy thing is, none of the people he took it from is missing any cash."

"Maybe it just *looks* like they're not missing cash. For all we know, whatever my dad put in the system could be wiping them clean."

I shake my head no. "If that were true, Tanner Drew wouldn't have been able to transfer forty million bucks. And if Drew was shorted a single dime, we would've heard it the instant it happened. Same with Sylvia and the rest. The richer they are, the more they inspect."

"So that's the big ultra-secret?" Gillian interrupts. "Some diddly computer virus that makes a few people rich?"

"We should be so lucky," I say, turning back to the blue glare.

Charlie watches me carefully. He knows that tone. "What're you saying?" he asks.

"Don't you see what Duckworth did? Sure, on the small stage, he invented some cash, but when you pull the micro-

scope back, it's far bigger than just adding a few zeros to
your bank account. To pull this off, he not only sidestepped
all of our internal controls—he also somehow fooled the
bank's computer system into thinking it was dealing with
real money. And when we transferred that money out, it was
good enough to fool the London bank, and the bank in
France, and every bank after that. In some of those places—
including ours—we're talking state-of-the-art, military-
designed computer systems. And Duckworth's imaginary
transactions fooled them all."

"I still don't see what's—"

"Take it to the next level, Charlie. Forget the private
banks and the tiny foreign institutions. Grab Duckworth's
program and sell it to the highest bidder. Let a terrorist
organization get ahold of it. Even worse, put it in a too-big-
to-fail."

"A what?"

"*Too-big-to-fail*. It's what the Federal Reserve calls the
top fifty or so banks in the country. Once Duckworth's
little worm digs in there, your three hundred million is
suddenly three hundred *billion*—and it's flowing everywhere—Citibank . . . First Union . . . down to the little
mom-and-pops across the country. The only problem is,
when all is said and done, the money's not real. And the
moment someone realizes that the Emperor's not wearing
any clothes, the pyramid scheme collapses. No bank trusts
its own records, and none of us knows if our bank accounts
are safe. The whole world lines up at the teller windows
and the ATMs. But when we go to make our withdrawals,
there's not enough *real* cash to go around. Since the
money's fake, every bank runs out of funds. The too-big-
to-fails implode first, then the hundred smaller banks that
they lend to, then the hundreds of banks below those. They

all crater at once—all of them searching for money that was never really there. *Sorry, sir, we can't cover your account—all the money in the bank is now gone*. And that's when the real panic begins. It'll make the Depression look like a quick stock market dip."

Even Charlie can't make a joke about this one. "You think that's what they want it for?"

"Whatever they want, there's one thing I know for sure: The only proof of what actually happened is right here," I say, once again tapping the screen.

Click.

Account Balance: $5,104,221.60.

The elevator pings behind us as ninety-one thousand new dollars stare back at us from the screen. Charlie checks the elevator, but no one steps out.

Glancing over his shoulder, I see it too. We've been here too long. "We should print this out . . ."

". . . and get out of here," he agrees.

"Wait," Gillian says.

"*Wait?*" Charlie asks.

"I-I just . . . we should be careful with this one."

"That's why we're printing it out. For proof," he says as he stares her down. This close, his fuse is shorter than ever.

There's an out-of-date laser printer right next to the computer. I flip a switch and it grumbles to life. Grabbing the keyboard, Charlie hits *Print*. On screen, a gray dialog box pops up: *Error in writing to LPT1: Please insert copy-card.* At the base of the printer is a handwritten card that says: *All copies fifteen cents per page.*

"Where do we get a copy-card?" he demands.

There's a machine in the corner. Two people are standing in front of it, stuffing dollar bills down its throat. Charlie's in no mood to wait. A few computers down, the porno kid has a copy-card sitting on his desk. "Hey, young sir," Charlie calls out. "I'll give you five bucks for your card."

"There's already five bucks on it," he tells us.

"We'll give you ten," I add.

"How 'bout twenty?" the kid challenges.

"How 'bout I scream 'Titty-freak' and point your way?" Gillian threatens.

The kid slides the card; I pull out a ten.

As I get up to make the trade, Charlie jumps back in the driver's seat. Leaning over his shoulder, I stuff the card into the small machine that's attached to the printer and wait as it whirs into place. The screen on the card-reader lights up. *Current balance: $2.20.*

We turn back to the porno kid. He sniffs the ten-dollar bill with a smirk. Charlie's about to stand up.

"Leave it be," I say, turning his head back to the screen.

Refocused, he once again hits *Print*. Like before, a gray box pops up, but this one's different. The font and type size match the ones on Duckworth's bank statement: *Warning— To print this document, please enter password.*

"What the hell is this?" Charlie asks.

"What'd you do?" I blurt.

"Nothing . . . I just hit *Print*."

"See, this is what I was talking about," Gillian says.

The porno kid next to us once again starts to stare. The elevator doors close in the corner. Someone's calling it from below.

Charlie tries to click back to the bank statement, but he can't get past the password warning.

"Ask the lady at the reference desk," Gillian says.

"I don't think this is from the library," I say, leaning in over his shoulder. "This may be a Duckworth precaution."

"What're you talking about?"

"We do the same thing on the important accounts at the bank. If you were hiding the smoking gun in the center of one of the world's most popular websites—wouldn't you bury a couple land mines just to buy yourself some safety?"

"Wait, so now you think it's a trap?" Gillian asks.

"All I'm saying is we should pick the right password," I tell her matter-of-factly. Charlie looks at me, surprised by my tone.

"Try putting in *Duckworth*," I say.

He hammers the word *Duckworth* on the keyboard and hits *Enter*.

Failure to recognize password—To print this document, please reenter password.

Crap. If this is like the bank, we've only got two more chances. Three strikes and we're out.

"Any other bright ideas?"

"How about *Martin Duckworth?*" I ask.

"Maybe it's something stupid, like his address," Gillian suggests.

"What about *Arthur Stoughton?*" Charlie adds, using the first name from the photos.

Gillian and I look at Charlie. As we nod, he quickly hunts and pecks *Arthur Stoughton* and smacks the *Enter* key.

Failure to recognize password—To print this document, please reenter password.

"I swear, I'm gonna put my foot through the screen," he growls.

Only one more shot.

"Try the guy with the cleft chin," I say.

"Try dad's account number at the bank," Gillian suggests.

"Try *Gillian*," I blurt, my voice and confidence already

wavering. I'm not the only one. Desperation settles across Charlie's face. He knows what's at stake. "*Gillian*," I repeat.

Charlie rubs his knuckles against his cheek. He's far from thrilled. Still, there's no time to argue.

Turning to Gillian, he studies her penetrating blue eyes and searches for the lie. But like always, it never comes.

"Try it," I say.

He looks down at the keyboard, types in the word *Gillian*, and goes to press *Enter*. But for some reason—just as his finger touches the key—he stops.

"C'mon, Charlie."

"Are you sure?" he asks, his voice shaking. "Maybe we should—"

"Just hit it," I demand, reaching over and pounding the key myself.

All three of us squint at the screen, waiting for the computer's reply.

There's a long, vacant pause. In the distance, I hear someone flipping pages through a magazine. The air-conditioning hums . . . the porn-kid snickers . . . and to all of our surprise, the laser printer softly purrs.

"I don't believe it," Charlie mutters as the first page rolls off. "We're finally getting a break."

With a wild grin across his face, he leaps out of his seat, dives forward, and grabs the top sheet from the printer. But as he flips it over, the grin suddenly goes limp. His shoulders fall. I look at the page. It's completely blank.

We spin back toward the screen just in time to see Duckworth's account slowly fade to black. We just jumped on the land mines.

"Charlie . . . !"

"I'm on it!" he says. Clutching the mouse, he clicks every button in sight. There's no way to stop it. It's almost gone.

"Get the web address . . . !" I shout.

Our eyes lock on the address at the top of the screen. I take the first half; he takes the second.

Gillian's lost. "What're you doing?"

"*Not now*," I snap, struggling to memorize.

The screen blinks off and a new image clicks into place. It's the Seven Dwarfs, and a red button marked *Company Directory*. Back at the beginning. But at least we're still in the internal employee site.

"Charlie, go to . . ."

Before I can finish, he's already there, anxiously clicking the button for *Directory*. Hundreds of company photos appear on screen. Like before, he scrolls down to the *Imagineering* section. Like before, he finds the black man with the cleft chin. And like before, he clicks on his face. But this time, nothing happens. The photo doesn't even move. "Ollie—"

"Maybe you have to go through all four," Gillian suggests.

"Hit it again," I say.

"I did. It's not going anywhere," he says in full panic.

"Put in the address."

Frantically passing me the keyboard, Charlie ducks out of the way as I type in the first half of the memorized address. Then he does his. The instant he hits *Return,* the screen hiccups toward a brand-new page.

"It's fine. We're still fine . . ." he says as we wait for the image to load. And for a second, it looks like he's right. But as the page finally appears, my stomach spirals. The only thing on screen is a plain white background. Nothing else. Just another blank page.

"W-What the hell is this?" I ask.

"It's gone . . ."

"Gone? That's impossible. Scroll down."

"There's nothing to scroll," Charlie says. "I'm telling you, it's not here."

"Are you sure you didn't type it in wrong?" Gillian asks.

He rechecks the address. "This is exactly where we were—"

"It's not gone," I insist. "It can't be gone." Crossing past my brother, I plow toward the nearest computer and yank the *Out of Order* sign from the keyboard.

Within seconds, I'm at the home page of Disney.com— *Where the Magic Lives Online*. "All we gotta do is start over," I say in full Brooklyn accent.

"Ollie . . ."

"It's okay," I tell him, already halfway there. Gillian says something, but I'm too busy clicking my way through the executive biographies.

"Ollie, it's gone. There's no way you'll find it."

"It's right here—just one more page." As I find the corporate pyramid, a dozen employee photos appear onscreen. For the second time, I make a beeline for Arthur Stoughton, slide the cursor into place, and click. When nothing happens, I click again. And again. The photo doesn't move. "It's impossible," I whisper. Trying to hold it together, I scroll down to the photo of the pale banker. Then I move to the redhead. Once again, nothing happens.

"C'mon . . . *please*," I beg.

Climbing out of his seat, Charlie reaches over and puts a hand on my shoulder. "Ollie . . ."

I gaze at the screen, hunched over in my chair. My elbows rest on my knees. "Why can't we ever get a break?" I ask, my voice cracking.

It's a question Charlie can't answer. He holds on to my shoulder and checks the screen himself. Teetering, he can barely stand. I don't blame him. Five minutes ago, we had everything that Duckworth had created. Right now—as my brother and I stare blankly at the screen—we've got nothing. No bank logo. No hidden account. And worst of all, no proof.

67

"Walt Disney World reservations—this is Noah. How can I help you?"

"Hi, I'm looking for Information Services," I say to the over-peppy voice on the other line as I watch Charlie squint in the Florida sun.

"Let me connect you with the switchboard—they'll transfer you from there," Noah says in a tone that's been genetically engineered for customer service.

"That'd be great. Thanks," I tell him as I give the thumbs-up to Charlie and Gillian. It doesn't calm either of them down. Crowded around me by the payphone across the street from the library, they're nervously checking over their shoulders, unconvinced I can pull it off. Still, big companies are big companies. By going through the switchboard, it's now an internal Disney call. We lost our proof once. I'm not losing it again.

"This is Erinn—how may I help you?" the switchboard operator asks.

"Erinn, I'm looking for the IS group that handles the Intranet for Disney cast members."

"Let me see if we can find that for you," she says, speaking in the royal Disney "we." As she puts me on hold, the song "When You Wish Upon a Star" floats through the receiver.

"Sir, I'm going to put you through to Steven in the Support Center," the operator eventually announces. "Extension 2538 if you get disconnected."

I grit my teeth and wait for the music to stop.

"This is Steven," a deep voice answers. He sounds young; maybe as young as Charlie. Perfect.

"Please tell me I have the right place," I beg in his ear.

"I-I'm sorry . . . can I help you?" he asks.

"Is this Matthew?" I say, pouring on the panic.

"No, it's Steven."

"Steven who?"

"Steven Balizer. In the Support Center."

"It doesn't make any sense," I say, ramming forward. "Matthew said it'd be on there, but when I went to pull it off, the whole presentation was gone."

"What presentation?"

"I'm dead . . ." I tell him. "They'll eat me as an appetizer . . ."

"What presentation?" he repeats, already swinging to my aid. It's Disney training. He can't help himself.

"You don't understand," I say. "I've got fifteen people sitting in a conference room, all of them waiting for their first look at our new online subscription service. But when I go to download it off our Intranet, the whole thing is gone. Zip. Nothing. It's not there! Now everyone's looking at me—the lawyers, the creatives, the finance boys . . ."

"Listen, you have to calm down—"

". . . and Arthur Stoughton, who's sitting red-faced at the

head of the table." All it takes is a single drop of the boss's name. That one I learned from Tanner Drew.

"You said it was on the Intranet?" Steven asks anxiously. "Any idea where?"

I read off the exact address where Duckworth's account was stored. I can hear young Steven jackhammering away at his keyboard. It takes an underling to know one—we're all in this together. "I'm sorry," he eventually stammers. "It's no longer there."

"No . . . don't say that!" I plead, thankful we picked an outdoor payphone. "It has to be! I just saw it!"

"I already checked twice . . ."

"This is Stoughton we're talking about! If I don't get his presentation up there . . ." I breathe heavy through my nose, trying to sound like I'm fighting tears. "There's gotta be some way to get it back. Where do you keep the backups?" It's a bluff, but not a risky one. Every sixty minutes, the bank's computer systems run an automatic backup to protect it from things like viruses and power failures. Then we store the copy somewhere else, purely for safety purposes. A company the size of Disney has to do the same.

"In the DISC building . . . in the North Service Area," he says without even thinking. "That's where they keep all the long-term stuff."

"Forget long-term—I need what was there three hours ago!"

There's a pause on the other line. "The only thing I can think of are the tapes in DACS."

I hate techno jargon. "What tapes?"

"Data tapes—the tapes we back up the site with. Since DACS makes a copy every night, that's my best guess to where they should be."

"And where's this place DACS?"

"In the tunnels."

"The tunnels?" I ask.

"Y'know, *the tunnels*," he says, almost surprised. "The ones below the Magic Kingd—" He stops and there's another pause. This one's longer. "What department did you say you worked in?" he finally asks.

"Disney Online," I quickly counter.

"What division?" he challenges. In the background, I hear him once again clicking at his keyboard.

I don't have an answer.

"What'd you say your name was again?" he adds.

That's my cue. Abandon ship. I slam the phone in its cradle.

"What'd he say?" Charlie asks.

"Are there backups?" Gillian adds.

Ignoring the question, I look up toward the blinding sun in the sky. I have to squint to see it. It's a few minutes past two. Time's running out. But I finally see the end in sight. The tapes don't just show reality—they show a reality that Duckworth invented . . . and that Gallo had clear access to. "Let's get out of here," I say.

"Where to?" Gillian asks.

"Is it far?" Charlie adds.

"That depends how fast we drive," I reply as I run toward the car. "How long does it take to get to Disney World?"

68

*W*hat?" Gallo asked. Pinching the cell phone between his shoulder and ear, he and DeSanctis raced up I-95. "Are you sure?"

"Why would I lie?" his associate asked on the other line.

"You really want me to answer that?"

"Listen, I already said I was sorry."

"Don't bullshit me with sorry," Gallo hammered. "Did you really think we wouldn't see you? That you could just sneak in without us getting a good look?"

"I wasn't sneaking anywhere. We were just reacting as fast as we could. We threw it together in about six hours—and once I got in, you were already gone."

"He still should've called."

"Can you please stop with the guilty mother routine?" his associate pleaded. "He said you already went through this—once Oliver and Charlie found what was in the remote, we were better off putting out the whole fire. After everything else, the last thing we need is to get burned by a loose end."

"He still should've dropped word with me—especially when he's just sitting on his ass in New York."

"No, no, no—not anymore. He flew in first thing this morning."

"Really?" Gallo asked as the Florida interstate whizzed past his window. "So he's close?"

"Close as he can get. But if it makes you feel any better, next time we'll send a Hallmark."

"Actually, you should send it to DeSanctis. He's the one that got gashed in the head."

"Yeah . . . sorry about that . . ."

"Sure you are," Gallo said coldly. Turning toward DeSanctis, he pointed to the sign for the Florida Turnpike.

"You positive?" DeSanctis whispered as Gallo nodded.

"Listen, I gotta run. I'm in demand these days."

Gallo rolled his eyes. "So you're sure they're going to Disney World?" he asked.

"That's where the backup copies are," she replied. "And the one remaining place where Charlie and Oliver can still prove what happened."

Gallo squeezed his phone as he thought about the tapes. "I still don't see why we don't clip their necks now and save ourselves the headache."

"Because contrary to what the macho portion of your brain says, torturing them isn't the way to get your hands on the money."

"And your way is?"

"We'll find out soon enough," Gillian said as her voice sank down to a whisper. "A few hours, to be exact."

69

"You sure we shouldn't rent a minivan or something more Disney-ish?" Charlie asks as he takes a full whiff of the gas station. He's tucked in the backseat and calling the questions out the driver's side window. I'm squeezing the nozzle and pumping the car full of gas. He already started to join us outside, but stopped himself before his foot hit the pavement. He's finally learned caution. The less seen, the better.

"And how do you plan on renting this van? With what credit card?" I ask as I squeegee the front window. Anything to keep us looking normal. "Remember what that guy said in Hoboken? It's the big purchases that get you noticed."

"Didn't he also say something about scorned women?" he counters.

I make a face. A week ago, I would've gotten into it. Today, it's not worth it.

The gas nozzle clicks, telling us the tank is full. Stuck in the backseat and lost in the fumes, Charlie looks like he's six years old. Back then, when dad took us to the gas station on Ocean Avenue, he used to always say, "Ten bucks, please." Not "Fill it up." He only said "Fill it up," when he closed a big deal. That was twice. Everything else was ten bucks. But—dad being dad—he still used full service. Just to prove we had some class.

"We ready?" Gillian asks, turning the corner and returning from the minimart bathroom. I nod as I slap the gas tank shut. Gillian hops in the driver's seat and readjusts the rearview. She glances at Charlie in the mirror, but when he catches her eye, she looks away, hits the gas, and sends us whipping back in our seats. Cats and dogs.

According to the guy in the gas station, it's a three-hour drive to Orlando. If we're fast, we'll be there before dark.

Fourteen miles later, we're at a dead stop in traffic. The Florida Turnpike may be the fastest route to Orlando, but as we wait in line at the Cypress Creek toll booth, nothing moves quickly.

"This is ridiculous," I complain as we inch forward. "They've got two hundred cars and four open toll lanes."

"Welcome to Florida math," Gillian replies. Swerving to the left, she angles for the one lane that actually looks like it's moving. Directly in front of us, while other cars roll forward, a black Acura sits still for about thirty seconds too long. "*Let's go!*" Gillian shouts as she pounds the horn. "Pick a lane and move!"

"Can I ask a silly question?" Charlie interrupts from the backseat. "Remember that Disney kid—the one on the phone who told us the backups were in this DACS place? Well, what if he got so spooked out, he started looking for the backups himself?"

"He's not going to do that," I answer, turning around to face him.

"How do you know?"

"I could hear it in his voice," I say. "He wasn't the type to investigate. And even if he was—he'd have no idea what he was looking at."

"You sure about that?" he asks.

Still facing Charlie, I feel a sudden, almost microscopic twitch in my eyebrow. He spots it instantly. "See what I'm saying?" he asks. "The Greene & Greene logo would be onscreen. All it'd take is a phone call to the bank . . . and another to Gallo and DeSanctis . . ."

As we roll toward the shadow of the toll booth, the sun fades from above. And it fades fast. It's only then that I turn around and notice our speed. The engine's revving. We're about to blow through the toll booth at thirty miles an hour.

"Gillian . . ."

"Relax, it's SunPass," she says, thumbing over her shoulder and motioning toward the bar code sticker on her left rear window.

Charlie stares out the windshield; I look up to follow. The sign above the toll says *SunPass Only*.

Damn.

"Don't go through . . . !" Charlie shouts.

It's already too late.

We glide through the toll booth and a digital scanner focuses coldly on the car. Charlie and I simultaneously duck in our seats.

"What're you doing?" Gillian asks. "It's not a videocamera . . ."

Out the back window, the toll booth fades behind us. Charlie shoots up in his seat.

"Dammit!" I shout, pounding the dashboard.

"Wh-What?"

"Do you have any idea how stupid that was?"

"What's wrong? It's just SunPass . . ."

". . . which uses the same technology as a supermarket

scanner!" I blast. "Don't you know how easy it is for them to trace this stuff? They know who you are in a heartbeat!"

Now Gillian's the one who sinks a bit. "I-I didn't think it was . . ." Her voice trails off and she tries her best to get my attention. She's not getting it. I flip down the visor mirror to check on Charlie.

What'd I tell you? he asks with a glance.

"Oliver, I'm sorry," she adds, reaching out and touching my arm. From the look on Charlie's face, he expects me to cave. I brush her away.

Finally. Good for you, bro.

"I'm serious—I'm really sorry," she continues. She touches me again, this time grabbing my hand.

Hold strong, Ollie. Time to claim victory, Charlie motions.

"Just drop it, okay?" I tell her.

"Please, Oliver, I was only trying to help. It was an honest mistake."

Between the bucket seats, Charlie shakes his head. He doesn't believe in honest mistakes—at least not when they're made by her. But even he has to admit, there's no real harm done. All we did was roll through a toll booth— which is why, as Gillian's fingers braid between mine, I don't hold her hand, but I also don't pull away.

Charlie shoves his knee into the back of my seat.

I flip the mirror closed. He doesn't understand. "Just next time, please be more careful," I tell her.

"I promise," Gillian replies. "You have my word."

Charlie turns around and stares out the rear window. The toll booth disappears in the distance. He's still watching our backs.

70

"'m sorry I couldn't be more helpful," Truman said as he escorted Joey back into the main lobby of Neowerks.

"No, you've been great," Joey said, tapping her pocket notepad against the palm of her hand. On the top sheet, she had written *Walter Harvey* and *Sonny Rollins*—Oliver's and Charlie's fake names. "So after you spoke to your co-workers, you could still only identify one of the photos?"

"Arthur Stoughton," Truman agreed. "But when I came back to tell Ducky's daughter, she and the two guys said their thanks and disappeared." Scratching nervously at his bushy hair, he added, "I only did it because I thought they were Ducky's friends . . ."

Joey knew that tone. She could see it in his manic movements—even the way he glanced at the receptionist behind the shiny black desk. "You don't have to worry, sir—you didn't do anything wrong."

"No . . . no, of course. I'm just saying . . ." His voice faded. "It was nice meeting you, Ms. Lemont."

"You too—but only if you call me Joey."

Truman forced a polite laugh, offered a fast handshake, and just as quickly scurried back to his office.

As the door shut behind him, Joey took a second glance at the receptionist, who didn't look up . . . even though it was her job.

Joey went straight for the shiny black desk. "Can I ask you a quick question?" From her purse, she pulled out two photos—one of Charlie and Oliver, and the other of Gillian and Duckworth. She slid them onto the desk, then placed her dad's badge next to them.

Lowering the magazine to her lap, the receptionist stared down at the photos and silently studied. "They're not rapists, are they?" she eventually asked.

"No, they're not rapists," Joey said in her most comforting voice. "We just want to ask them a few questions."

"You know they have different color hair, right?" she asked, still staring at the photos.

"We know," Joey offered. "We're trying to figure out where they went from here."

"You mean *after* the library?"

"Exactly—*after the library*," Joey replied, nodding like she knew it was coming. "Which reminds me—what library was that again . . . ?"

Hearing the familiar beep as he pulled back onto the Florida Turnpike, he flipped his cell phone open and saw the words *New Message* on the digital screen. Assuming it was Gallo or DeSanctis, he calmly dialed the number for his voicemail.

"You have one new message," the computerized voice said. "To listen to your message—"

He pushed a button on the phone's keypad and waited for the message to play.

"Where are you? Why aren't you picking up?" a female voice asked. The man grinned as soon as he heard Gillian. "I just spoke with Gallo," she explained. "He was happy to hear about Disney, but he's definitely getting suspicious. I'm telling you, the man's no moron—it doesn't take two blenders to the head to know what's going on. Whatever you told him at the start, he sees the chessboard moving. Anyway, I know you wanted to throw him and DeSanctis a bone, but from where I'm standing, it's two against one. So if you really plan on pulling this off, it's time to get your ass up here and help me out. Okay? Okay."

As the message faded, he hit *Delete*, slapped the phone shut, and put his foot on the gas. He was trying to stay away as long as he could, but like he always said back at the bank, some things required a personal touch.

"Whattya want?" Gallo asked as he picked up his cell phone.

"Agent Gallo, this is Officer Jim Evans with the Florida Highway Patrol—we just got a hit on that blue Volkswagen you were looking for. Apparently, it's registered to a Martin Duckworth—"

"I told *you* it was registered to Duckworth."

There was a pause on the other line. "You want the info or not, *sir?*" Evans challenged.

This time, Gallo was the one who stayed silent. "Tell me what you got," he finally said as he and DeSanctis raced up the Turnpike. He could hear Evans's quiet gloating on the other line.

"We put the name in SunPass, just to take a look," Evans began. "Apparently, about forty minutes ago, a pass registered to a Martin Duckworth went through at Cypress Creek."

"Which direction?"

"Headed north," the officer said. "If you want, I can send a few cars out—"

"Don't touch 'em!" Gallo shouted. "Understand? They're CIs—confidential informants—"

"I know what a CI is."

"Then you know I want 'em left alone!"

"Do what you want," Evans blasted. "Just remember you're the ones who contacted us." With a click, the line went dead.

Next to Gallo, DeSanctis shook his head. "I still don't think you should've called that one in."

"It was worth it."

"Why? Just to confirm she was going north?"

"No, to confirm she wasn't going south."

Nodding to himself, DeSanctis rubbed the back of his head, where a thin white bandage covered the still throbbing cut Gillian had given him earlier. "You really think she's turning on us?"

"It's definitely a possibility . . ."

"What about you-know-who?"

"Don't even say it," Gallo interrupted. "She said he flew in this morning."

"And you believe her?"

"I don't believe anyone," Gallo said. "Not after all this— I mean, how does he put her in the house and not even tell us? What the hell is that?"

"I have no idea—I just want to make sure we still get our cash."

"Don't worry . . . when all's said and done and it's time to split the baby, I guarantee we'll be taking a few extra arms and legs."

* * * *

"This one?" Joey asked, pointing to the middle computer.

"No, to the left," the woman behind the reference desk answered.

"Your left or mine?"

The librarian stopped a moment. "Yours," she answered.

On the fifth floor of the Broward County Library, Joey walked past the row of computers and approached the one on the far end. The one that—according to the sign-up sheet—had just recently been used by a Mr. Sonny Rollins. From the three chairs that were gathered in front of the desk, Joey knew which one it was as soon as she walked in, but that didn't mean she shouldn't double-check. Just to be safe.

"There you go—that's it," the librarian called out.

Pushing the two other chairs aside, Joey took a seat in the center one. Onscreen was the homepage for the Broward County Library—"Broward's Information Gateway" it said in black letters. Wasting no time, she moved the cursor to the button marked *History*, the computer equivalent of looking at an itemized long-distance telephone bill. She gave it a quick click and watched as a full list loaded in front of her. It had every website the computer visited in the last twenty days, including the last page viewed by Charlie and Oliver. Starting at the top, she clicked on the most recent.

Mickey and Pluto popped onscreen. *Disney.com—Where the Magic Lives Online.*

"What the hell is this?" she thought to herself.

She clicked the next on the list and found more of the same. *About Disney.com . . . Executive Bios . . . Executive Bios for Arthur Stoughton . . .*

Arthur Stoughton?

A high-pitched ring erupted and Joey reached for her cell phone. Every person on the fifth floor turned her way.

"Sorry—my bad," she waved to the onlookers as she stuffed her earpiece in place.

"You still at the library?" Noreen asked in her ear.

"What do you think?" Joey whispered.

"Well, get ready to shout, because I just got off the phone with your friend Fudge, who just got off the phone with some woman named Gladys, who just happens to be friends with another woman who is absolutely less than satisfied with the way her boss talks down to her at the Florida Highway Patrol."

"This better be good," Joey said.

"Oh, it's good. Let me put it to you like this: For a mere five hundred bucks, Gladys's friend happily put the word *Duckworth* into their computer system . . ."

"And . . . ?"

"And she quickly found out that a SunPass registered to Martin Duckworth was last used going north on the Florida Turnpike."

"North?" Directly in front of her, Joey stared at the official website for Disney, the number one tourist attraction in Orlando. North on the Turnpike.

Springing out of her seat, Joey made a mad dash for the elevator.

"What're you doing now?" Noreen asked, hearing the noise.

"Noreen . . . I'm going to Disney World."

71

It's the sign that does it to me. Not the green-and-white highway signs that take us off the Turnpike and onto I-4, or the brown-and-white directional signs that twist and turn us along World Drive. All this time, Charlie, Gillian, and I have been relatively calm. Small talk in the car, hunting for stations on the radio, staring out the window for our first glimpse of the park. It's just a typical trip to Disney World. But as the pink, purple, and blue sign rises in the distance . . . as the enormous blue letters arch across the eight lanes of perfectly paved road . . . as the stylized words "Magic Kingdom" come into focus and the car passes directly under them, all three of us crane our necks skyward and stay dead-man silent. Gillian's mouth gapes open. Charlie's huff-and-puff breathing gets loud enough for me to notice. And the tightened excitement in my own chest feels like an elephant stepping on my heart.

I look back at Charlie just to make sure he's okay. He puts on a smile I know is fake. I give him one right back. We did the exact same thing the first time we were here, when he was excited and used to puke on the Mad Hatter's teacup ride, and I was scared of meeting Captain Hook. Sixteen years later, I'm tired of being scared.

We're stalking Snow White. Watching the way she moves and who she talks to. I lean back against the wall. Gillian's next to me, pretending to make chitchat. Charlie, more nervous than usual, flutters in and out around the crowd. But all we do is stare . . . study . . . make our mental notes. Naturally, Snow White has no idea we're there—and as we stick to the shadows behind Cinderella's Castle, neither do the autograph-seeking kids and photograph-snapping parents who currently surround her. Right now, the swarming crowd is six kids deep, which makes her hard to miss.

From the moment we entered the park, we were hunting for characters. Up Main Street, through the castle, and straight into Fantasyland. But it wasn't until we heard the six-year-old shriek behind us—"Mom, *look!*"—that we spun around and saw the insta-crowd. There she was at the center of the storm: Snow White, the fairest of them all. To the kids, she appeared out of nowhere. To us, well . . . that's the whole point. If you want to find the employee tunnel, you have to start with the employees.

One by one, she lets each child have his moment. Some want a signature, others want photos, and the smallest ones simply want to hold her skirt and stare. Next to us, a mop-haired teenage boy is wearing a *"Why do they call it Tourist Season, if we can't shoot 'em?"* black T-shirt. That's Charlie when he was fifteen. Next to him, a brother and sister are in the middle of a vicious slap-fight. That's us when we were ten. But as Snow White waves to all three of them, they can't help but wave back. I clock it right from the start. Eight minutes after Snow White appears—just as the crowd hits critical mass—a college-aged kid with a Disney polo shirt arcs around to the back of the mob and gives the signal. Snow White looks up, but never falls out of character. That's all she wrote. Stepping back and throwing goodbye kisses to the crowd, she makes it clear it's time for her to go.

"Why's she leaving?" a clearly displeased curly-haired girl asks.

"She's late for her date with Prince Charming," the college kid announces as pleasantly as possible.

"My ass," Charlie whispers. "I hear they divorced years ago. She got everything but the mirror."

Gillian slaps him on the arm. "Don't say that abou—"

"Shhhh—this is it," I tell them.

A few flashbulbs go off, a last-second autograph is signed, and one final photo is taken by a parent who begs, "Please, just one more . . . *Katie, smile!*" Then, like a movie star waving to her fans, Snow White recedes from the crowd, all of whom are still grumbling until . . .

"Winnie the Pooh!" a little boy shouts as everyone turns. Thirty feet away, the familiar red-shirted bear magically appears and gets enveloped by tiny hugs. I have to hand it to Disney—they certainly know how to throw a distraction. The crowd runs. We stay. And that's when we see the old wooden door. Snow White and the college kid go straight for it—behind Cinderella's Castle, to the left of the Cinderella fountain—just under the arches, it's on the back corner of Tinker Bell's treasure shop. The way it's set off from the main path, it almost looks like a bathroom. But it doesn't say "Men" or "Women." It's just blank. A blank old door that's right in front of our faces. Perfectly designed to be overlooked.

The college kid takes a last-minute glance over his shoulder and checks for stragglers. All three of us look away.

Convinced no one's watching, he pulls open the door and escorts Snow White inside. Just like that, they're gone.

"Open sesame," Charlie says.

"You think that's it?" Gillian asks.

"That's the question, isn't it?" I ask, barreling forward.

"Wait!" Gillian calls out, grabbing me by the back of the shirt. "What're you doing?"

"Getting some answers."

"But if there's a guard . . ."

". . . then we'll say 'Oops, wrong door,' and walk away." I yank myself free and continue toward the door.

"Suddenly you're worried about our safety?" Charlie asks her.

Gillian doesn't answer. She's locked on me. "Oliver, this isn't something we should just rush into," she adds as I step forward.

I'm not listening. I just drove three hours on the promise I'd get my life back. It's all on the tapes. I'm not leaving here without them. I grab the door and check behind us. The crowd's on Pooh. It's now or never . . .

I pull open the door and turn to Charlie and Gillian. Both of them hesitate, but they also know there's not much of an alternative. As soon as Gillian moves, Charlie follows. I'm not sure if he's suspicious or just scared. Either way, all three of us slide inside.

Barely lit by a fluorescent light, the concrete landing is dark and empty. No one's here—no guards and no sign of Snow White. I check the ceiling and walls. No videocameras either. It makes sense when you think about it—it's Disney World, not Fort Knox.

"Check this out," Charlie whispers, staring over the metal railing on our left.

I squeeze between him and Gillian to see it for myself:

paved stairs that wind down four levels. The entrance to the underground.

"If I were six years old, you know what kinda bad dreams this would cause?" Charlie asks.

Without a word, I head down the stairs. It can't be much further.

"Just take it slow," Gillian warns as we spiral down into the depths.

At the bottom, we hit another door, but unlike the one up top, this one doesn't match the medieval feel of Tinker Bell's Treasures. It's just a standard, industrial utility door. I open it and peek my head into a short corridor. On my right, perpendicular to us, dozens of people crisscross back and forth in an even bigger hallway. Bright costumes rush by in a flash. Echoed voices ricochet off the concrete. There's the action. Time to jump in.

Slipping out of the stairwell, I march down our corridor and make a sharp left into the main hallway, where I nearly collide with a skinny girl in a Pinocchio costume, minus the Pinocchio head.

"Watch it," she warns as I step on her oversized foam Pinocchio shoes.

"S-Sorry . . ." Catching my balance and cutting around her, I notice Snow White on her right—a different one, with brown hair pinned back, a black wig in her hand, and chewing gum in her mouth.

"Kristen, you doing the parade tonight?" Snow White asks, poorly masking a Chicago accent.

"No, I'm done," Pinocchio answers.

I turn around as they pass, but quickly catch the eye of Charlie and Gillian, both of whom are staring me down.

Take it easy . . . please, Charlie glares, clearly unnerved.

I nod and continue up the hallway. They're a few steps

behind me, but they know what it takes to stay invisible. Keep it fast and keep it moving. It's the same as when I used to sneak Charlie into R-rated movies. The moment you look like you don't belong, that's the moment you don't belong.

Back on track in what looks like a pedestrian subway tunnel, I glance up the concrete hallway, which is about the width of two cars. All around us, we're swallowed by the colorful back-and-forth rush of Disney employees who're dressed in everything from the cowboy boots and hats of Frontierland, to the silvery, futuristic shirts of Tomorrowland, to the simple unmarked collared shirts of the janitorial staff. I pull off my tie, stuff it in my pocket, and undo the top button of my shirt. Just another Disney employee on his way to a costume change.

"Narc . . . ten o'clock," Charlie warns.

Following the dial, I look up to my left and spot two cops patrolling the tunnel. Damn. Instinctively reaching toward the back of my pants, I tap my waistband and check to make sure Gallo's gun is still there. Just in case.

"They're not armed," Charlie adds, knowing what I'm thinking.

As the Disney police get close, I realize he's right. They have silver badges and blue shirts, but that's where it ends. I glance at their holsters. Neither of them has a gun. Still, that doesn't mean we can afford a confrontation. As one of them looks my way, I lower my gaze to the ground. Stay focused . . . don't look up, I tell myself. Thirty seconds later, it's more than enough to do the job. The cops blow by without even a second glance, and I raise my head to once again face the labyrinth. The problem is, I don't have a clue where I'm going.

Picking up speed and trying to cover as much ground as possible, I walk up the hallway, inhaling the damp, underground air. From the faded purple stripe that colors the bottom half of the corridor, I'd say this place hasn't been painted in ten years. It may be the headquarters for all Magic Kingdom employees, but like the cheap industrial carpet we use in the nonclient areas of the bank, Disney keeps its money onstage. Still, the nuts and bolts of the park are clearly down here: exposed air-conditioning ducts overhead, random piping along the walls, and metal door after metal door marked with signs like "Maintenance," "AVAC/Trash control," and "Danger: High Voltage." Straight above us, kids hug Pooh, and parents marvel at the cleanliness of paradise. Down here, Pinocchio's a girl, and the trash chute rumbles so loud, you feel it in your back teeth. That's what magic's made of.

On my right, a black man dressed like a Tiki bird steps out of a door marked "Stairway #5—Legend of the Lion King." Across the way, a blond female elf comes through "Stairway 12—Ye Olde Christmas Shoppe." Every fifteen feet, people pop out of nowhere—and no matter how calm I'm trying to act, I can't shake the feeling we're starting to stand out. I scour the pipes that cover the ceiling and search for security cameras. There's only so long you can run around without a costume or nametag. If anyone's watching, we're running out of time. And worst of all, running blind. Three blind mice.

The further we go, the more metal doors we pass; the more doors we pass, the more the hallway seems to curve; the more the hallway curves, the more I feel like we're walking in circles. "Park Maintenance West" . . . "First-Aid" . . . "Break Area" . . . Where the hell is DACS?

"This is ridiculous," Gillian eventually says. "Maybe we should split up."

"No," Charlie and I say simultaneously. But it's clear we need to change strategy.

Up ahead, an older woman in a Pilgrim costume steps out of a room marked "Personnel." She looks about fifty years old. I motion to Charlie; he shakes his head. The older they are, the more likely they'll ask for Disney ID. Behind the Pilgrim is a girl in jeans and a Barnard T-shirt. Charlie nods. It's not my first plan, but we need to make a move. We both know who's better with strangers.

"Can I ask you a stupid question?" Charlie says, approaching Ms. Barnard as he bubbles up the charm. "I usually work over in EPCOT—"

"So that's why they let you keep the dyed hair," she interrupts.

Never fazed, he laughs out loud. "They don't let you have that around here?" he asks, running his hand through his blond locks. He's trying to sound relaxed, but from where I'm standing in the corner with Gillian, I see the shine of sweat on the back of his neck.

"Are you kidding?" she asks. "That's bad show."

"Yeah, well, there's something to be said about bad show," he nervously teases. "Anyway, they sent me down here to pick something up from some place called DACS . . ."

"DACS?"

"I think it's some kinda computer room."

"Sorry—never heard of it," she says as I bite the inside of my lip. "But if you want, you can check the map."

Map?

She points over her shoulder. Right around the corner from Personnel.

"That'd be great," Charlie says as he moves toward it. "And if you ever get to EPCOT . . ."

Don't make jokes with her!

". . . the tour of the giant golf ball is on me."

"I look forward to it," she says with a wide Disney smile.

Charlie waves goodbye; Ms. Barnard heads back to the maze. As soon as she passes, we calmly tear around the corner. There it is—up on the wall. *"Map to the Magic Kingdom Utilidor."*

Studying the layout, I go right for the "You Are Here" sign. The tunnels spread out from Cinderella's castle like spokes on a wheel and weave their way under almost every major attraction. Eventually, it looks like the face of a clock. Frontierland is at nine o'clock. Adventureland is at seven. To make it even easier to read, each land is also color-coded. Tomorrowland is blue, Fantasyland is purple. We're in Main Street—burgundy—which corresponds to the burgundy stripe that runs along the wall. Six o'clock position. Tinker Bell's Treasures was at twelve o'clock. We ran halfway around the clock.

"I told you we were making a circle," Gillian points out.

"And look what's at the far end of the hallway . . ." Charlie adds. He pounds a finger against the top of the map. The letters practically jump out and bite me on the throat.

DACS.

Dead ahead.

72

Weaving between two princes, Cruella De Vil, a railroad engineer, and Piglet, I'm ahead of Charlie, but trail Gillian, who seems to have no problem cutting through the dozens of cast members who're pouring out of the area marked "Character Zoo." On our right, she bolts up a short carpeted ramp that leads to a glass door. "DACS Central," it says in bold black letters.

"You sure you want to go alone?" Charlie asks me, purposely running slow. There's no doubt which of us is faster. He's just trying to stay by my side.

"I'll be fine," I insist.

Surprised by my tone, he studies me carefully. "See, now you're getting cocky."

"I'm not cocky. I just . . . I know what I'm doing."

He shakes his head. He doesn't like being on the other side. "Just be smart, okay?"

"Fine. Smart it is."

As we reach the ramp, Gillian's studying the fingerprint scanner that's next to the intercom outside DACS. Charlie stiffens. Of all the doors we passed, this is the only one with any sort of security measure. "Is there anyone who *doesn't* have one of these anymore?" she asks, pushing some buttons on the scanner.

"Don't touch it," Charlie warns.

"Don't tell me what to do," she adds.

Charlie knows better than to pick a fight. "Just ring the bell," he says.

She shoots him a look that'll ache tomorrow morning. I'm about to break it up, but I'm not even sure what to say anymore. The closer we get to the backups, the more the two of them are primed to explode.

"Ring it again," Charlie orders.

"I already did," she blasts.

"Really? Then why didn't anyone answer?"

She rolls her eyes and once again thumbs the button.

"*Can I help you?*" a female voice squawks through the intercom.

"Hi—it's Steven Balizer . . . from over in Arthur Stoughton's office," I say, once again dragging out the big names.

"Extension?" the woman counters.

"2538," I announce, praying I remember Balizer's direct dial.

Squinting to see through the translucent glass, I spot the woman staring at me from her desk. Thanks to the smoked glass, though, I'm just an amorphous blob with dark black hair. I smile and give her my best Mouseketeer wave.

There's a short pause, followed by a croaking ringing buzzer.

Behind me, Gillian reaches for the doorknob, then quickly catches herself. She's not the one going inside.

I step forward; she and Charlie step back.

"So you're all set?" she asks.

"I think so."

"And you know where to meet us?" Charlie asks, walking backwards down the ramp.

I nod and go for the door. The longer I'm out here, the more suspicious it gets.

"Knock 'em dead, bro," he whispers as I twist the doorknob. Just as I'm about to step inside, I take one last look over my shoulder. Charlie and Gillian are already gone— lost among the crowd of riverboat captains and fairy godmothers.

"So how you doing today?" a sweet maternal voice calls from inside.

Following the sound to the reception desk, I find a petite woman with plastic blue-rimmed glasses and a Little Mermaid embroidered shirt. But as I approach her desk, I look to my left and spot the computer servers and video screens that line the other three walls. In the center of the room, back-to-back servers form short library-style aisles and cover up most of the brown-and-white checkerboard floor. From their size alone—each server comes up to my neck—they remind me of an old rack stereo system, or one of those oversized super-computers from an old NASA movie.

Of course, my eye goes straight to the row of equipment that's the most outdated. On the front of each glass case is an unmistakable sticker: *It's a Small World* . . . *Carousel of Progress* . . . *Pirates of the Caribbean* . . . *Peter Pan* . . . Each attraction in its own antique mainframe. Unreal. They have a computer system that senses storm clouds so they'll know when to put out umbrellas, but when it comes to their most famous rides, Disney still drives a Studebaker.

"Amazing, isn't it?" the Little Mermaid asks. "But if it ain't broke . . ."

I nod and turn back to her desk.

"Now what can I do for you today?" she adds.

"I called about an hour ago—I'm here to get those back-ups for Arthur Stoughton."

She flips through a stack of paperwork on her desk. "And do you remember who you spoke to on that?"

I take another quick scan of the room. There's a closed door on my right. Nameplate says Ari Daniels. Under the door, there's no light. "It was with an A— Andre . . . Ari . . ."

"Typical Ari," the receptionist moans. "He's already gone for the day."

"Then how do I—?"

"I'll show you how to sign it out—I just need your ID."

I pat my chest, then my shirt pocket, then the back of my pants. "Oh, don't tell me I—" I pull out my wallet and pretend to frantically search through it. "It's sitting on my desk . . . I swear to you—you can call them right now. Extension 2538. It's just . . . when Stoughton loses his cool—you don't understand—if we don't get this reloaded, he'll—"

"Relax, darlin', I don't want the migraine either." Shoving her chair back, she crosses around her desk and heads for the double glass doors in the righthand corner of the room. Even in Disney World, everyone's afraid of the boss.

Through the glass, it's a computer nut's wet dream. Beige lockers filled with state-of-the-art mainframes and servers line the walls. Spools of uncut red and black wires twist along the floor. And in the center of the room, a laboratory-style workbench is covered with six computers, two laptops, a dozen keyboards, backup power supplies, and a mess of stray motherboards and memory chips. Forget the ancient stuff up front—here's where Disney's spending their cash. As we enter, two tech guys—one heavy, one skinny, both surprisingly handsome—are hunched over a flat-screen monitor. The receptionist waves hello. Neither looks up.

"Friendly," I whisper.

"That's why we don't let them near the guests."

Midway down the righthand wall, there's a closet marked "Supplies." Above the doorknob, I count three locks. The last one is a punch-code. Just like The Cage. Supplies, my tush.

"I still don't see why they don't keep this stuff in the North Service Area," she complains as she pulls out keys and punches in the PIN code.

"Most of it is," I say, checking to see if the tech boys are watching. They're still lost in their flat-screen. "It's just safer to have the dailies down here."

With a twist of the knob, the door swings wide. Inside, two black metal storage racks are filled with hundreds of cassette tapes. Tapes we want; tapes we get. There must be four hundred in total—all set side by side, so only the spines of the cases are sticking out. At first they look like short, squatty cassettes, but as we step into the closet, they're more like the digital audiotapes Charlie used to bring back from his old recording sessions.

"What was it you were looking for again?" the receptionist asks.

"T-The Intranet," I say, trying not to sound overwhelmed.

She runs her fingers across the laser-printed labels that're scotch-taped to the edge of each shelf. *Alien Encounter . . . Buzz Lightyear . . . Country Bear Jamboree . . .*

"Dis-web1," she announces, pointing to a collection of seven tapes. The spine of each case is labeled with a different day of the week, Monday through Sunday.

"Which day do you need?"

If I had my choice, I'd take them all, but for now, it has to be one day at a time. "Yesterday," I tell her. "Definitely yesterday."

She slides out the case marked "Wednesday," checks to make sure the tape's inside, then unhooks a clipboard that's Velcroed to the side of the storage rack. "Just fill it out," she says, handing me both the clipboard and the tape. "And don't forget to put your extension."

My fist wraps around the plastic case of the backup, and I have to fight myself to stay calm. There's still plenty to do before we—

A high-pitched chime rings from the front room. Doorbell.

My groin aches. I start scribbling as fast as I can on the sign-in sheet.

"Can one of you guys get that?" the receptionist calls out to the tech boys.

Neither of them looks up.

The doorbell rings again and my guide rolls her eyes. "Excuse me one sec," she says, heading out to the front room.

Alone in the closet, I lean outside and try to hear who's there. No arguing, no commotion. It's still okay. Over my shoulder, I eye the other six tapes. The rest of the proof— and the only way to be absolutely safe.

I take one last look at the tech boys. They couldn't care less. Then I turn back to the tapes. If I'm going to pull this off, it'll have to be quick.

Yanking the "Tuesday" cassette from the shelf, I pop the case open, stuff the tape in my pants pocket, and shove the empty case back on the shelf. Tape by tape, I work my way through the week, until my pockets are full, and all six cases are empty. When I'm done, I grab the Wednesday tape and—

"Steven . . . ?" the receptionist calls from the front room.

"Coming!" I answer, racing from the closet as soon as I hear my fake name. Trying not to look too rushed, I slow it down through the double glass doors and calmly reenter the main room.

"Just in time," she says. "Your friends are here."

I turn the corner and stop mid-step. My hands bunch angrily into fists.

"W-We just wanted to make sure you were okay," Charlie stammers.

"Yeah," Gillian adds. They're both standing by the receptionist's desk, but neither of them is moving.

What're you doing here? I glare at Charlie.

He shakes his head, refusing to answer.

"So it sounds like you're having quite a party tonight," the receptionist says.

Party?

And that's when I see them. They turn the corner and move in close behind Charlie and Gillian. Oh, God.

"There's our boy!" Gallo sings, stepping forward with a limp and a dark grin. "We were starting to get worried about you."

73

As I read the fear on Charlie's face, Gallo envelops me in a huge bear hug, purposely squeezing me tight so I feel his holstered gun against my chest. "Fuck you," he whispers in my ear.

"So I guess you got what you needed," DeSanctis adds, just as jolly.

"Of course he did," Gallo says, noticing the Wednesday tape in my right hand. "That's why he's Disney's best employee. Isn't that right . . . *Steven?*" He says the name with his rodent smirk, then extends an open hand out between us. "Now let's see what you got there, buddy-boy . . ."

Thinking about the gun in the back of my pants, I turn to Charlie. Directly behind him and Gillian, DeSanctis moves in even closer. I can't see his hands. Charlie's stomach flinches forward—like someone jammed something in his back.

"I don't mean to interrupt," the receptionist says, clearly unnerved, "but what department did you say you were with again?"

"Don't worry—we're all friends here," Gallo teases, still staring at me. "Now let's take a look at that tape . . ."

I hold on to it. Annoyed, Gallo reaches down and rips it from my hands. I don't put up much of a fight—not with a gun in Charlie's back.

"Oh, now why'd you go and get Wednesday?" Gallo asks, reading the day on the spine. "I thought you said we needed the other days as well . . ." Pointing to the receptionist, he adds, "Can you help us find Thursday through Tuesday?"

Clearly freaked out, the Little Mermaid starts to panic. "I'm sorry, sir, but I can't do anything until I see your ID."

"Y'know, I left mine in my other jacket," Gallo says. "But you can use our friend Steven's."

"Actually, I can't," the woman replies.

"Sure you can. You already let him have the one for—"

"I can't, sir. And since this is a restricted area, if you don't have ID, I'm going to have to ask you to leave."

"We're just looking for the other tapes," he says, still trying to keep it friendly.

"Did you hear what I said, sir? I'd like you to leave."

Gallo tightens his jaw. His voice is sandpaper. "And I'd like you to be a good employee and get us what we need."

"Okay, that's it," the receptionist says, reaching for her phone. "You can have the rest of this discussion with Security. I'm sure they'd love t—"

Gallo pulls out his Secret Service badge and holds it up. "Here's my ID. Now please put down the phone and get us the tapes."

Her eyes go from the badge, to Gallo, then back again. "I'm sorry, but you're going to have to speak to a supervisor . . ."

"I don't think you understand," Gallo says. He pulls his gun from his jacket and points it square at the receptionist's face. "Put the phone down and get us the tapes."

The receptionist drops the receiver as tears stream down her face. "I-I have a four-year-old . . ."

"The tapes," Gallo growls.

Her hands tremble as she raises them in the air. "They're in the back," she stutters.

"Show us," Gallo demands. Motioning to DeSanctis, he adds, "Go with her."

Nudging Charlie and Gillian aside, DeSanctis steps between them, holding his gun. As soon as the receptionist sees it, the tears flow even faster.

"Mickey Mouse smile—gimme a nice Mickey smile," DeSanctis warns, forcing her to pull it together as he pushes her toward the glass doors in the back.

"C'mere . . ." Gallo says, grabbing me by the front of my shirt and shoving me toward Gillian and Charlie. I stumble toward my brother. Our eyes lock.

The tapes aren't there, are they? Charlie asks with a glance.

I brush my hand across my pants pocket. Gillian sees it and grins along with us.

"Stand still," Gallo insists as I regain my balance and stand next to Charlie. He points his gun at me, then Charlie, but never at Gillian, who's back to staring silently at the floor.

"You okay?" I whisper to her.

"What'd you say?" Gallo asks.

"I asked if she was okay," I growl.

Gallo suddenly starts to laugh.

"What?"

He can't stop himself. The grin is ear to ear. "You still don't know, do you?" he asks.

"What're you talking about?"

"You're serious, aren't you? You really don't—"

". . . which brings us to DACS Central—the brain of the entire body," a cheerful voice announces as the door to

DACS swings open. Behind us, a man with sandy blond hair and a "Backstage Magic" collared shirt leads a group of twenty tourists into the already cramped reception area.

Gallo ducks his arm behind his back to hide the gun. The group presses forward, shifting their necks to get a look inside. As they pour in, a heavy woman in a pink shorts outfit and a matching pink sun-visor cuts in front of me, Gillian, and Charlie, and—without even knowing it—leads the whole crowd directly between us and Gallo.

"I'm sorry—were we interrupting?" the sandy blond asks in perfect tour-guide tone.

"Yes. You are," Gallo rifles back. He glares at us through the still moving crowd. He's ready to pull his gun, but he has to know what'll happen if he does.

"Hey, now," the guide teases as we step back. "Guests around . . ."

"Get the fuck outta my face," Gallo says, pushing him aside. He tries to rush toward us, but the crowd's too thick.

Charlie eyes the door. Any second now, DeSanctis is going to realize there's nothing in those cases . . .

Go, I nod to him. Charlie takes off.

"Don't move!" Gallo shouts, lifting his gun.

That's all it takes.

"Gun!" a woman screams. The crowd ruptures—everyone's shoving and shouting. The stampede's on. We fly for the door as the entire frenzied crowd follows.

A shot explodes as we hit the threshold. The glass door shatters, scattering shards of glass across the floor. Plowing forward, Charlie zigs and fights his way through the chaos of screaming tourists. Behind me, Gillian's tucked down and holding on to the back of my shirt. No one's hit. The room empties into the hallway—and the yelling echoes through the concrete tunnel.

"*Keep going!*" I shout, shoving Charlie in the back. We bottle-rocket out of the crowd and race up the neck of the tunnel. My feet pound against the concrete. Charlie looks back to make sure I'm okay. That's when he sees Gillian, who's still holding on to the back of my shirt.

His face says it all. *Lose her.*

What?

Lose her! he insists.

She lets go of my shirt and starts running on her own. Not stumbling . . . not slowing us down. She's running. Her clear blue eyes search for a way out. Her lips hang open in fear. He thinks it's so clear-cut. It's not.

"Let's just get out of here," I tell him.

Charlie clamps his jaw and kicks in the speed. As we launch ourselves up the tunnel, he's only a few feet ahead of me. He's faster than that. "Charlie, *go!*" I insist.

"Stay . . . with me," he says, cutting between Pocahontas and a Dracula from the Haunted Mansion.

"Up the stairs!" Gillian calls out as the doors whiz by on both sides of the hallway.

But Charlie just keeps running. It's not until the tunnel starts to curve to the left that I understand what he's doing. Behind us, the screams of the crowd muffle and fade—quickly replaced by the echoed footsteps of whoever's chasing us. I turn back to see what's going on, but thanks to the arc of the hallway, we can't see them. Which means they can't see us.

"Now . . . !" Charlie says, making a sharp right into a short corridor. At the end, he rips open the metal utility door and holds it open for us. Inside, yellow-painted stairs head straight up. I dart in first, followed by Gillian. Charlie's in the rear. I bound up the stairs two at a time, spiraling toward the top. Gillian's doing her best, but she's not as fast.

"Move!" Charlie barks. Squeezing past her, he scrambles upward, putting himself between me and Gillian. He touches my shoulder and nudges me forward.

"I'm going as fast as I can," I tell him.

At the top of the landing, both of us stop at a closed metal door. Our breathing's heavy. Charlie's is heavier than mine. It's been almost three days since he's had his medication.

"Are you sure you're—"

"I'm fine," he insists. But as I put a hand on the metal bar that'll open the stairwell door, he says two words that, as long as I've known him, have never left his lips.

"Be careful."

I nod—and with a soft push—inch the door open. Thanks to all the twists and turns of the tunnel, we have no idea where we are. Sticking my head inside, I can barely see anything. The room's dark, but it appears to be empty. We're in a back room . . . or maybe an oversized closet, if I had to guess. Sliding inside, I step lightly and search for context clues. Over my shoulder, Charlie and Gillian close the door to the stairwell and the rest of our light vanishes. At first, I'm completely blind, but as my eyes adjust to the dark, I spot a thin sliver of white light straight ahead. It's coming from the other side—another door.

Frankenstein-walking with my arms straight out, I reach the wood paneling and feel my way down to the doorknob. A twist leads us to the next room, which is just as dark. This time, though, there's someone in the—

BAM!

A gunshot roars and I duck down as fast as I can. Behind me, there's a thud against the floor. I spin around and reach out—but I can't find Charlie.

74

"C'mon—*let's go!*" Joey shouted as she punched her horn, honking wildly at the blue Lincoln Town Car with the "GRNDPA7" personalized license plate. Trapped in the enormous line of rental cars and overstocked minivans that were slowly filing into the Walt Disney World parking lot, Joey was ready to rip the steering wheel from the dashboard. "Yes—*you! Pump the gas and pull your rolling boat into Dopey 110! Just follow the other cars! Dopey 110!*"

"Are you not enjoying your Disney experience?" Noreen asked in her ear.

"Finally!" Joey announced as she reached the front of the line. She was about to hit the gas, but a Disney employee with a Day-Glo yellow vest was blocking the road and waving her to the left like an airline runway guide.

"All vehicles to the left, ma'am," he called out as nice as possible.

Joey stopped short, refusing to turn. "I need to get to the front gate!" she called out.

"All vehicles to the left," he repeated.

Joey still didn't move. "Didn't you hear what I—?"

Within seconds, two other employees approached her window. "Is there a problem, ma'am?"

"I need to get to the front gate. Now!"

"Y'know our trams run every few minutes . . ." the shorter employee pointed out.

"I'm sorry, ma'am," the other employee added. "But unless you have a handicapped sticker, you'll have to park right here like everyone el—"

Joey pulled her dad's badge and rammed it in his face. "You know what this means, Walt? It means I'm *not* parking in *Dopey 110!*"

Silently, the two employees backed away from the car and motioned for the man in the yellow vest to step aside. Without a word, Joey slammed the gas and sped for the front gates of the Magic Kingdom.

75

"Get down," Charlie urges, yanking me by the leg.

I hit the carpet hard and a hot rug-burn scorches the tip of my chin. On our far right is the silhouette of our attacker—standing in the corner, trying to blend into the shadows. He's bent over. Reloading . . .

There's no way I'm giving him the chance. Pouncing forward, I leap up toward the silhouette. Another shot rings out. Not a gunshot . . . an explosion . . . one after the other . . . popping . . . like fireworks. Before our attacker even realizes I'm there, I crash into him and wrap both arms around his waist. It's like tackling a vacuum cleaner. We slam into the floor with a metal clank.

The house lights slowly rise and I get my first good look at the person I've got pinned to the carpet. It's John F. Kennedy.

"In this Hall of Presidents, we look upon a mirror of ourselves," Maya Angelou's recorded voice booms on the other side of the blue curtain. Along the wall, there's an Andrew Jackson robot without a leg, a wicker basket full of ties and bow ties and a Styrofoam head with a fluffy blow-dried wig

that's labeled "Bill Clinton." Backstage—it's only backstage.

"*Ladies and gentlemen . . . the Presidents of the United States!*" Maya Angelou announces. Trumpets blare, the crowd applauds, and I glance up at the ceiling, where automated pulleys raise the main curtain. The velvet blue one that hides us is still in place.

"Let's go, Oswald," Charlie says, reaching down to help me up.

To our right, a man in a Paul Revere outfit bursts through a side door. He gets one look at the three of us standing over JFK. The walkie-talkie goes straight to his lips. "Security . . . I got a twenty-two over here . . . I need someone at the HOP."

Charlie tugs on my arm, and as I fight to get to my feet, I step over JFK's animatronic chest. Gillian's already heading toward the side door on our left. Charlie pauses, weighing whether to follow, but the only other choices are toward Paul Revere, under the curtain and past the five hundred people in the audience, or back the way we came. Running past Charlie, I grab the back of his collar and push him forward. Even he knows when there's no choice. We both follow Gillian.

Racing through the side door, she leads us into a red-carpeted room filled with fake antique furniture and phony Colonial American flags. Charlie grabs a rocking chair and wedges it against the door we just left. Paul Revere pounds and shouts, but he's not getting anywhere.

Across the room, there're three more doors along the walls. The two on the right have no visible light shining underneath. Those lead back into the theater. The one straight ahead has the last gasp of sunlight flickering across the foot of the carpet. That's outside.

Gillian shoves the door open and we're overwhelmed by the sudden expanse of space. Compared with the confining gray walls of the tunnels and the darkness of the Hall of Presidents, the bright openness of Liberty Square has me squinting through Disney's fake Revolutionary era town.

"Follow the crowd," Charlie says, pointing toward the human wave of people flooding the streets. On my left, dozens of kids wait in line to stick their head through a fake stockade so their parents can snap a photo. On my right, hundreds of tourists line up for the world's safest riverboat ride. Everyone else is in the streets—thousands of them milling toward the Old West township of Frontierland. It's the week before Christmas in Disney World. Getting lost is the easy part.

"Just take it slow," Gillian warns as we dive into the swarm of people bottlenecked in front of the Diamond Horseshoe Saloon. Within a few steps, the red, white, and blue of Liberty Square has been replaced by the muddy browns of the old-fashioned Frontier Trading Post. Gillian lowers her head and matches the pace of the moseying crowd. Wanting no part of it, Charlie runs ahead, weaving his way through the mob.

"Charlie . . . wait . . . !" I call out.

He doesn't even turn around. I take off after him, but he's already four families in front of us. Jumping up for a better view, I follow his blond hair as it swerves through the crowd. As he passes the Country Bear Jamboree, he glances back to make sure I'm with him, but the more I try to catch up, the further Gillian falls behind. Straddling between them, I try my best to keep it even, but sooner or later one has to give.

I look over my shoulder at Gillian, who's finally finding

some speed. "*C'mon!*" I call out, waving her forward. Cutting past a family with their stroller, I start to accelerate. But as I scope ahead to find Charlie, he's nowhere in sight. I crane my neck and scan the heads of the crowd, hunting for his blond hair. It's not there. I check again. Nothing. I don't care how mad he was; there's no way he'd leave without me.

Feeling that twitch in my stomach from when we got separated before, I punch the panic button and race forward. "Excuse me . . . coming through . . ." I call to the crowd as I angle and shove between them. As Gillian catches up, I'm still searching the swarm of heads for Charlie's hair color. The short-haired blond with the J. Crew–preppy family . . . the messy strawberry blond with the Louisiana State baseball hat . . . even the dyed blond with the visible black roots. I check each one. He's got to be here somewhere. Across the street, a ten-year-old boy shoots a cork popgun straight at his sister's face. Behind me, two kids chase each other with purple cotton-candy-colored tongues. Next to me, a boy cries and his father threatens to take him home. "Yankee Doodle" blares from the speakers in the lampposts. I can barely think straight. Gillian reaches out to hold my hand. I don't want it right now. Up ahead, the street bears to the left. I'm running out of space. I give it one last shot.

"*Charlie!*" I shout.

Twenty feet in front of me, a familiar blond mop-top juts out from behind the coonskin cap kiosk. Charlie! "*Charlie!*" I call out, waving both hands over my head.

Get down! he motions, patting the air, palms downward.

What're you—?

Get down! Now!

He looks back across the street and I follow his gaze—

through the mob—on the far corner of the Pecos Bill Cafe. I spot the two dark suits that stand out amidst the Mickey Mouse T-shirt crowd. And then they spot me.

Gallo's eyes narrow into a jet black glare. Shoving his way between a young couple, he plows into the crowd. DeSanctis is right behind him.

76

You had to yell, didn't you?" Charlie asks as Gillian and I blow past the kiosk.

"Me? I wasn't the one who—" I cut myself off and focus back on Gallo. Across the street, he's fighting through the heart of the throng. And we're almost out of running room. In front of us, the road dead-ends at a waist-high swinging wooden gate. On our left, Gallo pushes even closer.

"Down here," Gillian says, pointing to the right.

Charlie shakes his head. It doesn't matter if it's the best path; he's not giving her the chance. With a sharp tug, he pulls open the wooden gate and runs up what looks like the incline of an asphalt driveway. He's headed straight for a green wooden wall that surrounds the whole park. It has to be at least eight feet high. There's no way we're climbing over this one.

"Is he nuts?" Gillian asks.

"Charlie . . . stop!" I shout, chasing after him. "It's a dead end!" As he clears the highest point of the driveway, the road slopes down toward the green wall. From where I'm running—just inside the gate—he's got nowhere to go. "Get out of there!" I yell. Charlie keeps going.

But as I hit the peak of the driveway, I finally see what's got his attention. I didn't notice it at first—the small sign on the wall that says "Cast Members Only."

"Whoa," Gillian says as she spots it for herself.

We couldn't see it from the front gate—the angle was all wrong. But as we clear the highest part of the incline, it's obvious that what looks like a single wall is actually two walls that overlap, but never meet up. Charlie steps forward, makes a sharp right, and disappears. It's not a dead-end— just another optical illusion.

Following behind Charlie, I zigzag through the gap and run down a long, paved driveway. It's like being on a back lot—the park fades behind us and all its colors and music are replaced by concrete grays and a creaky silence. Next to us, a compact, green building reeks something fierce, making it blatantly obvious where Disney tucks its garbage. At first, Charlie runs toward it—if we plan on walking away from this, he knows we have to get out of sight—but the stench keeps him on the driveway, racing down toward the back of the lot.

Up ahead, it doesn't get much better. The closest buildings are a few scattered construction trailers, and an old warehouse with a faded blue sign that says "Magic Kingdom Decorating."

"The trailers . . ." Gillian says.

Charlie goes right for the warehouse. A few steps ahead of me, he spins around to check if Gallo's made it through the gate. That's when I see the pain on his face. He's as gray as the concrete, completely drained. Gillian and I start catching up. Even *with* his medication, he can't keep up this pace.

Just a few more feet, bro—almost there.

Outside the warehouse, fifteen parade floats are parked in

three neat rows under a rusted, metal awning. The smell of fresh paint surrounds us, and next to the glittering, shiny floats, dozens of empty paint cans tell us where everyone is. It's drying time. No one's around.

Rushing past the floats, we duck into the gaping mouth of the warehouse's enormous garage door. Inside it's like a giant airplane hangar—skyscraper ceiling, arched roof, and plenty of dark, dusty space—but instead of planes, it's packed with more floats. Five rows of them fill the entire righthand side of the hangar, but unlike the painted ones out front, these are all covered with tightly strung Christmas lights. Disney's Electric Light Parade. At night, it's all lit up. In the shadows of the warehouse—alone in the dark—it's dead and lifeless. I already don't like this place.

On the left, cluttered along the floor, it's a mess of leftover storage: giant rocking horses, an oversized treasure chest from *Aladdin,* two rolling popcorn carts, chandeliers, and even a few disco balls that're stacked up in the corner.

Wasting no time, all three of us scout for hiding spots and—

There's a muffled running in the distance.

Charlie and I lock eyes. He scrambles to the left; Gillian tugs me to the right. I go to fight, but Gallo's too close. Time to get out of sight. Stumbling behind Gillian, I hide behind a huge float that's shaped like Cinderella's coach; Charlie ducks into a storage closet against the wall. He shuts the door behind himself. And right there, my brother's gone.

Don't ever pull me like that again! I glare at Gillian.

She doesn't care. She's still focused on Gallo. "Did he see us?" she whispers, crouched down behind the float.

Quiet! I motion with a finger in front of my lips. Outside, the rumbling gets louder. Bent down and peeking diagonally between the wheels of the coach, I see Gallo's and

DeSanctis's tall shadows stretch out across the floor of the entrance. Gallo's arm slithers into his jacket and he pulls his gun.

As DeSanctis follows him inside, neither of them makes a noise. They may be killers, but they're still Secret Service. Gallo motions toward his partner and they slowly pick apart the room. They're slow, methodical. They go for the hiding spots first: the treasure chest from *Aladdin*. A giant teapot that looks like it's on wheels. Gallo flips open the chest. DeSanctis flings open the door on the side of the teapot. Both are empty. Like alley cats stalking dinner, they move deeper into the warehouse, circling around and slowly devouring every detail. They're trying to dig around our heads . . . figure out where we—

Gallo points to the closet.

My whole body goes numb.

DeSanctis nods with a know-it-all smirk. Approaching the door, he holds up three fingers. On three.

Gallo points his gun at the closet.

One . . .

I reach under the back of my jacket and pull out the gun we took from Gallo in the train station.

Two . . .

DeSanctis grabs the knob on the closet. I silently creep down the aisle, toward the front of the floats. Gillian looks at me like I'm crazed, but there's no way I'm letting them—

Three . . .

DeSanctis pulls on the door, but it barely budges. Charlie's holding it from the inside. "They're in there," DeSanctis says. He pulls again and it clamps shut.

"You're only making it worse!" Gallo warns.

Fighting with the door, DeSanctis is raging.

"Enough of this," Gallo says, pushing his partner out of

the way. He raises his gun to the doorknob and fires two quick shots. I go to scream, but nothing comes out.

With one final tug, DeSanctis rips the door open. A bent folding chair dangles from the inside doorknob—and then goes crashing to the floor. I angle my head, struggling to see the rest of the damage . . . praying to hear Charlie's voice. But all I get is silence.

"What the hell is this?" Gallo asks, confused as he stares into the closet.

It's not until DeSanctis steps aside that I finally see what they're looking at: the dark-tiled floor . . . the electrical boxes along the walls . . . and no sign of Charlie. There's another door that's already open on the other side. It's not a closet. It's a room. A room that connects to the other half of the building. I laugh to myself and my eyes well up. Go, Charlie, go!

DeSanctis and Gallo rush in after him. I spin around to share the news with Gillian. But just as I do, I step on a stray Christmas light that's hanging off the side of the float. There's a sharp crack and I freeze in place. Crap.

"What was that?" Gallo asks.

I duck down and search the aisle for Gillian. She's not there.

"You coming?" DeSanctis asks.

"I'll be there in a sec," Gallo says as he turns back toward the parade floats. "I just want to check something out."

77

He decided to wait for the little girl to stop crying. Tucked back on the wood porch of the Pecos Bill Cafe, there was no sense calling attention to himself. And as long as the little girl across the street kept screaming—as long as she and her consoling mom were blocking the swinging gate that Gallo and DeSanctis had just ducked behind—he wasn't going anywhere. Of course, there was something to be said for taking it slow. From here on in, there was no reason to rush. Oliver and Charlie . . . Gallo and DeSanctis . . . he found them earlier—he'd find them again. Last time, all he had to do was wait around the corner from DACS. He knew they'd come running by. Just like Gillian had said.

He grinned to himself at the thought of it. *Gillian*. Where'd she get that name anyway? Shrugging it off, he didn't much care about the answer. As long as they got their money, she could call herself whatever she wanted.

Scanning the crowd, he kept tabs on every stray glance and every lingering look. He didn't like being alone in Disney World. If he were younger, maybe, but at his age—without kids—it was a guaranteed way to stand out. And right now, standing out was the last thing he wanted to do. Eventually, he hopped off the porch, shoved a hand in his pocket, and calmly headed across the street with the purposefulness of someone rejoining his family. In front of the swinging fence, the little girl had stopped crying. And the crowd had stopped staring.

"I'm sorry—are we in your way?" the mother of the girl asked, kneeling down and wiping her daughter's nose.

"Not at all," the man said with a friendly nod. Stepping around them, he opened the fence and crossed inside. As it closed behind him, he never looked back.

78

I squat down behind the Cinderella coach float, and the door to the closet slams shut. In the distance, I hear Gallo slowly spin around. His shoes scrape like glass against the pavement, then pound like a dinosaur against the warehouse floor. He lumbers and limps slowly. Just waiting for a sniff of my reaction.

I don't give him one.

"I know you're here," Gallo calls out, his voice echoing up the aisles. Thanks to the enormous ceiling, it's like shouting in a canyon. "So who am I with?" he asks, still facing my direction. "Charlie . . . or Oliver?"

Across the room, three or four aisles down, there's another snap and a quick shuffle of footsteps. Gillian's moving.

"So there're two of you in here?" Gallo asks. "Am I really that lucky?"

Neither of us answers.

"Okay, I'll play along," he says, taking a step in my direction. "If it's two of you . . . and one's alone in the other room, well . . . I know I don't got Oliver and Charlie. She'd never let that happen. On top of that, I saw who was odd man out in Duckworth's backyard . . ."

I take the tiniest step backwards. I swear, I hear Gallo grin.

"So whattya say, Oliver? You and Gillian having fun yet?"

The room is dead silent. He takes another step toward me.

"That's the problem with threesomes," Gallo warns. "It's always two against one. Isn't that right, *Gillian?*"

Hunched over behind Cinderella's carriage, I scramble like a crab back up the aisle. I hear Gillian moving toward the front. Gallo leaps into my aisle. But all he sees are two empty rows of abandoned parade floats.

Crouching behind a float shaped like a pirate ship, I sneak into the next aisle. I'm leaning in so close to the ship, the barrel of my gun brushes against the tips of the Christmas bulbs. On the side of the hull, I stick my head up and stare across the bow. Gallo's still in my old aisle.

"C'mon, Oliver, don't be stubborn," he warns. "Even I'll admit we're past our bedtime. It may be a hike for the Orlando cops to get on Disney property, but even out here— even in the back lot—it's not gonna take forever. The clock's ticking, son . . . they're gonna find us soon."

As he wanders down the aisle, there's a noticeable change in Gallo's voice. Quieter. Almost anxious.

"I know you're the smart one, Oliver. If you weren't, you wouldn't have gotten this far." He pauses, hoping the compliments soften me up. "Don't forget: It took Brutus to kill Caesar. You may've been a few steps ahead, but we were always close. Real close. Like in the same room. D'you understand what I'm saying, son? It's time to make some hard decisions—and if you're smart about it, the first one you'll ask yourself is: How much do you trust Gillian?"

"Don't listen to him, Oliver!" Gillian's voice booms through the room. "He's just trying to confuse you." I look to my left, hoping to trace the sound, but the acoustics make her impossible to pinpoint.

"I told you it'd be a hard one," Gallo adds, sounding like he's moving further up the aisle. "But all you have to do is use your brain. You were in the tunnels under Disney World. How do you think we found you?"

His footsteps are close, but he's headed in the wrong direction. I duck under the front of the pirate ship and blanket myself in silence.

"Didn't you ever wonder why you couldn't find any of Duckworth's relatives when you worked at the bank?" Gallo asks. "He didn't have any, Oliver. Never married. No kids. Nothing. If he had, we never would've used his name in the first place. That was the whole point of creating and keeping his name on the account. If anything went wrong, no one was there to complain."

"He's a liar!" Gillian shouts.

"Oh, she's getting pissed now, isn't she?" Gallo asks. "I don't blame her either. I saw what she did to Duckworth's old place—from the photos . . . to the soft-touch bedsheets . . . You have to give 'em the A-plus for effort—they pulled it together pretty quick."

They?

"Personally, I think the paintings were the nicest touch. I'm betting those were to win over Charlie. Am I right, Gillian, or was it just part of the show?"

For the first time, Gillian doesn't answer. I try to tell myself it's because she doesn't want to reveal her location, but as I'm finally starting to realize, every lie takes its toll. Especially the ones we tell ourselves.

"Time to make a choice," Gallo says, his voice coming from everywhere at once. "You can't do it all by yourself anymore, Oliver." Like before, he lets the silence of the room pound his point into my brain. "It's time to get out of here, son. Now which one of us do you want to trust?"

79

The first thing DeSanctis noticed were the heads. There were two when he walked in—Goofy's and the Mad Hatter's. Neither was attached to a torso; they were just two colorful costume heads lying lifeless on the bright white linoleum floor. From the small folding table that was knocked over, DeSanctis knew where they'd fallen from. That much was simple. The hard part was seeing where it led. Exiting the closet and stepping into the hallway that ran perpendicular to it, he held his gun with both hands. On his right, toward the back, was a rolling laundry cart. Straight ahead was another room that smelled like bleach. On his left was the front door to the building, the easiest way out.

DeSanctis headed for the door, but as he tried to pull it open, the single deadbolt was locked. He took a quick scan for windows or other doors. Nothing that led outside. Wherever Charlie was, he was still here. Hiding. Turning around, DeSanctis raised his gun and studied the long white hallway. There were a few yellow gym lockers along the walls, the knocked-over folding table up ahead, and the same rolling laundry cart in the back. Through the walls, he could hear Gallo's muffled shouts at Oliver. On his left, next to the folding table, was the room with the bleach smell. On his right, past the maintenance closet, was a room he must've missed. Those were the only choices. One room on his right; one on his left.

As he learned in training, when choosing between the two, the majority of the population favors their right. Of course, this was Charlie. DeSanctis started on the left, where the door to the bleach room was slightly ajar. As carefully as possible, he used the tip of his shoe to edge the door open— just enough so he could peek in between the gap by the hinges. He angled his head to double-check. Nothing there.

He nudged the door open further and slowly inched his way into the room, finger still on the trigger. His back was against the doorjamb as he slid around it. Inside, he aimed his gun at the only thing in the room: an industrial-sized washer and dryer that took up most of the back wall. The machines were as big as DeSanctis had ever seen. Big enough to hide in.

With his gun cocked straight in front of him, he carefully crept toward the closed metal door of the washing machine. Over his shoulder, he could still hear Gallo shouting at Oliver. Letting it fade, he pulled back the hammer on his gun and carefully reached for the handle on the washer door. Leaning in, he didn't make a sound. The sharp stench of bleach filled the air. Just as his fingertips hooked around the handle, the washer sprang to life with a loud motorized whir, churning into its next cycle. DeSanctis jumped back at the noise, but as the machine flipped from *Soak* to *Spin*, he raced forward and tugged the door open. A pile of colorful clothes tumbled to the floor with a wet smack. Green leotards . . . bright red Santa pants . . . red, white, and blue skirts. Nothing but costumes.

Kicking them aside, he slammed the door shut and headed straight for the dryer. Again, he cocked his gun. Again, he pulled open the door. And again, he found nothing but a pile of bright multicolored costumes. Without a word, he angrily tossed a fistful of clothes to the floor.

Reentering the hall, he was about to cross into the next room when he noticed the one thing that was out of place. Up the hallway. Against the wall. The rolling laundry cart that was in the center of the hall . . . was now on the right. Something moved. Or someone moved it.

DeSanctis grinned and edged sideways up the hallway. *Not smart, Charlie-boy . . . not smart at all,* he thought to himself as he pointed his gun at the cart. But as he finally got in close—as he stretched his neck to peek inside the cart—he realized it was empty. Still, carts don't move by themselves. DeSanctis looked up the hallway. At the end, a tall wooden folding screen blocked access to the rooms in back. Shoving the cart aside, DeSanctis went right for the screen.

Ten steps later, he cut around the screen and skidded to a stop. In a room that felt like a smaller version of the warehouse, he stared at row after row of rolling wardrobe racks. In front, a red-and-white polka-dot dress hung from a hanger labeled "Minnie." One rack over, on a hanger labeled "Donald," the blue suit and white fuzzy tail of Donald Duck's butt was hanging in the air. In front of the suit, Donald's head hung upside down on a specially made hanger. Another Donald head sat on top of the rack, and a third sagged sideways on the floor where DeSanctis walked in. Throughout the room, the heads were the one thing DeSanctis couldn't miss—from Minnie, to Donald, to Pluto, to Eeyore, to all seven of the Dwarfs, the empty heads seemed to be staring blankly at him.

Trying his best to ignore them, DeSanctis did a quick scan

of the aisles. The costumes draped to the floor and blocked every clear view. If he wanted Charlie, he'd have to flush him out. Methodically moving forward, DeSanctis squeezed between two sequined butterfly costumes and entered the first aisle of racks. With every step, a kaleidoscope of colored costumes brushed against both shoulders, but DeSanctis didn't seem to notice. His eyes were locked on the floor, searching for Charlie's shoes. Every few feet, he jabbed his gun into the side of a costume that looked too lumpy, but otherwise, nothing slowed him down—that is, until he reached the end of the aisle and saw the familiar black tuxedo with the bright red shorts. Two white gloves, specially stitched with four fingers, were clipped to the sleeve. Raising his head, DeSanctis traced the costume up to the top of the rack, which held the head of the world's most famous mouse. Instinctively reaching out, DeSanctis tapped a knuckle against Mickey's smiling face.

"Couldn't help yourself, could you?" a voice asked behind him.

DeSanctis spun around, but by the time he caught sight of Charlie, it was already too late. Wielding an industrial broom like a caveman's club, Charlie swung away. Just as DeSanctis turned, the broomstick sliced through the air. There was a loud thud as it collided with DeSanctis's head.

"That's for messing with my mom, asshole," Charlie said, already winding up for another. "And this one's for my brother . . ."

80

With a mechanical crank, the turnstile somersaulted as Joey rushed through the main entrance of the Magic Kingdom. This late in the day, the lines were shorter than usual, but there were still plenty of tourists to get in the way.

"How's it look?" Noreen asked through the earpiece.

"Like a haystack," Joey said as she thrust herself into the center of the slowly meandering crowd. Surrounded by a group of overtalkative high school kids on one side, and crying baby twins on the other, Joey pushed her way through the insanity, ran under the overpass that housed the railroad station, and found herself face-to-face with the sixty-foot Christmas tree and colorful storefronts of Main Street, U.S.A. "Are you sure it's here?" she asked Noreen.

"I'm looking at their online map right now," Noreen answered. "It should be directly on your l—"

"Got it," Joey said, pulling a sharp left and running upstream against the exiting crowd. Straight ahead, next to the bright red firehouse, was the main entrance for City Hall. With a quick check of the surrounding area, Joey hit the brakes, tucked away her earpiece, and forced her best panicked look onto her face. "Oh, no . . ." she began, starting out soft. "Please don't tell me . . . Help!" she shouted. "Please, someone . . . help me!" Within seconds, she heard the rumbling of footsteps from inside City Hall, which was not only the home for Guest Relations, but also happened to be one of the closest places patrolled by Walt Disney World Security. "Why go to them," Joey had asked Noreen, "when they'll come right to you?"

Joey counted to herself. Three . . . two . . . one . . .

"What is it, ma'am? What's wrong?" a tall guard with a crewcut and a silver badge quickly asked.

"Are you okay?" a black man in a matching blue shirt followed.

"My wallet!" Joey shouted to both men. "I opened my purse and my wallet was gone! It had all my money . . . my three-day pass . . . !"

"Don't worry—it's okay," the tall guard said, putting his hand on her wrist.

"Do you know where you had it last?" the second one followed. As the two guards calmed her down, Joey noticed the way they watched the gawking crowd. The show, clearly, must go on.

"She's fine, folks," the tall guard announced to the onlookers. "Just misplaced her wallet."

As the crowd broke up and continued on its way, the guards huddled around Joey and helped her to a nearby wooden bench.

"Did it fall out on a ride?" the black guard asked.

"Or maybe in one of the restaurants?" the other added.

"Are you sure this isn't it right here?" the first one asked, pointing to the wallet that stuck out from Joey's purse.

Joey stopped and looked down. "Oh, God," she said, forcing a laugh. "I'm so embarrassed . . . I could've sworn it wasn't there when I—"

"No worries," the tall guard said. "I do the same thing with my keys all the time."

Standing from the bench, Joey thanked the two men and once again apologized. "I really am sorry—next time I'll be sure to . . . uh . . . to check my purse."

"Have a nice night, ma'am," the tall guard said.

Stumbling backwards up the block, Joey stepped into the crowd and let the guards disappear. The instant they were gone, she spun around, shoved her earpiece back in place, and plowed with a determined gait directly up Main Street.

"Well?" Noreen asked.

"It's like I always tell you . . ." Joey began. She reached into her jacket pocket and pulled out a black police radio with the word *Security* written on it. "Whenever you're on vacation, you gotta watch out for those pickpockets."

She turned up the volume and held the radio up to her ear. All she had to do was listen.

81

We can get you out of here, Oliver—all you have to do is have a little faith," Gallo says, his raspy voice scraping from the back corner of the silent warehouse.

Tucked down behind the bow of the pirate ship, I shut my eyes and replay the last two days: from the moment we met Gillian . . . to our night diving . . . to everything in between.

"It's the truth," Gallo calls out. "Even if you're afraid to believe it."

Once again, I listen for Gillian to argue. Once again, she's nowhere to be found.

"C'mon, Oliver, are you really that surprised? You know what's at stake—you found the worm . . ." The way his shoes grind against the concrete, it sounds like he's turning down one of the back aisles. "It's pretty amazing, don't you think? All from a bit of computer code. Cut it in half and it just keeps growing back." Gallo laughs to himself. "When you think about it, that program is Duckworth's *real* baby."

Wherever she is, Gillian doesn't say a word.

"So what's with the silence, Oliver? You got your feelings hurt? You've never had a knife in your back? Please, son—

I met your bosses at the bank—you're paid to grab your toes and take it from behind every day. And with all those rich clients who pretend they like you? You should be an Old Master at being lied to. From that alone, Gillian's stuff should roll right off. You had to know her whole background seemed fishy—or did you never bother to wonder where she got a New York accent? Besides, you've only known the girl two days—how upset could you possib—"

Gallo cuts himself off. And once again lets out a deep, throaty laugh.

"*Oh, Oliver . . .*"

I shut my eyes, but it won't go away.

". . . you really thought she liked you, didn't you?" Gallo asks.

Sinking down to the ground, I scrape my back against the ship.

In the corner, Gallo stops short and turns around. He knows I'm there. Like the best predators, he can smell the despair.

Within seconds, he heads my way. "So how'd she get you to bite the hook?" he asks, taking way too much joy in the question. "Was it the bullshit story, or something more physical?"

From the sound of his footsteps, he's back toward the front of the aisles.

"Let me guess—she fed you the whole orphan thing, then served up the chance-to-date-the-pretty-girl-you-were-afraid-to-ask-to-the-prom thing for dessert. Add that to all the running around, and suddenly you felt like your whole miserable life was coming alive. How'm I doing, Oliver? Starting to sound familiar?"

Still stuck on the floor, I trace the volume of his voice. He's now one aisle over. I should run. But I don't.

"What about her age?" Gallo adds. "What'd she tell you? Wait . . . let me guess . . . Twenty-six? Twenty-seven?" He pauses just enough to rub it in. "She's thirty-four, Oliver. Does that break your heart, or just make you feel like a bigger sucker?"

Knowing the answer, I slowly climb back to my feet. I'm not sure where Gallo is. And I'm not even sure I care.

"And let's not forget the name—Gillian . . . Gillian Duckworth—pretty good when you consider how quick they had to paste it all together. Of course, if she used Sherry, no one would've known the difference."

Sherry?

At the front of the aisle, two cheap black shoes turn the corner and slow to a halt. I look down the row. Gallo stares straight at me. His gun's up; mine sags at my side. Wearing his typical rat-faced grin, he shakes his head in one last machismo tease. But the whole time, he's studying my face.

"You really never even had an inkling, did you, Oliver?"

I don't answer.

"All this time, you thought you were flying first-class, and then the stewardess slaps you awake and tells you you're strapped in with a kamikaze . . ."

As he reads my reaction, I stare down at the floor. It's caked in dust. Just like her end table. Charlie said it all along.

"To be honest, I didn't think they could pull it off," Gallo adds. "But if you never met her before, I guess there's no way you could've known she was his wife."

I quickly pick my head up. "She was *whose* wife?" I blurt, finally breaking my silence.

Gallo smirks at the question. "Oh, c'mon, Oliver—use your brain for once—how do you think we got Duckworth's program past Securi—"

Behind Gallo, there's a deafening boom. Before I even squint, his chest explodes, spraying tiny flicks of blood up the aisle. I'm a good thirty feet away as the last few bits of blood spit across my face and shirt.

As I look up at Gallo, his eyes are wide open. His body teeters slightly—then slowly falls forward. He hits the ground with an unnerving thump, but my eyes stay glued straight up the aisle—just beyond Gallo. Gillian stares directly at me—her gun still pointed my way. I don't know where she got it, but as she grips it with both hands, a twist of smoke curls from the barrel.

Lowering her gun, she glances down at the oozing wet hole she's shot into Gallo's back.

"Wh-What're you— What the hell are you doing!?" I shout.

She's still focused on Gallo—tracing the path of the bullet.

"Gilli— Sherry . . . whatever your name is—*I'm talking to you!*"

"Watch yourself," she says, motioning to the body. "Don't step in the blood."

I look at her like she's nuts. "What're you talking about? What's wrong with you?"

She points to the door that leads outside. "C'mon, Oliver, we should get out of here . . ."

"*Don't move!*" I shout, taking my first step toward her. "Didn't you hear what Gallo said? It's over, Gillian—no more bullshit!"

Now she looks at me like *I'm* nuts. "Wait a minute . . ." she begins. "You don't think— Don't tell me you actually believed him. He was *lying*, Oliver."

No. No more mindgames. "Tell me who you are," I demand as I move toward her.

"Oliver . . ."

"Tell me who you are!"

She actually has the nerve to cough up an innocent laugh. "Don't you see what he was trying to do—he just wanted to pit us against each other, so he cou—"

"Do I really look that gullible to you?"

"Oliver, it's not about being gullible. Look who you're listening to—the man was trying to kill us!"

As I charge up the aisle, her words bounce off. From the instant she said my real name, I should've swam the other way. That's a mistake I made once. Not again. "Your name's not Gillian. You're not Duckworth's daughter. And you certainly don't give a crap about me. *Now tell me who you are!*"

Face-to-face, she reaches out to touch my arm. With my gun, I backhand her away. She's not getting any closer.

Right there, her expression flips. The soothing smile . . . the innocent blue eyes . . . they fade and disappear. I notice a deep crease along her forehead. She shakes her head, like I've made a mistake. "I'm sorry you feel that way, Oliver. Just remember, it's your choice . . ."

Raising her gun, she points it at my chest. "Just give me the tapes," she says coldly.

Refusing to answer, I raise my own gun and aim it at her heart.

She stares down at it, then checks my eyes. I don't flinch. Grinning, she lets out a shrill, piercing laugh that razor-slices through me. *"Please*—even on your worst day, you can't be who you're not."

Unmoving, I keep my finger on the trigger.

"Haven't you learned your lesson yet?" she asks. "Or are you always going to be Oliver—forever the boy who wanted more?"

My jaw shifts off-center, but my gun doesn't move.

"I know your feelings got hurt, but if it makes you feel any better, it wasn't all an act," she adds, suddenly playing nice. As she shifts her hips, everything I knew about her evaporates. The barefoot hippiechick . . . the daring free spirit—they're long gone. Her shoulders no longer dangle loosely at her sides; now they're pitched, almost barbed. I don't know how I missed it before. But like everything else in my life, I saw what I wanted to see. "I really did have fun with you," she says, trying to flip back to sincere mode.

"Really? Which part was more fun—lying to my face, or just betraying my trust? Actually, I keep forgetting . . . you're such a down-to-earth, granola gal, you must like the simple moments—like jamming the sword in my spine."

"Lash out all you want, Oliver. I meant what I said. You can still get out of here—but not with the tapes—and not with our money. So why don't you join us back in reality and put the gun away. We both know who the daredevil is in your family, and just because you want to play the part, doesn't mean it's happening."

Like that night on the boat, she's hoping to push my buttons. Too bad for her, all it does is focus me more on Charlie. He's next door, alone against DeSanctis. And the only thing stopping me from helping him is Gillian.

I pull back the hammer on my gun. "Get out of my way."

"Why don't we start with the tapes . . ."

"I said, get out of my way."

"Not until we get—"

"My brother's in there, Gillian. I'm not asking you again." My gun's aimed straight at her chest. My finger tightens around the trigger. I thought my hand would be shaking. It's not.

"Enough with the outlaw drama, Oliver. I mean, do you honestly think you have the balls to shoot me?"

It's a simple question. He's my brother. "You really don't know me at all, do you?" I ask her. Without waiting for her answer, I lower my arm, hold the gun to her knee, and pull the trigger.

The gun fires with a bright flash and a sharp hiss. But instead of screaming or falling to the ground, Gillian just stands there, a cocky sneer on her face. Confused, I look down at the gun, which is only a few inches from her knee. I pull the trigger again. The gun goes off with a violent bang—and again, Gillian's unharmed. I don't understand.

"Haven't you ever heard of blanks before?" Gillian gloats. "Sounds and smells real, but when you hold it to your head, the worst you can do is singe your sideburns."

Blanks? My eyes dissect the gun, then go back to Gillian's sneer.

"To be honest, I'm amazed it took you this long," she adds.

It doesn't make any sense. All this time . . . The gun isn't even ours—we got it in New York from Gallo—right after he shot—

Oh, God.

On my left, a brand-new shadow slides into the warehouse's open garage door. When Gallo said he had help, I always assumed it was Lapidus or Quincy. But never him. I turn as he enters. Just the sight of him is like a meat-cleaver in my stomach.

"Whatsa matter?" Shep asks with his boxer's grin. "You look like you seen a ghost."

* * * *

82

W e're all clear at Pecos Bill," a voice with a Southern accent squawked through Joey's radio as she weaved her way through the Frontierland crowd.

"Same at Country Bear," another voice crackled back.

Hidden among the tourists in the street, Joey watched as two clean-cut men in matching blue shirts stepped out onto the porch of the Pecos Bill Cafe. Another two appeared from the Country Bear Jamboree. Their walks were the same: strong and purposeful, but never too fast. Just enough to stay inconspicuous. That was all part of the training, Joey realized. Never panic the guests.

Out of the corner of her eye, she saw a man and woman moving through the crowd. They weren't wearing matching shirts, but Joey saw it in their walk—more Security. Within seconds, all three groups headed in different directions, checking the surrounding restaurants, storefronts, and attractions.

"We'll take Pirates," a female voice said through the radio as the man and woman team headed around the corner toward Pirates of the Caribbean.

At the center of the crowd, Joey didn't follow. Charlie and Oliver were smarter than that. It's one thing to lose yourself in the herd of people; it's quite another to purposely run into a potential dead end like a restaurant or a nearby attraction. Squinting as she turned her head from left to right, Joey carefully scrutinized the rest of the area. Packed souvenir shops . . . equally popular impulse-buy kiosks . . . and a never-ending stream of buzzing tourists. The only calming moment in the whole hurricane was up ahead, where a swinging wooden gate blocked part of the street. Watching it carefully, Joey couldn't take her eyes off it. The Disney cops were preoccupied with protecting paying guests, but if Charlie and Oliver were still running, they couldn't afford to be out in the open—they'd need someplace quiet and tucked away. Joey took another look at the swinging gate. Just beyond it was a sign with the words "Cast Members Only" on it.

"Quiet and tucked away," she whispered to herself.

"You got something?" Noreen asked through the earpiece.

"Maybe," Joey said, heading for the gate and leaving the Disney cops behind. "I'll tell you in a minute . . ."

83

Wha ... H-How're you ... ?" My mouth's gaping open as I stare at a dead man. "What the hell's going on?"

Lumbering toward us, Shep points his gun at me, but he's far more concerned with Gallo, who's got a black hole blown through his back. Shep lobs one of his scolding glares at Gillian. She shrugs like she didn't have a choice.

On the concrete, Gallo's body is facedown in a slowly widening puddle of blood. The same exact position I last saw Shep in.

"Look familiar?" Shep asks, reading my thoughts.

Still in shock, I can't take my eyes off him. The sausage forearms. The jagged nose. It's almost like it's not him. But it is.

"C'mon, Oliver—say something," he teases.

My fist clenches around the gun. If Gallo shot him with blanks ... and Shep knew it was coming ... That's who Gallo was working with. That's how they got Duckworth's worm into the bank. "You were their inside man."

"See, now that's why they pay you the big beans."

My face flushes red and reality slowly settles in like a block of ice melting down the back of my neck. "So all this time . . . How could you . . . You were watching all along . . ."

"Oliver, this isn't the place for this."

"So you were there from the start? You knew they'd try to kill us? Or . . . or was that the goal from the beginning—invite us in and create some scapegoats?"

"Let's just get out of here and we can—"

"I want an answer, Shep. Is that why you brought us in? To take our heads off?"

"Why don't we—"

"*I want an answer.*"

Realizing that I'm not moving, he checks the entrance to the hangar. Still clear. "What did you want me to say, Oliver? *I'm so glad you found our secret. Now let's swipe this three mil, because there's another three hundred million piggybacked on it?* Once you saw the honeypot, I didn't have a choice."

"You tried to kill us, Shep."

"And you tried to hijack our money."

"Everyone's a sinner," Gillian jumps in. Shep glares at her and she quickly backs off. Even though I've barely seen them together, it's clear who drives the relationship.

"When it all comes down, Oliver, this was *your* choice," Shep says. "If you weren't on your revenge fantasy with Lapidus, me and Gallo and DeSanctis would've walked away just fine. Besides, if you wanna start calling spades, *you're* the ones who worked one over on *me*."

"What're you—?"

"I checked that Antigua bank Charlie showed me on the Red Sheet. The cash was never there."

"That's the only thing that saved our lives. If Charlie didn't do that, we wouldn't even be standing right now."

"No, you wouldn't be standing if I didn't save your ass back at Duckworth's," Gillian once again interrupts.

"You only did that to help yourself," I shoot back.

Once again, Shep quiets her with an angry glance. "I'm not saying I blame you, Oliver. In fact, I kinda respect it. We all take our opportunities where we find 'em," he explains, his eyes still on Gillian. "Especially when money's involved."

"So you were never going to share it with anyone, were you?" I ask. "Not us . . . not Gallo . . . nobody."

"Let me tell you something, Oliver—Gallo may've gotten his mitts on the best idea in the world, but without a bank to put it in, Duckworth might as well've reinvented Pong."

"Then I guess that makes it okay to kill everyone along the way."

"Like I said at the start—there're only two perfect crimes: the crime that never took place, and the job where the criminal dies. It's a pretty good trick if you can pull it off. But if I was gonna be the body they blamed it on . . . well, to the martyr go the spoils. The only splinter in the eye was when they let you walk out of that train station."

"And that hatched your great plan? Follow us to Florida, screw over Gallo, and bring in your wife?"

"She fooled you, didn't she?"

I look at Gillian; she stares right back. She has no hesitation facing me. Like Lapidus always taught—business is business. I just can't believe I didn't see it before.

"It's not the end of the world," Shep says. "You've still got the goose and the golden eggs. Now it's time to decide what to do with them."

There's a brand-new pitch in his voice—like the moment he first offered to split the money with us at the bank. He's back to Big Brother Shep. Sure, he'll show us how to hide the money . . . then, the instant he gets what he wants, he'll slice us at the kneecaps. It's the same tone Gallo used two minutes ago. I'm sick of hearing it.

"Don't say no yet, Oliver. You haven't even heard the offer."

"Oh, I haven't? Let me guess—you'll wave your gun in my face, and in the process, become the fifth person this week to threaten to kill me unless I tell you where the money is."

"Just hear him out," Gillian says, her gun still on me. "We can all get what we want."

"I already know what I want—and I'm not getting it from you."

"Then who're you getting it from?" Shep asks. "The police? Lapidus? All your friends at work? This is bigger than you and Char—" He cuts himself off and quickly glances around. "Where's your brother?" he asks me.

There's no way I'll give him an answer.

"Next door," Gillian says.

"Go get him," Shep orders.

"*You* go get him," she challenges.

"Did you hear what I said?" Like before, the argument's over. Hiding her gun in the back of her pants, Gillian heads for the passageway that leads next door.

The instant the door opens, I scream the warning as loud as I can. "*Charlie, she's a li—!*"

Shep grabs me by the jaw and clamps his hand over my mouth. I fight to break free, but he's too strong. Gillian stares me down and shakes her head. "You really are a wuss," she says, turning away and entering the closet. She slams the door in my face, and the boom bounces against my chest.

Gripping my mouth, Shep holds tight until I finally stop

struggling. "Just listen for once, Oliver. If you don't calm down, none of us'll get out of here. We've got three hundred million to deal with—we might as well—"

"Do I look that stupid?" I ask as I pull his hand from my jaw. He latches on to the shoulder of my shirt. He's not letting me get far. "You really think we'll help you?" I ask. "It's over, Shep. We're fine where we are."

"Really? And you actually believe that?" he shoots back. "You haven't even stopped to think about this, have you, Oliver? The second you step back in that bank, you're fired. Lapidus'll bury you faster than you can say 'professional embarrassment.' And when you go to the police—even if you can avoid going to jail—even if you give back the money—you think they're throwing you a victory parade? It's still your signature on the original wire request. From that alone, your life is over. So now you've got no job, no money, and no one who'll ever trust you again. Worst of all, by the time the lawsuits are done and all your savings are devoured, your mother's not gonna be able to afford a spool of thread, much less the rest of her credit card and hospital bills. Who's gonna pay those now, Oliver? And what about Charlie? How long you think he can survive without your help?"

As he says the words, I know he's right. But that doesn't mean I'm getting in bed with a viper and his—

"Nobody move!" a female voice shouts behind us.

Spinning around, we trace the sound to the warehouse door. There's a woman with a gun. The investigator from the condo . . . the redhead . . . Joey . . . She points the gun straight at us—first at me, then at Shep.

Flushed with relief, I take a step toward her, away from Shep.

"I said, *don't move!*" she shouts as I raise my hands in the air.

"It's about time," Shep says, sounding relieved. "I was wondering when you'd get here."

"Excuse me?" Joey asks.

I expect to see some recognition on her face. Shep's alive—she's smart enough to fill in the rest. But instead, she seems confused. "Who the hell are you?" she asks.

My arms go numb as they stretch toward the ceiling. I don't believe it. She has no idea who he is.

"Me?" Shep asks with a crooked grin. He scratches at his forearms and lets out a deep, relaxed laugh. "I'm an investigator—just like you."

"He's lying," I blurt. "It's Shep!"

"Don't let him fool you, Ms. Lemont . . ."

"How do you know my name?" Joey asks.

"I told you—I've been investigating this from the start. Call Henry Lapidus—he'll explain everything." As he says Lapidus's name, there's a new calmness in his voice. He reaches into his jacket . . .

"Don't even think it!" Joey says.

"It's not a gun, Ms. Lemont." From his chest pocket, he pulls out a black leather wallet. "Here's my ID," he says, tossing it at Joey's feet. She reaches down to pick it up, but never lets us out of her sight.

"I swear to you, Joey—his name is Shep Graves . . ."

"Ms. Lemont, don't listen to him . . ."

". . . he faked his death so they'd put the blame on us!"

She glances down at the ID, then slaps it shut.

"So you're working with Lapidus?" Joey asks skeptically. Shep nods.

"And he'll back up your story?"

"Absolutely," he croons.

I'm not sure if Shep's bluffing, or if he's got a whole new card trick up his sleeve. Either way, Joey's come too far to leave without the truth.

"Noreen, are you there?" she says, speaking into the microphone that's clipped to her shirt. Nodding to herself, she adds, "Get me Henry Lapidus."

84

"Charlie . . . ? Charlie, where are you?" Gillian whispered as she cut through the utility closet and stepped into the perpendicular hallway that connected to it. Kicking aside the Goofy head, she surveyed the hall and shoved her way past the knocked-over folding table. On her far left was the door that led outside. Not a chance, she thought. DeSanctis wouldn't leave without telling them. A sharp scratching sound confirmed the rest. She spun around and followed the noise. Toward the back—beyond the laundry cart and the folding screen. She knew that one. Like someone running. Or hiding.

Scrambling up the hall, she kept an eye out for DeSanctis. He was still pissed about the blender to the head—but not enough to ruin it all, she decided as she slid past the folding screen. Still, better to stay quiet and figure out the lay of the—

Gillian stopped right there. From the floor to the tops of the costume racks, Minnie, Donald, Pluto, and dozens of other character heads stared back at her, each one with its own empty, frozen smile. Purposefully avoiding their glare, she cautiously stepped deeper into the room. "Hello . . ." she whispered again. "Anyone there?"

Again, no one answered. And then she realized why.

Straight ahead, at the end of the first aisle of costume racks, DeSanctis was facedown on the floor, his arms tied behind his back with what looked like a jump rope. Gillian couldn't believe it. His nose was covered in blood; his left eye was swollen shut. He wasn't moving. She nudged his shoulder with her foot, but it was like kicking a brick. Surprised, she squatted down for a better look. Was he—? No, she realized as she saw his chest rise and fall. Just unconscious.

There was another noise, this one from a few aisles over. Jarred by the sound, Gillian shot straight to her feet. But as she heard it again, she cracked a small grin. This sound was different than the first. Deeper. More guttural. Like someone breathing . . . or panting. Someone out of breath.

She glanced around and made her way across the back of the aisle. "Charlie!" she called out. "It's me—it's Gillian!"

The breathing stopped.

"Charlie—are you there!?"

Still no response.

She crossed over to the next aisle of costumes, then the next. Except for the colorful sequined outfits and a set of Chip 'n Dale costume heads, both aisles were empty.

"Charlie, I know you heard the gunshots—Oliver's been hit!"

Again, nothing.

"He's been shot, Charlie! He hit Gallo, and Gallo shot him in the thigh—if we don't get him to a doctor—!"

"Gillian, this better not be bullshit," a voice warned behind her.

She wheeled around as Charlie stepped out from the aisle

she just passed. He held the broom in his right hand, and while he tried to put on a strong face, he was clearly wheezing with each breath. Between the running and the fighting, it was all too much. "Are you okay?" she asked.

He studied her carefully. Her hands were empty. Nothing out of place. "Just show me where Ollie is," Charlie demanded. Turning his back to Gillian, he headed for the door—but before he could take a single step—there was a muffled click behind him.

Charlie froze mid-step.

"Sorry," Gillian said as she aimed her gun behind him. "That's what you get for trusting strangers."

Refusing to face her, Charlie closed his eyes. He wasn't going down without a fight. His fingers tightened around the broom—and Gillian's tightened around the trigger. Charlie spun around as fast as he could. He wasn't nearly fast enough.

85

Joey's got her finger on the trigger, and her eyes on me and Shep, but she's clearly focused on whatever's coming out of her earpiece. My arms are up above my head, but I can still see my watch. It's already past seven. Lapidus is in his car, on his way to Connecticut. There's no way she'll be able to—

"Hello, Mr. Lapidus?" she says into the microphone. "This is Joey calling . . . right, the private investi— No, we haven't found the money yet . . . No, I understand, sir, but I have a quick question I was hoping you could help me with. Do you know anyone named . . ." She looks down at Shep's ID. ". . . Kenneth Kerr?"

There's a long pause as Joey listens. The longer it goes, the more she watches Shep. He doesn't flinch. He thinks she's bluffing. So as long as he stays calm, she can't prove him wrong.

"No . . . I understand," Joey says. "Of course, sir. No, I just wanted to be sure."

She unhooks the cell phone from her belt and pulls out the earpiece. She's got her gun in her right hand and the phone in her left. Holding the receiver out for Shep, she adds, "Lapidus wants to speak to you . . ."

Shep glances at me, then back to Joey. Without the slightest of pauses, he steps forward, studying Joey's reaction. Joey smiles playfully, studying his. I stand there motionless and realize these two are playing in a different league. I have no idea who's got the advantage.

As Shep approaches her, Joey watches for the tell. A twitch in his eye . . . a shift in his shoulder . . . anything she can latch on to. But Shep's too good to give it.

The closer Shep gets, the more he towers over her. I expect Joey to step back. She doesn't. "Here you go," she says, reaching out to hand him the phone. Her gun is cocked as he steps close to her.

"Thanks," Shep says as he goes to take it. There's no fear in his voice. He's perfectly calm. They're close enough to touch. Neither one backs off. I can see it on Joey's face— he's passed her test. But just as he reaches for the phone— as their palms brush against each other—Shep widens his grip, seizes the phone and Joey's whole hand, and thrusts both their fists and the phone against Joey's face. It's all so fast, I barely realize what's happening. Joey staggers backwards as the phone cracks against the floor. Joey tries to lift her gun, but Shep never gives her a chance.

Lashing out with another punch, he buries his fist in her face and she reflexively pulls the trigger. There's a loud bang as the stray shot ricochets off the concrete, making a pinhole in the metal wall. Joey crumbles to the floor, unconscious. Her head hits the pavement with a hollow thunk. Standing over her, Shep reaches for his own gun to finish the job.

"Get away from her!" I shout, tackling Shep from behind. It's like tackling a motor-home. I plow into him, but he barely budges. I don't have a prayer. He whips around, back-handing me so hard across the face I almost black out.

"Do you realize how easy this could've been!?" he yells.

I'm on my feet, but as I fight for equilibrium, he grabs my neck and tosses me back toward the parade floats. As I crash into the float that's shaped like a train engine, hundreds of tiny Christmas lights shatter. I swing furiously to hit him back. He blocks my punch and lashes out even harder than before. "No more chances!" he shouts, raging toward me. "I want my money!"

With a violent pop and a neanderthal grunt, he plants his whole fist in my left eye. Then he pulls back and does it again. My eye twitches and burns, somehow moving by itself. It's already swelling shut. "Tell me where it is, Oliver!" Shep growls as he pounds me once more. "Where's my fuckin' money!?"

Something wet runs down my cheek. In the background, I hear a gun go off in the other room. Then I hear my brother scream. I try to look over Shep's shoulder to see what's happening. But all I see is Shep's fist, once again crashing toward me.

86

As Charlie tried to complete his swing, the gunshot thundered from Gillian's gun. The bullet whistled through the dusty air. There was a quick sucking sound. A spurt of blood erupted from Charlie's shoulderblade just as the broom stung Gillian in the hand and sent her gun sliding under the metal clothes rack. Charlie screamed. A snakebite of pain ran down to his elbow.

Feeling his left arm go numb, he gripped the broom in his right fist and squeezed it tight to kill the pain. Gillian reached down to chase the gun, but Charlie wasn't letting her get there. Not after all this. As adrenaline took over, he raised the broom over his head and swung vertically toward the ground.

Jumping back out of the way, Gillian fell backwards into a row of costumes and tripped on the bar underneath. As she tumbled between the costumes, Charlie's broomstick smashed against the concrete. Already feeling light-headed, he tried to raise the stick for another shot, but he didn't have the strength. He gasped for air. His shoulder was dead at his side, pulsing with its own heartbeat. Reading the pained look on his face, Gillian kicked the legs of the rack and tipped the whole thing forward. Dozens of character heads—from Mickey to Pluto to Goofy—all rolled to the floor as the metal rack crashed between them.

Before Charlie could react, Gillian was back on her feet, plowing over the costumes. She tackled him around the waist and knocked the wind from his lungs. Lost in momentum, they barreled toward a spare laundry cart that sat against the far wall. Refusing to let up, Gillian rammed Charlie's lower back into the metal edge of the cart, but at the pace they were moving—like a seesaw tipping—they went right over the top.

In mid-flip, though, their combined weight was too much, and the cart flipped forward, slamming Charlie to the floor. He landed on his back, his head banging hard against the ground. Gillian landed right on top of him, a pile of brightly colored costumes from the cart spilling over her shoulder.

Climbing up so she was sitting on Charlie's chest, Gillian bunched the tips of her fingers together like a dull dagger and aimed for the open wound on Charlie's shoulder. "Don't black out on me," she warned. She raised her arm back t—

A thunderbolt of a blast detonated in the other room. A gunshot. The echo rumbled along the metal walls of the warehouse.

Jolted, Gillian turned at the sound. That was all Charlie needed. Reaching up, he threw a single punch and plowed his fist into her neck. With Gillian off-balance, he turned on his stomach. Ten feet away—beyond the character heads wobbling along the floor—Charlie spotted the gun under the clothes rack. Scrambling on his elbows, he tried to reach it, but Gillian was still on his back. From behind, he felt a sudden shift in weight. A blur of orange and black fur flashed in front of him. And before he knew what was happening, something furry wrapped around his neck. Pulling Tigger's tail like the reins on a horse, Gillian leaned back as far as she could.

Gasping for air, Charlie clawed at his neck, trying to wedge his fingers under the costume tail. That's when he felt the wire. It was curled inside the tail—a thin metal spring, like a Slinky. On most days, it convinced thousands of kids that Tigger could really bounce. Today, as Gillian looped it around her hands and pulled it taut, all it did was dig deeper into Charlie's throat.

Arching upward on his stomach and scratching ruthlessly at his own neck, Charlie twisted and turned, but Gillian wouldn't let go. The more he bucked, the tighter she pulled, and the harder it was for Charlie to breathe. Gagging from the pressure, he felt the blood flood his face. He gritted his teeth, trying to suck in one last breath. Nothing came. Across his throat, the metal wire sliced against his Adam's apple.

His nose started to bleed and a dribble of blood matched the one on his lip. In front of him, floating gray spots cartwheeled through the air. But even with his vision blurred . . . even with Gillian on his back . . . he couldn't shake the mental picture of Oliver. Or his mom. Blinking back to consciousness, Charlie let go of the wire around his neck. Some strings had to be cut.

Across the floor, past Mickey's and Pluto's wobbling heads, he could still see the gun. It was too far. But there was one thing closer. With one final burst from his good arm, Charlie reached out, grabbed the leather strap that was attached to the inside of Pluto's head, and turned as hard as he could on his side. The wire was still digging into his throat. This part would definitely hurt. Ignoring the burning against his neck, he twisted around, held the strap with everything in him, and swung Pluto's head back toward Gillian. Arcing through the air, the head clipped her on the side of her face like a fifteen-pound cannonball and sent Gillian crashing to the floor.

As Charlie rolled over on his back, Gillian let go of Tigger's tail, but she didn't let up.

"You're a dead man!" she roared as Charlie coughed in a chestful of newfound air. She quickly climbed to her feet. Searching for balance, so did Charlie. But he still couldn't catch his breath. Bent over with his shoulder throbbing, he could barely stand, much less hold off another attack. A thin stream of blood ran down from Gillian's nose. "Feeling it now, aren't you?" she asked.

His breathing sputtered, and his mouth hung open, sucking in air. He knew he couldn't take another hit.

Unsure of what to do, he thought about running . . . He searched for the door and then— No. Enough running.

Planting his feet, he turned back to Gillian and tightened his grip on the leather strap. She rushed toward him in a rabid rage. Unmoving, Charlie arched his arm back. His eyes narrowed. He was holding the strap so tight, his nails were digging into his palm. *Not yet . . . not yet,* he counted to himself. She was almost on top of him. *Now!*

Pushing off his back leg and throwing all his weight into it, Charlie swung for the bleachers. Like an ancient mace on a metal chain, the fifteen-pound head tore through the air. There was a loud pop as it bashed into Gillian's ear. The graphite head cracked on impact, sending a lightning-shaped fissure across Pluto's eyes—and sending Gillian straight to the floor. She crash-landed on the concrete, right at Charlie's feet. This time, she didn't get up. But as Charlie finally took a breath, he felt a familiar ripple inside his chest. Lurching forward, he let go of the leather strap. He had to.

He couldn't hold on. Pluto's head thunked on the ground, and Charlie staggered sideways as a needle of pain stabbed him through the heart.

He crashed into a clothing rack, knocking another set of costumes to the ground. His heart bubbled and thumped. It felt like there was a bag of worms twisting inside his chest. *Please . . . not now . . .* he begged. Turning to run for Oliver, he gripped the costume racks and fought his way down the aisle, past the wooden folding-screen. The worms multiplied, clamping around his windpipe.

"Hhhh—" A sharp wheeze climbed through his throat. "Hhhhh—" Charlie gasped for air as his heartbeat quickened, then started pounding. Faster and faster, it was a drumroll inside his chest. He shut his eyes . . . felt for his pulse . . . *God* . . . it was at full gallop . . .

"O-Ollie . . ." he called out as his voice cracked. "*Ollie!*" Stumbling back along the main hallway, he crashed through the utility closet, set his shaking hand on the doorknob, and tugged the door open. All he had to do was step through. He held on to the wall and tried to pull himself forward. It seemed so close, but it somehow kept moving away . . . He felt his neck soaking. The worms squirmed, digging and squeezing like a fist around his heart. Charlie tried to breathe, but nothing came in. Through the doorway, Oliver and Shep were fighting. *Shep!* Now he knew it was a dream. Still, as Charlie looked on . . . *Ollie* . . . Ollie was winning. The tears flooded his eyes as Shep and Ollie both disappeared. *You got 'em, bro . . .* The fist tightened, gripping his heart. His whole face clenched to fight the pressure. It was about to pop. And then . . . as he sagged to his knees . . . it did.

"Ollie . . ." he stuttered with one last wheeze. He tried to add a goodbye—but as his face hit concrete—it never came.

87

"Oliver, I'm not asking you again," Shep warns. "Where the hell's my money?" Staggering backwards from his most recent punch, I move away from the floats and toward the side wall.

Behind me, I'm all out of running space. Tripping through the minefield of hula-hoops, ringmaster hats, and dozens of other random props that're piled along the floor, I frantically search for something . . . anything . . . I can use as a weapon. The only thing close is an ornate candelabra—but when I pick it up, it weighs less than a pound—all Styrofoam. I almost forgot. Disney World.

Rushing straight at me, Shep rumbles through the piles of props and grabs me by the lapels. "Last chance," he warns, his hot breath smothering my face. *"Where. Is. My. Money?"*

My head's ringing like a firehouse. I can barely move it side to side. "Drop dead, dickhead. You're never getting a dime."

Enraged, he flings me backwards toward an enormous rocking horse. My head bangs back against the wooden saddle, but Shep doesn't let go. "I'm sorry, Oliver. I didn't hear what you said."

"Drop . . . *dead*."

Spinning me around, he sends me face-first toward an oversized jack-in-the-box. My face pancakes against the front of it, and the sickening crunch tells me my nose is broken. "Wanna try that again?" Shep asks, now holding the back of my neck.

I look up at him with one good eye. My voice barely comes out. "D-Drop . . ."

Snarling like an animal, he whips me around and hurls me toward a rolling popcorn cart. I thrust my hands out to protect my face, but I'm moving too fast. I smash through the glass, and as it shatters everywhere, my hands are sliced by the shards. Crashing on my stomach inside the cart, I notice a triangular, stray fragment of glass right above my chest. There's a dull edge on one side, from where it fit into the edge of the cart.

Shep grabs my legs and yanks me backwards. Shards of glass claw against my stomach. Ignoring the pain, I reach out for the fragment. I clutch it so hard, it almost slices the palm of my hand. And just as my feet hit the ground—before he knows what's happening—I spin around and stab the jagged scalpel straight into his stomach.

His face turns white and he grabs his gut, staring down at the shiny blood that slicks his hands. He can barely believe it. "Motherf—" He looks up to face me. "You're dead . . . dead . . ."

Reaching inside his jacket, he goes for his gun. I slash at his arm and slice him right above the wrist. Howling from the pain, he can't hold on to it. The gun drops to the floor, and I kick it underneath the rocking horse. I'm not giving him another chance. His eyes burn bright red. And like a wounded bear, Shep thrashes forward, lunging for my neck. I slice the blade through the air and it tears his chest. My hand's bleeding from gripping the sharp sides, but it's clear who's taking the brunt of it. For the first time, Shep stumbles. As he gets closer, I wind up with whatever strength I have left. For everything he did . . . everything he put us through—I ignore the blood, bury the consequences, and move in for the final blo—

I hear a loud wheeze back by the closet that leads next door. It stops me dead in my tracks. I know it like I know myself. To my left—inside the closet. Charlie's holding his chest and gripping on to the wall to stand.

"Ollie . . ." he stutters, his mouth wide open. That's all he gets out. Gasping for air, he crumbles to the ground. I turn for just two seconds. For Shep, it's a lifetime.

Just as I turn back, he's already barreling at me. My chest caves in as he pummels me like a tackling dummy. Crashing on my back and slamming into the concrete, I take a sharp jab to the kidneys. Shep pulls the jagged blade from my hand, slicing my palm even deeper.

As I scream out in pain, Shep doesn't say a word. He's done talking. Crawling upward, he sits on my chest and pins my biceps back with his knees. Thrashing frantically, I fight to pull my arms free. He weighs too much. I search his eyes, but it's like no one's there. Shep doesn't care anymore. Not about me . . . not about the tapes . . . not even about the money.

Digging his knees into my biceps, he raises the blade like a guillotine. His eyes are on my neck. I'm not going to survive this one. I whisper an apology to Charlie. And to my mom. Shutting my eyes, I turn my head and brace for the impact.

But the next thing I hear is a gunshot. Then two more in

quick succession. I look up just in time to see the bullets cleave through Shep's chest. His body jerks violently as each one hits. A belch of blood dribbles out of his mouth. In his hand, the glass blade falls and shatters on the floor. Then, as his arm slumps to his side, Shep's body wobbles slightly and collapses backwards.

Following the sound, I trace the trajectory. That's when I see her, sitting up on the floor. Not unconscious . . . awake . . . Joey . . . The way the light shines behind her, all I see is her shadow. And the wisp of smoke that rises from her pistol.

She climbs to her feet, races for the wall, and smashes the butt of her gun against the glass case of the nearby fire alarm. The shrill alarm screams through the silence and within a minute, I hear sirens in the distance. Joey spins around and heads for my brother. Oh, jeez . . .

"Charlie!" I shout. "*Charlie!*" I try to sit up, but my whole arm is on fire. None of my fingers move. My body's shaking as it goes into shock.

Back by the entrance, half a dozen Disney security guards come streaming into the warehouse. They all come running at me; Joey stays with my brother. "Please sit still, sir," one of the guards says, holding my shoulders to keep me from squirming. Next to Charlie, four other guards kneel down, blocking my view.

"I can't see him! Let me see!" I shout, straining my neck wildly. No one moves. They're all focused on Shep's lifeless body.

"He's got V-tach! He needs mexiletine!" I scream in Joey's direction. She's doing CPR, but the more I thrash around, the more the room starts to turn. The world tumbles and somersaults on its side. My lifeless arm elongates like a rubberband above my head. The guard says something, but the only thing I hear is static. *No, don't pass out*, I tell myself. I look up at the ceiling. It's already too late. Life turns black and white, then quickly fades to gray. *"Is he okay!? Tell me if he's okay?"* I yell at the top of my lungs.

Another dozen officers race into the warehouse. They're all shouting static. And as gray blurs to pitch, lifeless black, I never get my answer.

88

Just like Charlie predicted, it's the staring that's the worst. Forget the whispering, and the unsubtle pointing, and even the way they walk past me as the gossip burns its way through the office. All those I can live with. But as I sit in the oh-so-pristine first-floor conference room and gaze through the plate glass window that separates me from my former bank co-workers, I can't help but feel like the monkey in the zoo. Scurrying through the maze of rolltop desks, they're trying their best to play it cool. But each time one of them passes—each time someone steps off the elevator, or races to the copy machine, or even sits back at their desk—their head turns for a split second and they hit me with that stare: part curiosity, part moral judgment. Some pepper it with shame; others add a smidgen of disgust.

It's been two weeks since the news hit, but this is their first chance to actually see it for themselves. And even though most of them have made up their minds, there are still a few who want to know if it's true. Those are the hardest ones to face. Whatever else Charlie and I did to save the day, it still was never our money.

For almost a full hour, I sit there and take the beating of their stares and whispers and awkward pointing. I try to make eye contact, but that's when they look away. On most days, only the lowest of the worker bees are caught in the hive of rolltop desks by the front entrance. Today, by the end of the first half-hour, almost every employee in the bank has found an excuse to come down and check out the monkey behind the glass. That's why they put me here in the first place. If they wanted to make it easy, they could've snuck me through the rock star entrance around back and whisked me upstairs in the private elevator. Instead, they've decided to put on a show and remind me that my private elevator days are over. Like everything at Greene & Greene, it's all about perception.

The traffic peaks when Lapidus and Quincy finally make their entrance. They don't say anything to me directly. Everything's done through their lawyer—a nasty mosquito with a high-pitched drone. He tells me that they're withholding my final paycheck until the full investigation is complete, that my health benefits are terminated effective immediately, that they'll seek legal recourse if I contact any current or former bank clients, and as a cherry on top, that they'll be contacting the SEC and the banking regulatory agencies with the hope that it'll stop me from working at any other bank in the future.

"Fine," I say. "Are you done?"

The lawyer looks to Lapidus and Quincy. Both nod.

"Wonderful," I say. "Then this is for you . . ." I slap a letter-sized blue-and-white envelope onto the desk and slide it across to Lapidus. It's blank on top. Lapidus glances at the lawyer.

"Don't worry, it's not a summons," I tell him.

Flipping it over, Lapidus notices his own shredded signature across the back flap.

It's the only reason I came back here today . . .

He opens the envelope and unfolds my business school recommendation letter.

. . . I wanted to see his face. And let him know I knew.

He keeps his eyes on the letter, refusing to look my way. The discomfort alone makes every second worth it. Folding it up, he stuffs it back in the envelope and heads silently for the door.

"Where're you going?" Quincy asks.

Lapidus doesn't answer. He and Quincy may've never been involved with the money and everything that happened, but that doesn't make them saints.

The meeting itself takes a total of six minutes. Four years to build this life. Six minutes to scrap it. The lawyer asks me to wait here while they gather my things.

As they leave, the door slams behind them, and I look out through the glass window into the lobby. Throughout the room, two dozen employees once again look away. The bandaged cut on my stomach stings every time I shift my weight. And my once broken nose stings every time I breathe. But this stings worse.

Twenty-five minutes later, nothing's changed. The zoo's still open. I throw a nod to Jersey Jeff; he pretends not to see it. Mary comes out of the elevator and refuses to acknowledge I'm there. For four years, I killed myself for the partners, made money for the clients, and immersed myself in every nitpicky detail the bank had to offer. But in all those years, I never made a single friend.

Trying not to think about it, I stare down at the inlaid mahogany conference table. It's the same table that I sat at to close my first client, which got Lapidus's attention and moved me from the first floor up to the seventh. Today, as my eyes trace the pattern of the antique mahogany, I angle my head and spot a nasty scratch that runs like a scar across the center of the table. I never noticed it before. But I bet it was always there.

Eventually exhausted by the waiting game, I stand up to leave. Yet just as I push my chair out, there's a loud knock against the conference room door.

"Come in," I say, though the door's already swinging open.

As it slams into the wall, I study the familiar figure who's carrying two cardboard banker's boxes. Unsure of what to say, Joey hesitantly steps into the room and lowers both boxes to the table. One's filled with management books and my cheap imitation banker's lamp, the other's filled with Play-Doh and the rest of Charlie's toys.

"They . . . uh . . . they asked me to bring you these," she offers, her voice unusually quiet.

I nod and flip through the contents of the box. The sterling silver pen set I bought with my first bonus. And the leather blotter I bought when I got my first raise. Naturally, the Art Deco clock I got from Lapidus isn't there. I'm guessing he pulled it off the wall last week.

"I'm sorry they wouldn't let you up there," Joey explains. "It's just that after everything that happened, the insurance company asked me to—"

"No, I understand," I interrupt. "Everyone has to do their job."

"Yeah . . . well . . . some jobs are easier than others."

"No doubt about that." I look her in the face. Unlike everyone else, she doesn't turn away. Instead, she stays with me . . . studying . . . absorbing my reaction. It's the first time I've seen her up close—and without a gun in her hand. "Listen, Ms. Lemont . . ."

"Joey."

"Joey," I repeat. "I just . . . I just wanted to say thanks for what you did. For me . . . and for Charlie."

"Oliver, all I did was tell the truth."

"I'm not talking about the testimony—I meant with Shep. With saving us . . ."

"I almost got you killed. That bluff about being on the phone with Lapidus . . ."

". . . was the only way to find out what was really going on. Besides, if you hadn't come in when you did—and then with Charlie's medication—"

"Like you said, we all do our jobs," she adds with a grin. It's the only smile I've seen all day. And means more than she'll ever know.

"So what happens now?" I ask her. "Were you able to get all the money back?"

"Money? What money?" Joey asks with a laugh. "That's not money anymore—it's just an assortment of ones and zeros assigned to a computer."

"But the account in Antigua . . ."

"Once you gave us the location, they sent every penny straight back—but you saw how Duckworth designed the worm. The three million . . . the three hundred million . . . none of it was real. Sure, the computers *thought* it was real, and yes, it fooled every bank you sent it to—that was the genius of the program—but that doesn't mean the money was actually there. Say hello to the cold hard cash of the future. It may look like a dollar, and act like a dollar, but that doesn't make it a dollar."

"So all those transfers from Tanner Drew and everyone here . . . ?"

"Were just the easiest way to make the money look kosher. It's brilliant when you see it up close. Completely random—completely untraceable. The hardest part is, once the worm gets in the system, it actually digs in and hides itself."

"Then how do you know what's real and what's fake?"

"That's the zinger now, isn't it? Too bad for us, it's like talking about time travel. Once Gallo brought the program in, and Shep unleashed it on the system, the worm burrowed in so deep, it created a whole new reality. The tech boys said it'll take months to purge everything. Trust me, Lapidus and Quincy may be smiling now, but for the next year of their lives, they—and every single client in the bank—are going to be under a magnifying glass the size of Utah."

She says it to make me feel better. And even though I can picture Tanner Drew's face when he's told about his audit, I'm not sure it works. "What about Gillian?" I ask.

"You mean Sherry?"

"Yeah . . . Sherry. Any word on how she's doing?"

"Besides the indictment? You know better than I do. You're the one talking to the U.S. Attorney."

She's right about that one. "Last I heard, she posted bail just in time to go to the funeral."

Joey's silent as I share the news. However it happened, she's still the one who pulled the trigger on Shep. Still, she's too bright to linger on the negative. Moving for a quick change of subject, she asks, "So what're you doing after this?"

"You mean, besides five years of probation?"

"Was that the final settlement?"

"As long as we deliver DeSanctis and Gilli— Sherry, the testimony sets us free."

By the crinkle in her forehead, she's wondering if it was a hard choice. Nothing in my life has ever been easier.

"What about you?" I ask. "Don't they give you a bonus or some sort of percentage for bringing everyone in?"

She shakes her head. "Not when a cheap-ass insurance company is paying," she says. "But there's always the next case . . ."

I nod, trying to sympathize.

"So that's it?" Joey asks.

"That's it," I tell her.

She looks at me like I'm leaving something out.

"What?" I ask.

Glancing over her shoulder, she makes sure no one's listening. "Is it true someone called you about buying the movie rights?"

"How'd you hear that?"

"It's my job, Oliver."

I shake my head, and for once, let it roll off. "They called—they said I had a lot of subplots—but I haven't called them back. I don't know . . . not everything has a pricetag."

"Yeah . . . well, I've got a lot of subplots too. And all I'm saying is when they cast *my* part, don't let it be with some soft beauty queen who runs around with a cell phone pressed to her ear—unless, of course, she's an asskicker, and has a normal body, and the final line someone utters to her is '*Thanks, Mean Joe.*'"

I can't help but laugh out loud. "I'll do what I can."

Joey heads for the door and gives it a sharp yank open. As she's about to leave, she turns around and adds, "I really am sorry they had to fire you, Oliver."

"Trust me, it's for the best."

She studies me to see if I'm lying—to her and to myself.

Unsure, she turns back to the door. "You ready to go?"

I look down at the two storage boxes that sit on top of the conference table. The one on the left has how-to-get-ahead textbooks, silver pens, and a leather blotter. The one on the right has Play-Doh and Kermit the Frog. The boxes aren't big. I can carry both. But I only take one.

C'mon, Kermit, we're going home.

Propping Charlie's box against my chest, I leave the other one behind.

Joey motions to it. "Do you want help carrying th—?"

I shake my head. I don't need it anymore.

Nodding slightly, Joey steps back and holds the door wide open.

I cross through the threshold and begin my final walk through the bank. Everyone's staring. I don't care.

"Knock 'em on their ass, kiddo," Joey whispers as I pass.

"Thanks, Mean Joe," I grin back.

Without another word, I step out into the crowd. Looking straight ahead, I already smell the Play-Doh.

89

So? What'd they say? Are we done?" Charlie grills me the instant I set a toe in his bedroom.

"Take a wild guess," I answer.

Sitting up in bed and readjusting the bandage on his shoulder, he nods to himself. He knew it was coming. If they didn't fire us, they'd be fools. "Did they say anything about me?" he asks.

At the foot of the bed, I dump the boxful of his desk toys all over his childhood comforter. "They wanted to make you a partner, but only if they could keep your Silly Putty. Naturally, I told them it was nonnegotiable, but I think we can counter with some Matchbox cars. The good ones, of course, not the crappy knockoffs."

As I say the words, he's completely confused. The result, he expected. But not my reaction. "This isn't a joke, Ollie. Whatta we do now? Mom can't support two apartments."

"I totally agree." I leave the bedroom and return two seconds later dragging an enormous army-green duffel bag. With a grunt, I heave it on the bed, letting it bounce next to him. "That's why we're downsizing to one." As Charlie whips open the zipper, he spots my neatly folded clothes inside.

"So you're actually going through with this? You're really moving back in?"

"I hope so—I just spent twenty-three bucks on my last cab ride. Those things'll cost you a fortune."

Narrowing his eyes, Charlie picks me apart. "Okay, what's the punchline?" he asks.

"I don't know what you're talking about."

"No, no, no," he insists. "Don't play that game show with me, Monty. I was there when you found that apartment and moved into your own place. I remember how proud you were that day. In college, all your friends lived in the dorms, and you had to live at home and commute. But once you graduated . . . once you signed that lease and took your first step on the yellow brick road of success . . . I know what it meant, Ollie. So now that you're moving back in, don't tell me you're not devastated."

"But I'm not."

"But you're not," he agrees, still searching my face. It may be a temporary move, but it's a good one.

"So you think this room can still sleep two?" I ask, motioning to the pyramid of speakers where my old bed used to be.

"Two's fine—I'm just happy it's not three," he says suspiciously.

"What's that supposed to mean?"

"Well, your girlfriend Beth called earlier. She said your phone was disconnected."

"And . . ."

"And she wants to speak to you. She said the two of you broke up."

This time, I don't respond.

"So who broke up with who?" Charlie asks.

"Does it matter?"

"Actually, it does," he says, touching the hairline scab that still hasn't faded from his neck.

"Since when're you so somber?"

"Just answer the question, Ollie." He won't say it, but it's clear what my brother's after. Life is always a test.

"If it makes you feel any better, I was the one who broke it off with her—"

"Ohhhh, Lordy, I'm *healed . . . !*" Charlie shouts, raising his shoulder in the air. "My arm—it works! My heart—it's a pumpin'!"

I roll my eyes.

"Mmmmm, baby, can I get a hallelujah!?"

"Yeah, yeah, she'll miss you too," I say. "Now how about helping me move the rest of my stuff?"

He looks down and grabs his shoulder. "Ow, my arm. Cough, cough, and more cough—I can't breathe."

"C'mon, you faker—get your butt outta bed—the doctors said you're fine." I yank the covers aside and see that Charlie's fully dressed in jeans and socks. "You're really sad, y'know that?" I say.

"No, sad is if I was wearing sneakers." Hopping out of bed, he follows me into the living room and spots my other duffel bag, two huge boxes, and some milk crates full of CDs, videos, and old photos. That's all that's left. The only piece of furniture is the one I brought over last night: my dresser from when I first moved out. That belongs here.

"Where's your Calvin Kleinish bed?" Charlie asks.

"Mom said she kept my old one in the basement. I'm sure it'll be fine."

"*Fine?*" He shakes his head, unable to accept it. "Ollie, this is stupid—I don't care how good an actor you are—I can hear the pain in your voice. Now if you want, we can pawn some of my speakers. That'll give you at least another month to—"

"We'll be okay," I interrupt as I grab the other duffel. "We'll definitely be okay."

"But if you don't have a job—"

"Believe me, there're plenty of good ideas out there. All it takes is one."

"What, you're gonna go selling T-shirts again? You can't make money doing that."

Letting the duffel slouch to the floor, I put a hand on his good shoulder and stare him straight in the eye. "One good idea, Charlie. I'll find it."

Charlie looks down at the way I'm bouncing on the balls of my feet. "Okay, so we're past the College Ollie, and the Banking Ollie, and the easily forgettable Dying to Impress Ollie with its very own Removable Soul. So which one's this? Entrepreneur Ollie? Go-Getter Ollie? Working at Foot Locker in a Month Ollie?"

"How about the real Ollie?" I ask.

He likes that one.

Crossing back into the dining room, I can already feel the energy rumbling through my stomach. "I'm telling you, Charlie—now that I have the time, there's nothing to get in the—"

Cutting myself off, my eyes dart to the torn-open envelope on the edge of the table. Return address says Coney Island Hospital. I know the account cycle. "They sent us another bill already?" I ask.

"Sorta," Charlie answers, trying to brush past it.

That's it—something's up. I go straight for the envelope. As I unfold the bill, it's all the same. Total balance is still eighty-one thousand, payment due at the end of the month is still four hundred and twenty dollars, and payment status is still "On Time." But at the top of the bill, instead of saying "Maggie," the name above our address now says "Charlie Caruso."

"What're you—? What'd you do?" I ask.

"It's not hers," he says. "It shouldn't be on her shoulders."

Standing there with his hands in his pants pockets, he's got a calmness to his voice I haven't heard in years. That being said, taking over the hospital bill is easily one of the rashest, unnecessary, and uncalled for things my brother's ever done. That's why I tell him the truth. "Good for you, Charlie."

"Good for you? That's it? You're not gonna grill me on the details: Why I made the change? How it's gonna play out? How'm I possibly gonna afford it?"

I shake my head. "Mom already told me about the job."

"She told you? What'd she say?"

"What's to say? It's illustration work down at Behnke Publishing. Ten hours a day doing drawings for a line of technical computer manuals—boring as watching shoe polish dry—but it pays sixteen bucks an hour. Like I said, good for y—"

Before I can finish, the front door slams behind us. "I see handsome men!" mom's voice calls out as we spin around. She's balancing two brown bags of groceries in a double-barreled headlock. Charlie races for one bag; I race for the other. The moment she's free, her smile spreads wider and her thick arms wrap around our necks.

"Ma, careful of my stitches . . ." Charlie says.

She lets go and looks him in the eye. "You say no to a hug from your mother?"

Knowing better than to argue, he lets her put a wet one on his cheek.

"Charlie told me he hates your hugs," I jump in. "He said he hopes you don't give him another."

"Don't start—you're next," she warns. She plants one on me and fights her way out of her winter coat. Noticing the crates and boxes all over the floor, she can barely contain herself. "Oh, my boys are back," she coos, following us to the kitchen.

Charlie starts stuffing groceries into the cabinets. On the counter, I take a long hard look at the Charlie Brown cookie jar. I'm already biting the inside of my lip. For almost five years it's been my most regular habit. I'm dying to open it. But for once, I don't.

Charlie watches me closely. *It's okay*, he says with a glance. *Everyone needs a day off. Including you.*

"And guess who I got a present for?" mom asks, grabbing my attention. From one of the shopping bags, she pulls out a blue plastic bag. "I saw it in the yarn shop—I couldn't resist . . ."

"Mom, I told you not to buy me anything," I moan.

She doesn't care; she's too excited. Reaching into the bag, she takes out a needlepoint canvas and holds it up. In thick, red stenciled letters are the words, "Bloom Where You're Planted."

"What do you think?" mom asks. "It's just a little coming-home gift. I can put it in a frame or on a pillow—whichever you want."

Like most of mom's needlepoints, the slogan is mushy and oversentimental.

"I love it," I say.

"Me too," Charlie agrees. Pulling out his notepad, he scribbles the words as fast as he can. *Bloom where you're planted*. As he writes the words, he looks good with the pen back in his hand.

"By the way, I saw Randy Boxer's mother in the yarn shop," mom adds, turning to Charlie. "She was so glad you called—it just made her day."

"Randy Boxer's mom?" I ask. "What're you calling her for?"

"I was actually trying to get Randy's number," he explains as if it happens every day.

"Really?" I ask, noticing the quickness of his answer. He's not fooling anyone. He hasn't seen Randy in at least four years. "So why the sudden high school reunion?"

He spins back to the groceries, refusing to say. "Not yet," he explains without facing me. "Not until it's all in place."

"Charlie . . ."

He thinks about it again. Whatever it is, it's got him nervous. But after a lifetime of telling me to eat the dandelions, he knows it's time for him to finally take his first bite. "We were . . . we were thinking of maybe starting a little band . . ."

I can barely contain myself. "A band, huh?" I ask, wide smile across my face.

"Nothing big—y'know, just something loud but smart. We figure we can get together after work . . . start at Richie Rubin's club over in New Brunswick . . . then maybe work our way into the city."

"No, that sounds great," I say, trying to keep it cool. "Of course, now you're gonna have to find something to call yourselves."

"*Please*—how d'ya think we spent our first three hours of practice?"

"So you've already got a name?"

"C'mon, baby, we look like novices? Coming to Shea Stadium early next summer—ladies and gentlemen . . . please give a Big Apple welcome to . . . *The Millionaires!*"

I laugh out loud. So does mom.

"You really gonna use that?" I ask.

"Hey, if I'm gonna be struggling to leap tall buildings in a single bound, I might as well be wearing a cool cape. Start low—aim high."

"That's very Power of Positive Thinking of you."

"Well I'm a very Power of Positive Thinking kinda guy. Ask anyone. Besides, who wants to see a band called *Pluto's Severed Head*? We do that, we lose the whole kiddie market."

Back by the sink, mom turns on the faucet and washes the daily grime from her hands. She's got Band-Aids on four of her fingertips. Behind her, I spot Charlie eyeing the Charlie Brown cookie jar. The paint's scraped off the nose. He reaches out and taps the ceramic round ears. "He's not nearly as big as he used to be," Charlie whispers my way. "I don't care how many drawings I have to do—this sucker's gonna be empty within the year."

"So you're ready?" mom interrupts, focused on Charlie.

"Excuse me?" he asks. At first, he takes it as a typical mom question. But as he reads her face—as I replay it in my head—we both realize it's not a question. *So you're ready.* It's a statement. "Yeah," Charlie tells her. "I think so."

"Can I come watch you practice?" she adds.

"Forget watching, we need star power like you on stage. Whattya say, ma—ready to bang some tambourines? We got our first tryouts tomorrow night."

"Oh, I can't tomorrow night," she says. "I have a date."

"A date? With who?"

"Who do you think, mushmouth?" I jump in. Cutting between them, I slide my arm around mom. "You think you're the only one who knows how to cha-cha? Dance lessons wait for no man. Hit it, sweet momma—and a-one, and a-two—right-foot-first-now . . ."

Swinging mom out and banging her into the metal stove, I laugh loudly and bounce to my own imaginary beat.

"Did someone actually teach you how to move that awkwardly?" Charlie teases. "You dance like a fifty-year-old man in a bad wedding conga line."

He's absolutely right. But I don't care.

After years of busting my ass at the nation's most prestigious private bank, I—at this moment—have no job, no income, no savings, no girlfriend, no discernible professional future, and not a single safety net to catch me if I plummet off the trapeze. But as I twirl our mom through the kitchen and watch her gray hair spin through the air, I finally know where I'm going and who I want to be. And as my brother angles in for the next dance, so does he.

"And a-one, and a-two . . . right-foot-first-now . . ."

EPILOGUE

With a twist of the Victorian bronze oval doorknob, Henry Lapidus stepped into his office, shut the door behind himself, and headed straight for his desk. Picking up the phone, he glanced at the Red Sheet in his in-box, but didn't bother to take it out. He learned that lesson years ago—like a magician protecting his tricks, you don't put every number on the sheet—especially the ones you know by heart.

As he dialed and waited for someone to pick up, he stared down at the letter of recommendation he'd written for Oliver, which he was still gripping in his left hand.

"Hi, I'd like to speak with Mr. Ryan Isaac, please. This is one of his clients from the private group," he explained. Lapidus couldn't help but be amused. Sure, his priority had always been to get the money back. Indeed, he was the one who personally called the bank in Antigua to secure the return of every last cent. Without a doubt, it was the right thing to do.

But that didn't mean he had to tell the Antigua bank about the theft, or Duckworth's worm, or the fact that none of the money was real.

"Mr. Isaac, it's me," Lapidus said the instant Isaac said hello. "I just wanted to make sure everything got there okay."

"Absolutely," Isaac answered. "It came this morning."

Three weeks ago, the bank in Antigua was surprised to receive a three-hundred-and-thirteen-million-dollar deposit. For four days, it was sitting on one of the largest individual accounts in the world. For four days, it was flushed with more cash than it had ever seen. And for four days, in Lapidus's opinion, Oliver had done at least one thing right. It was one of the first lessons Lapidus taught: *Never open a bank account unless you're getting interest.*

Lapidus nodded to himself, enjoying the moment.

Four days of interest. On three hundred and thirteen million.

"One hundred and thirty-seven thousand dollars," Isaac clarified on the other line. "Should I put it in your regular account?"

"That'd be perfect," Lapidus replied as he swiveled around in his seat and stared out the window at the New York City skyline.

Hanging up the receiver, Lapidus knew that once the principal was returned, the government would be far too preoccupied with tracking the worm and figuring out how it worked. And now that they were knee-deep in that, well . . . thanks to a well-placed payment to the Antiguan bank manager, all records of the interest were long gone. Like they never existed.

His eyes still on the skyline, Lapidus crumpled up Oliver's recommendation letter and tossed it in the eighteenth-century Chinese porcelain vase that he used as a garbage can. *One hundred and thirty-seven thousand dollars,* he thought to himself as he leaned back in his leather chair. Not a bad day's work.

As he took in the shadows of the late afternoon, a ray of sun gleamed off the Kamakura samurai helmet that was hanging on the wall behind him. Lapidus didn't notice. If he did, he would've seen the twinkle of light just under the helmet's forehead, where a silver object barely peeked out. To the untrained eye, it looked like a nail holding the mask in place . . . or the tip of a fine silver pen. But nothing more.

Except for the occasional glare of sunlight, the tiny videocamera was hidden perfectly. And wherever Joey was, she was smiling.